# COLD RECORD

# COLD RECORD

Eric Ferguson

ISBN: 9798368260587
Library of Congress control number: 2023905315

Ferguson, Eric, 1964-
Cold Record / Eric Ferguson
1st ed.

1. Fiction. 2. Fiction – American. 3. Fiction –
Contemporary. 4. Fiction – American Contemporary. 5. Fiction –
Crime. 6. Fiction – Mystery. 7. Fiction – Legal. 8. Fiction –
Courtroom Drama. 9. Fiction – Legal Mystery.

Technical and editorial assistance by Mike Goodenow Weber
Cover design and illustration by Hampton Lamoureux – TS95 Studios
and Jerry Todd – Studio TWL

Printed in the United States of America
Published September 2023

*To the three loves of my life –*
*Susanne, Evan and Julianne*

*But never a truth has been destroy'd;*
*They may curse it and call it crime;*
*Pervert and betray, or slander and slay,*
*Its teachers for a time;*
*But the sunshine aye shall light the sky,*
*As round and round we run;*
*And the truth shall ever come uppermost,*
*And justice shall be done.*

Charles Mackay (1814-1889)

# PRETRIAL

# 1

**(John Patrick Howland)**

IT'S A FRIGID JANUARY AFTERNOON, a month and a half after Haylee's murder, when Marta Branch brings us the remnants of her daughter's life in a silver box.

The Christmas decorations still line State Street in Millsford, California, ice pellets crust the courthouse lawn, and snow – a sporadic visitor – has begun to flutter. Marta has driven more than an hour over the forested, suddenly-treacherous roads of Contenta County to meet Assistant District Attorney Sonya Brandstetter, who will prosecute Andrew Rodarte. But she's a few minutes early, Sonya's not quite back from lunch, and we certainly won't leave Marta in the lobby. So the first allied face Haylee's mother sees this day is mine.

From a single online photograph and the accounts of those who knew, Haylee Branch, a college sophomore, was beautiful – willowy dark blonde, wide-mouthed, sparkle-eyed, graceful. Marta, by contrast, projects absolute strength. Even wracked and hollow, enduring the unthinkable, she is tall, lean and long-necked, with thick sloping shoulders and yellow-gold hair in a knot to her shoulders. But her light blue eyes are the one vulnerable part of her, and the smile she manages is an obvious act of will.

Turning back her apology, I soon launch into lawyer-speak – the delay of Rodarte's preliminary hearing, his first legal safeguard. Then I drop in a "we," I guess, and her great pale eyes widen with hope.

"You too? We'll have you both?"

"Well, I'm more of the sidekick. But I'll do all I can to help."

"Wonderful," she says, lowering her gaze but clinging to her smile. "The good news, I guess, is that we aren't a crowd. It's really just me and Ash, my younger daughter Ashlyn. You might meet a friend or an aunt or a cousin, but it'll mostly just be us. And a lot of what you learn is probably gonna come at random."

"I'd like to learn a lot." Now I've heard the back door, and Sonya's in the hallway. She pauses at District Attorney Tom Winston's door, leans in with a thought, he murmurs back – deferential as ever to his supreme subordinate. Her heavy coat hung, her purse tucked away, she comes out to greet Marta with a smile of frozen fire.

SIX YEARS INTO my languid, rural DA career I have never before come near a murder case, nor much wanted to. And I've assumed, I think, that those who do seek justice for the dead and their sleepwalking, empty-handed survivors must hold back just a little, keep a cautious distance even as they care.

But here I've been enlisted, so I follow Marta into Sonya's office, and as I perch to the side and watch as they empty the box, it wallops me. No adjudication can ever fill the marble emptiness, let alone transcend it, and this one certainly will not, whatever becomes of Rodarte. Yet long before the afternoon ends it is plain to me that in the forge of Marta's loss they have been permanently fused, no matter how it ends – that Sonya, back to the calling she'd once abandoned, will expend all of herself in the cause of justice for Haylee Branch.

And I'll hover on the fringe, for the most part. Barely in the frame at all. Perfect.

HAYLEE WAS FOUND in the guesthouse of an estate along Horsefall Creek. The property was about fifteen miles south of Millsford, the unmemorable seat of our rustic county, which lies in the mountainous inland reaches well north of San Francisco and the Bay.

She was not a local, there only to visit her unlikely friend Jacinta Cantrell on her way home from school at Thanksgiving break. Jacinta's father, immensely rich, owned but barely visited the estate. Haylee had been strangled and sexually assaulted, and Jacinta had been found in a coma, drugged and abandoned.

But there was daylight, too, in all the darkness, because by the time the coroner's van took Haylee to the morgue, the first responding detective – our best – already had Rodarte in his sights.

THE BOX IS heavy, its lid ornate. Sonya *wants* to reach its bottom, learn all of the story it tells, yet I also see Marta's slight hesitation, her apologetic fingers, as she hands things across. Worried, no matter what, that this is more of her lost child than we need.

There's a preschool art project, birds brightly crayoned, stuck to a slab of blue construction paper. A plush hand-puppet of a lion, her favorite early friend, snug to sleep with. Paper dolls, homemade rings, cards from her grandparents. A single school photo, first grade, wide-eyed. The list she made of invitees to her seventh birthday party. A story she wrote about Christmas, another – a eulogy – about a cat.

Drawings, poems, even cartoons. Age eight, says Marta's jot: a five-panel strip on the upside of culinary courage, a bunny-faced protagonist reciting her recent samplings to a chum: "HOT peppers, raw zukini, cottage cheese, pea pods, chicken on skewer, cantalope, mustard . . ." Then the punchline: "Now my mom will let me complain!"

Sixth grade, Haylee's report card. A, A, A+, A, A-. The last comes with a comment about a single indifferent quiz. Seventh grade, flawless. A picture of her father, paper-clipped to his funeral handout.

A playbill, tenth grade. *The Crucible*, Haylee as Elizabeth Proctor. A painting of wildflowers on a tiny square canvas, impressionist, purples and yellows, probably out her back door. Her learning permit to drive, nothing but a battered DMV printout.

Her high-school ID card. Ticket stubs from a volleyball match, a regional championship, and a clipping. Haylee starred, but lost. Her address book, meticulously filled with birthdays. Notes in the back, her month-by-month plan to pay off her Visa card, some $900.

Recruitment letters from mid-range colleges. A draft of an application essay. Her favorite book – *Watership Down*.

And photos, of course, from every era. That will be another day.

ALONG THE WAY Marta apologizes. "It's all random, and I couldn't imagine how to organize it for you. But I guess that wouldn't be the point."

"All that matters to us is that it matters to you," Sonya says softly. "This is just the place we're starting from, together. And everything that tells us more about Haylee is going to light the path."

Marta trembles now, but conquers it, resilient like a rumbled-over bridge. "Well, don't expect objectivity, and we'll all be fine. But there's a lot to tell. I mean, she was an honor student, and a volunteer, and my barely-paid assistant, and a shade-tree animal doctor, and an athlete and a mentor and a cook and an artist, and a thinker and a heart bigger than all outdoors, and humble about every part of it, and a beauty while she was at it, who hardly tried. And more than anything, her own mother's best friend."

Sonya's three are grown but still near. She smiles with her eyes, her mouth unable. "How beautiful. I understand completely."

"I know you do." Marta takes a deep breath. "And I'm scared of getting her *corrupted*, somehow. Does that make sense?"

"Sure. You're afraid they'll tell lies about Haylee to try to help him. Or he'll make up some story himself. They'll try, somehow, to obscure who she was. But know we'll expect that, and the judge will too. And if any lie gets out there, we will beat it to a pulp."

Marta nods. "They've been trying to brace me. The lead detective told me look, we have to dig down to make sense of this, and we never know quite where that leads. He's kind as he can be, but I realize he's afraid she knew this guy, that maybe she'd done things I never knew about, because that's what young girls do. I might have to hear that Lee was doing drugs, losing control, sleeping with half the world, maybe breaking laws. And it's because they know Jacie and her fancy house, and that things have gone on there. So he's worried it could get worse, and whether I can handle it.

"Of course he gets mama bear back. I say *no*, not a chance, and I'm as sure as I sound, because I knew my girl so well. But even after the arrest, I'm scared that the cops will keep clinging to this idea that she had secrets. And that nothing a mother might say would ever be able to overcome that."

"I get it." Sonya raises her chin, includes me in her glance. "Which is why we're going to pave a road to the truth, all of us together."

I linger another hour, overpowered and superfluous, then finally ease away. But Marta and Sonya are in there through the last light of the afternoon, well after the snow has begun in earnest. We all make it home, but it's a ten-year storm, and the next morning half the courthouse calls in helpless and marooned in the mounds of white.

BUT THIS ISN'T where the story begins, of course. Even the worst of it comes to us in methodical, two-dimensional form – already seen, lived and processed by the people who get there first.

# 2

## (DETECTIVE MARK WADE)
## (Contenta County Sheriff's Department)

NOVEMBER 21, 2003, the Friday before Thanksgiving week, had been chilly and slow. I'm rereading a report for about the seventh time, leaning back in my chair and testing its wobble, debating whether to zap my coffee, and somebody calls in a worry just before midnight.

Word goes out over dispatch, and it's a snoozer even for a slow night – the door to a guest house ajar on a wine estate, a light-colored SUV hauling off in a hurry, a neighbor talking about recent burgs but no alarm going off. But out it goes, and two deputies respond: a bright young bulb named Logan Akers, and a veteran, Angie Laird, who just finished training him and happens to be nearby.

It's me and Bill Porter, our rumpled Texan, paying half-attention. I'm off at two, in theory. He's here all night. Then all of a sudden the night turns upside down.

WE ALREADY KNOW the house, a custom rebuild on a beautiful piece of land. It's a sprawling Italian-style two-story above a slight, winding incline, with grapevines to the north and east, orchards to the south, Horsefall Creek below it to the west – wide and roaring after early-season rains. I've never met the owner, a private equity hotshot from SF who isn't around much and isn't serious yet about wine, but we're on pretty familiar terms with his daughter.

There's a big iron gate at the bottom, but it's wide open. We're figuring on tracks from the beginning, so we park on the dirt shoulder, walk up to Laird, she leads us down the path and inside to the room, and the body on the bed. And for a long moment we both just stare.

The girl is brutally young – recently 20, it turns out – yet somehow a grownup, no lingering child. She is slim, tall and long-limbed, her hair a tangled beige mane, her blue-gray eyes sort of quarter-open, left a little more than right, pockmarked with tell-tale red. She lies there with her blouse unbuttoned and yanked open but not ripped away, a bra half pulled off, and nothing else beyond underwear half up her left leg. There are two sets of marks across her neck, deep bruises and then what had to be a ligature, some fabric knotted tight, maybe a belt.

By cliche Laird would be tearing up, I guess, while us males stay firm-jawed.  In fact Angie Laird – a great patrol cop – is normally about five degrees above freezing.  But here, for a moment, she nearly gives way.

What got her, she said later, is how she knew right off this girl wasn't a usual, wasn't a tweaker, probably wasn't even a local.  And she wasn't trying to make an *effect*.  She had a big wide mouth that must have smiled, one little silver bracelet, a well-used pair of beige flats, half a minute's worth of makeup.  When we find her purse it looks like $20 at Walmart.

Making fixed judgments about people at first glance is a great way to go broke, even when you're in the incomplete-information business, but I did it anyway.  Just the shell of her – sightless, degraded, left behind like a pizza box – could tell me she'd never hit the pipe, never ripped anybody off, never passed out in the street, never left somebody hanging, never embarrassed herself at all.  She'd have been a mother, a friend, a light.  I mean, we've all seen fresh, warm corpses, but this was a crusher.  You'd have sworn you could rouse her, even with the horrible marks on her neck.  But she was gone.

MY FIRST QUESTION is obvious, for the surroundings, but there's nobody around to answer it that night, and when I eventually confirm the truth I say many uncharitable things.  This is a rich man's country estate, newly rebuilt, he has his own flaky daughter living there practically unsupervised, he has artwork all over and a cellar full of wine, he has grapes and outbuildings and amenities galore, but he bought the property without a video security system and in three-years-plus he's never gotten around to installing one.

The main house, up a slight rise to the north, somebody dubs the Crystal Palace, what with its giant windows and display cases full of glassware, God knows why.  And there they have Jacinta Cantrell, the actual resident, oxygen over her nose, on the far end of semi-conscious.

Laird had found Jacinta on the couch, easily visible through the window, saw her inert and thought she was a second corpse.  So it's paramedics, and she can't tell us anything right now.

Jacinta has been on our radar for a while. The house is far too big for her, the property's a den of pandemonium, and she's made all the wrong friends. We know she boozes, flirts with meth and pals around with slackers and druggies of all stripes, rich and poor. We just missed hooking her up once when we busted a dealer, and I pressed her hard another time about a burglary that a couple of her cronies might have been involved in, but all it got me was a well-rehearsed blank look.

Cloudy and neglected as she appears to be, though, her dad's about a half-billionaire – I looked it up – and I've assumed that on basic brains and money she'd slide through, even if she's at Contenta Valley College (home of the Pioneers) when she ought to be at Stanford or Yale or someplace.

Porter will go with her and wait till the cloud lifts. Which means I can start looking for tracks. And I get lucky ten feet from the front door.

IN CASE THIS WASN'T CLEAR, Contenta is the sticks. It's a full-on backwoods county – for all its glitz, California has dozens – that you could basically drop straight down in Kentucky without anybody noticing.

The highlight is a pair of middle-sized natural lakes, Crown and Marsh, separated by a narrow hilly rise where many of our affluent dwell. They're surrounded by pine forests, farmland, trailer parks and marijuana grows, and a scattering of wine estates in the foothills to class things up.

But it's rural, first and last, which means plenty of open ground and unpaved road, so we spend a lot of our lives tracking shoeprints and tires. And sometimes the fates are with us.

THERE ARE BEAUTIFUL TREADS up near the front door, where the driveway has a turnaround, and it's easy to see they don't match either the Hyundai still parked there or the Acura in the garage. These are SUV-size tires, all right, 245s, in a nice clean pattern, thanks to a low spot at the top of the drive that gathered up rainwater – lousy paving work, pure gold. Everything going up or down passed through, and you can see a Hyundai pulling up to park, and the Acura too, passing up to the garage.

But there is a third set, right up to near the house, fainter making the loop to leave, then strong again coming down past the trough. And when we get to the bottom there's another puddle, then firm mud, then asphalt and tracks that turn to skid marks. So the SUV turned south, as reported.

Better yet, though, he had to *stay* on Sundown, because it turns out the driveway to the house is the last one before the creek bends to the road and the slope on the west side turns sheer, meaning that for the last mile into Ray's Valley there are no turnoffs on either side. So unless he made a three-point turn in the middle of a high-speed, pitch-dark two-lane road, he got to the highway and passed the all-night Arco. Which means cameras, and when the manager hits rewind it's almost as simple as that.

We narrow it down right away to a white Chevy Suburban – other than somebody towing a trailer it's the only thing that's the right size for the tires, not to mention the right color, and it also happens to be hauling ass. Dim light and tint mean we can't make out anyone inside, and when we go frame-by-frame some of the license plate still blurs, but three of the characters are clear, and the Suburban does stay south onto the highway – the fast, logical road out of the county. So we head to the Shell a few miles down and manage to decipher the rest.

We run the plate on the spot, of course, and my language doesn't improve. It comes back to an address in San Ricardo, near Oakland, a solid two and a half hours away. Only later do I realize how considerate he was – if Rodarte had ever updated his DMV address, or wasn't on his way to the old one, God knows when we might have found him.

IT ENDS UP BEING five of us, in two unmarked units. Our barely-there sergeant, counting down his last few weeks before retirement, stays back to "oversee the investigation" with his thumb up his ass and his nose in a coffee cup. Bill Porter is at the hospital with Jacinta Cantrell, and the crime scene will be hours yet. But it's an all-hands-on-deck night, obviously, and we've left a whole backseat for Rodarte, if we find him, the stars align and we end up with enough to arrest him.

We also get a break. I find myself on the phone with the watch commander down in San Ricardo, who by the luck of Irish cops has a connection to our captain. And in half a minute he's on board, sending an unmarked detective car over to sit on the house and wait, and he's checking Andrew Marcelo Rodarte's history, which shows no record of arrests in Alameda County but a few misdemeanors scattered around the state.

The record doesn't much matter, though, because of the beautiful fluke of the tracks. Andrew Rodarte. We're rolling in hope.

◆

YOU CAN'T REALLY BURN the first 40 miles or so, which is all two-lane, winding and mountainous, constant tight curves. Later we pick it up but the roads are muddy and damp. So we're still a solid hour out when San Ricardo reports great news – the Suburban pulling up, and a guy climbing out who in dim street light seems to match Rodarte's DMV photo.

We're there by 4:30, parked two houses down. It's a decent neighborhood, well-tended postwar bungalows, large lots, old shade trees, and we decide we'll wait for daylight. So at a quarter past seven, the other four fan out around the property and I ring the bell.

HE GOT HER SKIN, light olive and smooth as a playing card. Terri Rodarte opens the door in a robe, but isn't fazed by a fatigued invader in a blazer and a government tie, thinning on top, with a little color of his own (my own mother is Native). And then and always she is class.

She invites me in, offers me coffee and a seat. The recorder's in my shirt pocket. I smile and apologize a little, knowing I look exactly like eighteen hours straight and an up-all-night.

Yes, her son is Andrew. He's there, she confirms, and asleep.

She woke when he got there, as mothers do – if she'd ever even drifted off at all. He'd hugged her, asked about the dog, gone to bed. He'd been in jail, up north, and she hadn't seen him in eight months, but they'd been in contact every week.

A MINUTE LATER, in silent agony, she goes to speak softly through a door. Maybe 20 seconds pass, and then he's out in the hallway, blinking and bedheaded, wearing a robe of his own over sleepwear. He's a big good-looking dark-haired SOB, but he has his mother's mild eyes and there's something passive about him. Unless that's just sleep.

It hits me like a winter gust, that quick and startling. I'd love to have something better, but I don't. In no time he's telling me how he met Jacinta Cantrell at a mini-mart and wound up at the house on Sundown Road. But the first thing I ever think, in the hallway of his mother's house, is that it wasn't Andrew Rodarte.

# *3*

**(JPH)**

WE'RE AN OFFICE of eleven lawyers, counting Tom Winston himself. Four of distinct importance, seven more – including me – who man our zones and follow along.

In November 2003, Tom is in his seventeenth year as the elected District Attorney of Contenta County. Before all that, long before my day, he had been the right-hand man for Bob Lacayo, who served two terms and landed a big-bucks lobbying job in Sacramento. It's said Lacayo was so cautious a politician he could barely order lunch, so even then Tom basically ran the operation. But when his chance to jump arrived, Lacayo got his handful of major donors to come through for Tom, and nobody ever looked back.

Through his constancy and personal warmth, Tom has avoided the usual bane of district attorneys, a palace revolt. And in a law-and-order county, this has meant a string of feeble opponents: an aged far-lefty of a judge, long relegated to civil court; a two-day campaign by a clueless sheriff's lieutenant with a nighttime law degree, pissed off over a case turndown; a carpetbagging defense attorney from San Jose, promising unasked-for "change" and bringing neither money nor charm to the show.

Tom is well into his sixties when Rodarte turns up, his energy down a peg or two, maybe leaning a little heavier on his smile than he once did, but still a sure thing. We all know we're blessed to have him, and in gratitude try extra hard to not fuck things up. In a crisis Tom would smother any grenade; we don't want him blown to smithereens.

SONYA, HIS RIGHT HAND, tried and lost a robbery case my first month in the office. And the shock – much greater yet for those who actually *knew* her – had an after-effect, because she pulled away from trial life. Now Rodarte and Haylee Branch have brought her back.

Petite, keen-eyed, silver-haired and elegant, Sonya is cool where Tom is warm, and more legally acute, a long-ago *magna cum laude*. Though younger, she is senior to Tom in service time, and with her force and smarts might have beaten him to the top in a completely objective world. But Sonya had family obligations that slowed a woman as it might not a man – and to his credit, Tom knew it, and made clear from the beginning that she was and would remain his firm number two, if not co-equal, and she gave him in return her equal loyalty. She liked him, too.

Yet every once in a while, maybe every year and a half, there would be a tiny moment – an exchange, a comment through a doorway, a crack in a meeting, and a thought the whole world could read would cross her face. *I should be in charge. Just a fact.*

While she doesn't micromanage often and has always carefully governed her moods, it is at times a visible effort. I have always thought, with no real evidence, that there is something down there that she doesn't quite trust, a fierceness she must always keep in check. For all intents and purposes, I don't yet know her, and don't expect to when it's over.

DOUG LAHTINEN, next in the collage, diffidently supervises all us "line" DAs, because someone must, in between the things he cares about much more. Doug is balding, bespectacled, brusque and orderly, just this side of OCD. The signs are everywhere – his unnervingly tidy desk, his kids' portraits at perfect slight angles to his computer monitor; his neatly printed desk calendar, with a full page for each day; his lean, cardio-fit frame; his shelf of hardbound law treatises and binders; his pin board, as carefully arranged as a mural, with cheat sheets of at least a dozen different things – "moral turpitude" offenses, statutory time frames, forms of theft, approved and non-approved drug treatment facilities, judges and their staffs, email backup and recovery procedures, and more.

Basic managing aside, Doug's primary job has always been the daily review and filing of "in-custody" cases, arrestees who must now be charged or released. It's a time crunch, and detectives sometimes frown at his restraint in charging, but he makes very few mistakes. Normally bunkered all morning, he just won't mangle a code section, or forget an element of a crime, or fail to subpoena a necessary cop for the preliminary hearing. His plea bargain offers always make math sense, his case law knowledge is our gold standard, he's our occasional crusader in the appellate courts, and he doesn't care for trial much, or glory at all. No wonder I always felt that he was the one who actually chose me, way back.

THE FOURTH INDISPENSABLE is Brian Flaherty, our trial alpha. He's first in line for any high-profile case, save this one, and rich in personality – instinctual, passionate, profane, hilarious.

He can be prodded, meaning occasionally his emotions burst their banks. But Brian also has a baseball closer's ability to forget, and considerable compassion for the everyday loser – he reserves his true ferocity for the people who do irreversible things. So even the public defenders get along with him about 28 days a month, and I've personally always liked him without reserve – his warm first-day greeting, his grins, his wicked wit and determination.

THEN MAYBE YOU GET down to me – five in seniority, if nothing else. Almost six years in I'm a level-three DDA, generally popular, adept at paper litigation, unremarkable in trial. But Tom did know that when he made the call.

I came here from Orange County in early 1998, after my father died and my mother moved back to New Hampshire to spend late days with my grandmother. Sensing freedom, bored with my gig, I began to thumb the fine print in the back of the *Daily Journal*, and one day there it was. I went straight to the map.

I DROVE UP for the interview, about six hundred miles.  Left on a Saturday evening, made a leisurely stop for the night, then sailed up I-5 the next day.

It rained for the first long stretch, but sun eventually emerged and the world brightened, in gradual stages, as I wore through the endless Central Valley.  Finally, in late afternoon, I turned off and climbed out of its northern reaches, and when the road flattened out again I continued west through a thick carpet of fresh wild-grasses among the live oaks, the hulks of a past fire season standing as incongruous black sentries amid rebirth.

Ten miles, fifteen.  Then around a bend and atop a ridge, as the western sky faded to a soft vermillion, I looked out at the green valley and the blue of the lakes, and saw a dreamscape – a place I felt sure I'd seen before, and would not want to leave.

For as far back as memory went, I'd returned in sleep to a vast, lush, nameless land, a tableau of valleys and rivers, forests and roads.  Still California, I knew – probably not more than an hour or two from home – and itself a sublime destination, a suburb of heaven.  Yet I returned every time convinced there was a deeper trail to seek, and that with luck and nerve I could pass out to a land of even greater light.

I'd comb the horizon, every crag and creek an option, and sometimes I would find a path and follow it, wide-eyed and thrilled – walking, riding, flying, floating.  But a few miles in, inevitably, I'd see a landmark or a signpost, and realize again that it was not the way *on*, but the way *back* – a return to the still green place I began, the headwaters of my own awareness.  On waking I would cling to the evanescent remainder, longing to map the trek for future reference, and find a parallel – to link it to something actual and near, to solve a mystery in the world that counted.  But it was futile.

The long Contenta Valley was the closest thing I would find to that nether-land, and I knew it right away.  So as I drove away again, having done OK in my suit, it was nearly a mantra in my buzzing head: *Let this be my life*.

IT TOOK TEN DAYS, but the call did come, Doug Lahtinen wondering about my pending lunch hour and how far I'd have to drive to enjoy it. "Up here, by contrast, we got about four acceptable eating joints, and sounds like one of 'em already burned your bacon." I'd made small talk about the Hard Luck Cafe. "But if you'd like to swap smog for meth fumes, we'd like to have you join us."

*I'll find the roads.* My estate-planning cohorts down at the firm in Mission Viejo snickered, my law school pals went tactfully silent, and I gathered my nondescript life and never looked back.

A year in, settled, I caught the early wave of subprime lending and managed to buy a house of my own, an aging, two-story affair on half an acre. Single, unhandy me, with a mishmash – two small bedrooms, elderly plumbing and a falling-down deck I'd have to replace, yet there was granite tiling around the tub and shower, a skylight, and a broad, airy kitchen facing directly east, across grazing land to the hills beyond.

I've loved it daily – the sweep of the horizon, the clean breeze, the trees and vines, the roads I've found and haven't. Yet as I drift into my mid-thirties, unattached, I sense the core years of my life beginning to shuffle past, like rail cars from a standing stop, as one event, one file, one string of laughs begins to blend into another.

Then here I am, suddenly at Sonya's elbow, with a fresh haircut and a new gray tie. (My best color, I'm often told, with no apparent irony.) Prodded, a little, by the looming ridges and the brilliant sky.

# 4

**(WADE)**

BILL PORTER WOUND UP camping all night and morning in the ER with Jacinta Cantrell. Fitting, I guess, since she had nobody else. Once they saw her vitals were all right, did a blood draw and figured it out, it was mostly a waiting game, and he was at the ready for whenever she made it back to earth. But she wasn't in a hurry. She opened her eyes a few times, he said, but the minute he made it to her line of sight she went right back to Nod. Which isn't surprising, if you've seen him.

We've tracked down her father, of course. I've left him a one-AM message, he calls back on the road down, and he tells me he's in Boston. By the end I'm tempted to make him prove it.

Once we're through the obvious preliminaries – they've got his daughter under observation, they're sure she will live and recover, here is what happened and where – he turns into the bright shining prick I figured him to be. He'll take the next plane out, of course, but he's worried about the PR. Mister Cool. *Detective, let's just stay calm, be reasonable.*

And in the next minute you'd think *he* was the victim. Wants to know if we're going to "release the address" where it happened. Never says a compassionate word about Haylee Branch, though I was told he met her more than once. He's worried about the "media impact," whatever that means, and what he needs to tell his business manager, and he wants to avoid a formal interview.

As we talk I'm thinking how perfect it is – Mister Private Equity Millions, cross-country absentee, stays awake nights over everything but his daughter. Now this. He's trying to win something, morning noon and night. Nine-alarm assholes don't tend to evolve.

THE UPSIDE OF Jacinta's long nap is that I make it all the way back before her eyes stick open and she can tell us her name. And even before she stirs I'm thumbing through her phone, where I find a predictable name in an unexpected place.

Tamara Roberge, about her age, drives a convertible Audi way too fast, sets up illegal raves on county property, has been gathered up wasted in the alley behind Hammonds Mercantile at four AM, and has a habit of mouthing off to authority every chance she gets – which is invariably about nine drinks in. There's rumored to be a pool for the deputy who manages to hook her up.

But her dad owns three car dealerships, a motel and a dockside restaurant, meaning she's only a *little* bit awed by the Cantrell compound. So they're a perfect fit. And since Tam is in Jacinta's "called" log not half an hour before the neighbor called 911, I'll have to make nice. I'm not looking forward to it.

A FEW MINUTES LATER Jacinta blinks, stares to the ceiling, coughs, tries to rise. After a nurse raises her bed she gradually focuses her eyes. She manages to identify herself, knows the month and the year and the president, figures out she's in a hospital.

There's something to be said for waiting, but I don't. Not five minutes later I show her a photo lineup, and after she goes straight to Rodarte I tell her that her friend is dead.

◆

THE TECHS HAD PROCESSED the body and the room, of course. And Rodarte had agreed to let me swab his cheek with a Q-tip, even though he didn't want to, so we packed off the one beer bottle in the bedroom for fast-track DNA analysis, since it could put him five feet from her body. The follow-up batch could wait – fibers and hairs on Haylee's blouse, scrapings from beneath her fingernails, even the condom on the carpet, which had been rinsed. But "rush" is a relative term for a small lab staring down a holiday week, and best-case scenario we were hearing three days.

Since the house has a hangout history, I'd be entitled to hope a few others passed through. But Jacinta can't tell me about a party, because she has no memory, and especially not once she learns that Haylee is dead. I've tried to build gently, but she collapses, cries for at least fifteen minutes out of half-open eyes, can't say a word beyond "no." And eventually she turns her face away, clenching her pillow, shaking her head.

I do have to push, and eventually – mostly by nods – she confirms the bare essentials. They fit. She did meet the guy in the picture in the

SpeedyGrab, at the gas station in Walkersburg. He did buy beer, she did invite him home, and she thinks he followed her there. But then it goes dark. She *doesn't know* what happened next, because she remembers almost nothing after getting back.

There was also no sign of a crowd, so the prospects were dimming. All we really had in the living room was about a dozen dead soldiers around the coffee table and a bottle spilled over on the couch. Which was luck, arguably, considering the mess it might have been on other nights – between the living room and the patio, there has to be room for a hundred shit-faced nineteen-year-olds, even if a couple dozen pass out on the tile. But Rodarte himself had narrowed the human universe to three.

MY MOOD DOESN'T IMPROVE at the SpeedyGrab. They do have cameras, of course – but their system is down, has been for an entire week. *For fuck's sake.* And the night clerk isn't in yet to look at photo lineups.

So on to the property, and I realize there's a downside to luxury: when Hell breaches your castle walls, there may be nobody close enough to notice, let alone care.

Most of the household employees are day-timers – a gardener, two guys who tend the orchard, a pool guy – who'd have been long gone if there at all this rainy Friday. There's a full-time cook/housekeeper on site and her thirteen-year-old son, but they live in a separate guesthouse, far north of the main house, went to bed by ten and heard nothing until us. And the mistress of the house was rendered unconscious. There are, in fact, no potential witnesses anywhere on what must be a fifteen-acre estate.

I'm wandering, more or less, aimlessly looking for footprints even knowing Rodarte was there, when Sergeant Short-Timer crackles through to alert me nobody's tried the neighbors, not even the guy who made the call. Suggests that we took too many bodies south the night before – possibly true, except he had signed off on it himself, and was perfectly capable of conducting interviews all on his own, but did not.

Things improve slightly. I ring three bells, they're civil to me, and the calling-in neighbor is solid and helpful. I've been awake almost 30 hours by the time I get there, but the take-away is simple. Rodarte described a calm, genteel departure from the house. But the SUV didn't glide away, it *tore.*

## (JPH)

I HAD BEEN DISTRACTED that Friday night, nervous for an intern who was getting his result on the bar exam. He managed to dawdle until nine o'clock before going online and learning he had flunked. When he called to tell me I felt a duty to meet him for a beer and a pep talk, since he lived only a couple of miles away.

I was back early and my light was out by midnight, rare for a Friday, but then nobody sent word of the murder around in real time. So we learned of it in a short blast email on Saturday afternoon, which also informed us that there had not yet been an arrest.

On Monday morning we got the picture. Wade and company had already tracked down Andrew Rodarte three counties away. Wade interviewed him, got him to admit he was at the house, that he was with the victim, that he was the only stranger there. Found nicks on him suggesting a struggle. Then left him there anyway.

The collective reaction was holy terror. We can all imagine it – he runs, science confirms his guilt, and now the hayseeds have to launch a second manhunt for a guy they already had by the scruff of the neck.

HE HAS NO SPECIAL TITLE, or special attitude, but Wade is the lead dog of the detectives. This means he sees all our murders, which are rare and usually very dull. A bar dispute goes nuclear once in a while, there's an occasional jealous rage, somebody runs afoul of tweaker logic in a drug deal here and there, and we've even had a wife calmly blast her husband with a twelve-gauge as he lounged blotto in a recliner, but yell abuse and self-defense. (Brian proved otherwise.)

But we've never seen anything nearly so cold as this case, at least in my time, and we can't possibly have ever trekked the better part of three hours to hunt down a murder suspect, seen the case get better once we found him, then decided that the smart move was to travel home without him. The solace, such as it is, is that we know Wade well enough to begin with trust.

He's confirmed a phone tap, Doug tells us as we crowd the hallway. And they're sitting on the house, and they're running DNA.

Brian grunts. "Let's hope he doesn't do the running first."

But Doug – usually the most cerebral – has a cowboy moment. "Let him run."

"Really?"

"Scary, but I see upside. Ten to one if he runs we catch him, with that many eyes, and I bet that seals it. And either way I say he gives up something on the wiretap."

He doesn't, though, and Sonya nearly goes mad.


**(WADE)**

THE REASONS I didn't arrest Rodarte were easy to list – I know because I got a lot of practice. And I might have seized his truck, or at least his cell phone. There were reasons for all of it, though in the cold glare of hindsight they may not have been good enough. I had just tallied what we had, thought about the process, and made a choice.

I was already hating it on the way back. Never mind that I'd missed a neon clue in the conversation, there was only one set of tracks, he was a stranger on the premises, they found her ten minutes after he left, and I'd seen his hitch when I asked for the DNA swab. Yet some contrarian instinct still talked me into waiting.


TWO DEPUTIES STAY BEHIND in the unmarked unit, eating and sleeping in shifts, as San Ricardo wastes umpteen of its own man-hours sitting at the other end of the street, and we get nothing – *zero* – from the tap on his cell phone. You'd think he knows. I sleep three hours in two nights, my brain a pinball machine. *Shoulda hooked him.* He'll run, and within an hour his DNA will come back on the bottle.

Nightmares, like dreams, occasionally do come true. At 6:45 on Wednesday morning, four days after I drove back to Contenta County without him, Rodarte climbs into the Suburban and sets off toward the 580 freeway, inland-bound. The call I get from the left-behind Taurus is more exhausted than enthused, but of course they put it in gear and follow.

By now somebody noticed that the Suburban's registration is expired, meaning instant probable cause for a stop, though it's no basis for an arrest. And I tell myself there's an upside – if he leaves the area, we'll have an argument he's fleeing. So the unmarked just follows, we make a few phone calls and in Millsford I jump in a unit with Gallardo, the toughest street deputy we have, in case we happen to catch up and one of us needs to wrestle Andrew Rodarte to the ground.

THEY FOLLOW HIM east on the 580, with the San Ricardo unit loyally trailing our unmarked, and Gallardo and I abandon hope of participating when we learn he branches south before Tracy, toward I-5.

Then we get the DNA report while I'm pondering the options. Rodarte on the bottle, of course. *Shoulda hooked him.*

THE WARRANT is mostly done but Porter finishes it, hunt and peck with his flabby, grease-stained fingers, gets it signed. Then a huddle, and somebody way above me makes a great decision for once, and after assorted high-level communication it all ends well.

A Kane County sheriff's deputy, forewarned, lurks above I-5 on the shoulder of an onramp, spots the Suburban and pulls it over. If he'd missed, the CHP was on the next bridge down. The deputy dawdles by the roadside, talks a few things over with the driver, then escorts him politely to the county seat, where the cuffs come off but the administrative wheels turn slowly. And maybe half an hour after he gets there, a rare bird swoops from the sky.

I'd like to be there, but so it goes. Porter and another of our finest climb out of Eagle One, arrest Rodarte on the warrant, and he talks. Then they strap him in and fly him north to justice.

The thought settles me better than single-malt Scotch.

# 5

**(JPH)**

RODARTE IS ARRAIGNED two afternoons later, a pure formality but the media's first crack. As Doug participates, several of us have trailed the handful of reporters down to the courtroom to lay eyes on him. And Judge Jim Bright brings him out last, after all the other cases have cleared.

Even disheveled in guacamole-green on the worst day of his life, he's a good-looking specimen. The arrest report has him six-two, 190, his hair is thick and dark, his eyes a curious tan. He's trim, though not especially buff, and I get the same vibe Wade did – there's something a little distant, even reticent, about him. His expression isn't a jail scowl but a sort of bleak meditation. There's even a hint of embarrassment. Sociopaths, of course, have many faces.

The judge takes no apparent interest in him. Even up here, Bright's probably arraigned 50 murderers over his long career. The Public Defender's Office is appointed, Deputy PD Marina Schorr enters not guilty pleas to all charges, and bail is set at a million dollars.

Judge Bright then sends the case, as expected, to the Honorable Anthony Vanzetta – our brightest, liveliest, most mercurial judge. He'll be part of the show, no question, but he'll set the boundaries and protect the record. There's not a whole lot more to ask.

◆

THE PUBLIC DEFENDER HERSELF, Abby Barnett, shows up for the first hearing, but you can nearly hear a car engine idling, and it's clear within half a minute that Rodarte will fall in Ted Stauber's lap. The allegation of a "special circumstance" – that this was murder in the course of a rape – means that we will seek either a death sentence or life without parole. The decision can be deferred, and we haven't announced it yet.

This gives their office an out, and Abby isn't going to miss it. With recent retirements to point to, not only are they short of bodies, but she can claim with a straight face that they have nobody fully qualified to undertake this, since a capital case hasn't been tried in the county since the 1930s. So the Contenta County Public Defender's Office makes a formal oral motion to be relieved as counsel.

In theory Vanzetta could save the county money by denying it and making Abby's own second-in-command put on his best suit and try the case, but not only would it cause no small injury of feelings, any hint of a death sentence puts every judge on high alert. Above all, naturally, the accused must be looked after well. So with little ado, he grants the motion and appoints the "conflict panel," the designated batch of private lawyers who step in when the public defender can't practically or ethically take a case.

Ted Stauber has headed the panel for a couple of decades by now, but it's his *third* act. He was admitted to the state bar in December 1962, seven years before my birth. He was a prosecutor for this office until I was, I believe, nine years old, then left, cashing in connections, to get rich in San Francisco. A decade or so later, well-situated, he returned as a defense lawyer and landed the lucrative conflict contract. And even well into Medicare, arthritic but masterful, he remains by consensus the best defense lawyer in Contenta County.

Ted accepts the appointment, of course. He later tells me it's a whopping flat rate, $75,000 just for LWOP, a hundred if we seek death.

IN A MEETING I DON'T ATTEND we decide against it. I'm told the vote is one somewhat equivocal yes from Brian, a stronger no from Doug, and then Sonya and Tom, as a united front, ultimately choosing no. So after Tom has communicated it to Marta Branch, we advise that we will seek only a sentence of life without parole.

It's no surprise, considering the obstructive circus that is capital litigation in California – I think I'd have voted against it too. Yet the contrarian in me rebels. *Why shouldn't he die, if he did this? Tell me, Andrew Rodarte, if we know you chose to throttle the life out of this innocent girl after raping her, left her dead and humiliated beneath a drab overhead light, what case is there for your life?*

In law school I remember defending the splashy federal law that sped it up, and my most patronizing professor looking down his nose. "Could *you* push the button, Mr. Howland?" And I did play it safe, gave some in-between answer, but wanted to say *fuck yes* – at least in the exceptional, soulless, arctic cases. A hood-eyed assassin, a Ted Bundy, a kill-my-wife-for-insurance, a child-killer – if you *know* –

But at the starting line, we don't. Certainty requires facts not yet in evidence. The case is strong enough, but not a concrete vault.

That decision made, Tom calls me in and explains that I'll be sitting at the table with Sonya.

I'M SURE I WINCE, even as the shock sets in and I mumble that it's an honor. But it doesn't take long to figure out.

The case is important enough to call for a second body. With Sonya trying the case, Doug will have to take over much of her job, and while Brian deserves the right-hand spot, Tom and Sonya both know he'd go nuts as second chair. Which makes me a plausible next-in-line, particularly since she'll mostly need technical help.

Still, Brian will be irked, and I get it. I'm not a fool, but I'm even less a warrior – I spend most of my life looking for common ground. At best I'll be the vice president at the State of the Union address, well-tailored and visible but mostly there just to listen, nod and clap.

HE DOES TAKE the afternoon, once the word comes down. The next morning, though, Brian turns up in my doorway, reconciled, and manages a mournful grin. *Tear him up, man.*

I smile back. *I'll have a front-row seat.* Then we settle in to wait.

♦

EVEN WITH DEATH off the table, it seems like the case ought to make bigger news, go national – a beautiful murdered girl, a handsome accused, a rape, a rich man's estate. But it never really does.

We do have big-town reporters from as far away as Portland and L.A., by the end, but that's about it, and it aggravates Brian Flaherty to the hilt. He googles every day, and will offer a fuzzy update – something picked up in Minneapolis, or was it Milwaukee? A call from Mexico? Somebody from *Holland*? But out here where the trains don't run, Haylee Branch – for worse or for better – does not join the brutal sorority of murder victims the nation will know by shorthand.

Closer-at-hand sources do have interest, of course, and they call and they hover, endlessly asking when the case will go to trial. The true answer, normally, is "when the defense is ready," because that's what ultimately decides. Ted isn't the type to stall, or for that matter to hurry. And he's working on a flat rate, so the process is methodical.

HE FIRST SEEKS a change of venue. Were we going for a death sentence, the logistics might require it, but here it's really just Ted covering himself. The argument, as usual, is that pretrial publicity will taint the jury pool, cause the good citizens to prejudge the defendant, and prevent a fair trial in our small-pond county. But he has no real evidence to offer, just the inherent luridness of the case and cursory copies of stories from the local paper and online.

Vanzetta's record is easy to make. At close to 60,000 we are small but not a flyspeck, meaning we'll have a pretty robust pool to choose from. Beyond that, the fact that neither Rodarte nor Haylee Branch were local is nearly enough on its own to deny it. Since nobody knew either of them (and few would have known Jacinta Cantrell, or even her father), nobody is likely to have a credible personal claim that they can't be fair. There's never a doubt that the case will stay.

Then routine things. Ted seeks funding for investigation. He moves for a standard psych evaluation on his client, for a few extra documents from the Lab in discovery, to exclude Rodarte's initial statement under *Miranda v. Arizona*. He brings a Penal Code 995 motion after preliminary hearing, challenging the rape charge.

I'm the lead author of our responses, and Sonya does insist my name goes on, above hers. Vanzetta, colorful by nature, issues a series of flat, predictable rulings. And we wonder, or at least I do, when Ted will come looking for a deal.

PLEA BARGAINS are comparatively rare in murder cases, because there is little ground on which to meet. Unless there is enough doubt about the killer's mental state to justify a reduction to manslaughter, our side is bound to demand at least the minimal "indeterminate" sentence for a second-degree murder, which in California means fifteen years before the inmate can be *considered* for release. And this alone usually guarantees that the case will go to trial, because a defense attorney, well aware that many who get "life tags" never do get it together and make parole, will rarely recommend that a client accept any life sentence.

Here, though, Rodarte's predicament is even worse, because if the jury accepts the special circumstance allegation, he will face life with no chance of parole. So even a 25-to-life deal on a first-degree murder, offering a shot at redemption and release by middle age, would be something of an upgrade, and from Ted Stauber's view a *second*-degree 187 may even sound attractive, assuming he expects Rodarte to go down. And if anyone might talk a murderer into a plea, it's Ted, whose "client control" is the stuff of legend.

IN ONE FAMOUS EXAMPLE, Ted represented a world-class dunce named Gerald Cavarette, who became aggrieved with his girlfriend and set her family's barn on fire one fall afternoon, in full view of four witnesses. The eager blaze not only devoured the barn and several beasts inside but skipped to an adjoining wooden fence, then along to the eaves of the farmhouse. Most of the second floor went up in smoke, and the girl's father broke his leg as he fled for his life, so in addition to charging the obvious arson, we alleged that the accused had caused great bodily injury, intended or not.

In due course the assigned DDA made a standard, move-things-along state prison offer, less than half Cavarette's potential exposure at trial. Brian had lightly given her shit about it, in fact, what with the slam-dunk evidence. Still on misdemeanors, I hovered in the room, probably awaiting some driving-without-a-license plea. The judge left the bench and Ted leaned toward his client, in the jury box, with a murmur. And we soon observed Cavarette shake his head disgustedly, the sort of shake that could mean anything from *I ain't guilty* to *I can't believe I'm quite this stupid.*

Yet here, incredibly, it meant a guy who couldn't even grasp that his case was worth a felony. "Frickin property damage," he muttered repeatedly, with increasing volume. "I didn't make him trip." Ted replied, tried to soothe, and a couple of minutes passed. Then there must have been one more head-rattle, because his voice cut straight through the stillness, seeming even to resound off the walls.

"Son, yer dog-paddling up shit creek with your arm in a sling and an anchor around your neck," he barked. "Exactly how deep in shit do you feel like sinking?"

Not two minutes later Cavarette was putting his initials on a plea form. And from that day on I'd remind Ted of his "special way" with clients whenever things got stuck.

BUT ANY HOPE of a deal is a reverie. The only direct conversation happens one morning before daily calendar. I'm not there, would be no factor if I was, and per the bailiff it didn't last a minute. It's days, in fact, before Sonya even gets around to telling me.

# *6*

**(JPH)**

BY EARLY SUMMER 2005 our side is ready for trial. But now Ted has a trip to Greece and Turkey – three full weeks, most of it a cruise. He'll be back in late July, says he'll be ready within a few weeks of that.

Rodarte stays calm in his scrubs as Ted lays out the plan. Vanzetta has a blank space on the calendar in late August. We'll probably run through Labor Day. But our witnesses are available, and Ted and his client have waived enough time.

"Firm," the judge adds. "I'll entertain further continuances if somebody loses a limb. Otherwise we go."

"Duly noted," Ted agrees.

Sonya just nods, grim and gleeful.

♦

IN MID-AUGUST Marta returns with a clear plastic bag of photographs – some from the original box, some others.

They've come from albums, the faint residue of adhesive from the clear plastic pages visible in Sonya's overhead light. I see Marta at her kitchen table, late at night – turning, absorbing, choosing, extracting. Thinking, surely, of how this collection would be not only the best of Haylee, but the last.

"We want one picture as the main image, for the overhead at trial," Sonya explains, in the gentlest of murmurs, when they've narrowed it down to a few. "We'll keep coming back to it. This attorney won't object."

Marta nods, turns and smiles at me. "John, what do you think?"

"No, no. Let me leave it to you."

"No, you get a vote," Sonya assures. "Speak up."

And for the second time I'm ravaged, because I'd never truly seen her – in many ways, even this far along, the living Haylee Branch was almost a myth. The one in the initial news report was a posed full-body shot from her high school yearbook, later used at her funeral. Past that I'd seen a couple of face shots on a memorial page, and photos of her dead on the bed, and – to the minimum extent possible – pictures from her autopsy.

Then these. There is Haylee in a formal blouse, made up, a close-up shot where she is leaning toward the camera over a banister, self-conscious and bemused – on her way to a student government meeting, maybe. There she is near a pool, the blue behind her, late afternoon light, just the hint of a freckle or three.

Haylee in her volleyball uniform. Haylee in cap and gown, sheepish and shimmering, high school graduation. Earlier, across a wooden table, maybe fourteen, a soda in a tall glass in front of her, beaming. On a swing, much later, feet crossed, in a checkered skirt and sandals.

Then the last of them. She's there in front of an oak tree the spring before she died, in a blue-and-white sundress, neck slightly bent, her hair the color of a dry summer plain, a hint of gangliness, clear-day exuberant and shy at once, mouth slightly open.

"I like the light," says Sonya right off, tapping the picture. Vote concluded.

AND AFTER THAT, a last couple of hours of communion – a little more to "learn." I'm still a third wheel, always will be.

Marta only met Jacinta once, she tells us, yet still felt as though she knew her. Her immediate diagnosis was that Jacie was lonely. The two girls met because Haylee was talking to her professor one day after class. Jacinta overheard, was lightly awed by her calm intellect, and sought her out.

"Lee was flattered, no question. And then Jacie invited her down there for the first time, which sort of blew her mind. She got the tour, they ate lobster salad, and she slept in this great big guest room, fit for royalty, with its own private bathroom with a sunken marble tub.

"And maybe she had a moment of seduction, as it went along, an idle thought of a necklace or a new car or a closet full of beautiful dresses. But it wasn't aspirational – they bonded because it worked for both of them, and because they each had a gap. Haylee lost her dad, my ex, when she was in ninth grade, and I gathered Jacie's mother was also long dead, and then there was some trophy stepmother for a while she didn't get along with.

"Lee dealt with her dad's death because she always dealt with things. She comforted Ash as much as I did, maybe more. Now I think in a way she comforted Jacinta, too."

Sonya's eyes are locked on hers, as always.

"It sounds like she had a gift."

"Her human skills were off the charts. And somehow the friendship did work. They were windows into different worlds for each other, I think, and there was something in it for both of them.

"One weekend Lee comes home, later than normal, I think, and she has two new pairs of high heels, ridiculous. But they're classy, and I know she didn't buy 'em herself. She didn't have the money to waste, of course, but I raised this girl, and apart from a pair of ballet shoes when she was seven, she has never gotten excited about footwear in her life. She's sneakers, sandals, work boots.

"Anyway, Jacinta would kid Lee about her height, not that it was that extreme, but that one day they'd been to the RiverPoint mall, window-shopping, and now she says to Lee, what you need to do is dominate. And when Lee sort of laughs it off, now Jacinta insists. You helped me raise my grades. Let me raise your stature."

Sonya laughs. "I can picture it."

"And I'm mind-reading here, but in this spot, my girl wouldn't say no because she knew the spirit it was offered in. She tells me hey, she really *wanted* to. It was about laughter and keepsakes, them both knowing Lee was probably transferring out to a four-year – she could've gone straight there, but wanted to stick around local an extra year to save money, and for me. And Jacie wasn't ready to, yet. Lee looked on this friendship as an experience, not a life to emulate, and she was never going to lose control of herself. She simply enjoyed it for what it was – because that's how she was."

Marta turns to the window, shuddering. Barely in the room, I'm haunted now. But when she turns back around, Sonya's gaze is direct and hypnotic.

Sonya reaches forward and takes Marta's hands.

"We are going to bring Haylee to a jury." She closes her eyes, softens, opens again. "And they will never want to let her go."

Eric Ferguson

# CASE IN CHIEF

Eric Ferguson

# 7

*August 24, 2005 – Morning*
**(JPH)**

THE GLOOMY, WINDOW-FREE room is nearly full, which is rare, and too warm, which isn't. Outside it's a fine, blue-sky, late-summer morning, but here on the second floor we could be anywhere – a basement, a warehouse, below decks on an aircraft carrier.

The county dates back to the Gold Rush, but Millsford burned twice and then got rattled by a major quake, so this is apparently the fourth courthouse, dour, aging and merely functional on its best day. And as the Honorable Anthony Vanzetta plows through the initial jury instructions and Sonya waits statue-still to my left, I ponder a question only a "second chair" has the time to dream up: *Would any of us be here in this room by choice?*

We can rule out Rodarte, of course, facing life without parole for the murder and rape of Haylee Branch. But the fifteen sworn to try the case after two long days of selection also surely wouldn't – not the twelve on the actual jury, nervous and blank, and especially not the three alternates, who are odds-on to sit through all of it and then go home, having no ultimate voice in the outcome.

Vanzetta, the judge, is in his mid-forties, tall, fit and irreverent, a natural-born charmer with a seemingly perpetual two-day beard. He enjoys his role, as a rule, and undoubtedly wants to rise to the occasion that is this trial. But since he isn't insecure to start with, I doubt his ego stands to gain, and by now it's clear that the case horrifies him. On balance, I decide, he'd rather be kayaking, or plunking the mandolin behind his desk, or brunching on a fifty-dollar steak.

The bailiff, cheery and plump, is always a picture of ease. He reads spy novels or history books every down-time minute on a normal court day, so I see him, given a wish, beneath a sun umbrella with a tall soft drink, his four kids in happy orbit.

For the moment he has a companion, a tall, lean-faced Black deputy named Aziz, new to the department, who for as long as the trial may take will sit with folded arms immediately behind Rodarte – there simply to make sure that the unhandcuffed defendant facing life without parole never decides that a couple of shoves and a bolt for the exit is the best of his limited options.

No court reporter has ever exuded love for the exacting task, so I can rule out Ellen Tomkins. Likewise the court clerk, Lucille Esch, a 35-year veteran who is down to her last few months before retirement, gleefully breaking it down to the minute for anyone who asks.

There are two spread-out pews of media, but the reporters – I tally eight, including our locals – look inert and faintly resigned, aware that a trial is tedium above all else.

Nearer the front sit Marta and Ashlyn, another relative and a family friend, and, across the aisle, Rodarte's mother Terri – all of them far beyond the point of hope or pleasure, able only to endure, connected by their different shades of suffering.

WHEN I FINALLY circle back to counsel table, I start with myself, and that's no close call. As pierced as I am by the case, by Marta, and by Haylee herself, I already know I'll be glorified scenery, not a full contributor, and would much prefer that Sonya's safety net was someone else.

Then Sonya, and the reasoning is different. Even after years away, I'm sure she would have no patience for the hypothetical. There *is* no option of that kind, I think she'd say. We do what *needs doing*, because it's essential. There is no luxury of choice.

But then Ted Stauber, last of all – did I plan it that way? And he's the exception. He claims it's the money that keeps him working, but that's not all of it. He is 70 now, hair a shiny silver, his glasses thick, but he plainly hasn't stopped enjoying this game – the everyday predictability of it, the formality, the reason it gives him to wake and dress, polish his shoes, hold forth in Vanzetta's chambers, stride confidently through the hall. And he is surely aroused by these stakes. *Yes.* He would choose to stand here and defend Rodarte. Even for the murder of Haylee Branch.

◆

TWENTY MINUTES LATER, opening statements complete, the cheerful bailiff – inaptly named Graves – peers out into the hallway and calls Jacinta's name in a crowd-control voice, then crinkles his face into a smile as he holds the door and she passes through.

Jacinta, now 22, is a spoiled child, a flake and an addict. Yet today, here to be submerged again in the darkness of Haylee's death, she wears a professional beige blouse and a maroon skirt, with stockings and reasonable heels. Her hair is not only washed and brushed, which is progress enough, but the skirt nearly matches it. The reddish-brown tresses are drawn back from her face, and she stands straight.

She moves cautiously but with a bit of grace, and her light brown eyes are clear. Not only is she scrubbed and arranged, she appears, in this guise, actually altered – as if she's turned her past off like midnight television, gone to sleep and awakened in the cold morning of adulthood. I'm startled, then laugh inside: *We can clean 'em up, too.*

A moment later, seated, she has given her name and oath. She smooths her hair back even though it is restrained. Her hands show white as they clench in front of her, and Sonya stands a second time and glides to the lectern.

THE PRACTICAL FIRST. She goes by Jacie – both the name and the initials, I guess. Where she lives, what she does. Finishing junior college. *JC for JC,* I think inanely. Hoping to transfer next year, wants to get an MBA.

The house was ten minutes west of Walkersburg, above the creek. Her dad lived in San Francisco, came up some weekends. She had a housekeeper who cooked and managed things.

Sonya eases into rhythm.

"Now, Jacinta, do you remember the details of November 21, 2003, from morning until a point in late evening?"

"Mostly, I think." She braces, eyes wide and grave.

"What can you tell us?"

"Well, it was a Friday. I went to class at CVC, then lunch. My last class was canceled, so I drove across to Target. When I was there I got a call on my cell phone."

"From who?"

Only a moment's pause. "My friend Lee. Haylee Branch."

"And what did she have to say?"

Jacinta measures it. "Well, she'd left, that school year, to college in Sacramento. She'd been living there, on campus, and had a job in the bookstore. So I hadn't seen her since the summer." Here a sigh. "She said sorry for short notice, but she'd just decided to leave that night to drive back up here for the holiday week, rather than the next day, and she had thought maybe she could stop and see me."

"And how did you respond to her?"

"I said great, sure, of course. I'm here. Great. Come on by."

"Was that something she'd done before, during your friendship?"

"Yes, when she was still up here she came over a lot of Friday nights. She'd stay the night, because her mom's place was so far away. We just normally planned it out ahead of time."

"Did she indicate she wanted to stay over with you that night?"

"I don't actually remember. I was in the checkout line when she called, so we kinda hurried it. She would have had a suitcase and clothes, I guess, since she was going home, so maybe we were just gonna play it by ear." She quivers now – the needless bags, the morning that never came. "But I'm not quite sure."

"So you left Target, then what?"

"I drove straight back. It took like 45 minutes. It was raining, got bad for a while, but it had lightened way up when I got home."

"Do you remember what time you got back?"

"Around dark, I think, whenever that would have been. Maybe a little after five."

"Now can you tell us who lived at your property, at the time?"

"Well, Marie, who kept house and cooked, and her son, his name's Kevin, I think he was in middle school. But they had their own separate living quarters up past the vineyards."

"Any other staff?"

"Not living there. Just people who came and went. There had been a lot of day workers for the grapes, but I think they'd all been harvested by then, and taken away for processing."

"So basically just you?"

"Pretty much. My dad was there a few days a month, and once in a while other people would come for the weekend to go fishing or wine-tasting, and they'd stay in the *casita* like a hotel. Family or his friends. But our paths wouldn't cross much."

"Would you often have people over yourself, in those evenings when your dad wasn't there?"

She nods, matter-of-fact. "Yes."

"So were you alone that night in the house when you got home?"

"Basically, yes. Marie was normally off at noon Fridays, though she was usually on the grounds if I really needed her. My dad wasn't there. He was planning to come up for Thanksgiving the next week."

"Now can you tell us how you came to know Haylee, where and when and why?"

"It was at the JC, Contenta Valley. We met in an English class, fall the year before. Both starting out, and we just sort of hit it off."

"And what kinds of things did you do together, once you were acquainted?"

"Well, we'd hang out on campus, grab coffee, study together, go to the library. Then sometimes stuff afterward, get a meal, even see a movie. But then she'd come over for the night maybe once a month, after Friday class."

"Where did she live, if you know?"

"On a horse farm way west of here, the back of beyond. I don't remember the road, or even the place name. I got lost the one time I went there."

SONYA NODS. "So what tended to happen on your Friday nights?"

"Well, things were always mellow in the early evening. Sometimes people would filter in later on, because that's just what tended to happen – a lot of people came over on the weekends, nights would kinda turn into parties. But when it was just us two we'd go in the pool, the jacuzzi, watch DVDs, see whatever's on cable. Shop online. Go get takeout. Even study sometimes. Just hanging out and talking, that was a lot of it."

"And you enjoyed that?"

She pauses, getting hold of herself. "Yes."

"What were those conversations like?"

"Well, she always had these little observations about things. She was quiet but she noticed everything, and things just struck her funny. Always mocking herself, which sort of cracked me up, because I never saw her do the wrong thing.

"Honestly, she wouldn't even come down on me when I deserved it. All I'd ever get was like, her eyebrows, a look. I'd tease her about that, say it was worse than getting yelled at. So on the nights when people would show up later on, I'd try to get her to loosen up and party a little bit."

"Now it could get rowdy at your place, right?"

"Sometimes. People coming over, you know, getting buzzed, making noise, cranking up music. Hooking up. Not when my dad was around, of course, but he usually wasn't. There was just a lot of space to hang out there, pool, spa, sauna. People liked it."

"I see. And you wanted Haylee to loosen up a little, on occasion?"

Jacie wrinkles her nose. "Kinda. I mean, if I could get a couple beers in her she would laugh, even talk a little crap about people sometimes. But anything beyond that was a wild night, and I never saw her full-on drunk. Or at least that I can remember."

Sonya smiles, takes a detour. "Who did she ever talk crap about?"

"Oh, people from school, mostly. And even that was just funny stuff we all were thinking. Like why didn't this one guy ever change his T-shirt, or what was up with this girl who'd talk out loud to herself on the quad, or why did a professor use the same lame phrases over and over. Or even, what was up with this one professor who was hitting on her, except she normally didn't want to believe it. Those kinds of things."

"Ah, OK. Now did other people sometimes spend the night at the house?"

"Yeah. I'd tell 'em to. Better than driving."

"Is it fair to say your house got a party-type reputation?"

This invites speculation, but Ted is happy to bring it in.

"Yeah, probably."

"In fact, the sheriff had been there a couple of times before that night, hadn't they?"

"Yes. I thought we were far enough away from the neighbors, but they said the sound was carrying, the music and shouting, they got complaints. Disrupting the peace. So we said sorry, turned down the music, people went inside. The cops would figure we weren't 21 and make us dump our drinks, but we had more."

"So you would drink. What about drugs?"

"Just – now and then." She's been warned the question will come, of course, and to tell the plain truth. "Joints, pills. Stuff people had. Or . . . meth a few times. Methamphetamine."

"All right.  And let's clarify something.  You have battled problems with both alcohol and drugs, Jacinta, haven't you?"

"Yes ma'am."

"That includes meth?"

"Yes.  I'm 174 days clean, though."

"You're in a diversion program through the court, correct, for a drug arrest?"

"Yes.  Inpatient first, 90 days, then outpatient for six months.  I'm almost done, and then I can get the case dismissed."

"That's good to hear."

SONYA LETS IT SETTLE, passes on.  "So Haylee called you, and then she got there.  When was that?"

"Well, sometime past dark.  Maybe 6 to 6:30.  I'm just – fuzzy about a lot of things that night."

"That's understood.  Do your best.  Now did you have other plans for that night?  Apart from being with Haylee?"

An unexpected blow.  Her chin falls, and she closes her eyes to hold the tears in.  Long seconds pass, and she lifts her head again, daubs with a tissue.  "I'm sorry.  That's just what's hard.  It's not real clear, but I know I'd wanted to party that night.  It was the start of holiday break, and I remember there was a big high school football game happening, people were gonna be amped up afterward, and I'd sort of figured things would happen.  I wasn't even thinking of Lee at all, and then she called."

"Had you stayed in touch, those months, you and Haylee?"

"Well, sort of.  We'd talked maybe twice since she left, I'd been bad about it.  But she still thought of *me*.  So when she called, I remember thinking well, it'll be nice to see her, we can hang out, but I wasn't quite ready to give up on other stuff."  She shakes her head.  "Even though she was my friend and I hadn't seen her in months.  Somehow it couldn't be that simple."

"OK," Sonya says, matter-of-factly. "So when she got there, do you recall what you did?"

"Not that well." Jacinta seems to regret it. "I mean, we hung out at the house. I think she was glad to be there again. I remember she wanted to see my cat, who was always hard to find because the house was so big, so we wandered through the rooms until we did.

"Then we walked out back a little, even though it was dark. Then we sat in the kitchen a long time, I think, just talking."

"Do you remember what you talked about?"

It's irrelevant, of course, but Ted won't object. Resisting bringing the victim to life would be bad psychology.

"Not exactly. Probably school – I'm sure she was acing it and wouldn't brag, and as usual I was just muddling through. I think I asked about her place, if she had a boyfriend and she said no. She may have asked me, same answer. I remember that she asked if I was planning to transfer to a four-year the next year. I think we talked about music."

"Anything else you recall doing?"

"We ate something, I think, probably leftovers from the fridge. I could never finish Marie's meals during the week, so Lee always loved seeing what gourmet stuff I had in there by Friday."

"Were you drinking?"

"A little. I know I had a beer, maybe two. I think she opened one, but she was still a sipper. But then I remember realizing we were low, and that was always an emergency. So, eventually, as it started getting later, we went out to get more."

SONYA'S SMILE is a masterwork – at once sympathetic, mildly disapproving and ever-so-faintly amused.

"Now neither of you was 21 yet, right? So how were you figuring you'd pull that off?"

"I had a strategy. I'd put on something flashy, go to the mini-mart in Walkersburg, and look for a guy who'd buy it."

"Inside the store, or outside?"

"Well, outside was harder. People were more suspicious, and you just look like a loser when you do that." Jacinta sighs, and her voice drops. "I was in there a lot anyway, so it was more natural to shop around for a few things and wait for a chance."

"How did it work?"

"The beer was in a separate cold room in the back of the store, not easy for the clerks to see, so if I hung out close by I could probably approach somebody. If they'd say yes I could just slide back out, finish my own shopping and wait around the corner. And I knew some of the clerks well enough that they wouldn't hassle me."

"So that's what you did?"

"Yes."

"Did Haylee go in with you?"

"No." Her lips quiver. "It wasn't something she wanted to be part of, going up to strange dudes, sweet-talking 'em. Not her style at all. But I didn't have any shame about it."

"And that happened that night – you met a guy who made the purchase?"

She nods, half-speed, looks away. "I did."

"How did that go?"

"Well, I mean, I asked him and he bought it. Later we met at his car, which was off to the side. But I realized I hadn't brought enough cash, like an idiot." Again she flails her head, hating herself. "And I'd been thinking he might be – I don't know . . ."

"Take your time. He might be what, Jacinta?"

"Might be – fun to hang with. And so I said to him, I remember saying hey, he should follow me home. So I could pay him, and whatever else."

"And he did?"

"Yes.  He had a big white SUV.  I remember him following me up the driveway, and – that's about where things go dark."

Sonya folds her arms, squints at the ceiling.

"Your memory pretty well goes blank after that point, doesn't it?"

"Yes."  Her voice is a croak.

"And it's dark and blank for the rest of the night?"

"Yes."

"Do you know *why* you don't remember?"

Jacinta closes her eyes and nods.

"Need you to answer out loud," Vanzetta puts in, kindly enough.

She opens them, well-earned tears.

"I do."

# 8

**(JPH)**

JACINTA SAYS THAT she was drugged. Ted could object at this stage, but sees no point.

"Now were you taken to the hospital for that?"

"Yes. That's where I woke up."

"That night, or the next morning?"

"Morning. Late morning – it might even have been noon. I was completely out."

"And that is from the time you came back to the house, and the man had followed you home?"

"Yes."

"You remember nothing at all?"

"Well, I can recall the guy standing in the kitchen. Just a snapshot. And a few other random things. Like that I was laughing at something on TV, and that I was on the couch at some point, and being in the bathroom for some reason – sitting on the floor. Maybe I fell down."

"Now understanding that, Jacinta, do you have *any* memory or knowledge of what happened to Haylee that night?"

"No." It takes her just a moment, but it's decisive. She shakes her head in a burst, sighs. "I don't remember anything at all that happened to her."

"And apart from being drugged, do you recall anything that involved you personally, any assault on you?" The exam was negative, but the jury will wonder.

"No. I just basically went blank after we came home."

"ALL RIGHT," Sonya says briskly. "Now, Miss Cantrell, when you woke late the next morning, as you remember it, were there police there to interview you? Sheriff's detectives?"

"Yes."

"Did they tell you that you'd been drugged?"

"Yes. They didn't say exactly what it was."

"And did the detectives tell you at some point that your friend Haylee had been murdered, there in your guest house?"

She closes her eyes. "Yes."

"But before that, do you remember looking at photographs of some men?"

"Yes. A page of them."

Sonya softens, a maternal look.

"Did you recognize any of them?"

"One, yes."

"From where?"

Jacinta lowers her head.

"The guy from the store, who followed me home."

Sonya leans in. "Miss Cantrell, do you see that man in court today?"

"Yes. I do."

"Can you point him out for the record?"

"In the blue tie and suit at the end of the table." She half-looks as she raises her left hand toward Rodarte.

"Thank you, Your Honor. Nothing further."

TED STANDS ELEGANTLY at the lectern, hands clasped behind his back.

"To ensure that I understand, you were not even in the same building as Miss Branch when she was killed, correct?"

"I don't think so. They found me on the couch in the living room. But I can't absolutely know where I'd been."

"At the very least, you have no recollection whatsoever of it happening, correct?"

Jacinta recoils, eyes wide. "God. No, I mean, I didn't see it, I couldn't have. I was completely gone."

"Meaning you have no direct information about who actually killed her, I assume?"

"Right, of course. I was – somewhere far away."

"In fact, you don't remember anything past – what time?"

"I don't really know the time accurately. Just from whenever it was we came back."

"But you do recall all the things you've told us about, yes, from earlier that night?"

Jacinta frowns, baffled. "Well, sure. I didn't imagine them."

Ted nods, conjures a bad-odor face. "Now you have met with the District Attorney's office repeatedly, haven't you, leading up to this?"

"Just one time lately. A couple of others, way back, but I don't remember much about it."

"You've been through your potential testimony with Ms. Brandstetter, I assume, and perhaps Mr. Howland as well?"

"Well, sort of. I was told what might be asked. But not what to say, other than the truth."

"And you were told you'd be asked about your memory loss?"

"Yeah, for sure. It's part of that night."

He should have a tough follow-up here, but stops short. "So this was otherwise a normal day in your life, wasn't it? That Friday?"

Jacinta frowns. "I guess so. It's hard to imagine it now."

"Right, of course. But routine events, then you're home, your friend is there, you go obtain beer and then you do get drunk and party, don't you? Isn't that what happened?"

Her eyes go wide. "I don't remember what happened. Things just went dark."

TED LATCHES ON. "Did that happen to you other times? For other reasons?"

"Sort of. I'd blacked out before, mostly from drinking. It's scary, but that was a little different."

"And drugs were around too, correct?"

"Yes."

"Even when Haylee was there, too?"

"Well, not usually. Not unless it got really late, she'd gone to bed and there were people still around getting wild. She didn't do drugs at all. I didn't even want her to know I did, either. And it wasn't an every-time thing."

"Did drugs ever knock you out the same way alcohol did?"

Again she pauses, measures her answer. "No, not that way. Not where I had no memory at all. I might've gotten groggy from weed a few times."

"Did you like to try new things, with drugs?"

Sonya is immediate. "Objection vague."

"Sustained."

"Were you interested in trying unfamiliar drugs?"

"Objection relevance."

Vanzetta stops to think. "Could go to credibility. Overruled."

Jacinta stares, confused. "You mean, like –"

"Like, when people would show up with things you hadn't tried. That happened, didn't it?"

Her eyes dull, and she gives a tiny shrug. "Well, once in a while."

It hangs out there, his gears turning. Ted could chance it now, suggest she took the roofies herself. But there's no evidence anyone else ever showed up that night, and a far better chance of a blank stare and an irritated jury than a bombshell.

"YOU DID TAKE RISKS in those days, didn't you?"

"Yeah. Far too many."

"And you didn't mind lying, correct?"

Jacinta hesitates, face working. "I don't know if I minded. I often did lie."

Ted pauses now, softens. "But telling us the truth now, you never saw Mr. Rodarte behave aggressively that night, did you?"

"No, but – I mean, I don't remember seeing him with her at all."

"All you know is he followed you back, is that right?"

"Yes."

"So that must mean you don't know when he left, correct?"

She processes it. "Umm, that's right."

"He could have left five minutes after you got back to the house, couldn't he?"

"I guess, sure."

"It's possible you just paid him the extra few dollars and he left pretty soon after that, isn't it?"

Jacinta thinks a long moment before she nods. Her expression is subdued, regretful. "Right."

"He never did anything menacing or intimidating toward you that you remember, right? At the store or in the parking lot – or later?"

"Nothing I remember."

"And you never saw him approach Haylee, assault or attack her in any way, during the time you can remember?"

"Right." She nods slowly, hesitates. "Not that I can recall."

A MINUTE LATER Sonya passes on redirect and Jacinta steps down, clumsy and spent, clothes rumpled, her mascara streaked. She is barely out the door when we hear her crumble into sobs.

# 9

*August 24 – Morning*
**(JPH)**

EVERYTHING WADE TOLD ME about Tamara Roberge is solid and true, but she turns up on time. She is short, plump and full-lipped, over-made-up, blonde hair piled atop her head. In her designer suit she is sleek yet frightened – a pale, shaky set of chins. Even today she probably has the sense to be scared of Sonya.

"Miss Roberge, are you familiar with Miss Jacinta Cantrell?"

"Yes."

"From where?"

"We met in high school, at the start of eleventh grade."

"Was that at Trowbridge Prep Academy?"

"Yes."

"Miss Roberge, did you visit her home on Sundown Road, near Walkersburg?"

"I did, yeah."

"How many times, do you think, total over the years?"

"Gosh, like probably twice a month for a couple of years. Whatever that adds up to. A bunch."

"Parties and such?"

A hint of contrition. "Pretty often. Yes."

"Were you still socializing as of November of '03, if you remember?"

"Yes."

"Now did you ever meet a young woman named Haylee Branch, there at that house?"

"Yes. Maybe five or six times."

"What do you remember about her?"

This is fuzzy, and again Ted could object, but there is no reason to fear a first-person impression of the murdered girl.

Tamara pauses, dry-eyed, but a shudder comes into her voice.

"Well, first she was tall and blonde and, basically, stunning – or could have been, anyway, but she didn't really advertise it. Not flashy at all, not looking to overshadow anybody. Didn't wear much makeup, dressed low-key. Didn't have to go to the salon every week. Sort of a natural, country-girl type."

"And personality-wise?"

"She was quiet, kinda shy, had a responsible sort of vibe. Smart, you could tell, and she could laugh, but she kinda stayed in the background. Just somebody who was nice to be around."

"You knew her through Miss Cantrell knowing her, then?"

"Yeah, only that. She wasn't really out and about. I never saw her any other place."

SONYA NODS. "All right. Now Miss Roberge, did you hear from Jacinta on the night of November 21st, that year?"

"Yes. I actually got two calls that night."

"From her own cell number?"

"Yes."

"Now you provided me a cellular telephone bill, correct?"

"Yes."

The projector flickers to life. "Is this it? With your name, the address redacted?"

"Yes."

"Miss Roberge, do you see an entry here for a call at 10:31 PM?"

"Yes."

"And it is from Miss Cantrell's number, even though we've redacted part of it out?"

"Yes. I confirmed that before you blacked it out."

"Thank you. Now this first time, what did she say?"

Ted objects. "Hearsay, Your Honor."

Vanzetta waves us to the bench, scowling. As we huddle he peers down at Ted.

"Enlighten me."

For a moment Ted is thrown. "Well, Your Honor, it is – it would be – I would deem it to be a *statement*, made *out of court*, offered for the *truth of the matter asserted*. Does that pass the final?"

"You think I remember law school?" Vanzetta says, grinning and ducking his head so the jury can't see it. Then business, still in undertone. "Strike that last. Continue."

"The statements are the product of an unreliable source, because their source is Miss Cantrell, and her remarks were made during a time that by her own admission she does not remember, because she was incapacitated by mysterious drugs. How can they be relied upon?"

Vanzetta turns his head with a well-practiced laziness. "People?"

Sonya rolls her eyes. "There's nothing here to rely on. All that matters is her condition, the scene, the time frame."

"How so, as to time?"

"It conflicts with his statement. The jury will hear him say it was at least 10:45 when they got back and started drinking. She wasn't supposed to be back, with him, and already intoxicated by 10:30."

Ted knows all this, of course, but he's protecting himself.

"Very well. But I will be compelled to renew my objection should she attempt to offer any factual assertions by Miss Cantrell."

Vanzetta's eyes narrow into a smirk. "I guess we'll see. But you'll get all the cross you need."

"All the cross I can *bear*," Ted mutters, timing the line just right as he turns away.

THE COURT REPORTER repeats the question. Tamara focuses.

"Well, it was a little hard to make out, because she sounded seriously blitzed. But she said hey, you should get over here. I think that was her phrase."

"Did she say why?"

"No, not that I can remember anyway.  She wouldn't have normally, though – it was just, come over, hang, party. I mean, you've seen the place.  It was the go-to."

"Sure.  Did she mention that Haylee was there?"

"No, I'd have been surprised – I knew she'd gone away to school."

"Did you hear any voices in the background?"

"Yeah, a guy – I mean, a male voice. Mostly just laughing, I don't know at what.  Maybe TV.  I couldn't make out anything he was saying."

"No *other* voices in the background, right?"

"Right."

"Did you recognize the one male voice, or think you did?"

"No, not at all."

"Did you ask Jacinta who was there?"

"No."

"And she didn't volunteer who it was?"

"No.  She wasn't really able to say much."

"So what did you say, about going over?"

Tamara thinks this through.  "Well, I said no, no thanks.  Kinda begged off."

"Do you remember why?"

"Umm, well, yeah."  Tamara squirms in the chair, resettles.  "I'd been partying more than I should have, and was trying to get my act together before the holidays – we had family coming into town.  Plus I had studying to do.  So I knew I needed a weekend off.  I could hear she was already completely hammered by 10:30, there's already some noisy guy hanging out, and I didn't know how the night would go.  So I just said hey, not tonight."

"And how did she react?"

"She's just kind of mumbled something and laughed, and then hung up without saying goodbye."

SONYA WAITS an extra beat, then taps the screen.

"Now a couple of lines down, do you see a call just under an hour later, at 11:28, also from Jacinta Cantrell's number, for just one minute?"

"Yes."

"Miss Roberge, did you answer that call, too?"

"Yes. I nearly didn't – I'd already turned out the light to sleep, and I could imagine what she sounded like now. But then I thought she'd just call back if I didn't pick up."

"Now when you answered, that second time, was Jacinta on the other end?"

She pauses, and I feel the room go still. For just a moment now Tam Roberge has gravity. She gives a wondering shake. "I don't think so. But it's hard to be sure."

"OK. Was *anyone* there? Any sounds like earlier?"

She twitches again, looks away and back.

"No, that was the creepy part – there wasn't any other noise. It was so quiet I looked at my phone again to make sure it was her and she hadn't hung up."

Sonya nods, carefully, letting it linger. "What did you think, when you heard it?"

"Well, that it was probably accidental, that she'd hit the button, didn't know she'd dialed. Something like that. But considering how it sounded earlier, it didn't make sense that she'd be in a completely quiet place. I'd figured things were only gonna get wilder."

"How did you respond?"

"Just, hello hello, but nothing back. And so after maybe fifteen seconds I hung up."

"Did it worry you in any way, that call?"

Tamara considers it, grimaces. "Not as much as it should have."

"Why not?"

"I guess, the same thing. She drank enough to pass out sometimes – we all did. So I decided it was nothing but a passing-out drunk call, whether by accident or on purpose. And I just went to sleep."

Sonya pauses now, weighs her words.

"Miss Roberge, when Jacinta called the first time and you could understand her, did she say anything at all about having taken drugs, including roofies?"

"No. To me she just sounded way drunk, but it could have been the other stuff for all I know."

"Had you ever heard her mention roofies, at any point?"

"No. I didn't know what they were. I don't think I really do now."

"And as far as you knew, she didn't either?"

Vanzetta sustains Ted's objection, but Sonya is smiling. A good place to stop.

TED LEANS on the lectern as he peers at her.

"You said you 'didn't know how the night would go' if you went over there when Jacinta called you. Can you elaborate on that?"

"Umm, well." Tam Roberge is savvy enough to flick a glance Sonya's way, hoping for an objection. "Basically, like I said, I was trying to pull myself together that weekend, and it was always kinda unpredictable with her. Things could get a little wild at her place, particularly if a lot of people showed up, and we could all lose the handle pretty easy. It sounded like she'd gotten off to a fast start, and there's already some strange guy there. It just wasn't what I wanted that night."

"Fast start meaning drunk and/or drugged?"

"Right."

"OK. Now to get this straight, at 10:31 you heard a man in the background, as well as television, and at 11:28, you didn't hear either of those things?"

"Yes."

"Meaning the male could well have left?"

"Objection, calls for speculation."

"Sustained."

"All right." Ted pauses, then takes a shot. "Now Miss Roberge, did you know of any males who hung around with Jacinta Cantrell?"

Sonya scowls. "Objection, irrelevant."

Ted tries a whopper. "As potential witnesses, Your Honor."

Vanzetta just waves us back to the bench, smirking again.

"I'd say we're a little past the discovery phase, wouldn't you?" He aims the stage-whisper right at Ted Stauber. "Here in mid-trial?"

"Investigation is an ongoing thing, Your Honor. This is simply–"

"Swinging at the *pinata*?" Sonya suggests.

"Base-covering, Judge. The witness declined to speak to us."

"But she also stated that she didn't recognize the male voice in the background. So you certainly can't expect her to testify to anyone in particular. And I'm not going to permit you to toss around names with no connection to this crime."

"Again, we don't intend it as evidence of third-party culpability. We're just trying to provide an accurate rendition of the conditions in that house. When witnesses won't cooperate, a certain amount of discovery *is* necessary on the stand."

"Maybe – when relevant." The judge turns. "People?"

"We stand on our objection, Your Honor. There is no reason to believe any person she could name was in any way involved. Miss Cantrell made clear that Mr. Rodarte was their one houseguest that evening. There's no evidence of any other person or vehicle."

Vanzetta nods as we retreat. "Objection sustained. Proceed."

"Thank you. Nothing more."

# *10*

*August 24 – Morning*
(JPH)

THE ONE USEFUL NEIGHBOR is a retired Army lieutenant colonel named Bern Dumaret. He will explain how – and when – Rodarte fled in a frenzy.

HE'S AT LEAST Ted's age, I'd say, but the picture of fit – sinewy and healthy-lean, not old-man skinny, with a dog-walker's tan, a white crew cut, and a squint.

He lives across the road from the Cantrell estate, on a rise.

"Mr. Dumaret, had you contacted the Sheriff's Department previously about activities at that house?"

"Yes, on two occasions."

"How recently?"

"Well, I can't pin the first one down – July or August, I think. Summertime. But the second was, I believe, two Fridays prior."

"Those were in regard to noise?"

"Yes. Pounding music, loud voices after midnight. Tends to carry right across."

"And the sheriff responded?"

"Yes, both times. That settled things down."

"All right. So what happened on this night, the 21st?"

"Well, I'm a widower, I live alone. It had actually been quiet over there that night, and I was on my way to bed at 11:45. Then I suddenly heard car doors slam and a truck, it sounded like, came barreling down the long driveway across the road. So I looked out toward the bottom of the drive, which is lighted, and saw what looked like a white sport-utility flash through, turn on the road with a shriek of tires and go tearing off south.

"Now since things had been quiet otherwise, I was a little puzzled, grabbed my binoculars. There's a smaller, one-story guest-house building south of the main residence, past the apple trees, and I could just make out that its front door was ajar, and that there was light coming from inside the building."

"I see. And then what?"

"Well, there's some background. We'd just had a couple of break-ins that month, one of 'em the property up from mine. So I'm on the lookout. It ends up I stand there a minute or two, watching, see no sign of anybody else, and decide I oughta call it in, even though it isn't much. Got the same dispatcher I'd had before, too, so I didn't even know how seriously they'd take me."

"I see. And you're sure it was 11:45 when you saw the SUV?"

"By my kitchen clock."

"And you're confident it's accurate?"

"Calibrated weekly."

"So you used the term 'tearing off' to describe the vehicle. Can you elaborate on that?"

Dumaret makes a sour face. "Zooming. In a hell of a rush."

"Even coming down the driveway?"

"From the noise, yes. I didn't have much of a view till it came to the bottom, but it was hauling, and then it peeled out into the road."

"Did you see or hear anything before the SUV tore off – for example, a female voice?"

Haylee shouldn't have cried out, but there's no harm in asking.

The old Army man does consider it for several seconds, but shakes his head. "Not that I could make out."

TED STAUBER was a Navy corpsman out of high school, just missed Korea. Maybe the helpful neighbor knows the scent of a swabbie, even now. Ted has a question on the tip of his tongue, it seems, but bites it back.

♦

LIKE ALL NEWBIES, the gangling, strawberry-blond deputy named Logan Akers started as a custody officer in the jail. Like the smartest of them, he'd sprung himself out onto patrol within six months. And before he knew it he was on Sundown Road at midnight.

This being his first murder trial, he should be sucking air, clutching his report like a life preserver and quavering through his answers, yellow-faced. In fact he's already a known pro.

The call was a basic "suspicious circumstances." He'd responded to one of the recent area burglaries, two properties north, so was prepared for more of the same. Had never been on the property but had seen it from the road.

"When you arrived on this night you saw a light, is that right?"

"Yes, visible through an orchard from Sundown Road."

"And you were alone?"

"Deputy Laird heard the call and happened to be very close by. She knew the property and knew I'd only been off field training status for a couple of months – she'd been my training officer. So she decided to meet up with me there, and we set out to investigate together."

Sonya smiles gently. Bracing him for it, maybe.

"Now what did that involve?"

"The light had been reported in a residential building near the southern end of the property, along with an unsecured door. And, as I indicated, it was faintly visible. So we entered from the perimeter of the property and made our way across toward it."

"Was the property fenced?"

"The orchard portion was not. There was a gate and a hedge border along the main driveway, as I recall, and I believe portions of the vineyard on the property were fenced."

"Now when you came out of the trees, could see the building?"

"Yes ma'am. The light we'd seen was above the doorway of a single-story, guest-house-type building. The door was ajar, and there was also light visible behind it, from inside."

"And what did you do, at that point?"

He sets his jaw. "We announced our presence, got no answer, then entered the building to ensure no one needed assistance."

"And what did the two of you find inside?"

"The outer room, the living area, was empty, but we observed a door to a bedroom that was also partially open. We looked through the door and saw a partially-clothed female figure lying on her back on top of a made bed in that room."

"What more did you observe about her?"

"Well, we found that she was non-responsive, had signs of hemorrhages in her eyes and had obviously been violently assaulted. She appeared to have been strangled."

"What did you do then?"

"We radioed for assistance and attempted CPR, with no success. Deputy Laird then set out to sweep the immediate area while I remained behind. When paramedics arrived they declared the young lady to be deceased."

Sonya clicks on the projector, and she is there under the oak tree.

"Is this the young lady you found on the bed?"

"Yes ma'am. It is."

"And did you learn her name to be Haylee Maureen Branch?"

Akers takes a solemn half-second, bows his head. "We did."

TED IS AMIABLE with him, meanders a little, then smiles.

"Now, Deputy, can you catalog for us any items you touched, came into contact with, at the scene?"

It's really just a prayer, but it's also a freeroll. Ted needs any inconsistencies he can find, anything that will let him argue that the investigation was careless.

As such, it's tonic. Akers straightens himself, cop-firm all the way.

"Let me try to be precise. The door to the building swings inward, and it was ajar but not entirely open. So I nudged it slightly without touching the handle. Once inside we found the door to the bedroom also ajar, and facing inward. I opened that slowly in the same manner to allow us to pass through.

"At that point we found Miss Branch. We immediately called for emergency medical responders. I touched her wrists, her neck and her chest, seeking a pulse. Deputy Laird assisted in that. There was none. However, we noted that her body temperature was still warm, and attempted chest compressions and CPR for several minutes as we awaited the paramedics.

"In sweeping the building we were obliged to touch several other doors, including a couple of closed closet doors. Then other personnel arrived and secured the scene."

"And what about Deputy Laird? What did you see *her* touch?"

"Well, she accompanied me as we entered the building, and was with me for some minutes while we tried to revive the victim. Beyond that, I can't speak to what she might or might not have touched."

"Well, what you observed," Ted attempts.

"Only what I've told you, to the best of my recall. And I'm sure you don't want me to speculate."

Genius. Ted, of course, *does* want him to speculate, to put out there the idea that Laird did something she might later deny doing.

"No, certainly not. So you were together in the bedroom?"

"Yes sir."

"When and where did you separate?"

"Just after we determined the building was secure. I returned to the bedroom while she went back outside."

"So you were left alone inside with Miss Branch, but touched *nothing*?"

"No sir, I was still new on patrol." He smiles discreetly, a kid flashing through again. "Figured it made better sense to wait."

♦

DEPUTY ANGELA LAIRD, a more fearsome redhead, takes the stand in an off-white pantsuit and sensible heels. The rare specific guidance from Tom Winston: urge formalwear for cops at trial, not uniform and gun. Makes them look more like a professional, less like a threat. She is not particularly softened by the look.

**(WADE)**

ANGIE LAIRD . . . There was a brutal winter day, maybe the year of the trial, when she pulled a teenager out of a car in the middle of a crashing rainstorm west of Hammonds, saved his life. A crappy old Dodge had slid off the road, flipped and landed upside down in a wash. She waded out there, found the kid's dad and little brother both dead, but he got wedged in just right and had enough to breathe, broken arm and collarbone, whatever it was, and so she dragged him out of there and ended up with a community award out of it.

But long before there's a photo op I remember her shaking her head and swearing, because she had stopped the car a week before, the registration was expired, it had two broken seat belts and the tires were so bald she wanted to impound it and drag the dirtbag dad's ass to jail for endangerment. And the younger kid, she said, had the balls to mouth off, a dropped apple if you ever saw one.

When horror struck, though, there was never a doubt – Angie, with two of her own in elementary school, went out in water to her waist and dragged the bigger kid out of there anyway, risking her own ass when she could've waited, and she'd have done the same for the smaller kid if there'd been any shot at saving him. The job is the job, get out of my way.

The bottom line is that she loves patrol, hates diplomacy and has that ancient handicap of being a woman in a man's world. With all that over her, I doubt she even wants to make sergeant. But I can still picture her running the station one day.

**(JPH)**

"After you discovered the body, what came first?"

Laird squints at the middle distance, wrinkling her freckled nose, then swings back to Sonya. "After contacting dispatch and attempting CPR, we very quickly swept the inside of the property, leaving the scene as undisturbed as possible, to ensure no one remained there. We then went outside the building to consider exit routes, possible paths of travel. We then determined that Deputy Akers should remain at the scene while I swept the immediate area."

"What was your state of mind at that time?"

"High alert." She can't quite repress a *dumb question* scowl, even for Sonya. "I'm trying to determine if there's a killer in my vicinity, possibly concealed in darkness, and I'm also mindful of not disturbing evidence he might have left. I'm wanting to examine pathways for possible tracks. Then I'm also generally wanting to reach the main house and see what's there. Lot on my plate."

"You had also been there before, you indicated?"

"Correct. That was on the eighth of November, two weeks prior, about 020 hours. Just past midnight."

"And how did that come about?"

"A standard 415 call – noise disturbance. Loud outdoor party with many underage attendees."

"On the prior occasion, do you remember who you met there?"

"I was greeted at the door by a young woman who identified herself as Jacie Cantrell and advised that she lived there. She appeared intoxicated but was compliant with solving the problem."

"Now on the night you found the body when you returned two weeks later, Deputy, did you look for shoeprints?"

"I did, as I moved toward the house. However, the only path leading away from the *casita*, apart from the short walkway to a dock at the creek, was of continuous concrete and stone tile from there to the main house. I could not make out markings along it."

"What about leading away from the concrete path, through the orchard?"

"I scanned a bit with my flashlight as I traveled toward the house, but there was too much ground to cover, and I could not make out individual tracks at that time."

"And so you traveled the path to the house?"

"I did."

"What did you observe when you reached it, if you recall?"

"Well, I approached with care, and edged along the perimeter to a large bay window, which was uncovered. When I reached it I looked inside, and I was able to make out a huddled shape on a white sectional couch. This proved to be a second young lady, whom I eventually recognized as Miss Cantrell. But to my relief she was breathing. And around that time my backup arrived."

ON TED'S TURN, he's scowling. "Deputy Laird, what did you collect from the main residence, when you entered?"

"Myself, nothing. After calling for backup and medical our focus was securing the scene, leaving the evidence for the detectives and techs. I touched only the bottom of the handle of the sliding door to the patio, which was unlocked, and that as minimally as possible to open the door. And once inside, of course, I touched Miss Cantrell to determine her physical condition and attempt to revive her."

"How many bottles did you observe in that room?"

"If you mean beer bottles, at least a dozen, but I didn't make an exact count."

"But you did touch some of them, surely, at least once?"

"No, myself none, either there or in the *casita*. They were left for the techs."

"Did you open the front door to admit your colleagues?"

"No, I advised them to come through the doorway at the side of the house."

"They parked at the top of the driveway?"

"No. They were advised to park at the base of the driveway, so as not to obscure possible tire markings."

"By you?"

"Yes sir, with emphasis. It was my job to preserve the scene."

Ted mumbles and sits, for the moment a beaten man.

◆

THE RESPONDING CRIMINALISTS, two of them, lay out what they saw and examined and what they took away in plastic bags, including one beer bottle from the *casita* and thirteen from the house.

Then the deputy coroner, who arrived, confirmed demise, arranged Haylee's removal when the scene had been processed, wrote the necessary report. His face remains fixed in a thin, firm line, his voice soft, even as he authenticates pictures of the scene. Even a Haylee Branch is routine.

Vanzetta winds it up, one fast quip to the jury. *Like a vacation tomorrow, folks — we're only here* half *a day.* They don't smile much, filing out pale and wary.

◆

BRIAN TRAILS ME into my office. On a contact high now, fully with the program.

"That was *solid*."

"I was fabulous," I agree, having not uttered a word on the record.

"Well, you just gotta sit there and look pretty."

"I'm *trying* to look badass."

He breaks into real live giggles.

"You are, man. You're as serious as a nuclear warhead. Your face is a polished rock. And you *do* look pretty, by the way. New suit?"

Somebody noticed.

◆

I HAVE A HANDFUL of tasks for Sonya, maybe two hours' worth. At the end she declines my offer to fetch her a sandwich, so I hit the Daily Grinder alone, then ease home, where I shed my jacket and tie and stagger out to my patio in the last salmon light of the day.

You'd swear it's the sun that's leaving, not us aboard the rocket ship, making every unfelt bend and turn, cavorting through the ocean of space. But one way or another, the black settles down and around, and a Coors goes half undrunk even as night takes charge.

# *11*

## *August 25 – Afternoon*
## (JPH)

VANZETTA IS OTHERWISE OCCUPIED on the morning of the second day of evidence, so we don't reconvene until after lunch. The room, though a bit emptier, seems more stifling than the day before.

Me in the second seat, sticky-shirted, does resolve a question. At trial the prosecution can designate one cop as its "investigating officer," which entitles him (her) to remain in the courtroom when other witnesses are excluded, and even to sit next to the DA. And at times having the lead cop at your elbow is helpful. But there's an argument that having armed authority next to the sober-suited prosecutor can, in some cases, look to the jury like ganging up. So it tends to be a point of discussion, even from one day to the next.

A second DA scuttles the issue. Instead of brandishing broad shoulders and a gun, I sit mild and unarmed, and Wade retires to the front row of the gallery.

ON MOST DAYS we sort out questions before the jury is brought in. They veer to the practical. Where can we stash our modest media during the breaks? Can we keep the reporters out of our office visitor lobby, where they want to hover as the day winds up? Can Ashlyn Branch wear a T-shirt with Haylee's name, if the jury can read it?

These have sensible answers, but Vanzetta worries most, as judges do, about the jury – their comfort, their timeliness, and above all their immunity from taint.

He not only reads the standard separation admonishment at every break, he often amps it up. "I must remind you not to discuss the case or form any opinion concerning the defendant's guilt or innocence until the conclusion of trial, when you have heard all the evidence and convened together in the jury room, and to refrain from discussing the case with one another or with others until that time. I mean by that you are not to discuss the case with your husbands and wives, significant others, children, mailmen, barbers, bartenders, bosses, babysitters, priests, handymen, bankers, sisters, brothers, cousins, nephews, aunts by marriage . . ."

He enjoys this shtick far more than the conscripts do, but he has the rake's confidence that he'll bring his audience around eventually. The best I ever see is a tight smile or two.

Beyond that, though, there's worry about passive exposure to outside influence. Jurors must not hear random remarks from spectators, bitter ones from Haylee's side, even a fast quip from a bored scribe. Or, just as dangerously, a quick, trailing comment by Ted to his investigator – or Sonya to me – in the hallway bustle.

Eventually it is rigged so that the jurors can enter by a side door from the sheriff's department each morning and afternoon, then snake through the back halls and out again, avoiding the artery altogether.

And, of course, we make extra-sure Rodarte is already dressed out and seated in place before the jury is brought in each morning. Despite the fact our defendant is charged with murder, and the awkward truth is sure to emerge soon enough, Vanzetta – like most judges – wants to divert attention from the fact he is in custody. So in these first days a slow-processing juror may conclude that Rodarte is simply punctual by nature, that the curious monotony of his suits arises from nothing more than a lack of style, and that the calm and restraint of his body language is natural – as opposed to being ensured by Deputy Aziz, who hasn't changed expression yet, perched two feet behind him.

♦

WADE IS PROPERLY GRAVE as he takes the stand. He's around my age, dark-eyed and middle-sized, with notable cheekbones and in-between coloring. And very well versed in the ritual.

It's an hour going through it, the scene, the tracks, the video footage, the muddy caravan, until the dawn in San Ricardo. And then Rodarte – exhausted but alert – on his belt recorder.

ALONE WITH RODARTE, in his mother's backyard with the patio door closed, Wade gave him a "Beheler" advisal – essentially an inverse Miranda, where the suspect is assured that he *isn't* in custody and may end the conversation, even leave the scene, at any point.

The key is that a defendant not yet under arrest need not be given the Miranda warning itself. And the hidden wrinkle is that this non-Miranda is only a transitory proclamation, because it is not rare for a conversation that begins as "informal" to end in an arrest, if the suspect's answers have now created probable cause where only suspicion lay before. But when the cops can afford to move slowly, it's a great place to start.

We begin there. Sonya passes out transcripts, hits play, and the voices crackle through the overhead speakers as we follow along.

### (*REDACTED TRANSCRIPT – RODARTE 1*)

| | |
|---|---|
| DET. WADE: | So hey, sorry. Not your average Saturday morning huh? |
| RODARTE: | Yeah, well no. |
| WADE: | Sorry about that, and walkin in on your mom. You live here, right? |
| RODARTE: | Well, moving back. I just got here again, few hours ago. |
| WADE: | This her place, I take it? |
| RODARTE: | Yeah, few years now. |

# Cold Record

| | |
|---|---|
| WADE: | That room you came from yours? |
| RODARTE: | Well, kinda mine by default. But you know, basically, wherever I'm not in the way for a few days, weeks, whatever. |
| WADE: | And your – what is it out front? Tahoe, or was it – |
| RODARTE: | Suburban. |
| WADE: | Serious wheels. You got a crowd to carry around? |
| RODARTE: | Ah, nah. Sorta did a while back, though, with my lady of the time. Her and her kids, came in handy. It needed work, but that's where I could help myself out. Now I just kinda drive around lookin dumb in it, I guess. |
| WADE: | So where'd you come here from, where you been? |
| RODARTE: | Well, been up north, along the coast. Palomar County. |
| WADE: | What were you doing up there? |
| RODARTE: | It's where my ex-girlfriend was, really. But then, since you asked, I'm fresh out of county up there – I wound up serving out a |

71

|  |  |
|---|---|
|  | probation violation, did four months actual. Figured I'd seen enough of the place. |
| WADE: | And so you just made it driving down here, last night? |
| RODARTE: | Last night. Way late. |
| WADE: | All right. Well, and hey, this is bound to be throwing you off, first thing in the AM, but I'm not here to dick around, really. Just had a question or two. |
| RODARTE: | Uh-huh . . . |
| WADE: | See, we're looking into something that happened last night, wondering if you might know anything about that something. Gonna ask lots of people, you're just one, and can't really tell you why right now. And people read off plates wrong every day, but it's the place to start. Did you maybe duck off 101 and take a bunch of back roads, heading down? Hills and dales? |
| RODARTE: | Yeah, I did. Yes sir. Lot of wandering. |

# Cold Record

WADE:       Now did you wind up coming on
            through my county, maybe?   Nice
            little corner of the world with
            lakes and mountains and broke-
            down jalopies, not much else?

RODARTE:    Man.   Right . . . how the hell?
            I did, absolutely.   But - what,
            CIA keeping tabs on me or
            something?

WADE:       No, no.   No black helicopters,
            really kind of a fluke.   Just,
            well, I basically have a long
            story about something that went
            down yesterday, and I'm trying to
            shorten it down a little.   So we
            talk to people, and we get the
            idea your vehicle and some other
            ones might have been in the
            immediate area.   So I'm going down
            a list.

RODARTE:    OK.   And you're wondering about
            something that went down?   Where?

WADE:       Well, let's make sure I'm in the
            ballpark.   When you passed there,
            you happen to come down a road
            called Sundown?

73

RODARTE:     Sundown . . . is that −?

WADE:        Road with a house where you might
             have stopped?

**It's four seconds on the tape, a good long time.  Then a laugh.**

RODARTE:     I did, if that's the house.  It
             must be.  See, here's the − the
             thing that went down, whatever
             sense it makes for you.  I stopped
             off at a mini-mart near there,
             whatever that nearest town is.  I
             go in and there's a girl who comes
             up, older girl but not 21, and she
             wants me to buy beer for her.  So,
             well, I went along and did it.
             Guess that's a crime right there,
             if you care.  But I bought it, she
             follows on out a minute later,
             comes up to my truck and she's
             short of cash, like five bucks.
             I'm thinkin fine, I'll just keep
             a couple beers, but she goes hey,
             you need to follow me to my place,
             I'll pay you and you can have some
             too.  It'll be a party.

| | |
|---|---|
| WADE: | Ah. Nice. And that's what you did, went to the house on Sundown? |
| RODARTE: | Followed her taillights, yeah. Got there and it was a damn estate. Long-ass driveway, big fancy house. |
| WADE: | And she invites you on in? |
| RODARTE: | Yeah. |
| WADE: | What time is it? |
| RODARTE: | I'm not that sure. I know it was already maybe 10:15 when we got to the mini-mart, because I'd been looking at the time and trying to calculate when I'd make it home before I stopped. Then that all takes a few minutes, then we talk at the truck, then the drive to her place. Had to be at least 10:45 when we got there. |
| WADE: | And who else is at the house? |
| RODARTE: | Well, I just saw this one other girl. No party yet, anyway. |
| WADE: | OK, tell me about the second girl. |
| RODARTE: | Well, she was somebody you'd notice. Blonde, slim, tall side, eyes sort of silvery-blue, long |

lashes. Gorgeous, basically, but also the quiet type, you could see that, used to letting the other girl take the lead. I first figured she lived there – she fit better than the first girl did.

WADE: All right. You get her name?

RODARTE: Yeah. Lee, she said. Lee.

WADE: When was that?

RODARTE: Well, quick. We were, fuck – I was just there a few minutes. She, the first one, said her name was Jacie, no idea how you spell it, she gets the few bucks she owes me, offers me a beer, I say OK. I sit down with em, drink it down, make small talk for a few minutes, take in the atmosphere. But I don't belong there, and it isn't any party, just two girls, so that's my cue. I'm there maybe 20, 25 minutes, and then I just kinda politely excuse myself, head back down the drive and start on the way here.

# Cold Record

| | |
|---|---|
| WADE: | So you'd figure what, 11:20-11:30 when you leave? Or could it have been later? |
| RODARTE: | Well, hard to say. I wouldn't – no. Shouldn't have been later. |
| WADE: | So for sure not 11:45? |
| RODARTE: | Not – no, not for sure. I just wasn't paying close attention. |
| WADE: | So you came straight on back, from there south? |
| RODARTE: | Well, I'm not great with directions. And I think – well, I got confused somewhere, wandered off the main road and it took a while to find my way back. |
| WADE: | Near the house, after you left? |
| RODARTE: | Well, I think so. But maybe that was earlier. I was pretty brain-fogged by the end of the day. |
| WADE: | Now, did you have direct contact with the second girl, Lee? Shake hands, anything? |
| RODARTE: | No, just kind of a wave at each other. Super casual. Sat down and made some small talk with her. |

WADE:    All right. OK. This helps a lot, for sequence. See, you happened to stop by this house down on Sundown Road. Then time goes by, there's a call to police and the next thing you know it's a full-on crime scene, and we're trying to figure out who might have been there when this shit went down, and *when* it happened, too. We're thinking a party, actually, so I'm kinda thrown by what you're telling me. We heard this was a party house, and thinking maybe it's something just got outta hand. But something ultimately went down. So we're trying to piece together the people that were there, because basically we got nowhere else to start. License plates, see what people know. That's why I'm all the way down here, wearing you out.

RODARTE:    Umm.

Wade is creative. Here, not for the first time, he pulls out an old booking shot of Tommy Hite, a tweaker who fell off a dock and drowned a few summers back. More than one suspect has eagerly ID'd him at a crime scene the night before.

WADE: So look, lemme show you one thing, in case it jangles. No right answer. Any chance you came across this guy last night?

RODARTE: No, no sir. I mean, guess he could've been somewhere I didn't see him. Big as the place was, people might've been tucked away, back rooms and stuff, but no. I mean - no.

WADE: He mighta lost the goatee. This isn't a brand-new pic.

RODARTE: Doesn't look familiar, no. Just the girls there at that main house, no dudes at all. I guess he could've passed me on the road or something.

WADE: All right. All right. Didn't really figure, with the time frame, but wanted to check. Now you said about 10:15-ish you reached the mini-mart and ran into

|  | Jacinta, then around 10:45 you got to the house? |
| RODARTE: | Yeah, at least. Had to be. |
| WADE: | OK. Let me ask you this, though. Did you touch anything there, in the house? |
| RODARTE: | The house? Well, what - maybe something here or there? Beer bottle, I guess? And I touched the beer pack, obviously. Can't think of anything else. But might have. Sure - could have. |
| WADE: | Now did you ever go outside, from inside? |
| RODARTE: | Like out to a patio or something? No, man, never. I just went in and out the front door. |
| WADE: | Didn't explore the property? |
| RODARTE: | Naw. I went to take a leak, guest bathroom. That's it. Guess I'd have touched things in there, too. |
| WADE: | OK. Now were the girls drinking, when you were there? |
| RODARTE: | Yeah. The first girl Jacie had seemed a little buzzed when I saw her in the store, and she pounded |

|            |                                                                                                                                                                                              |
|------------|----------------------------------------------------------------------------------------------------------------------------------------------------------------------------------------------|
|            | it hard when we got back. The other girl Lee was just sipping, didn't really seem like a boozer.                                                                                              |
| WADE:      | All right. So did you and Lee ever break off, leave the room? Go somewhere else, just the two of you?                                                                                         |
| RODARTE:   | Well, no – I mean. No.                                                                                                                                                                        |
| WADE:      | You're not sounding sure.                                                                                                                                                                     |
| RODARTE:   | Just trying to get it right. But – no, not at all. We talked a little, it was nice, but just right there. And like I said, I didn't stay long.                                                |
| WADE:      | So you wouldn't have carried a beer into another room, anything like that?                                                                                                                    |
| RODARTE:   | Well, the bathroom? Or maybe set one down somewhere? I'm not – I don't think so. But not sure.                                                                                                |
| WADE:      | Hey, memory ain't perfect. I'm just trying to get the lay of the land. Now you got here when?                                                                                                 |
| RODARTE:   | I lost track. Way late.                                                                                                                                                                       |

| WADE: | Long after midnight, right, since you were still up there until at least 11:20-11:30? |
| RODARTE: | Ahh, again, can't really say for sure. But, yeah. Maybe 2:30? |
| WADE: | I'm just trying to fit things together. So by midnight you're a good way gone, anyhow? |
| RODARTE: | Well, it's hard – I just don't know. Like I said, I didn't take all the right roads, so I wandered around a little. Don't know quite when I got to anywhere. But yeah, I must have been pretty far away by then. |
| WADE: | Sure. Thanks. Hey, could we go out real quick to your Suburban? |
| RODARTE: | You mean for – like what? |
| WADE: | Well, just covering my bases. You've watched TV. |
| RODARTE: | Well – sure, man. |

(END OF RECORDING)

# *12*

**(WADE)**

I THOUGHT PICTURES of the tire tread would be half the case, putting him there. No idea he'd just admit it. We'll need 'em anyway.

The jacket's just sitting loose in the back seat, plain sight, dark blue cotton-fleece sort of thing. Very strange he didn't ditch it, looking back. I do think he looks a little nervous when I fish it out, tell him I better take it, I'll give him a receipt.

Back inside I want to see his room – he'd been there what, three hours? He could make me get a warrant, but we're still being friendly. I see a pile next to a hamper – gotta be last night's dirties. Jeans, a gray flannel shirt with the cuffs rolled one fold. And he says yeah, it's mine, from the trip down. Obviously hasn't had time to wash yet.

Recording again, I tell him I better snag those, too, but he just says sure, take 'em all. Nonchalant about it, almost. So, thanks, I say, and then go Columbo – oh, guess I better ask you for your drawers, too.

And for a moment I'm sure. In my fantasy it was too late to wash them without waking his mother. There will be all of it – spunk, a hair from the girl he raped, maybe even her blood.

But he just shrugs, goes to the hamper and comes right out with a dry gray pair of boxers. "All yours," he says. "I don't go without 'em."

"May I?" I say, opening the hamper lid, half wanting him to challenge me, demand a warrant – I think I'll *know* if he does, for whatever that's worth. I figure half a dozen pair, maybe more – he'd have brought his laundry home, right? But he doesn't, just gestures with open hand, and there's nothing in there but a single pair of socks. Otherwise he hadn't unpacked.

Yet another reason to arrest him would be to do a sex kit, a swab of his privates to see if any of Haylee adhered to him. But he tells me he showered, too, and shows me the bathroom, the washcloth and towel, all that. I don't *have* to buy in, but somehow I'm sure it's true.

Finally I ask him to take off his shirt, looking for signs of a life-or-death struggle. The best I do is a couple of scratches.

**(JPH)**

NOT A WEALTH, but slightly suggestive. Rodarte has nicks on the back of his right hand, a scrape on his right wrist, a couple of faint lines on his neck, a bruise above his sternum.

"Did you ask him about those blemishes, these signs of injury?"

"Well, he volunteered a partial explanation."

"I see." Sonya's tone is velvet skepticism. "What was that?"

"He stated he had gotten scraped up in a basketball game while confined."

"All right. What then?"

"At that time, I believe, I asked his leave to take swabs beneath his fingernails, on the chance biological material might be present. Once again he agreed. I also obtained his fingerprints."

"I see. And was there anything else, before you left?"

"A last thing." Wade pauses. "I asked if he'd mind me collecting a DNA sample."

**(WADE)**

ON THE TAPE it's here you do hear a slight hitch. *Umm, well, sure . . . I don't know how any of that works.*

Shit, me neither, I say back, cheery. Just something we ask about, these days. I pull out the kit and swab his cheek, a ten-second job.

Keeping it light, my strange decision already made, I tell him he's the closest thing we have for a witness, get his cell number (which we'll need), tell him not to vanish without letting us know.

He's already nodding, relieved as hell. "Sure man, whatever I can do. Here I am out two fuckin days and lo and behold, talkin to a detective. Johnny on the Spot again."

"Yeah, must be weird."

"Well, that's kinda my normal."

## (JPH)

TED STAUBER'S CROSS is predictably brief. There aren't many facts in dispute, and given a choice, he's always preferred to hurry solid cops off the stage. Wade, in particular, is no help.

"Now, you saw just that single set of tracks turning out into the road from the driveway, correct?"

"Yes. Mr. Rodarte's."

"But you can't swear there was no *other* vehicle in the driveway at the time, that might have left before you did?"

"Well, that's hard to imagine. Because there was only the one set of unfamiliar tracks, and the water was still puddled when I got there."

Ted's face reddens – he rarely loses track of a key fact. "Yet despite that information, you did not arrest Mr. Rodarte following the conclusion of the interview, correct?"

"Yes."

"Which would mean that at that point you were not satisfied of his guilt, correct?"

Vanzetta instantly denies Sonya's relevance objection – curious himself, no doubt.

Wade goes stock-still, spends a solid five seconds gearing up.

"I strongly suspected him of guilt. And I believe I could rightfully have arrested him on the spot, but I chose to wait."

"Why?"

"Because, above all, we have the burden of proof. I wanted to be that much more confident."

"Confident in your case, the path to conviction?"

Wade's brows rise a quarter of a centimeter, but I know the whole room sees it.

"Confident that we had found the man who killed Miss Branch."

♦

THE KANE COUNTY DEPUTY on the traffic stop is a classic old mustache named Richardson, easily retirement age, tired but good-humored after the long trip north.

He confirms making a stop of a white Chevy Suburban on southbound I-5 on the morning of November 26, 2003.

"Do you see the driver of that vehicle in court?"

"Gentleman at the far end of the table, dark brown hair, suit and blue tie."

"Record will reflect identification of the defendant," Vanzetta murmurs.

"Thank you, Your Honor." Sonya shuffles pages. "Now when you made contact, did you ask him for his registration?"

"I did, yes ma'am."

"And was it current?"

"It was not, in fact. It had lapsed two months prior, as the tags showed. That was my stated basis for the stop."

Then the bonus.

"What about his identification?"

The deputy's mouth twitches north. "At my request he produced . . . a California driver's license."

Sonya bites her own smile back. "Putting that aside for a moment, did you ask where he was from, and where he was going?"

"Yes. He advised me that he was from the Marin County area, but he was headed to Long Beach for work purposes."

Sonya clicks, a picture of the license now looms on the wall, and I swear I hear a juror giggle.

"Deputy, is this an accurate copy of that driver's license?"

"Sure looks to be."

"How does the license identify him?"

He clears his throat. "As you will see, the name listed on the driver's license is partially redacted, but the last is Castaneda, and the first two names did not correspond to the actual driver, Mr. Rodarte. The day and month have been redacted, but his birth year is given as 1962. His height is given as five feet nine inches, his weight 180. The address has been redacted, but the city is shown as San Rafael, California."

"And did you conclude that the driver wasn't the man in the license photograph?"

"I did, yes. It seemed self-evident. And the registration on the vehicle was in the name of Andrew Rodarte, not Mr. Castaneda."

"So this was a false form of identification, in your view?"

"Yes ma'am. When confronted, the driver admitted it and acknowledged that in fact he was Andrew Rodarte."

"In light of the expired registration and the false identification, what did you do?"

"I said we would need to tow the vehicle, and that he was being detained and would need to accompany me to our station, which was about fifteen miles distant."

"Did you mention the warrant for his arrest?"

"I did not."

TED WON ONE SMALL BATTLE, gets to ask the obvious. "This was part of a plan, was it not?"

Deputy Richardson smiles. "After a fashion. We'd been advised earlier that morning, as had other agencies, to keep a lookout for this particular vehicle. Later we'd learned that an arrest warrant for the driver was now active. We'd also gotten updates from this county as to his progress south, and had been told the tags would support a stop as well."

"But you did not arrest him on the warrant, correct?"

"Correct. Earlier in the day we'd been asked simply to detain him for a reasonable time if a stop was required. Your county advised us that he had no prior history of violence and was not believed to be armed. After the warrant went active, a felony arrest became a strong option, but in the moment he was highly cooperative, and I judged that the detention could be accomplished without risk. So I did not formally arrest him at all, and removed his handcuffs at the station. Your detectives then arrived by helicopter and completed the arrest."

And Ted has no real follow-up, because "pretext stops" are normally legal. If a cop has a valid reason to pull someone over, it's irrelevant that there's a larger objective.

THE HELICOPTER is a shiny lure. The jury is late-afternoon resilient as Bill Porter ambles to the stand.

# *13*

*August 25 – Afternoon*
## (DETECTIVE BILL PORTER, CCSD)

MY GENERAL GAME is to put 'em at ease. Helps that I'm bald, homespun and three years older than dirt, plus I've learned a few sympathetic faces over the years. So I try to stay steady and calm, get their guard down. Sooner or later they usually decide they have a few things to tell me, and a trickle has a way of turning into a stream, or even a flood.

Down in Kane County it's me and a second corporal, Gerardo Vasquez. Half my age, basically, one big ball of adrenaline. But he went all over hell in the Marines, and he doesn't miss much of anything. We pair up funny, when we do pair – Tortoise and Hare. It's been known to work, though, and now here we are when it counts.

It's a hell of an entrance, really, swooping down from the sky and marching on in to tell him he's under arrest. Then a search of his Suburban. Then we talk.

WE ACTUALLY HAVE THE IDEA he might be bright enough to clam up now, under the circumstances, but he waives Miranda right off. I get the feeling he's about given up, which is a great place to start.

If this was the first interview, we'd start slower, trying to get him comfortable, but here he's barely escaped getting hooked once, he's tried to run, and now he's under arrest. You meet people so deluded they imagine they can talk their way out of anything, but all along I think he knows he's finished.

I'm nearly right.

## (JPH)

PORTER IS CLUMSY, triple-chinned and Texas-slow, but he's as reassuring as a St. Bernard in a blinding blizzard. *I'd* talk to him, too. For a second time Sonya hits play.

## (REDACTED TRANSCRIPT – RODARTE 2)

PORTER:    Look, first let me apologize for the dramatics. We just reckoned the bird would make life easier. And I know you already explained all this once, but we need to try and work through it some more, before everybody goes off half-cocked.

RODARTE:   Okay.

PORTER:    You know where we are, no point in playing around. You're under arrest and takin a ride back on up with us. But we're here and talking first because we're hopin to understand things a little better. Us and the DA.

RODARTE:   You mean, like – you lost me.

PORTER:    That dog won't hunt, Andrew. Simple as that.

RODARTE:   Hunt?

PORTER:    Well, that's my east Texas. But like I say, we've heard the story you told Detective Wade, and it ain't completely ridiculous.

|  |  |
|---|---|
|  | It's just we know now it couldna gone down that way, and that means we're hoping we can get to the truth together if we try again. |
| RODARTE: | Look. I mean, I'm lost. But here's the thing. I didn't, basically, I had no good way to explain this, and I was scared stiff. So I mean, yeah, I held some things back. |
| PORTER: | Looks that way to us. Wanna fill in some of the blanks now? |
| RODARTE: | Well, the story doesn't change. I didn't do this. But I shortened it a little. |
| PORTER: | All right. People been known to. |
| RODARTE: | Starters, like I said, I met the first girl in a mini-mart, bought her beer, got invited and followed her home. Get there and meet the second girl, Lee. Who, you got the picture, she's like nine-point-five gorgeous. And so I don't, I didn't leave quite as fast as I said. I sat down for a little while. The first girl is |

gonna get drunk fast, you can tell, and after I pound the one bottle she goes hey, you need another one, and I look around, feel like pinching myself, and go yeah, OK, don't mind if I do. The second girl Lee, she gets it for me, and when that's gone there's a third one. Kinda movin fast.

VASQUEZ: *Dude.* It's like they're planning to take advantage of you.

RODARTE: Sheesh, yeah. Whatever.

VASQUEZ: All right. And this is what time, you get there?

RODARTE: I don't really know. I'd stick to what I said before – maybe 10:45 or so.

PORTER: So point being, you were there a lot more than fifteen minutes, right? You settled in there with the two ladies for a while.

RODARTE: Yeah, a while. Long enough to drink three beers, at least. And sitting there I'm checking out the place, basically in awe. Knowin

|  | I probably won't ever be anyplace like it again. |
| PORTER: | So you're with both girls. What was the first one's name again? |
| RODARTE: | I ask, she says Jacie, I didn't get clear how it's spelled, but she goes it's short for Jacinta. |
| VASQUEZ: | And she's what – pretty hot herself, all in all? |
| RODARTE: | Well, yeah. Kind of out there, a mess, but – |
| VASQUEZ: | Lot more attractive than the chow line up in Palomar, right? |
| RODARTE: | Oh man – |
| VASQUEZ: | Aw, dude, sorry, had to throw that one in. |
| PORTER: | He's a nice guy by nature. But you were sayin? |
| RODARTE: | Yeah, well. The truth is I'm there maybe 40, 45 minutes all told. But it's weird. I oughta be foaming at the mouth, place like this, two girls. But I'm worried too. This Jacie, she's pounding beer, not exactly in control. It's a scary setup. |

|              | Being there in a house like this, the girl who lives there wasted, pretty easy to imagine how wrong it could go. |
|--------------|------------------------------------------------------------------------------------------------------------------|
| PORTER:      | All right.  But what happens?                                                                                    |
| RODARTE:     | Well, thing is, Jacie, she's been sittin around there, talking, slurring, getting louder, then gets quiet, and then she just kinda zonks out all of a sudden, slides down flat on the couch, and now I think that's my cue to go. But then, right as I'm getting up, Lee says hey, don't stress too much, this is what she does, this girl.  She overdoes it.  And I'm like yeah, I get it, but I have to go. |
| PORTER:      | All right.  Then what?                                                                                           |
| RODARTE:     | Then . . . shit.                                                                                                |
| VASQUEZ:     | Lay it on us.                                                                                                    |

# *14*

**(JPH)**

WE HEAR HIM CLAIM that Haylee Branch grabbed his bottle of beer, and put it to her lips, and looked at him as she drank from it, and then he says that with no warning, she leaned in and shoved him against the wall – cheesy, over-the-top BS all the way – and came at him, kissing him, reaching down and grabbing him as she did. And he says she told him there were lots of bedrooms, she knew the house, they could go right down the hall.

Rodarte's voice is low and scratchy, his breath heavy. It's a monologue, it's ridiculous and when it ends it's the silence you hear – I picture Porter giving him an earnest, don't-that-beat-all sort of face, just prodding him with his eyes and gestures. Then a little more nothing, but finally Vasquez breaks it.

| | |
|---|---|
| VASQUEZ: | Damn, dude, I'm looking for the downside. |
| RODARTE: | Yeah, well. |
| PORTER: | So then what? |
| RODARTE: | Look, fuck. I see how it all fits your picture. It's all I've been thinkin about. Of course I went online to find out about this, and I nearly passed out. She's killed, in that very house? I know exactly how it fuckin looks. But the truth is I didn't push it |

at all. I mean, I didn't mind being kissed, and it's hard for me to believe myself, but I pulled away. I didn't have sex with her, didn't hurt her, I sure didn't kill her. I just - left.

PORTER: OK. But see it from our side. You're there, you've got contact with the young lady, there's sex in the air, and right after you leave, Andrew, she's found dead in the middle of a sex scene. You tellin us some phantom snuck in after you?

RODARTE: I don't - Christ, how am I supposed to make sense of it? Maybe there was somebody else there. Or they came right after - she'd expected that, she said. Jacinta. People to show up.

VASQUEZ: And that's really all you got?

RODARTE: What the fuck do I need, if it's the truth? And one more little thing, whatever it's worth. Believe it or don't. Somewhere before she passes out Jacie says to Lee something I kinda halfway hear, and sounds like, look, we just need to hang because *Glenn* said he might make it. Or maybe *Len,* or *Lynn.* And Lee says something like, hey, we know how that worked out the last couple times, all that waiting around. I get the vibe this is a dude they're both interested in, but he sure ain't there while I'm there, and that's all I have. Now I'm sitting here, but God as my witness it wasn't me. I don't see a guy anywhere, anywhere else, any sign of him. Easy to make somebody up, right? But no. It's me and two girls, that's it, the whole time I'm there. Then somebody else had to come along. But she's been saying other people are coming over.

PORTER:                Sure. All right. I'm just tryin to picture you turning this girl down, though, dude. And I ain't.

RODARTE:   It's too much to make up. The whole thing's crazy. First being there in that house, then a dream girl in my face. But I'm just too far from the world I know, and I can see it going bad, so vivid. So the fact is I told her, Haylee, thank you very much, flattered. But I better pass.

VASQUEZ:   Aw, come on. You played hard to get, for reals?

RODARTE:   Fuck. Like it was that, dude. She wanted me, though. I don't know why, but she wanted me.

PORTER:    See, you guys, you've got way too many moves. Nobody's ever just offered me sex on the half-shell. Not even my wife.

We should have redacted this, probably, but at least two male jurors laugh out loud.

PORTER:    All right. So you're saying that Lee steps up, and even though you're wowed by her you say no, partly because there's some mention of another guy. You

understand he's come around
before, maybe they have something
working with him. That right?

RODARTE: Pretty much, as to him. But the
bigger part was me being afraid.

PORTER: But when she offers herself up you
tell her no.

RODARTE: Yeah, man. I said no. If it's
another time and my shit was
together, I mean . . . different
answer. But I gotta be smart for
once in my damn life.

PORTER: Well, OK. And she's good with it?
Or heartbroke?

RODARTE: She just went quiet, really. I
mean sure, maybe disappointed,
but then she doesn't know anything
about me, least of all that I'm a
jailbird. So then I grab my
jacket like to go, and she grabs
at it and tugs, practically
ripping it.

PORTER: And what do you do?

RODARTE: Well, I struggle right on back and
there's like a scuffle. A stupid
one, us tugging at the jacket, and

|           |                                      |
|-----------|--------------------------------------|
|           | then I win and she kinda breaks up and laughs at me. And so I say goodnight, thanks for the beer, and I'm out the front door. |
| PORTER:   | So no hard feelings?                 |
| RODARTE:  | Shit. I don't know.                  |
| PORTER:   | Now where was this?                  |

It's an inspired question, and there's an obvious, audible hitch, gears frantically turning.

|           |                                      |
|-----------|--------------------------------------|
| RODARTE:  | You mean –                           |
| PORTER:   | Just, where'd you break her heart?   |
| RODARTE:  | I'm still there. In the room there.  |
| PORTER:   | Still in the living room?            |
| RODARTE:  | Yeah.                                |
| PORTER:   | And when you left Lee was still wide awake, but Jacinta was down for the count? |
| RODARTE:  | Yes.                                 |
| PORTER:   | Well. All right. But when did you go to the other place? |
| RODARTE:  | I – what?                            |
| PORTER:   | The other room you went to, with her. |
| RODARTE:  | I didn't.                            |

PORTER:    Ah, c'mon. You've been doing so
           damn well getting straight. You
           *did*, Andrew. This didn't go down
           in the living room. You got to a
           bedroom, dude. We *know* it. And
           man, *you* know we know it. Because
           you know good old cop brain. We
           like the obvious, and here, man,
           the obvious plays. You're gonna
           keep denying it, when we got proof
           in our hand?

RODARTE:   Like what? Like – I mean, you
           want to tell me?

PORTER:    I can, or do you wanna just get
           straight now, Andrew? You wanna
           tell me some other names, people
           who might have been there, might
           have pushed it along? Or just
           you? See, we been around, me a
           few more laps than Junior over
           here, and even out in Sticksville
           we seen a full-on sociopath now
           and again. You aren't that,
           Andrew. I'm in the figure-people-
           out business, and from what I see
           you make normal human sense. And

that means I can start to understand.

RODARTE: That what?

PORTER: That you probably never meant to kill her at all, man. How you just planned on a fun time with her, like any red-blooded guy woulda been inclined to do in the unlikely event he got the chance. I mean, you say nine-five, this Lee, and maybe my ol' bald-headed ass ain't the best judge anymore, but I'd call that pretty spot-on. Girl next door, not dressin to kill, but look, I've been to see her mama and her sister, and we saw some pictures in the house. Prom, vacations, family stuff. That girl cleaned up something else, didn't she? Girl next door and then some. Blonde, long legs, blue eyes. The kind you *didn't* say no to, Andrew, because you're wired like any straight dude with two eyes is wired. You saw her –

RODARTE: No.

PORTER: C'mon now. You saw her, and then
she sees you, and after all, she's
got eyes of her own. Not that I'm
an expert from this vantage point
either, but you are one handsome
young heartbreaker of a dude.
Six-two, are ya?

RODARTE: Yeah, about.

PORTER: I'm gonna say she did light on
you, like you told us, reckoned
maybe you were the best thing
*she*'d seen in a long damn time. I
mean, our county, I don't wanna
knock it, but you got a truck that
runs, ten workin teeth and you're
off parole, you're a major fuckin
catch. She doesn't realize you're
just flashing through, I bet. And
why shouldn't she want you, too?

RODARTE: I told you that. I told you – she
did, she came to me – fuck –

PORTER: So look, I get you holding back.
When something goes as crazy wrong
as this thing did, of course it
ain't easy to get straight about.
But now is the time, and that

|            | starts with you and this beautiful girl, there in that bedroom, doin what comes naturally. |
| RODARTE:   | No. No. I – fuck, I didn't. I *didn't* go down there, to that room, to any room. I didn't do anything to her. |
| VASQUEZ:   | Sure, dude. But it's your bottle, man. You know it is, and we know it is – because it's got your DNA on it, Andrew. Not to mention your prints. |
| RODARTE:   | Well, sure. I mean, I had at least three beers, maybe more – |
| PORTER:    | Except it's *in the room*, Andrew. Not just anyplace. You're on a bottle found not ten feet from where this went down, where we found her throttled to death, even though you say you never went to any bedroom, right? Wanna explain that for us? |
| RODARTE:   | I – no. *No*. I don't – I can't figure any of it out. If the bottle's in the bedroom it's in the room, but I didn't take it |

there. I — *Christ*, no. I couldn't — Jesus.

PORTER: All right. Well, lemme recap. You're saying you end up at the house, even though you're a stranger, cause you did a favor for the girl who needed beer, then she came up short. You get there and meet her friend, who's even better looking. Then you say they ply you with alcohol to loosen you up when you get there, and then you say that after the first one passes out, then the second girl, who's about as pretty as they make em, comes on to you just like that. She's all over you, she wants to drag you to a bedroom on the spot. But you just say no ma'am, no thanks.

RODARTE: It wasn't — I don't —

PORTER: And then, after you've turned her down, some *other* dude winds up with her in that bedroom, havin the sex she offered *you* — and so does your beer. That makin sense?

But there is only a short pause.

RODARTE:  Well, fuck.  Laugh if you want to. I'm just telling you it wasn't *me*. I couldn't kill this girl - she was a dream, man.  A fuckin dream, a knockout.  You should've seen her.  She was all that and more.

VASQUEZ:  Dream you turned down?

RODARTE:  Yes.  God strike me down, I never fucking touched her that way. You ever hear about truth stranger than fiction?

PORTER:  Ripley's Believe it Not, that what you're sayin?  Sure.  But I got another one for you, Andrew. Didn't wanna get there yet but guess it's time.  See, we tested more than bottles.  We tested *her*, Andrew, and people know where to look.  And under her *fingernails*, man - whaddya think we found?

All we could actually identify was bits of blue fabric, but it's his chance to crack.  There's a long, long wait.

RODARTE:    Yeah, well . . . no, man. No. Fuck this game. I wasn't ever naked with her, not touching her, *none* of that. Fingernails, fuck. That's BS. Didn't rape her, didn't kill her, I didn't do any of that. I just –

PORTER:    Look, let's settle a minute. The way I see it you're in the throes of it all, chokin her for the thrill of it, maybe even cause she wants you to. And she's dying but you don't know it. She starts grabbin at you, tryin to breathe. Those scratch-marks you got start makin sense . . . *That*'s what happened. Tell me I'm wrong, Andrew. Tell me they ain't fingernail marks.

RODARTE:    They aren't. I *wasn't* –

PORTER:    You *were*. You were there in that room – putting it to her, this girl, and you start squeezing the breath out of her, so she fights. I mean, you got another theory for

|  |  |
|---|---|
|  | us? How a little of you could be under her nails? |
| RODARTE: | Theory, no. I have no theory, cause it didn't happen. I never touched her. I'm just – |
| VASQUEZ: | But thing is, Andrew, *somebody* killed her. And what do we have to show that anybody was ever there other than you? Didn't you tell us no other cars up by the house? Didn't you say it was just you and the two of them there, dude, except maybe some crap about a mystery man from a phone call? |
| RODARTE: | I said that – yeah, the truth. Never saw anybody else. But I didn't kill her – and I know I don't have to prove things. It's you, I know that much. |
| PORTER: | Well, that's true when you get to court, but we ain't there yet. I'll tell you right now, though, that we're gonna make this case. You're gonna have a lawyer get up and talk about circumstantial evidence, that kinda thing. But |

that ain't rare. Most murders
don't have an eyewitness, and
unless it's a long goodbye, the
victim ain't here to tell. So
it's all the other stuff that
makes the case, and it makes it
here, pretty well plain as day.

RODARTE: It doesn't, it can't –

PORTER: Oh, it does. But thing is,
Andrew, we need to take a long
hard squint at everything. And
that includes what was goin
through your head. Even when you
killed somebody, worst act there
is, well, we still have to figure
out what was happening in the top
story. And here we're pretty sure
*how* she died. What we don't know,
though, is *why*. So this is your
chance to tell us how something
as plain as rape and murder wasn't
as obvious as it looks.

RODARTE: Obvious? Like how?

PORTER: Personally, look, if this started
as willing sex, I got no earthly
idea how you'd suddenly want to

intentionally choke the life out
of this girl. And yet, if I
stretch, I think I can just barely
imagine a scenario in which this
happens by a fluke. And because
of that, I'm giving you every
chance in the world to explain.
Admit she died right there when
you were banging her, Andrew, then
take your shot to explain. Tell
us how it wasn't intended, killing
wasn't in your mind. Crazy-ass
shit's been known to happen. But
has to start with the truth.

And here he's an inch from surrender – he *has* to be. Cornered,
pummeled, tag-teamed. *Knowing* he's finished. I count off the seconds
– eight, nine, ten, eleven . . .

RODARTE: Man, *no*. . . . No. No. Fuck no.
It's wrong. It's a – a made-up
story, a lie, a lie I'm under her
fingernails. I can't help myself.
I can't escape . . . what I did
or didn't do doesn't even matter,
you'll just go with what you

```
            believe.  So that's it.  Shut off
            the tape.  I'm done, and when we
            get   there   I   want   somebody
            appointed.
PORTER:     All  right,  sir.   All  right.
            That's  your  right,  and  that's
            understood.  And you've invoked
            your right to silence.  So this
            interview is concluded.
```

A true pro – stopping cold when the suspect invokes, playing no angles, dropping no hints. They get on the bird, buckle in, and nobody says another word.

◆

PORTER TIES A FEW LAST THREADS, Ted's cross again is quick, and ten minutes later we've reached a three-day break. As usual, Vanzetta plans to leave Fridays dark to handle other business.

Sonya smiles down the hallway, deflecting the media as I follow, two full steps back. When we've reached sanctuary, I pause at the threshold as she hangs up her coat.

"Little tired?" I venture, offering a mild, concerned face.

"Out of practice," she answers, warmer than I expected. "And starting to feel it."

"Nobody'd ever guess you've been away."

# *15*

**(JPH)**

THERE IS A TACT among DAs – lawyers in general, I'm sure – about bringing up past defeats. However true the notion that comedy is tragedy plus time, a not-guilty verdict on a case you believe in has no levity to it, no lightness. It knocks you flat. And the losses are always easier to remember than the wins.

I push on anyway. "The last one was when I was a stone newbie, wasn't it? Early in 1998?"

Sonya sighs, half-smiles, leans back in her chair.

"You were, weren't you? So you wouldn't know the story."

"A robbery case, right?"

"Yeah, Midtown Drug and Discount, if you remember it, here in Millsford. Sporting goods store is in there now, but before Rite Aid got here they were the only game in town. The drive-through pharmacy went 24-hour; the main store was open until two in the morning or something.

"Anyway, we get to midnight some Saturday, and they get jacked by a tall guy, six-two at least, in a Freddy Krueger mask. He's mostly covered up, but there's enough visible here and there to tell he's on the pale side, like 93 percent of this county.

"He waves a gun around, all right on camera, and gets just a couple hundred bucks, mostly small bills, and some garbage like clock radios and eight-dollar watches, bottles of cheap champagne, sweeps all this junk into a trash bag. It's all over in seconds. The cashier kept cool, but she didn't dare look close and he barely talked, so no way she can make ID.

"Now the thing is, mystery dude *knows* there's a camera. Hence the mask. He may even suspect there's an outside camera, which there is, but he's got the brains to leave his getaway car in the pitch-dark empty lot next door.

"What's not so bright, though, is that when he gets outside, he pulls off the mask. His back's to the camera and the lighting's not good, but it gives away a little about his hair and skin color, which pretty well confirm he's a white boy. And what he really doesn't count on is that there's another night cashier out on a smoke break, around the back of the building, and that guy gets a pretty good look at him when he comes through."

Sonya's eyes go wide. I get the feeling she's enjoying herself, and surprised by it.

"Fast-forward maybe three days, the sheriff does a warrant search down in Ray's Valley, targeting another moron who isn't even there, and in one of the bedroom closets they find three or four clock radios and a couple of watches that match the stolen stuff, store labels still on 'em. They ask whose room it is and find out it's Danny Tarrant."

"Ah," I nod – I had retained the name.

"Now you know all the Tarrants, whole family of skinny tweakers. And Danny even has a prior robbery, though in the end we don't get to bring it in, because there's no match at all to the MO and it's way back, he was barely an adult. But on the whole everything is making pretty decent sense.

"The cops hang around until Danny wanders in, a few hours later, loaded and defiant. They wave the stuff at him, ask the questions, but in a minute he invokes his rights. All he's said is that he bought 'em from a guy in a truck outside the supermarket, somebody he'd dealt with once or twice before, and gives a half-ass description of a white tweaker with bad skin. Admits he figured they were stolen, but didn't know for sure.

"He gives consent to search, since now the warrant wouldn't stretch, but they find no mask, no gun and no serious cash. That hardly matters, though – any moron will toss the mask, he could've stashed the gun anywhere, and Danny looks like he's been on a bender, just now coming down.

"Now because of some questionable scheduling the detective's shift is about up, and the sheriff was clamping hard on overtime that month, so you have just what you don't want – an in-progress investigation getting handed off. But that's what happens, and when it does it goes to Mitch Marks, who's a story all his own.

"Marks is a moron, plain and simple. Basically a god-awful patrol deputy, couldn't write a report to save his life – and then one day he gets promoted to corporal, and we all about pass out."

"How'd that happen?"

"Well, you remember Blankenship, of course." Dade Blankenship had been defeated for reelection as sheriff, in a cloud of controversy, my first year. "Things got fast and loose under him, and sometimes the Constitution was a bit of a rumor. There was a little tune-up a couple of patrol deputies gave a dealer one night when he acted out – got him a few broken bones, and he brought a claim against the county. Marks had been at the scene, nowhere near the action, but the story was he got promoted for toeing the party line.

"But anyway, he's working the overnight, so it comes to him when the first detective goes home. And Marks, giving him credit, does latch onto the weakness in the case, and goes right after it. Can this clerk outside the building actually ID the guy as Danny? So he figures it out. He'll put together a photo lineup with Danny Tarrant – and *both of his brothers* – and then he'll show it to the clerk."

I CHORTLE ALOUD. "The usual suspects."

"Exactly. It's the three Tarrants and three others, who best I recall weren't much of a match. But to make it worse, it turns out that when Marks does go show it to the clerk, he manages to garble the standard photo lineup admonishment beyond all recognition.

"Sure enough, the clerk can't immediately pin anybody down. What happens, though, is that he hovers between Danny and his younger brother Brett. With just a *little* prodding he says he thinks it's one of the two.

"And so at this point ol' Marks figures some further subtle persuasion just can't hurt, and so he asks him if the guy had a limp. Because Marks knows that Brett rolled a motorcycle earlier that year and has a gimpy knee. The clerk thinks and says no, no he didn't, at which point Marks says, literally, 'Well then!' And next thing you know he has the clerk making positive photo lineup ID that it's Danny. This is the testimony we get from the clerk *at trial*."

"That's when you found out?"

"Sure, what better time? Hell, if we knew we would've had to disclose it long before trial, and even Stan probably wouldn't have been making offers."

"Whew. And that's all you actually had?"

"Well, the stolen property has to be worth something, whatever his story is, and then we got lucky and found witnesses saying he'd blown a wad at the bar the night before. Like most tweakers, he was perpetually broke, and didn't normally go paying retail price for anything – and they seemed to remember him having lots of singles and fives. If we still had a strip joint I guess he could've gone there.

"So he's come into some money, he's come into stolen stuff, he matches the description. And of course we haven't gotten the full picture from Marks's report, so we think we have a decent ID. On the whole the case looks at least medium-strong."

"All right."

"The wrinkle, though, is that the owner of the drugstore was Mary Trapp, and we had been friends since junior high. Not quite *best* friends, but maybe the next circle out. I knew her through high school, college, baby showers, social functions. We both joined Kiwanis when it opened to women. We did the gardening club, fundraisers. She even walked the half-marathon one year after I got her motivated. We had the same hairdresser, both had kids in college, and we'd both had cancer scares in our forties – hers worse than mine.

"But one place we differ is a bad one, because she was a widow. Summer before, her husband Rick had gone out drunk in his boat one evening, gunned it and smashed into the rocks up near Sumter Point. He was in a coma for three weeks, brain-dead by consensus, before she decided to pull the plug.

"And before she pulled the plug, well, she called me. Partly to ask about the law, but also just to unburden, talk it out.

"So we were friends. Not every day, not weekly, not best pals. But we had a real history together."

SONYA HAS TURNED toward the window now, but swivels slowly back.

"So bottom line, Mary's already a wreck, and then this. It guts her. Not a few bucks, obviously, not a little inventory. But she's haunted. Lost her husband, who was a lovable SOB for all his flaws, and now she's in absolute horror of the thought that this guy will come back. Probably thinks that next time she'll be at the register herself. Or that word will spread she's an easy target. It all builds and builds, some of it irrational, all made worse by her state of mind in the first place.

"Now the good news is how quick we've come up with Danny Tarrant, and it's not the worst case in the world. For sure we can make a receiving for the stolen items, but from the report we also have a solid six-pack ID, the one witness who saw the guy's face making him as Danny. We didn't find a gun, but Danny had a million chances to dump it, and Tarrants are Tarrants, not that we get to argue that to the jury. So on paper we feel OK.

"The problem is that Mary calls me up the morning after it happens, and like I say, she is a wreck. She needs somebody to tell her it's under control. So . . . I tell her it will be, and then, lo and behold, I look like a prophet, because we nail Danny the next day.

"But what I do, like a fool, is call her right up when we have him in custody and say hey, we've got him dead to rights. She buys right in, and naturally, she asks who will handle the case on our side. At which point I tell her I'm going to take care of it myself."

"But that was still pretty common, wasn't it? You trying cases?"

"Well, not unusual. We'd had turnover, gotten kinda bottom-heavy, and sometimes a case was a little more than the default person could chew. So mostly bigger stuff – life cases, Three Strikes when that came along.

"And this was a full-on armed robbery, nobody got hurt but obviously a state prison case. The problem was just that I was a little too close, and I set myself up."

"How, though? If it looked like a righteous case?"

"Well, right. We're allowed human feelings, and most juries actually want to see a little passion in a victim case, not just the facts and the logic. The thing was, though, Stan Bartlett had the case for the public defender. You remember Stan."

"Sure, of course. He retired that same year, didn't he? I was there for his going-away dinner. You told an old story about a dog."

"Christ, that's right – Barney the terrier, found in the rubble of an arson fire. How interesting you remember that. But bottom line, Stan is a man of decency. Was, still is. I see him at Friends of the Library. He has balance issues and gets around with a cane, but still has a twinkle in his eye, and I'd trust him with my life.

"The thing is . . . well, as you know, the defense can always try to get us recused from a case by claiming we have a conflict. But it has to be a real conflict that *matters*. You know the law on that.

"Now up here, obviously, the circles overlap. Other than college and law school, I've lived my entire life in this county. Even as we've grown, I doubt there's ever been a single jury pool in this courthouse where I didn't know at least two or three people pretty well, and often it's five, six people on a personal level, not to mention everybody I know by reputation. More than that sometimes."

"BUT THIS WAS DEEPER. Mary and I had a 40-year history, not only acquaintance and shared history, but legitimate friends. I could look at her, see her big green eyes and go right back in time.

"I remember us sneaking together out of a high school dance, meeting up around the back of the building with her boyfriend, a college guy – this was before she settled on Rick. He pulled up in a great white Chevy, the one with the taillights that looked like wings, with a bottle of whiskey and paper cups and we sat in the back seat, gulped it down and started laughing like the world was gonna end. Then I went back in and I tripped over the edge of the bleachers and tore a beautiful silk dress. Fall of 1960.

"I knew her husband from grade school, I'd see her when I came back from college. I knew the names of her kids, roughly their ages. So we'd talk, catch up, meet for coffee. And when her nightmare came, I realized it was deep and it really counted with her to have me there."

"OK. But still nothing wrong, right?"

"Right. Not fatal. We are bound by truth, and by ethics, and I'm telling myself to make it just another case. And so when Stan, who knows the history, delicately brings it up, well . . ." She looks down. "Well, I blew my line. I told him that I had no conflict that really matters, and how the statute says that even when there is an *appearance* of impropriety, they've still gotta prove there's something there.

"And I said then that, with all of that in mind, Stan, look, I have no conflict. You can't win if you claim I do. I am prepared to be fair and reasonable and broad-minded, but you can't show how any of this means we can't be fair to your idiot Danny Tarrant."

"So you talked him out of it?"

She nods, very slowly.

"Yes. He withdrew the motion the next morning. And he told the court, off the record, that it was due to my assurance that I wouldn't be affected. Old-school all the way.

"Then he tells me Danny swore he was innocent of the robbery, but he knew full well he was buying stolen stuff and wasn't going to snitch that guy off.  So he would plead to the high term on it, and then an added *second* count of receiving just to stretch it out, if we would dump the robbery, so he wouldn't get a 'strike' conviction out of it.  This meant three years, eight months, and he'd do half of it actual, so he'd serve a little less than two years."

"And then?"

Sonya clicks her teeth, half-smiles.  "Then, I'm afraid, I said no."

"Well, you didn't believe him.  Was that wrong?"

"Not in principle, of course.  The problem was I didn't do my job.  The case had issues, but I was pretending it didn't.  We have the clerk picking him out of a lineup, and we have him with a few items.  But the ID is by a stranger in bad light, late at night, and there's nothing else to prove he was *actually there*.

"Tall skinny white tweakers aren't exactly in short supply around here, and by now we've all heard enough about problems with stranger ID – worse when it's cross-racial, and the store clerk was from Jamaica or someplace, God knows how he ended up here.

"So Danny had stolen stuff on him, but he had an *explanation*, lame as it was, which pretty much left us with one nighttime witness and some circumstantial evidence of him coming into money."

"NOW, AGAIN, I didn't realize how badly Marks had botched the investigation.  But I did know what a gold-plated dimwit he was, and I should've taken a much harder look at everything.

"And what I should have been asking was that awful question – do I truly believe in the case?  Do I have enough to satisfy *myself* before I go try proving it to twelve people?  Maybe yes – there's no dispute he's connected in some way.  But maybe no, and what I really did is shove the question away.

"And then the second thing, which is the goal.  What was I really trying to accomplish there?  Well, I was trying to make Mary feel better.

"When he offered the plea I could have gone to her and said, look, he's going away, solid couple of years, and when he gets paroled he'll have a full no-contact order. Knowing Stan he'd have upped it a little bit, too, if I countered with something reasonable. A deal would have been something tangible, maybe enough to get her through.

"But instead I acted out of plain old adrenaline, and against Stan of all people. I said no to the deal, didn't make a counter at all, showing Mary by God I was serious. And Stan nodded in his accepting sort of way, and off we went to trial.

"It was barely a day of evidence. I told you how the clerk testified. Then Marks was an imbecile on the stand, hadn't prepared, contradicted himself, got practically struck dumb on cross. At the end of it the judge granted Stan's motion to exclude the ID evidence entirely. The flaws all came out in the worst light, and they walked him in less than an hour – not just on the 211, but on the receiving too, which I had assumed we could never lose. The jury was flat disgusted, they told me so, and they wanted us to know it."

I try a smile. "About all I remember is people being surprised."

"Well, lesson one – *anybody* can lose a trial. Should have given you a little peace of mind when you were starting out, right? But this hurt, and the worst of it is what I'm telling you. I ended up rejecting a fair deal in a case I didn't entirely believe in myself. All I thought about was the math and showing strength and being tough to protect Mary, and when I did that I presumed Danny was good for it. Then I lost, and I think I deserved to lose – but Mary didn't.

"The worst part was calling her, of course, and hearing her try to comfort *me*, practically as if I was the crime victim. I damn near broke down. And she only stuck around about a year after it, sold off, moved to Montana. Her first couple of cards I almost didn't want to answer. We email a little now, seen her just a couple times. Neither one of us is really over it."

AND AFTERWARD she told Tom she was taking a break from trial life.

"Well, you had plenty else to do."

"Sure, that was a good rationale. I also told him he needed somebody more nimble, more able to detach, plus our newer people needed more cracks. I'd been cherry-picking, too. And I knew I'd just gotten what I deserved."

"Whew. No fun."

"No, but it really goes deeper. I'm sure you've been in this spot yourself. The fact is, between Marks screwing up and the ambiguity of the whole thing, when I sat down from rebuttal I hadn't proven the case even to myself. I wasn't sure that Danny Tarrant robbed the store."

THE END – and now she smiles, squints, looks square at me. Suddenly, unexpectedly, there's a challenge – do I have the nerve to ask? *What about now? Would you ever dare doubt?*

But the answer is right there in her eyes – and anyway, I *wouldn't* have the nerve.

# *16*

*August 29 - Morning*
**(JPH)**

THE CHIEF MEDICAL EXAMINER of Contenta County is a small, balding Chilean immigrant named Eduardo Baltierra, who moved here to retire after decades in Arizona, then got the itch back when the job suddenly opened up. He's maybe three years in and has rarely needed to testify, but Tom likes him, calls him "Steady Eddie."

Sonya eases him through the autopsy protocol, the sequence of steps and the subsequent report. He reviews the deputy coroner's report, schedules time and place for the brutal task. Suspected homicides are a rush job.

There's the external – her wounds, bruises, scratches – and then the rest of it. Haylee Maureen Branch was a "well-nourished white female adult whose external physical characteristics appeared consistent with her reported age of 20." She measured five feet nine, a hundred and thirty-three pounds in death. She died of strangulation.

The key is the petechial hemorrhages. These are the tiny reddish spots in her eyes. One awful picture of it, and the explanation. When the airway is constricted the blood can't flow back out of the head normally, so blood vessels behind the eyes swell and finally burst.

With no knife or bullet wounds, the pictures aren't otherwise too horrible, though one downward-looking image from her neck toward the sternum reveals the beginning of her breasts, and the defenselessness of it hammers my heart.

SHE HAD BRUISES, obvious and ugly. Man hands. And a dark, circling redness just above them.

"What do the bruises tell you, Doctor?"

"Well, I find them to be highly consistent with attempted manual strangulation."

"And what of the redness in the same area as the bruise marks?"

"Those were, in my opinion, most likely made by the wrapping of a thick cloth or similar object tightly around the neck. This is consistent with strangulation by ligature, as opposed to hands. By means of a fairly broad sort of article."

"Wider than a cord or a wire, or even a rope?"

"Certainly wider than a wire, which would also create deeper ligature marks. A cord of some kind, conceivably, but with something that firm I would anticipate more bruising as a result, though with the other bruising there could be overlap. And wider also than a simple piece of twine. A thick rope possibly, but if it were of a standard coarseness I would expect more damage to the skin, more punctures, more pronounced redness."

"What about a cotton or similar fabric?"

"Cotton is more consistent, perhaps a knotted towel. Or perhaps acrylic. A softer fabric, wrapped very tightly."

SO IT EMERGES – the hands, almost certainly first, and then some sort of cloth, wrapped around her neck and twisted as he bore down on her, his sizable frame holding her in place.

And then her broken hyoid bone.

"What is the hyoid bone?"

I expect Latin words, but he's clear. "That is a rather unique bone in the upper neck, below the chin and above the larynx."

"What is its purpose?"

"It helps to support the tongue and it is important in the process of speech, the production of sound."

"I see. Have you seen it broken on any previous occasion?"

"Yes, quite a number of times. I would estimate once or twice per year over my 28 years conducting autopsies. Perhaps 40 times in total."

"What does it mean to you?"

"It is observed in many cases of strangulation, especially when done manually. The hyoid is normally the first thing to yield when severe pressure is applied to the neck and airway."

"Are there other ways to break it?"

"Very few. Fracture is also occasionally seen in suicide by hanging, but otherwise the hyoid's location typically protects it, and there is very little risk of it being broken by accident, save perhaps in a severe trauma like a car accident."

There's another artful lull here as Sonya turns a page.

"Dr. Baltierra, did you examine the body of Miss Branch for possible signs of sexual assault?"

"I did, yes, with the aid of a colposcope."

"And what did you find?"

"I detected mild bruising at the vaginal opening. There was a small laceration in the vaginal roof, and there was also internal discoloration and bruising."

"Have you seen injuries of this type before, at autopsy?"

"I have, yes. With some frequency."

"Doctor, what significance did you attach to them here, if any?"

He pauses, arranging his words.

"They were, I will say, suggestive of a forceful and nonconsensual sexual activity."

TED IS WISELY NARROW, comes up with a smile.

"Had you mastered the English tongue before you came to this country, Doctor?"

Baltierra smiles back, self-deprecating. "That overstates it. And I arrived more than 30 years ago. But it has been my professional language for a very long time now."

"And I'm happy to rely on it. Your term 'suggestive' describes a fact that gives a *hint* that something else is true, but does not actually amount to proof, is that correct?"

"That expresses it well."

124

"And since something merely suggestive is not proof, it certainly can't be proof beyond a reasonable doubt, can it?"

"Correct."

"So you can't at all say the evidence you found proves rape, can you?"

"No. I could not make such a claim on the basis of the physical evidence alone."

◆

ANALYST NOREEN SAWYER hunted the DNA.

Noreen, who is the lab director, arrives looking exactly her scholarly part – a short black coif, a long, frumpy blue dress, thick glasses. A veteran witness.

It's a short briefing – one headline. Rodarte's saliva was on the single beer bottle found in the room he denied ever entering. Or, that is, a DNA profile perfectly matching his own chromosome, and expected to occur at random in one of every 23 million males of Southwestern Hispanic origin.

Sonya changes the subject, almost lightly.

"Did you also receive a condom as an object for testing?"

"I did, yes."

"Did it yield any DNA profile?"

"No, it did not. It contained no testable biological material."

"No semen, therefore?"

"Correct. The item appeared to have been used, and then rinsed. It showed signs of – stress, for want of a better word."

"Consistent with having been used in sexual intercourse?"

"I would say so, yes. While noting that I'm unfamiliar with any other purpose it might have." For some reason this gets the biggest laughs of the week.

ALL TED HAS is a half-court shot.

"Correct me if I am wrong, but multiple beer bottles were collected, were they not?"

"Yes sir. However, I personally analyzed just one."

"And the bottles were all Miller Genuine Draft?"

"I believe so. That was certainly the brand of the one I analyzed."

"And of the same size – twelve fluid ounces?"

"Mine was, and I believe that was true of them all."

Ted pauses – steeling himself, maybe.

"So would it be possible, then, that the bottle you examined was *not* the bottle from the *casita*, but in fact another?"

Sonya rises effortlessly. "Objection, assumes facts not in evidence. Chain of custody has been established."

The judge thinks, nods a bit. "Sustained."

I glance over and see Rodarte, for some reason, nodding along as if he agrees. Ted also sees it, and as he sits he flashes his client a look normally reserved for three-inch piles of dog shit on a city sidewalk.

♦

A SECOND CRIMINALIST inspected Haylee's fingers. Arnold Schrain probably isn't 80 yet, but you'd say he looks it, and many a defense attorney has tried aggression. It tends to fail.

There is no tissue or DNA beneath her nails, but there is something else – tiny dark blue fibers under three of them, which Schrain found to perfectly match three other fibers that were found, after intense inspection, on the bedspread.

These they compared to the cotton-fleece fibers in Rodarte's jacket.

"What did you conclude?"

"Well, fibers of this kind can't be correlated in the manner of genetic profiles. But I found them to be consistent in texture, consistent in the weight, density and shape of the fibers, and consistent in color."

"What significance is there to finding similar fibers under the victim's fingernails?"

He pauses – I expect an objection, but it doesn't come.

"Well, assuming they came from the jacket, considerable force would be required. The jacket was not torn or obviously damaged, as might make it easier to pull out threads or stitches. I would take that to mean that there was some sort of a struggle in progress as it happened."

TED TENDS TO over-enunciate when the fight is going badly.

"Forgive my per*sis*tence. But just to achieve clarity, you cannot say pos*itively* that the fibers found under Miss Branch's fingernails in fact came from Mr. Rodarte's jacket, can you?"

"Well, if you're asking my opinion –"

"As an expert in forensic science. I'm asking you whether you can say with certainty that they came from that source."

"In my professional opinion, they are very likely from the same source. They are a perfect match for one another. And factor in the connection to this individual –"

At this stage Ted's fuse is short. "*Sir*, I am not asking you to do the jury's job. They get to figure out what the evidence means, not the rest of us. I'm asking you whether it is *certain*, in your view, that the fibers under her nails came from the jacket collected as evidence."

"Well, no. No sir. That's a big word. I'd say very likely."

"Likely," Ted repeats. "All right. Nothing further, thank you."

◆

A COUNTY TOXICOLOGIST named Ephraim Stanley is next. He's another regular, a great tall Black guy in his fifties, a friend of Sonya's from their gardening club. Juries love him. He detected and measured the flunitrazepam and alcohol in both girls' blood.

The drug's brand name is Rohypnol, and it's a benzodiazepine on steroids, developed in Europe, many times as strong as Valium. It's often colorless, has a quick onset and a long half-life, and dissolves right into a drink.

"Now beyond putting you to sleep, can flunitrazepam have an effect on recall?"

"Yes. In sufficient doses it can cause what is known as anterograde amnesia."

"Meaning what, in layman's terms?"

"It means you temporarily lose the ability to form memories, similar to an alcoholic blackout. Which, in theory, makes it ideal for sexual assault."

"Is it known for that?"

"It has that reputation, yes, though its actual prevalence is not entirely clear. And in this country it has no other claim to fame, because it's never been approved for medical use in the United States."

Sonya's eyebrow arch is beautifully subtle. "Meaning it's strictly a street drug?"

"Yes."

"And does Rohypnol or flunitrazepam have a street name?"

"Yes. The drug is widely known as roofies."

♦

LUNCH BREAK. Trial is the world's best appetite suppressant, even for a benchwarmer, but Sonya is aglow. Ted has made no dents, and the path is brightly lit. We are on time and on course.

# 17

*August 29 – Afternoon*
**(JPH)**

OUR SIDE CAN'T normally use a defendant's history of bad conduct, or even his criminal convictions, as stand-alone proof that he's guilty of what he's accused of now. But there's more wiggle room in a sex crime. And we do have a witness.

**(WADE)**

Her name is Alina Nieves, and she called us out of nowhere, saw the defendant's name in a news story, figured the rest of it out. And so the next afternoon I'm interviewing her up in Tehama County, turning it into a supplemental report.

I expect that by the time I get there she'll be nervous and starting to backtrack, but no. She's still in her coffee-shop uniform with a wad of dollar bills to count, her four-year-old in the bathtub. Doesn't matter – she's nails. Ends up an hour together, most of it me trying to get a better window into the guy, but the relevant part is simple enough.

Her generous and helping spirit earns her a free vacation in Millsford, California, the following summer, including one complimentary night at the White Feather Inn and all the mini-muffins she can eat, where she gets to describe the most vulnerable experience of her life to strangers under oath. Such is the nature of this grind.

**(JPH)**

WE'VE SENT our own senior DA investigator, Steve Waterford, to pick her up. He finds her standing on the sidewalk in a business suit she found in a thrift store, wearing it ahead of time to get used to how it fits her. She tells him she has a spare blouse to go with it the next day, and another in case it takes two days.

She is young, this Alina, bright-eyed and serious, very slender, delicately beautiful. From a distance she could be much less than 23. Onstage she has the calm and bearing of a royal.

Sonya starts with the obvious, and Alina's ID of Rodarte is quick and sure.

"Miss Nieves, where do you know Mr. Rodarte from?"

"I met him and went out with him for a couple of months, in the summer of 1999."

"Where did you meet him?'

"Working at my family's farm stand on Colusa Highway. He stopped by one day, chatted me up. Then he came back the next day and asked me out."

"And what did you say?"

She smiles, very softly. "I said yes. But I let him know first I was still seventeen."

We've cleared all this.

"And how did he react to that?"

"As if it was fine. He said he was barely 22. I didn't sense any pressure."

SONYA PAUSES, cocks her head cheerfully. "So what did you do? Going out?"

Alina Nieves smiles a little, shrugs. "Small town thrills. I was too young for bars, so it was mostly movies, lunch and dinner, walking by the river, going for drives. Simple stuff on the weekends. I was still in high school."

"And there was chemistry between you two?"

She sighs. "Yes. We connected."

"I see. Did he do things you associated with love, romance?"

She nods, gently and wistfully. "He brought me flowers. The first two times."

"How did you respond?"

"Well, flattered, I guess. Happy. Like I was important to him."

"All right." Sonya pauses. "This lasted how long, if you recall?"

"Around two months, I think."

"Now did something cause the relationship to end?"

The witness smiles again – still philosophical. "Sort of."

"Can you tell us about that?"

A deep breath. "Well, I had told him after we hit it off that I didn't want to sleep together until I was eighteen. I said it was better for him too. I told him that this wasn't something brand-new to me, but I was kind of a bookworm, only been with high school guys, just a couple of times. And he was different, adult, out there in the world. He was working construction, he said, temporary job, but – grown. Drove a cool blue truck. Another league, kind of. I wanted to . . . grow into it, I guess."

"OK. And how did he react?"

"Well, he was patient for a while. But – not forever."

"What happened, specifically?"

Crunch time. But her strength is obvious.

"Well, I met him at the end of July, I think, and we'd gone through August, and now it was late September and he knew I was only a few weeks from my birthday, in October.

"He picked me up on a Saturday, a gorgeous clear day when the valley was finally cooling down, and we went up to Lake Oroville, took a walk, had a picnic. Then we circled across the valley to the 5, and on the way back down he suddenly pulled off and stopped at a motel."

I see a woman in the jury box nod her head. Sympathetic.

"What was your reaction to that?"

A distant look, something lost. "Well, a mix of emotions. I mean, fear and thrills and whatever else, all together."

"Did you repeat that you weren't ready for sex with him?"

"I don't really remember the words I used.  But I know he could see me hesitating."

SONYA BOWS HER HEAD.
"Can you describe for the jury what happened there?"
"Well, we drank.  That was first.  He had a couple of things with him, something called Mickey's Big Mouth, which I'd never even heard of, and a bottle of something, Bacardi rum I think, and shot glasses.  Of course I'd drunk before, even a little with him, but I wasn't a pro.  And all I really had was a shot, shot and a half and then, you know, he started trying to move on, get me to go along."
"With having sex?"
"Yes."
"Had he tried that before?"
"Talking, yeah.  He'd say I was older than my years, more interesting than anybody his own age, and what was it but a formality, when I was so close to being legal age.  But I'd tried to hold back, and this was on a whole new scale."
"Sure.  Now do you recall what happened next, once it was clear what he wanted?"
"I was just – going along.  Our clothes were like half off, and then he came up over me and then he said something like hey, this is where it gets good, and . . . his hands went around – and then, it's so strange, because all of a sudden I was somewhere else, in a cloud."
"Like a dream?"
"Well, it seemed like it.  And it went on and on, no memory other than how far away it took me, and then I came back to, eyes open, he was up there above me, and in me, and like, smiling, saying hey, you all right, you seem to like that, hey . . . things that didn't seem to mean anything to me right then.  It's like I'd come back from the other side of the moon or something, to end up on that bed, and there he was."
"Did you believe you lost consciousness?"

"Yes . . . I had to have. I knew it then, where he'd put his hands. But I didn't know how long I'd been gone – five seconds, a minute. Guess it couldn't have been much more, but it felt like hours."

"What did you do, when you had your bearings back?"

"Well, it was all too much to process. I was scared. I remember that I yelled at him right away, what was that? What did you do? And he wouldn't answer."

"And then what?"

"Well, I shoved him away, and remember hunching up on the bed, my head on my knees, him there just saying stuff I didn't want to hear."

"Apologizing?"

"Not really. Just more like excuses, that he didn't want to push me, but thought I'd like it. That he wouldn't let anything happen to me. He had this big, self-pitying sort of look, like I should see how he'd been deprived, but was trying to be correct. Stuff like that."

"Was he angry?"

She sighs, closes her eyes. "Hard to say. Probably mad it happened that way, but still sort of acting happy with me. It was all just strange, and too much. Too much, too soon."

"And that ended your relationship?"

"Well, yeah. I felt like I didn't actually know him, and he didn't make me feel better. I couldn't see a way to go forward after that. So that night was it."

TED'S EYEBROWS are busy, his demeanor calm.

"You described that after you came back to full awareness, you stopped the activity and put on your clothes, correct?"

"Yes."

"And he did the same, correct?"

"After a little while. He wasn't really in a hurry."

"But once dressed, he took you home to Marysville?"

"Yes."

"And he *did* apologize, did he not?"

"Well, sort of.  He seemed embarrassed, but he had excuses for himself, too.  I got the idea he was used to having his way, and I had the feeling I'd have just been a name on a list."  Her face is weary now.

"But he really wasn't angry, was he?"

"I don't really know.  After a while I was the pissed-off one.  I don't remember much past what I felt, all my fear and discomfort about it."

"But once more – and please do your best to listen to my phrasing," Ted says, clearing his throat.

"Are you listening to mine, though?" Alina asks in a soft, clear voice.

"I – what?"  Completely off balance, Ted forgets even to object as non-responsive.

"I mean, does what I say count?  Do you really want the truth, or is it your job just to make it sound different than it actually is?"

I DOUBT THERE IS any real way to recover from that, but Ted Stauber is a professional to the core.  He ends with all he has – that she never reported it.  She did not call the police to report a sexual moment, without witnesses, in a county not her own, after she went there willingly and knowingly with the handsome guy she was dating, less than a month from legal adulthood.

After flashing the last of her tiny eyebrow-arches and being excused readily by Sonya, Alina steps down, careful and unobtrusive, eyes to the floor.  She's there in our lobby, as Sonya asked her to remain, when we get there a few minutes later.

I leave them to speak alone for a moment, and try to read Sonya's look.  There is great warmth in her face as she bends her head over, says a few words, and then leans into a hug – maybe the first I've ever seen her give.

♦

AND NOW, FOR LAST, Sonya calls Marta Branch.

A little stagecraft is usually tolerated here. Most defense attorneys, especially the veterans, don't object when the DA asks an anguished survivor to look upon a picture of the lost and name the face, and if tears result there is no deceit to it. So the sundress and the tree – *I like the light.* My own heart skips. A minute later Marta is at the county morgue in the middle of the night.

"And my apologies, Ms. Branch, but we have to get through it. There at the coroner's office, did you identify your daughter by her remains?"

Ted stands, folding his hands in front of him. "That's cumulative, Your Honor."

Vanzetta is baffled. "Can you elaborate, Mr. Stauber?"

"Ms. Branch should be spared recounting that moment," Ted says. "We're in no dispute she lost her daughter Haylee and identified her remains. We will gladly stipulate to that effect. There is no need for testimony of that event."

A sudden flash – of *course.*

I had forgotten. Completely forgotten. But I look at Ted and see what Sonya sees – the shimmer of tears at the edge of his eyes. Vanzetta abruptly calls a ten-minute recess, tells the jurors to go stretch their legs, and they dutifully file out.

"Spend a minute," the judge says then, kindly. "Use my chambers."

Ted nods, grateful. "A moment will do."

THE DOOR CLICKS behind him, Vanzetta turns to his clerk Lucille, and I stare back at Sonya.

"His daughter, right?"

Sonya nods. "Yes."

"When was it?"

"Winter of '93. I'd just become a grandma. February, I think. Out on the cutoff road north of Crown Lake."

"How old was she?"

"Wanna say she was 24. Her name was Kelly . . . Kelly Irene Stauber. When she was younger Ted called her Kissy, because of the initials. Had long frizzy golden-red hair, battled her weight a little, long-legged like Ted but really looked more like her mother."

"So you knew her."

"More in her younger days, we'd see her here and there. She came around with fundraisers, Girl Scouts. Saw her do community theater when she was still in high school.

"Went off to Oregon State, I think it was, but didn't finish, left about her junior year. Ted was sick over it. She chased a guy all the way to Colorado, and Ted had a long few months, but ended up she came home no worse for wear. She was still getting her life together when it happened, working up at the old North Shore resort, back living at Ted's place but seeing her mom all the time."

"Christ. What happened?"

"Wee hours of a Sunday morning, she's driving home from a late shift, gets smashed into on a curve, basically T-boned by a kid in a truck who fell asleep and didn't turn the wheel."

"Jesus."

"Yeah. The kid was just a high school senior, a Mormon, coming home late from a youth event up in Grace Canyon, stone-cold sober. The CHP had a hard time believing it, didn't know him but thought maybe he'd been huffing up there with some usual suspects. But it checked out.

"There was nothing to file on – no jury was gonna convict for that, and the kid was distraught, came to Ted with his mother and father to apologize to his face. He was gonna wear it forever, you could tell – saddest thing you can imagine." She frowns. "He had a Scandinavian name, can't quite remember it . . . he'd been at the camp . . . first name was *Jason*, that's right, but I can't remember his last. Just that it was as long as mine."

"So no charges."

"No. And Ted did his best to forgive the kid – said she'd have wanted it. He'd say *there but for the grace of God go I*, which in a way made sense, because Ted had done his share of drinking, back in the day, coulda fallen asleep some nights himself. Though if he could still sense God after it happened, I don't know.

"He was long split from Janette, who was Kelly's mom, had already been remarried and divorced by then. But the really horrible thing that night was he couldn't reach Janette, no matter what he did. This is before we all had cell phones, of course, and she'd gone away someplace overnight, so all he could do was leave a message on her machine. Then he had to wait for a call back, could come any minute, any second, to tell her their only child had been killed. Ended up taking eighteen hours, at least. Can you imagine that? But before any of it, he had to go down there and have them pull back the sheet."

"Ugh."

"And." She shudders. "He needed somebody to keep him standing upright when he did it."

Now it clicks. "Which was you."

"Yes."

Jesus *Christ*.


SONYA HAD brief places to go with Marta, but she sees the gain in sparing her. She walks over to explain it, and a minute later we wind up with a quiet stipulation to the necessary facts – Haylee's age, where she lived, where she went to high school, where she went to JC, where she went for four-year college. That she formed a friendship with Jacinta Cantrell, that she is the girl in the oak tree picture, that Marta learned of her death and went down to the morgue.

I doubt Ted had a cross planned, in any event.

Eric Ferguson

The faces in the box are ashen as Marta, struggling, gathers herself and steps down in silence. However good the intentions, the moment is crushing in its emptiness.

"NEXT WITNESS," Vanzetta says, forgetting she's the last. We have blitzed.

"Thank you, Your Honor. The People rest."

♦

SONYA'S PHONE RINGS at the moment of farewell, so I walk Alina Nieves out to Steve Waterford's unmarked car for the trip back north. It seems an honor.

"Back to your boy?"

"*Yes*," she says, decisively. "I bet he'll be mad at me."

"For leaving?"

"Right. First night we've ever been apart."

"He's with your sister, though?"

"Yes. And four cousins, three of 'em teenagers."

"Can't be that bad, right?"

"Well, it depends. I brought crackers and made her promise to heat up a bean burrito for him, but she's a flake. He'll be lucky if he gets milk and Cheerios."

"So you were always the responsible one?"

"Seems that way. But there are three others."

"Five in all? Five sisters?"

"Well, three and two halves. And no boys. Pity my stepdad."

"Well, he had you in the group. I'm guessing that helped."

Alina gazes off, distant for a moment, then turns back toward me as we come to the car and lean against it. I see Steve coming out the back door, fifty yards off.

"What about rebuttal?" she asks me, then reddens. "I mean, if you need to."

138

I can't help grinning. "Have you learned this whole process?"

"A little. Just to have a clue."

"Excellent. They get to make a case first, if they want to. Then rebuttal is our shot back, to answer theirs."

"Does it mean you might need me?"

"I wouldn't think so. And we'd give you a heads-up."

She nods, somberly. Her voice goes soft and small. "The thing is, I don't completely know what happened. I didn't really know *him*, even. But I also knew I was there voluntarily. I wasn't of age, but he didn't push me that hard, and we didn't just go straight to it. It just got . . . out of control."

"Right. I can understand."

Alina nods again as Steve strides up, rustling keys, and raises her wide, self-conscious eyes. There's a tiny squeeze in her feather-soft handshake. "Thanks for getting me through."

I'm well-cast as a liaison.

"Thanks for being here."

◆

YOU CAN'T GET WRAPPED UP in the moment. The witness after your star may fall on his face. A great court ruling on evidence may be followed by a plainly idiotic one. After you tear apart one witness on cross-exam, the next may say things you never got discovery about. So DAs tend to exult on the quiet, during trial, because today's triumph can always turn to ragged madness tomorrow.

"Nice job," I tell Sonya.

She considers it, quarter-smiles. "Witnesses did well."

I nod. "So did you."

HEADING BACK IN I hear cackles in Tom's office – Tom, Brian and the narc lieutenant, chortling about the previous night's sweep, a huge random haul of meth.

"But it ain't the show *you* have," the lieutenant says, voice dropping into a serious octave.

Which is true. But if it required a ticket, I know I would've scalped mine long ago and watched on TV.

# <u>DEFENSE</u>

Eric Ferguson

# 18

WE HAD NEVER BEEN SURE what to expect from Ted. It seemed a coin flip whether Rodarte would take the stand, and their potential witness list was very short. The defense can always call no one and rely entirely on reasonable doubt, of course, but here it would have been a shock. In the end the first witness for the defense has hair a bottled shade just this side of orange, too short a skirt, and a run in her hose. But for all that she does well.

Her name is Renae Winter. She's from Bay City, in Palomar County, well up the rocky coast, a cashier in an auto parts store, divorced, a mother of two. We're the ones who found her. We took a report and provided it in discovery, but in the end we decided not to call her ourselves.

Ted, with few options, decides there's enough to work with, and his offer of proof is "to humanize and normalize" Andrew Rodarte. Sonya rewards that with a hundred-watt scowl. Vanzetta rolls his eyes too, but there's little doubt he'll allow it.

THEY MET ONE MORNING in her store. He needed a battery. They went out, they had fun, he moved in. He had work as a boat mechanic, she had told us, and a sense of humor, and was kind to her kids. Took them for fast food, to the park, out to the shoreline. Grilled hot dogs. Played Nintendo.

Ted's gone through this slowly, almost meandering, then suddenly blurts out the money question.

"Miss Winter, how was your sex life, with Andrew?"

She raises her eyebrows and shrugs. "Well, what are you asking? We slept in the same bed."

"For what length of time?"

"We – let me think. I guess it was a year and a quarter. March to June, I think, '02 to '03. Not far from the record, on my end." She flashes a likable, self-aware smile.

Ted hesitates, and you can see the gears grinding. Restrained by his generation, he can't think of a polite way to get to what he wants, even with his own witness.

"Miss Winter, would you describe Mr. Rodarte as 'normal,' in his sexual tastes, or unusual?"

"Objection, vague, lack of foundation," Sonya murmurs.

"Sustained."

Ted stands stiffly at the lectern, looks at the ceiling.

"During your time together, was Mr. Rodarte interested in anything that *you* would consider to be – off the beaten path, intimately speaking?"

"Uh, well." She sighs, a little theatric. "I'd answer that – yes and no. He liked standard things, absolutely, and he sort of liked role-playing. He liked to be somebody, me to be somebody else. That was part of it."

"And you did that together, or were they his ideas? His direction?"

"Most of the time, I guess. We'd think it over first, even sort of rehearse. School play stuff."

"Can you give us examples?"

"Umm," and then again, fleetingly, the appealing smile. "Boy, this is fun. Cliches, really. Teacher and student, staying after class. Doctor and nurse. Boss and secretary, except I got to be the boss. Animal trainer." Here she blushes.

"What animal?" asks Ted, stiffly.

"Oh, like a tiger. Or a lion."

"Hmm. How do you train a lion?"

"Well, you know – it takes a whip."

"It would, wouldn't it?" Ted smiles, but it's queasy. "Who whipped who?"

"Andrew was the trainer. I made growly noises until I needed a whack."

"As play, I assume?"

She nods. "Just fun. Not a serious whip."

"No welts? No bruises?"

"No. Stings a little, of course – it's supposed to."

ANOTHER LONG PAUSE. Ted Stauber is like a cowboy on a skateboard. "Okay. What else?"

"Not a lot. Slap and pull hair a little. Pretty normal."

"I see. All right. Now, Ms. Winter, thinking back, did these games ever involve restriction of the airway, by either of you, on purpose?"

The witness shrugs, then nods – matter of fact. "Now and again."

"Was this his idea, or yours?"

"Well, he brought it up, but it wasn't brand new to me."

"And how did that go?"

"Good enough, I guess. It's dumb but it can get you lightheaded, boost the intensity. Give you a rush."

"Were you ever actually knocked unconscious?"

"Well, I don't remember ever coming back from far away, so if it happened it was just a few seconds. That's not the goal. You get the effect pretty quick, and we only did it a handful of times."

"And the relationship itself – it ended in June of '03?"

"Right in there."

"What terms were you on when it ended?"

She hesitates, raises her eyebrows, puzzled. "Well, lousy. What else? I mean, if it was peace and harmony we'd have kept with it. But it was mutual. Never claim I'm a full-time beam of light, either."

"And no harm came to you from these games, I trust?"

"Right. Just – games."

SONYA ASKS FOR A SIDEBAR when Ted is done. Vanzetta nods, we stroll off. As the chamber door closes he grins and says *no*.

Renae Winter has not "opened the door," in the age-old analogy, to Sonya bringing in the fact – known all along to both sides – that Rodarte went to jail for a domestic battery against her. He had left her with a black left eye, the reports said, and the charge had initially been a felony. But it was also plain that she'd landed blows of her own, and the Palomar DA had resolved it downward.

"You are saying it's irrelevant what caused the breakup? That he smacked the fuck out of her, excuse me, and got a misdemeanor because she's the hitting-back type?"

"Well, first, I don't think it did cause the breakup. There's a six-month gap, if I have the dates right. And otherwise what's to impeach? She didn't paint a rose garden."

Sonya scowls. "It's probative, and we get some latitude under the statute, don't we? It's a window into his head, how he problem-solves. And it might help this jury."

Now Vanzetta smiles again, and for a moment I see a slightly awestruck kid, back in the day, watching her as I do now. "Look, that's my ruling for now, Ms. Brandstetter. But I can't foretell the course of Mr. Rodarte's defense, so maybe it comes back around."

Ted smiles weakly. "I will content myself with endorsing your current ruling. And I will let the pageantry unfold from here."

WITH NO CLEAR OBJECTIVE Sonya is careful and quick. Renae Winter is excused three minutes later.

"Next witness," says Vanzetta.

Ted stands and looks at him, curiously still. I feel a sudden adrenaline rush.

"May I ask your indulgence, Judge? Perhaps ten minutes?"

It's only 3:30, but Vanzetta shrugs and turns to the jury. *We're making good time. We'll call it an early night.* There's no hint of disappointment from the box.

♦

AT MY DESK I grab a highlighter – there are several things to go back through.  The green ink is drying up when I suddenly see it.

♦

AN HOUR LATER I'm standing along Sundown Road, inhaling the evening.  Twilight yields slowly, the great green-and-gold hills looming behind and in front of me.  The creek is still in full throat here in late summer, crackling, crystal and unending, just passing through. The broiling day notwithstanding, it's dipped into the sixties by now, the heat on a fast wane here at 3,000 feet.  I'm on the dirt shoulder, looking west at the orchard, then ambling southeast along the roadway, to the base of the land, grateful for the approaching dark.

We had assumed Frank Cantrell would put the property on the market, but he didn't, probably still hoping to raise the stock of his vineyards.  So it's a tenant who raises the grapes there now.  The pear and apple trees remain, dense and heavy, not far from harvest.  And while you'd certainly think the *casita* would have been flattened and built anew, apparently he just remodeled it – you can see the bottom of the cottage through the straining trees.

On the way there I've realized my mistake – even if nothing has changed, the trees would have been much thinner in November than they are now, fat with fruit.  But a kind of hum settles over me anyway. *Good enough.*  I can't wait for morning.

# *19*

*August 30 – Morning/Afternoon*
**(JPH)**

SONYA IS TAPPING OUT an email when I reach her office, an hour before our scheduled time. I get a vague wave to sit. A few last clicks and I learn that we've lost another half day – another judge is sick, Vanzetta has to cover her calendar.

I'm deflated, but her eyes are bright. Excited.

"Got something for me?" she asks, seeing paper in my clutch.

"Well, maybe." I hand her the first interview transcript, tabbed to the key page. "First interview, with Wade. See anything here? His answer to the bluff question about Tommy Hite."

It's strange to give Sonya even the slightest direction, but she's absorbed, runs her finger along the page.

"'Doesn't look familiar, no. Just the girls there at that main house, no dudes at all.'" A squint for five seconds, not more – then her eyes light up. "Wait, is that it? *Main* house. He shouldn't have known?"

"Right. Wade hasn't said anything about a second building, and by Rodarte's own account it's dark. He explicitly said that he never went out the back or explored the property at all. And there was an orchard blocking the view from the driveway or the road. The deputies could see a light through the trees, but no details of the building. The orchard's still there and you still can't see much through it. Plus he is clearly thinking of it as a second *house*, as opposed to some indeterminate building– or else he wouldn't be drawing the contrast. And this is right after it happened. He couldn't have learned it on TV."

Sonya bends her head, raises her brows, smiles with her eyes. "Very nice. We all missed it. Or – almost all." Her mouth joins in.

I try for an aw-shucks face. "Just a cherry on top."

Her mouth tightens. "We're gonna take our shot."

IT ENDS UP two o'clock before we get started. Vanzetta apologizes at length to the jury and looks to Ted, who looks at his client. And then Rodarte stands up to testify in his own defense.

◆

THE FIRST THING is his size. The jurors have seen him stand with Ted as they enter and leave the courtroom, but they would be avoiding his eyes. Now he passes feet from them – stepping carefully, desperate *not* to scare anybody, undoubtedly failing.

The second thing, naturally, is how damned handsome he is. Every defendant dresses in clean-cut masquerade, but on him it sells. He looks like he's on his way to an audition – somebody's new boyfriend on a sitcom, maybe, or the center fielder who overcomes addiction. Sonya had looked hard for swooners when we sized up the panel in jury selection.

*He killed Haylee Branch.* There ought to be a subcurrent, menace just below, but I've never really felt it, and I don't at the time.

RODARTE IS FROM the bottom of the Central Valley, south of Bakersfield. Family farm, stone fruit and nuts. Left high school during his senior year, headed down to Long Beach, near L.A. Got a job working on big rigs.

That was ten years ago. Then Ted asks him when he started having trouble with the law.

This isn't the shock it might be in another case, of course. The jury's already heard him talk to the cops about going to jail in Palomar County. In another spot they might not have, but Ted decided that trying to redact it would sabotage Rodarte's own attempts at explanation. Sonya, somewhat to my surprise, opted against a formal motion to impeach him with any of his past, figuring it could be dealt with in the moment. But it didn't dawn on me Ted would be subtle enough to bring it in himself – the portrait of a *loser*, not a killer.

"Well, I messed up senior year in high school, that's incident one."

"What can you tell us about that?"

"Basically, we got blitzed and decided to bust up the school cafeteria one Saturday night. Me and a couple other guys, but it was my idea."

"How did you do that?"

"We hopped the fence, busted out a window, made idiots of ourselves. Tore the place up. Simple as that."

"Were you angry when you did that?"

"Yeah, plus drunk. Angry at the whole place."

"Because why?"

"Teenage stuff, I guess. Wasn't doing that well, school-wise, and had some teachers I didn't much get along with. They were on my ass, I smarted off and got the principal himself on my case, threatening to suspend me. Then on top of that I got thrown out of the cafeteria the day before, two bites into lunch. I kinda got to a hostile place."

"This is while you were still a minor, correct?"

"Yeah, barely. We all were. Thought about that before we did it."

Ted nods. "Now did they charge you with a felony for the damage?"

Sonya turns, eyebrows arched. The world is at an angle.

"They did. Yes."

"And you spent time in Juvenile Hall?"

"Nine days, I think. Did a whole week of school locked up, I remember that."

"Now they eventually worked it out as a misdemeanor, not a felony, and you paid restitution?"

"Yes sir."

"In full?"

He goes sheepish. "Eventually."

"OK, DUMB MOVE number one," says Ted. "What was your next mistake?"

Rodarte pauses, but just to remember. "Shoplifting down in SoCal. Orange County. Pair of sneakers – hard to hide."

"I see. And more informal probation?"

"Yes, pretty much."

"OK. Then what next?"

"Umm, well, got a DUI, up in Sacramento."

"What was the story there?"

He snickers. "Nothing good. Split with my girlfriend that day, got wasted at a friend's place and tried to get home. It's lucky it didn't go worse – I clipped a parked car before the cops ever saw me."

Now Ted again clears his throat, transparently reading from his RAP sheet. "Would this last episode have been around the summer of 1998? Perhaps August?"

"Sounds right. I pled guilty right away. More probation."

"Thank you. And what is the *last* thing we can find on your record?" Sharp, as usual – *last* conveying *least*.

He pauses now – nervous? Or maybe not. "That was me and Renae. Getting drunk and having a fight up in Bay City."

I steal a look at Vanzetta, and he does give an extra blink or two. Since Ted is bringing up that which we were just forbidden to raise.

"That would have been December '02?"

"Must have been."

"Let's go back to that. What happened?"

Now he sighs, rolls his eyes. "On me. We were actually decorating the house for Christmas. Argument, goes from bad to worse. Says something I don't like at all, repeats it a few more times. I snapped, kinda shoved her against a wall, and then she came and belted me on the ear, and I swung back with my open hand."

"And connected?"

"Yes." Eyes downcast. "Not proud of it."

"Well, of course you aren't," Ted says, peeved. "We're speaking of her face?"

"Yes. Side of it."

"No broken bones?"

"No. Lot of swelling and bruising."

"Now as a part of that, did they have a no-contact term between the two of you, or did they leave it so you could remain together?"

"They let us stay together, but said if there's any sign of trouble, any call to the cops, I'd go in regardless, as a violation. Basically, I had to keep the peace – any argument I'd be responsible."

"That solved the problem?"

Rodarte grimaces. "Sort of. We kept it in check for the next few months. Then we broke up, but that wasn't the reason."

"I see. But did something else happen during that period of probation, Mr. Rodarte?"

"Yes sir. What happened was I'd gotten 90 days to serve and a date to report to jail. I blew it off. I wanted to work a few more weeks, that turned to months, and then Renae and I broke up. I got a month-to-month on a studio apartment, but I was already thinking of leaving the area and was trying to keep my head down. Then like a moron I got pulled over for a stop sign, the warrant came up and I went in."

"And your probation was violated, correct?"

"Yes. The judge terminated probation and gave me 180 for admitting the violation."

"Basically six months?"

"Correct."

Ted looks at his papers. "Would that have been July 23, '03?"

"Sounds right. And I got credits, so I basically did four months."

"NOW WOULD IT BE November 19 that you got out, November 19th of '03?"

"Yes sir."

"And two days later you were all the way down here?"

"Yes sir.  On my way to my mom's place, kinda taking the scenic route.  Spent most of the afternoon lost."

I like his tone – not mordant, not whiny, not carefree.

"And along the way you stopped at the house on Sundown Road.  On the property where Haylee Branch was later found dead, as we have heard.  Correct?"

"Yes sir."  A look momentarily flashes over his face, and I seem to recognize it from the end of the second interview, when he finally punched back.  *Perfect,* I think.  *Stick your chin out.*  He will never see it coming.

"And now we're here on the charge that you murdered her?"

"Yes sir."

"Mr. Rodarte, did you kill Haylee Branch?"  Ted's tone is carefully offhand – get the obvious into the record right away.

Rodarte clears his throat.

"Yes sir."

# *20*

*August 30 – Afternoon*
**(JPH)**

IT ISN'T REALLY HOLLYWOOD. I'm not sure Vanzetta even owns a gavel to bang. But the average DA never sees it happen in a lifetime, and I feel my own face go numb and slack, trying to believe my own ears.

Marta and Ashlyn aren't there. Rodarte was the one thing they couldn't squarely face. But right behind me I hear audible gasps, a sob and a voice – a family friend, I think – muttering "Praise God." To her left I hear the intake and holding of breath, and from further back, a muttered word – it sounds like *animal*.

Then I glance across to where Rodarte's mother sits alone, her head bowed, her hands folded in her lap – maybe praying. But it seems wrong to look at her, or even to wonder if she's surprised.

Sonya Brandstetter could be in line at the bank.

TED STAUBER LEANS BACK, his tone conversational. "You killed Miss Branch, yourself?"

"Yes sir." Rodarte's face is red, his breath shallow. He pauses, and a little hiss of air begins to leak from the balloon. "I didn't mean to. It shouldn't have happened. But I'm to blame."

Ted nods, slowly. "In what way, Andrew? How are you responsible for her death?"

"Because her wind got cut off," he says softly. "I – we did it, together – the thing. Her throat." He clenches his eyes, five seconds pass. More. "And it went too far, too long. I didn't mean for it to happen. But I did it. I'm responsible."

Now Ted nods vigorously, though his face is pale. This is a terrible risk. *All right*, he says, like it happens every day. *Let's come back to that in a moment.* And he goes right back to the start.

BACK ROADS, Rodarte agrees, through our collective daze. The scenic route. *He killed Haylee.* Taking 101 straight down would have saved him hours, but he says that day, free again, he was in the mood to wander, take new roads. *No more mystery.* Not in a huge hurry to return to his mother's house, failed again.

After a long afternoon of rugged, bending mountain roads had dissolved into dark, he says he came at last to the northwest edge of Crown Lake and stopped to eat. He even remembers the name, a popular greasy-spoon about eight miles north of Hammonds. *Before he killed her.*

He left there maybe 9:30, went out into the darkness, having figured out a general route the rest of the way. Southeast.

TED SMILES NOW, tightly.

"Mr. Rodarte, did you eventually reach the town of Walkersburg?"

"Yes."

"Did you stop at a gas station, mini-mart place, as you stated in your interviews and Miss Cantrell described?"

"Yes."

"Why?"

"Well, bathroom stop. But then I looked around a little."

"Did you end up buying anything?"

"Some water, I think, and then the beer, like she described."

"Jacinta, you mean?"

"Yes sir."

"Did you find her attractive?"

Rodarte is settling in. His expression is earnest. *He killed her.*

"Generally so, yes sir."

"And did you sense some degree of interest from her, too?"

"Well, maybe a little. But then she wanted something from me."

"I see." Ted flips pages, gathering himself. "Now did she give you money, Andrew?"

"Not inside. Thought it might look bad if someone saw it. I went up and bought it, went out to my truck. A couple minutes later she went up, bought her own stuff and then met me there."

"And then what?"

"Well, thing was, we – I'd parked around the corner from the main door, kind of outta sight. So I figured, let's square up right here, or down the street or something."

"I see. And how did she answer?"

"She goes, she says, you *need* to come back with me, follow me to my place. Those words. She tells me she only has like fifteen bucks on her, which would leave me at least a few in the hole, and I wasn't exactly rolling in money. She goes, it'll be a blast. And she says, too, that this way I can't get busted, nobody's gonna see the handoff. So it's a big sales pitch."

"I see. And you agreed to do that?"

"Eventually, yeah. I followed her to that house. Had to haul to keep up with her." *But you did, and then you killed her. Haylee. And Wade found you before dawn.*

TED MAKES A STUDY of his notes. "Now you told Detective Wade that you reached the house at about 10:45. Is that accurate?"

"Well, no. That can't be right. Must have been earlier, like 10:15, maybe 10:20."

"And who's there, when you get there?"

His eyes widen, like this was unexpected. "Well, I mean, just me and the first girl, Jacinta, and there's her friend, who is – you know."

"Haylee Branch?"

"Yes sir. She used Lee." He closes his eyes. *What does he see?*

"So you're there at Jacinta's invitation, and for the moment it's just the three of you?"

"Right. I asked – she said, umm, it was a football night for the high school, out of the area, and there'd probably be more people along later. But for then – yes. Just them. Me and them."

"And then what? Do you start drinking?"

"Yeah, we start right in on the beer. Or she does, and we follow, sort of."

"You and Lee?"

"Right. I gulp a couple fast, then a third, start on a fourth. She starts with one, but the first girl Jacie, she's like four down in the first 20 minutes, and keepin at it."

"And the girls are giggling, happy?"

"Well, I thought so. Jacinta more. But after a little while she starts to fade out."

Ted pauses, innocent-faced. "Now did you know why that was happening?"

"No sir. I mean, she was drinking, but she went from laughing and loud down to passing out super-quick."

"Did it occur to you drugs might be involved?"

Sonya won't object, and Rodarte's eyes are wary.

"I wondered, I guess. But I didn't really know."

"Not drugs you gave her, right?"

Sonya rolls her eyes. "Objection leading."

"Sustained."

"Did you have roofies in your possession that night?"

"No sir. I'd never seen em, even."

"Meaning you can't have administered them to either girl?"

"Right, sir. I didn't." *Bullshit – you killed her. You –*

TED NODS AND SQUINTS, as if learning new things. "And when she starts fading out, Andrew, then what?"

"Well, I *did* want to leave, like I've always said. I wanted to get out of there." Now he's queasy-faced, not quite natural. "But what happened is . . . after she's drifted off I go to the bathroom, and then, when I come out, the second girl, Lee, she's there. Sort of sudden, with a lot of purpose. I mean – words, a look, her body language, all that."

"You explained this in your second statement, didn't you?"

"Yes sir."

"And you've explained when you were interviewed that she was very beautiful and appealing, haven't you?"

He drops his head, contrite. "Yes sir." *And still you* –

"I see. Now what did she say to you, if you remember?"

"Well, like, 'Don't go, I need you to stay,' that sorta thing. Then I'm wondering about the first girl, but she goes don't worry, she's out. And I can see she is."

"All right. And then what?"

WHAT HAPPENED THEN, he says, is that Haylee Branch led him out from the gleaming living room through a sliding door and down a broad set of shallow stairs to a lighted pathway. They walked down it, her leading him, and he could hear the rush of water below.

And then, with frozen muscles and a faltering face, he says they came to the *casita*, and that she had a key to the door and the lights were already on. He says he brought a beer down there, though he can't remember if she did, and he says that when they got inside and the door was closed she came straight at him.

He says that Haylee, there in the last half hour of her life, shoved him back against the doorway, rammed her body against his, kissed him violently and then, as he was only beginning to respond, grabbed him and shoved him toward the bed, and began to undress him by force. He says that meant she had to pull off his outer layer first, which was that dark blue jacket with its obliging fibers, and that they had a little "game" over it, and she really had to "tug and yank" at it.

Only now do I get angry.

HE SAYS THEY WENT immediately to sex – no pause for l
no questions asked. Simple lies, on balance, are easier to manage
elaborate ones.

He says he stood over her, and that as more "play" they foug
over him pulling off her panties, and that she may have "pretended t
resist," but all the time she was actually laughing, and then it was on.

Her underwear must have gotten tangled up over the left leg,
somehow. He can't remember.

Ted is rigid and stern, reaching for words.

"Now you began intercourse with her?"

"Yes sir."

"How would you describe it?"

"Well . . . intense."

"From the beginning?"

"Pretty much, I guess."

"And what was her – state of awareness, at this point?"

Rodarte actually shrugs. "Well, alert. Right there, you know."
Now just the hint of a smile. "Involved."


SUDDENLY I'M PAST FURY, on to a riper and fouler thing, as if
I'm hearing it through Marta's ears. I feel like a passenger told to brace
for a water landing, being reminded that if the 737 doesn't smash into
two million shards, the seat cushion can double as a flotation device.

# 21

RODARTE'S FACE is white now.

"Now, you recall the discussion of the condom found there. Was it yours?"

"Yes sir."

"Did you bring it with you?"

His eyes go wide and stunned, for some reason. "I don't – well, I did. I carried it in my wallet."

"So you put it on and then resumed – intercourse?"

"Yes. I guess so."

"Please don't guess if you can do better. Are you sure?"

A tiny shrug. "Yes."

"And what happened from there?"

"Well, then it went . . . next level. She told me to grab her, around the neck." Shaking his head now, sweating.

"How exactly did she do that, Mr. Rodarte?"

"She grabbed my hands one at a time, put 'em there. Then she said something like do it, do it and keep doing it, and tighter and tighter, just watch me if I fade out."

"And this was not something new to you, then? As per the testimony of the last couple of days?"

Even on direct you can feel his desperation. Could this possibly have been a good idea? "No, but I wasn't – serious, you'd say. I mean, I'd had fun with it a few times. But not – with danger."

"All right." Ted forces himself. "Now you saw the picture of bruises around her throat. Haylee, Miss Branch. Did you make those, with your own hands?"

The words can barely escape his mouth. "Yes. Yes sir."

"In the course of asphyxiating, is that what we're talking about? Cutting off air?"

"Yes."

"Now what did she do, physically, if you can remember?"

He's shaking his head, eyes away.

"She, well, she made me squeeze firm. That was the main part. I mean, with the sex itself."

"OK. And the sex continued, for how long?"

"A while. Two minutes. Three, four. Even five maybe. I don't really know."

"OK. And then what?"

A BIG HEAVE, and suddenly he's just pathetic – a man nine days on a raft, begging for rain. *Didn't think it all the way through, did you?*

"Well, she goes hey, let's do it another way. And she points to a plastic bag behind me, on a table. So I grab it."

"What sort of bag? To carry your groceries?"

"Umm, the kind they give you, I guess. Plastic with flaps." Sudden alarm. "But you could see through it."

"OK. And then you did what with it, Mr. Rodarte?"

His face remains frozen and blank, but it nearly works as pure horrified disbelief. And his voice is strong, almost resolute.

"I put it over her face. And pulled it down tight, and tied it with the flaps. But not too tight – or, I thought."

Ted Stauber nods, slowly and grimly.

"So the redder marks in the photograph were made by a tied plastic bag, not a rope, not something else?"

"Yes. Yes sir."

THEN IT WENT ON. Harder and faster, he says. And from what he could hear Haylee loved it, bag over her head, and wanted it to go on and on, and so he pounded her hard for several minutes, and we are to hear her gasping moans and whimpers, there in those last minutes. With a bag over her head.

My own stomach still churning. Could any sane person credit *any* of this – and would it matter, really?

But we need all twelve.

"Weren't you concerned about her, about the risk?"

"I was – yes, I asked her – are you sure, do you know this? She says yes. It's what she wanted, what she was telling me to do."

"But let's clarify, Mr. Rodarte. This was a thing you already knew how to do, correct?"

"Umm, well, not really – not with the bag, at least. That was new."

I see Sonya half-turn, almost involuntarily. Maybe trying not to burst into flames.

"All right. Did you discuss anything else with her?"

"Well, she had said to pay attention to her. That she was OK."

"And . . . you did, Andrew? Or you didn't?"

It's quick – agonized, then almost bored. "No. No, I didn't."

As Ted frowns and gathers himself once again, I see a different angle. Yes, he'd rather be here than almost anywhere else, but that only takes into account the possible. He must once have imagined tall iced teas, island shirts and buffet suppers, grandchildren on his knee – and all he had was his daughter. He buried her and endured, and his portion instead is to stand here firm, with that and two of my lifetimes behind him, as his client more or less admits to murder.

TED FOLDS AND RESTS his hands.

"So, Mr. Rodarte, did you climax with the bag still over Miss Branch's head?"

It's a squeak. "Yes."

"Now at any point, did the intensity fade away, what was happening between the two of you, while it was still in progress?"

Rodarte's shoulders shrink, a head shake.

"I felt . . . like she went quiet. Like it faded out a little . . . like it slowed."

Ted sighs – forcing himself. "Now did you slow down too?"

"Umm. I don't quite know."

"But you did not stop, correct? Until you climaxed?"

"No. No, I didn't."

"And was the bag still over her head?"

Now what you notice is his audible breath, shallow and fast. He puffs his cheeks just slightly, lets air escape. It should be ridiculous but it isn't, quite.

"Yes."

"And it ended, Andrew, and then what?"

"Then I . . . went blank a minute. I just collapsed there, forward – worn out."

"Where's the bag, while you're out of it?"

Rodarte clenches his jaw. "It was there. Right where it got tied, around her throat."

Ted nods. "And how did Miss Branch look to you now?"

He just quivers for a moment, then emits a small sound. Finally he does tear up. *Fake.* "All wrong. Just all wrong."

TED LEANS BACK, folds his arms. "So, Mr. Rodarte, what did you do when you discovered that?"

"I tried . . . to get the bag. To remove it. But it was hard to do."

"What was hard about it?"

Rodarte shakes his head, looks to the far end of the room. "It was tight. I mean – I thought it wasn't. But I had to grab something, like a pen," – *like* a pen? – "went ahead and punctured the plastic."

"And what did you see?"

"Her just not responding. Not seeming to feel anything, hear anything – her face frozen, eyes like half open, with those spots in them. And not breathing now."

"What did you do then?"

It takes a while, as it should, him shaking his head, almost disintegrating – *hoping* to, I'm suddenly sure. "I mean, I shook her, slapped her cheek, shouted, all of that – for like, I don't know, a minute. I couldn't believe it was true. And then, I . . . tried to find out whether she was, you know. Whether she was gone."

"ALL RIGHT." Ted Stauber smiles brightly now, lets it dissolve. "So you are in the guest house, in the bedroom there, Miss Branch lies on the bed, and you have discovered that she is unresponsive, possibly dead, as a direct result of what just happened between you. Correct?"

"Yes sir."

"But you did not call 911, correct?"

"No. I – I think it was just too much to take in."

"I'm not sure I understand that." That quickly Ted has gone quiet and frosty. "Can you be clearer?"

Another sigh, and Rodarte looks square at his lawyer, but I think his eyes flash first over the jury box.

"I was just scared. Terrified. I could picture how it would look, and go. And I thought they'd start hunting, find my history, see I'm just out. They'd find out how we met up, how we, everything – how I ended up there. And then I was sure . . . well, that they, people, wouldn't believe. What happened."

But Ted stays distant. The facts have to come first.

"So no call. What *did* you do, Mr. Rodarte?"

Again gathering himself. "I panicked. Just fled. Ran to my truck and just took off, tore out down to my mother's place."

"That being in San Ricardo?"

"Yes sir."

"Now were you shocked when the sheriff got there so fast?"

Rodarte hesitates, shakes his head. "Not really. Not sure why."

"Had you expected to just vanish, never be found?"

"I don't think so. I couldn't picture that. And for however long I'd just be in fear."

"But couldn't you have packed up and left then, Mr. Rodarte?"

"Well, I could have. But – I didn't."

TED EASES OUT from behind the lectern, hands behind his back. "Now let's get straight one more time. When Detective Wade spoke to you, Andrew, why didn't you tell the true story?"

"Because I didn't dare. I just couldn't see how any of it, ever, would get believed."

"But you did admit you went to the house, and told the true reason. Why?"

"Well, I thought they had me trapped. I thought they had me on a camera, already knew I was there. So I figured I'd better be honest about that."

"Then what did you do – that day, the next day?"

"I barely remember. I felt paralyzed. Deep breaths, just talking myself into staying where I was, hoping somehow time would pass and the spotlight would fall off me. Magic-type thinking. And I guess I was scared to call attention to myself, if I left."

"But eventually you did leave, correct?"

"Yes. Eventually."

Ted nods, folds his fingers in front of him. "Now were you assuming you were under surveillance?"

"Well, pretty much. I barely left the house, but when I did there were cars around, sometimes marked, sometimes not. Wasn't hard to figure out, though."

"All right. And so after a couple days you made a plan?"

He looks down, nods. "If you can call it that."

"Where were you headed, Mr. Rodarte?"

"I didn't know. I'd thought of Mexico, but I wasn't sure how I'd get back – I don't have a passport, and anyway I'd be a fugitive. I was just gonna head south, I thought, get at least to L.A. and figure it out."

"And you didn't realize your registration had expired?"

"No, I knew. The overdue notice was in the mail pile my mom gave me. But I decided I couldn't even wait. It was like my panic had a slow fuse, then blew up.   First I was paralyzed, then suddenly I decided I just had to risk it, no matter what, and get the hell out."

"What about the false ID?"

"He was a guy I knew in Bay City, actually – fellow grease monkey. He'd kept his old license after he renewed and changed his address, offered it to me for 20 bucks. Seemed like a dumb thing to do, and I wasn't sure why I'd ever need it, but I said OK."

"And so you decided to employ it if you got stopped?"

"Basically, yeah. Didn't make sense, but that was all I had – hope they don't look too close, hope they don't see it's expired too. Couldn't do anything about the picture.   But I also figured there might be a warrant now."

Ted pauses. "What was your state of mind then, Mr. Rodarte?"

"Well, trying to escape, trying to forget." Now stronger. "Guilt."

Nodding and shuffling now, Ted, stalls, runs the clock, and it works. We break for the night with the defendant still on direct.

♦

I FLOP IN SONYA'S corner chair, old-pro style.   In fact I'm shocked senseless, even now.

*"Well.* Have you ever seen that move before?"

Sonya doesn't pretend to think about it. "No, not even close."

"And after his outrage on the tape."

"It was good outrage, while it lasted."

"Fierce, even."

"That's a good word for it. But he's had all this time to think."

"And Ted." It may or may not sound like a question.

"Ted's always thinking. Way ahead of his client, normally."

*But do you think – am I going nuts –?* The words stall.

"Can you make any sense of it?"

Now a smile forms. She purses her lips, and her eyes answer the unasked question. "I don't know that we're meant to."

## Cold Record

THE DANCE BETWEEN US keeps our meetings short. I don't quite ask things, she doesn't quite answer, I say yell if you need me and drift back down to my own office.

On a normal night I'm there until nine, maybe, complete small tangible tasks, come up with a plausible question or two. When I duck my head back in for good night, she never seems to have moved, and her eyes seldom rise from her screen.

Tonight it's nearer ten. I assemble five or six pages of bullet points, pretty well-crafted, possible directions in which to drag him on cross. I'm kinda proud of it, like a decent term paper, and it's enough to make her raise her eyes and give me a solid half-minute of engagement before I amble out into the night.

THE NEXT MORNING, looking in, I see her own notes – an inch-high bound assortment, rich in tabs and highlights in her small, flowing script. And next to it on the desk is her own set of bullets, in fourteen-point type.

Again a riddling smile, but this game's rigged against Rodarte. For several strange seconds I feel sorry for him.

# 22

*August 31 - Morning*
**(JPH)**

WE'RE EXPECTING a strong finish, but to my surprise Ted arrives with the haggard look of a senator who refuses to concede on election night, then wakes to find the margin has doubled. I suspect they've bickered.

"So Mr. Rodarte, where we left off – you lacked awareness of what you did?"

"Yes sir. Completely."

"In a situation of consent?"

"Yes. Yes sir."

"Now, you've admitted familiarity with this practice. Did you mean to render her unconscious, Miss Branch?"

He pauses. "For a few seconds, at most. Then pull back."

"That is the goal of this – approach?"

"Well, to the brink."

"And you are acting at her direction?"

"Yes."

"While she is awake?"

"Well, right. Leading up."

"But the unconsciousness was sustained, somehow?"

"Umm, yes sir."

Ted pauses an extra beat now. "So would you regard her death as an accident, Mr. Rodarte?"

Incredibly, Rodarte stalls in his tracks. "Can you repeat that, sir?"

Ted Stauber looks ready to complete the trial by murdering his client.

"You would call Haylee Branch's death an accident. *Correct?*"

Sonya has to object to leading, finally.

"Sustained."

Ted actually needs a moment to calm down, turns away, then back. "Do you have a word to describe what happened to Miss Branch, Mr. Rodarte?"

He's scared straight.

"Yes. Umm, yes sir. It was inadvertent. An accident. I never meant to harm her at all."

"Thank you, Your Honor. Nothing further."


WITH THE LIGHT DOWN, Sonya begins with the postmortem photograph of Haylee's neck, brutal and immediate.

"So your hands made those marks, Mr. Rodarte?"

"Yes ma'am. Yes."

"How long did that take, again?"

An immediate road-fork. If just a few seconds, of course, the force had to be immense. If longer, he is moving toward the timeline of killing her intentionally. But he finds the third way.

"I'm just not sure. I totally lost track."

"I recall that you estimated earlier something like two to five minutes of the initial sex, correct? With your hands, not the bag?"

"I, well . . . maybe two minutes, maybe three? But it could've been more."

"Throughout, though, you are pressing strongly enough to leave these marks and bruises, correct?"

"I must have been."

"And she's not complaining of pain?"

"She, well – I mean, I don't remember. She was drifting in and out."

"But you recall switching over to the bag, don't you, *after* the hands?"

"Yes, yes – sure."

"And you told us she was awake at that point, correct?"

"Yes."

"In fact you said she talked to you about doing it, didn't you?"

"Right. Yes."

"So she must have been awake, earlier, when you bruised her throat, right?"

A helpless shrug. "She must have."

"Did she cry out in pain, Mr. Rodarte? Under that pressure?"

"Objection, vague, speculation. Argumentative."

No chance. "Overruled."

"I don't . . . I don't remember."


"ALL RIGHT. Mr. Rodarte, when did you break Haylee Branch's hyoid bone?"

Another head flail, he looks away. "I don't know that either. I have no memory."

"So you don't remember it breaking?"

"No, no ma'am. I do not."

"Which means you don't remember her having any reaction?"

"No, I guess – no. I don't."

"So she had to have been unconscious, right?"

"Speculation, Your Honor." Ted's voice is scratchy, sleep-deprived.

"Sustained."

"I'll move on. Now we're agreed that you constricted her throat in two ways, hands and with the bag?"

"Right. Yes."

"And the bag was simply an air-restricting device?"

"Yes, that's all it was for."

"Did it seem to you the bag was tight enough to actually constrict the airway, as opposed to just limiting oxygen?"

"No. I mean, it wasn't supposed to be. I had left some slack."

Fish in a barrel.

"So doesn't that mean, Mr. Rodarte, that you must have broken Miss Branch's hyoid bone with your hands?"

"Objection, speculation," Ted tries again.

"Overruled."

"Mr. Rodarte?"

"I – no. I can't imagine. I can't believe I did."

"But you have no other explanation, do you?"

He gives it several seconds, appearing to think. "No ma'am."

SONYA'S EYEBROWS ARCH, ever so faintly.

"Now where was the jacket you mentioned?"

"Well, close, right there. Like on a chair."

"All right. How far away was the chair from the bed?"

"Maybe, I don't know, a few feet. More than five, maybe eight feet, maybe ten."

"Which direction?"

"Toward the wall."

Now she plays frustrated – a decoy scowl. "And you *never* placed the jacket around her neck and knotted it?"

He shudders, eyes wide and appalled. "No, no ma'am. I didn't do that."

"Are you sure it wasn't right there next to you, on the bed, right there to grab when you got frustrated?"

"No ma'am."

"So you never grabbed it, never knotted it up in your hands?"

"No ma'am." Despairing. "Never."

"You never teased her by pulling it around her neck?"

"Never. Not that. No, never. The bag – that's what it was. That's all that was wrapped around her."

She leans back, raises her eyebrows.

"Then can you explain how three fibers matching your blue jacket wound up on the bedspread, inches from where her body was found, and three others wound up under Haylee's nails?"

171

Rodarte shakes his head wonderingly. "It must have been earlier. When we wrestled over the jacket."

"But that was in another part of the room, wasn't it? Are you suggesting that you wrestled and she yanked out fabric from your jacket, then carried it to the bed and it fell out there, near her neck, during sex?"

"No, I mean – I don't have any idea, really."

"Couldn't you be forgetting that *you* used the jacket, too?"

"*No* – no, I didn't –"

"You were intoxicated, though. You may not remember, right?"

He flails, opens his hands. "I remember. How could I forget, no matter what? I remember all the important things. I *didn't* – I did not ever knot that jacket, did not ever put it around her neck." He hitches, nearly adds something, can't work it out.

SONYA FOLDS HER ARMS.

"OK. Now you did bring a beer down with you to the *casita*, right? Even though you initially denied it?"

"Yes ma'am."

"What do you know about DNA, Mr. Rodarte?"

Momentarily relieved to shift topics, he tries a smile, answers almost lightly. "Umm, not very much. Next to nothing."

"Heard of it, though, haven't you?"

"Well, sure. TV, I guess."

"Have you seen stories about DNA in criminal law?"

He turns it over for a moment. Remembering standard advice – *when you're feeling pressured, don't hurry. Pause and think.* He nods slowly, carefully. "Somewhere."

"You're aware it gets used in criminal cases, aren't you? Sometimes to convict people, sometimes to exonerate?"

"Yes, I guess. Heard of that."

"You're aware DNA is in blood, correct?"

"Yes . . . yeah, I know that."

"Semen?"

"Must be."

"Saliva?"

"Object!" Ted barks. "Invites speculation. Beyond the knowledge of the witness."

Vanzetta shakes his head. "I think that's what we're testing. Overruled."

"Do you know that saliva contains DNA, Mr. Rodarte?"

"I guess, right."

"Fragments of skin?"

"I would think so."

"Do you remember where you learned all that?"

Rodarte shrugs, cartoonishly. "Ah, not really. Just stuff you pick up. Some of it I learned here, really."

Sonya's eyes take on a gleam.

"But some of it you learned quite a while ago, isn't that right?"

It dawns on him now – the search history on the laptop found in the Suburban when he was arrested, collected and disclosed in the early days, teed up for rebuttal if he denies it.

"I . . . checked it out. Sometime back then."

"Back then," repeats Sonya. "Maybe two Novembers ago?"

"Well, it could be."

"In fact you went online to read about it on Yahoo, didn't you?"

"I – did a search. I remember that much."

"Clicked a link?"

"I guess so. I don't really recall."

"When do you think it was, relative to Miss Branch's death?"

Now Rodarte sits a long time, then nods. "OK, it was afterward. Obviously. It was that day. It was after he came and left again, when I realized what I was up against. That's when I went to look."

"NOW, YOU WERE RELIEVED you weren't arrested, I assume?"

"Yes. Yes. Of course I was."

Sonya smiles brightly. "Did you think it was because you told a pretty good story?"

"Objection, argumentative, calls for speculation."

"Sustained."

"Fair to say you didn't tell the whole truth, correct?"

"Yeah, of course."

"But it seemed to work, didn't it? On that day?"

"I guess. They didn't take me away."

"They *did* ask you for a DNA sample, though, correct? As Detective Wade testified?"

"Yes, right. The cheek thing."

"Then, when they had gone, the *first thing you did* was go to your computer and read about DNA, isn't that right?"

"Well, maybe." His voice has gone quiet. "I mean, it might have been that day, maybe the next. I can't really know, not now."

Sonya pauses, half-smiles at him. "Mr. Rodarte, you knew that DNA test on the beer bottle was going to put you in the room where Haylee had died, didn't you?"

He remembers to wait, squints toward the floor, and comes up with a pretty good answer.

"I'd been there a while. I'd touched things, drank things." He clears his throat again. "I mean, sure. I knew there was still something there of me."

"But you had made no mention of the *casita* to Detective Wade, isn't that so?"

He freezes, probably trying to remember what was on the recording. "I'm not sure."

"Based on what you'd told the police, there was no justification for your DNA being there in the room, was there?"

"Well, I don't – I'm not sure."

"And you knew there was a good chance they were going to find it through a DNA test, didn't you, and probably come back and arrest you for murder?"

He's nodding now, slack. "I thought – yes, I was afraid of that."

"And so you made your plan and hit the road before that could happen, didn't you?"

Rodarte waits again, but the sea around him is dark and wild. "I didn't plan. Not that way."

Sonya smiles. "What, you woke up in the driver's seat, with your old work buddy's driver's license in your pocket?"

There's an audible snicker, probably from the box.

His eyes are glassy. "It wasn't a real plan."

♦

NOW A BREAK. Forcing myself to move, I walk down to the first floor and step out the side door into the small hedged courtyard, more or less the only appealing feature of the building. Its battered stone bench might be original courthouse equipment, but it is reliably quiet.

Rodarte is in the ancient fix – when your story is lies, it's hard to keep them all straight. Let alone with a Sonya in your face.

A few minutes later, a brief sausage rush behind him, the guy who runs the hot dog cart comes wandering back for a cigarette. He grins when he sees me seated and inert.

"Ya got him on DNA, right?" By reflex, I glance around for anybody with a juror button, but we're alone. "Shit don't lie, do it?"

"It don't," I agree, grinning but keeping it low, wishing him gone.

"So why didn't you try and send this fucker over the rainbow?" he asks. "Save a prison bed. Or maybe you can't talk about it while it's going."

"Better I don't." I shrug. "And the answer would be complicated."

175

"Well, right. Just 'cause they *make* it complicated, right? I mean, this oughta be simple. Fuck that needle bullcrap. Do it Old West style, right here behind our fallin-down old piece-a-shit courthouse. Big tourist attraction, right? Hell, I'll get here six in the morning, bring my snow-cone machine too. Make a day out of it."

"Ah, I don't know," I say, reluctantly amused. I look around. "You're right – there's room for a scaffold. Anybody know how to build one, around here?"

"Well, shoot, I do decks on the side," he says, with a throaty chuckle. "Just lumber and nails, ain't it? Hinges for your trapdoor, sturdy beam for the noose."

"The rope's tricky, though. Gotta get it just right."

"Well, I got a nephew in the Boy Scouts. He could help."

I close my eyes, smiling in the shady warmth – and then, incredibly, drift away for a moment. When I come to with an awful start, for the first time ever I have kept the court waiting in the middle of trial – just a minute or two, but that's an eon.

The jury is still settling, though, and Ted has his head turned to Rodarte as he rises to resume the stand. Once in plain view I make a face and pass a hand, very subtly, over my stomach.

◆

"YOU USED A CONDOM, isn't that correct?"

"Yes ma'am."

"And you stated you climaxed inside that condom, the green one found in the bathroom area?"

"Yes. Yes ma'am." I can imagine Ted's advice during the break – *take a breath, keep it simple.*

"And you're engaging her sexually for some minutes, correct? Haylee?"

"Yes."

"And you say she is *aggressive*, right? And full of energy?"

176

"Yeah, pretty much."

Sonya's eyes are as deadly and ruthless as a firestorm. "Until the point when you really started squeezing her neck, yes?"

"I guess, yes."

"Because until then she's awake and into the whole thing, right?"

Sagging now. "That's how it seemed."

"Now how are you doing with it, while she's awake and aggressive?"

"Objection, vague."

"Let me rephrase. Are you nearing orgasm, while she's fully awake?"

He takes many seconds. "Yes."

"But then you *don't* finish right away, correct?"

"Yes. I mean, no, I didn't –"

"So your pace slowed, your climax?"

"I guess. It must have."

"And when you really squeeze is when she goes quiet, right? When she *stops* being loud and aggressive?"

"Yes. Well, but the bag –"

"She's gone quiet, your pressure increases, but it takes you some time to finish?"

A crack for Ted. "Objection, vague as to 'some time.'"

Vanzetta turns to us. "People?"

Sonya scowls. "I think we've established that he can't do better, haven't we?"

He thinks about it, nods. "Overruled."

"It takes you at least a couple of minutes to reach orgasm, yes?"

"Yes, ma'am."

"Yet you were already near orgasm back when she was fully engaged with you, correct?"

"Yes."

"So this was slower, calmer sex, wasn't it?"

There's no way out. "Than – the earlier. I guess. Yes."

"But your testimony is that it happens, you're done, and you fade out?"

"Yes . . . yes ma'am. For a minute there."

"Even though this was *less* frantic, slower activity?"

"Yes."

"With a bag over her head, by your testimony, and your hands around her neck?"

"Yes ma'am."

"Or, *wait*." This is art. "You said earlier the bag came *after* you were choking her with your hands, didn't you?"

He can't remember, of course. "I don't – it runs together."

"You'd remember choking her through a bag, wouldn't you? Wouldn't that be *double* choking?"

Eyes closed. "I don't know. I just –"

"So there was the together sex, with her awake, featuring the choking by hand, then the bag later?"

"It must have been, yes – I can't exactly – I don't remember."

"And when you faded out, by your description, with the bag over her, it was some minutes since the frantic sex with her awake and responding, wasn't it?"

"Vague, Your Honor." Ted forgets to stand, desperate to interrupt.

"Overruled."

"Can you repeat it?"

"So it was after the rough awake sex with your hands restricting her that you went to the calmer sex with a bag tied over her face, and *that's* when you faded out of consciousness, and in that time she died?"

He shrugs, a terrible image. "I – those are your words."

"What words do *you* have for it?"

Rodarte's throat constricts, he looks down, he cries. At least ten seconds drip by. Vanzetta could prod him, doesn't. "I don't have words."

SONYA PAUSES, presses her hands together, squints at the ceiling.

"OK. Now do you have any medical training, Mr. Rodarte?"

He shakes his head slowly, pathetically. "No."

"Ever seen somebody check vital signs?"

He thinks. "Well, TV. Pulse, I guess. Neck, wrist, those places."

"Did you do that?"

"I tried – I mean, basically. Not knowing what I was doing. Just tried to find any sign, like a breath or a heartbeat."

"Even though it had only been, what, five minutes since the peak of your sexual communion, when she was right there with you, responding, even with her airflow being restricted?"

"Well, I just can't say about the time. But – right. Not long."

"OK. Now can you remember how long before your orgasm it was that you sensed her going weak, not responding?"

"Like, a minute at most. Probably less."

"And then how long, if we are estimating, did you fade out after you climaxed?"

"That's . . . that's the harder one. Somehow I just zoned. The beer didn't help, I guess. Can't have been long. I mean maybe I closed my eyes and two minutes passed, but I don't think so."

"And she died while you were zoning out?"

Rodarte stares wonderingly at the far wall, then back. His voice shakes. "That has to be what happened."

Sonya is nodding before he's even said the words, as if it were a formality.

"All right. So you did not realize her condition until you had climaxed and come back from a little mental detour, and when you're out of your fog you look down at Haylee Branch, and just like that Haylee is dead. Correct?"

"Yes. Pretty much."

"You've had this happen, she's dead by accident, and you – panic, lose your composure, is that right?"

"My judgment," Rodarte says, trying to rally. "Whatever word."

"And you run, straight out the door, is that right?"

"Yeah. Pretty much."

"ALL RIGHT," Sonya says, and turns her back on him for a moment, strolling behind the lectern Hollywood-style. It's obvious once more that she's enjoying herself. "And then outside – where did you go, again?"

"Up to the house, to my truck."

"What about the door to the *casita*? You left it open, correct?"

"I must have."

"Why would you do that?"

Rodarte pauses, exhales.

"Just, hard to say. Hard to make sense of. Panic state."

"You weren't quite yourself?"

"No ma'am."

"Is it hard to even remember it all?"

He realizes the necessary answer. "No ma'am. It's with me permanently."

"And in your panic, you just fled?"

"Yes," Rodarte says, and sighs. I think he feels like he's crested the summit.

"And you were not thinking straight, is that right? Flying blind, frantic?"

"Yes. I mean – I wasn't."

"All right," says Sonya. "So when did you take the time to rinse out the condom?"

It freezes him, five seconds at least. Finally, twitching his shoulders, a dry croak. *I don't exactly know.*

SONYA GIVES HIM a slow, sage nod.

"OK. Now let me see if I have most of it straight. You met Jacinta at the SpeedyGrab mini-mart in Walkersburg, followed her home, and met Haylee Branch when you got there, correct?"

"Yes."

"Then they ask you to stay and you sit on a couch, drinking beer?"

"Yes."

"And Haylee is where – opposite you?"

"Right. It's a huge couch, like three sides of a square. I'm on one, she's across."

"And where's Jacinta?"

"Well, kinda here and there."

"But Haylee stayed put, far as you remember?"

Another great sigh. "I think so."

"Who was bringing you beers, Mr. Rodarte?"

"I, heck, I don't even remember, really. They were just around, after they cracked a pack. I think Jacinta brought me one herself, maybe I grabbed one."

"And you sat there, aren't sure how much time went by, but then it's Jacinta who starts fading out, getting quieter?"

"Yes."

"But not Haylee, because she is awake and interested in you?"

Shrugging now, but nowhere to go. "Right."

"Now you never saw any roofies, is that right?"

"No, not at all."

"Which means you sure didn't bring them there yourself, correct?"

He shakes his head vigorously. "I've never touched 'em, never seen 'em –"

"And so you certainly didn't see Haylee take them herself, did you? Or Jacinta?"

"No," he says, but here's where it dawns on him. You can see him think better of it, too late. "I – no, no, I didn't."

"You just don't know where on earth they came from, right?"

Resigned now. "I don't."

Sonya nods – closing a book.

"OK, thanks for clarifying. So to go back a little, you are released from jail, and head south from Bay City just a day or two later, correct?"

"Yes ma'am."

"And this unbelievable thing happened on your way home, toward a new life?"

"Yes."

"And after it happens you make it home, but it's the middle of the night and you left Haylee Branch dead in a house at least a hundred miles away?"

"Yes . . . I did, yes."

Her voice takes on a honeyed sound. "Were you upset?"

"Absolutely. Beyond belief."

"And then the detectives showed up after you'd just had a very brief sleep, right?"

"Almost none."

"Which means you must have woken up still upset, correct?"

"Well – right. Plus scared, of course."

"You feel panic, at that time?"

"Yeah, more or less. I don't know what better word."

"But you heard the recording. We heard your calm and natural voice here in court, didn't we, on the recording of that interview?"

He twitches. "I'm good at . . ."

"Pretending?" asks Sonya softly. "Faking it?"

His muscles go slack, and he breathes heavily out of his nose. *I can't answer that, ma'am. I don't know what answers you want.*

"ALL RIGHT, MR. RODARTE.  So to you, then, this was an accident, yes?"

"Yes," he manages, his gaze far from Ted Stauber. "I can't believe what happened, even now."

"And it was an accident in the course of a sexual game that Haylee initiated with you, even though you've played it yourself?"

"Yes ma'am."

"And so you start with hands, and then the hands weren't enough for her, even though they'd already left huge bruises on her neck?"

"I guess."

"So you went to the bag, because she told you to, and never used the jacket at all?"

"Yes ma'am."  He nods his head like it especially matters.

"And you don't know how Haylee's hyoid bone was broken?"

"I – no.  It just had to happen along the way, somehow."

"Though you don't know when?"

"I don't."

"And you testify that the bag was over her head too long, and then you missed any signal she might have given you to stop."

"Yes."

"But you went into it because she demanded it of you?"

"Yes."

"And you took the lead from her, correct?"

"Yes."

"Yet you acknowledged you've experimented with this very thing yourself, and Miss Winter testified to that, didn't she?"

"Well, right."

"And what happened to Alina Nieves, her passing out – that was an accident, holding a moment too long?"

"Yes ma'am."

"Has it happened to you any *other* times, these accidents?"

You can see his eyes glaze.  "No.  No ma'am."

Now Sonya nods very slowly, shuffles a page or two for show. "Nothing further, Your Honor. Thank you."

Neither of us is surprised when Ted declines redirect, and rests the defense's case.

♦

SONYA PERMITS HERSELF an apple for lunch today, I drop a burrito in the microwave. When I wander back past her office, a few minutes later, she is laughing on the phone.

AT 1:35 PM we are asked about rebuttal evidence.

Sonya rises up ever so slightly, queenly in her designer heels.

"With the Court's permission."

Vanzetta gives an awkward smirk, suddenly subordinate even as he looms above the room.

# REBUTTAL

# Eric Ferguson

# 23

*August 31 – Afternoon*
**(JPH)**

LONG BEFORE WE FOUND Alina, Wade came up with the other girl. Sonya wanted to use them both in the case in chief, but Vanzetta said pick one, so she chose Alina. Ted then decided to risk Renae as his answer, knowing this could follow. After Rodarte's bomb I thought Sonya's plan might change, but it didn't.

The witness sits mannequin-still and spells out all three names, Tanya Dawn Melendez. She's about Rodarte's age and nicely dressed, in a ruffled, lilac-colored blouse and black slacks. She is tallish, her long black hair in a swirling wave. But the rest of her, to me, is almost jarring – a long face with a crooked nose, a dark red mouth and sulky, sleepy eyes. We haven't hit it off with her, to say the least. No matter.

Sonya looks a bit world-weary as we resume. I wonder if it's a very subtle act, a way of telling the jury the rest is a formality. Equally bored, to appearances, the witness identifies Andrew Rodarte.

"THANK YOU. Where do you know him from?"

"Umm . . . up north. Where I live."

"Which is where?"

"Bay City."

"Up along the coast?"

"Right."

"How do you know him?"

"We went out a few times, for like a month."

"When, if you remember?"

"The summer of '01. I'd just finished college."

"Miss Melendez, did that relationship reach the point of having sexual contact with him?"

If the witness had been civil enough to have a real conversation with us, Sonya would have worked up to it gently. But that's not how it went.

"Yes," she says, distantly.

"How many times, if you remember?"

"A few. Hard to say exactly, after all this time."

"Did that include full sexual intercourse?"

"Yes."

"All right," says Sonya. "Let me build on that. During that contact, Miss Melendez, did Andrew Rodarte ever cause you to lose consciousness?"

She looks down at her nails, and we wait. When she does raise her head again, though, her eyes are no longer bored or sleepy, but wet with tears.

"Yes, he did."

Sonya nods, in stride. "More than once?"

"At least four times," she says, and now she bows her head and her body shakes, and she reaches out with a blind hand toward the box of tissues.

Ted Stauber, his voice quavering with anger, asks to approach. I see Vanzetta nearly deny it, annoyed by the delay, but then he gets a good look at Ted's expression.

IN CHAMBERS Sonya's tone is flat and soft. "Ted, we're both surprised. We gave you what we had."

"You had a grudging, halfhearted admission," he says, spitting the words out, syllables precise. "The report provided to us said once or twice in the course of a consensual relationship. Now it's a pattern of behavior and Niagara Falls. I will object for all I am worth. I've been caught completely unawares."

Sonya tries to force a smile. "She did say 'a couple of times,' Ted. If you look. But I've had one short conversation with this witness since the day I got Wade's report, not counting about three minutes of indifference this morning. We have been regarded as hostile from Day One. Even pleasant Mr. Howland."

Nothing witty comes to mind. "Confirm."

"So how does that help me?"

"Just that we've held nothing back. I showed her the report this morning and she agreed it was correct. I told her she'd be asked this question and she just nodded. If she'd expanded on it, we'd have told you. Or if she started making excuses for him. None of that. You knew what we know, just hadn't yet felt her personal warmth."

Vanzetta smiles. "Not the first nasty surprise you ever got, I'm sure, Mr. Stauber?"

"Oh, I have a special *gift* for it. And the timing always seems to be precisely calibrated to wreak destruction on the defense."

"But not by this prosecutor, surely?"

Ted scowls at Vanzetta, but then he sighs, the match already burning down. We're past the apex of his fury, and he realizes he's in a box. "Ms. Brandstetter was certainly not a prime offender in that regard, back when she trod these boards with regularity. But this is a two-by-four in the chops with no discovery, and it's my duty to ask that it be limited, and for an appropriate instruction to the jury."

"Inconvenient," agrees the judge, only half-smirking. "Regrettable, even. But we all know stuff sounds different when the lights are on. I'm making no limitation on the testimony at this point, and we aren't ready to talk about an instruction. If it's the truth, it's entirely relevant. If not, I'm confident you'll make that clear with your cross. And if we get somewhere very strange, we'll revisit."

"If we knew, we'd have tried harder to get it in up front," Sonya adds, her voice flat. "We knew it happened, we didn't know the extent. She didn't volunteer that to us. So we're finding out together."

"On equal footing," Vanzetta says, and he stands. Meeting over.

Ted bites his tongue. His knees crackle as he follows suit.

TANYA MELENDEZ has tried to fix her makeup.

"You said four occasions. Were these on separate days?"

"Yes."

"And how did that come about?"

"Well, first because he talked me into it. The first two times. Then I said to stop."

"Now how did he cause you to lose consciousness?"

"He choked me. He pressed under my chin."

"And what did he say about that?"

The witness sighs, her voice small. "That I'd think it was exciting. And it kinda was, at first. But he just went too far with it."

"It took more than one no to make him stop?"

"Three times, after the day I went along. The first day was like fun, the best things ever got. We were into each other. It was after the second time I told him to stop it."

"But he did it again a third time, then a fourth?"

"Right. I could've been clearer, I guess. Less soft about it. After the first no he tried to play it off the next time, like he didn't really understand. But the time after that he knew. I guess he was thinking that because I'd been into it once he could get me back to it. I'm not wired like that, though. I make my mind up about stuff."

"And the relationship ended then, after the third no?"

She swallows. "Yes."

"By your decision?"

Mouth firm. "Yes. I was done."

I remember a curious lightness at this exact moment – the relief, I suppose, of the unambitious. *We can't do worse than a second-degree now,* I think to myself. Even if they looked past everything else, they'd surely convict Rodarte for killing her out of extreme recklessness – a "depraved heart," in the old words. Second-degree murder, meaning fifteen years to life even if they don't convict on the rape. And if they do, it's everything.

Then I realize Sonya would have turned down a second if it had been offered, and that was long *before* Andrew Rodarte admitted killing Haylee Branch on the witness stand.

TED STANDS, groping for inspiration.

"Now Ms. Melendez, this was a consensual relationship, correct?"

Shrug. "How do you define that?"

"You were voluntarily seeing him, spending time with him, being intimate with him, were you not?"

"More or less."

He'd normally make her explain, but she's made him gun-shy.

"And this one issue was the cause of your split?"

"If it even deserves the word. Basically we just had one long hookup." She studies the floor. "But this scared me, and I shut it down. Doesn't that make sense?"

"Did you believe he lacked respect for you?"

She frowns. "I don't think I thought that far."

"How did he react when the relationship ended?"

"I don't – I can't really say I thought about it."

"Didn't even think about it?"

"Was I supposed to?"

Ted finally snaps. "Ms. Melendez, can *I* ask the questions, and you try to answer?"

Her expression is worth a million bucks.

"If that's how it has to be."

♦

STANLEY, THE TOXICOLOGIST, is back for a single purpose.

"You are familiar with the toxicological report and its results for alcohol and flunitrazepam, as earlier brought out. Dr. Stanley, in your professional opinion, in light of those levels, and particularly the

191

flunitrazepam, is it likely that Haylee Branch could have been entirely alert and fully engaged in a sexual encounter at roughly 11:30 PM on the night of November 21, 2003?"

Ted objects, of course. Vanzetta instantly denies it.

Stanley clears his throat. "Considering the quantity of flunitrazepam detected post-mortem, I do not find that likely at all. There are a few reports of paradoxical effects in the literature, but the extent of the other victim's incapacitation, at only slightly higher levels, illustrates the power it is known for."

"And can you remind us how the alcohol in her system would be expected to affect things?

"Her post-mortem levels of blood alcohol were moderate, as you know. But considering that she was a female of modest weight and from what I understand a very light drinker, and had no known history of drug abuse, I'd judge it very probable that she would be heavily affected by the combined effects, with flunitrazepam being augmented by the alcohol. Both depress the central nervous system, and their combined effect is typically highly sedating. I can't know to a certainty, but in my view she would probably have been semiconscious at best, and not able to engage in any activity, sex included."

"How would you characterize a 'semiconscious' state?"

"Well, I'd see it as a state where perhaps the eyes are open, but she would have a lack of responsiveness, lack of awareness, limitations on her motor skills, limited response to stimuli."

"So again, not likely to be engaged in any vigorous physical activity?"

"Extremely unlikely, yes."

"What about speech?"

"I would not expect her to be verbal, and if she could speak at all, the words would almost certainly be badly slurred and difficult to understand."

TED DOES HIS BEST. Dr. Stanley was not present that night, didn't observe her, hasn't seen a video of her condition, people don't all respond alike. But after Sonya passes on redirect and Stanley steps down, there's a clear "we get it" look on the faces in the box.

A guy in the front six gazes intently toward Sonya, nodding faintly. Works for the road department, gave mild, middling answers, but had a square jaw, a pleasant squint of self-awareness and a history, three prior jury trials to verdict. Two of them, we learned, guilties for our trial hound Brian. I'm sure he expects us to stop here.

I do too. But Sonya hedges, does not rest.

"Your Honor, there's a prospect of a further rebuttal witness, but it will require discussion first, and likely a ruling by the Court on admissibility."

Vanzetta's eyes widen. Mine too – I know nothing. "Is defense counsel in the loop on that, just yet?"

Sonya is in the act of handing Ted a police report. "I'm providing discovery as we speak."

♦

I'M THE USUAL TWO PACES BEHIND as we reach her office door. I hang back, then see the crease of a smile, and she looks up at me with a conspirator's face, handing over another copy of the report – a stone-cold secret she kept all afternoon.

"This you'll like."

I see Wade's name at the bottom of the page, and a very familiar name marbled through the text. My mouth sags open. "Oh, it *can't* be. Too perfect."

She stands, just to stretch, smiling, raising her small arms over her head. For a moment there's an elfin flash, a glimpse of her as young, brilliant, dead alluring. I'm thrilled to be in the room, finally coming to know her. "That's the very word Ted used."

# 24

*September 1 – Morning*
**(JPH)**

NEW DISCOVERY in the middle of trial frightens a judge even when it won't seal a fate. This might. So we start the next morning with a standard pre-jury hearing, where Vanzetta will hear the testimony for himself before deciding whether to allow it – assuming, of course, our witness can manage to say the same thing twice.

Jail-bedecked, our unlikely offer of proof comes in sheepishly, stands and swears, and endures half an hour of questions, cluttered with objections and records and rulings. At the end Ted argues with a special note of outrage that can only be caused by the truly absurd. This is dropping your wallet down a storm drain, a flat tire that makes you miss your flight to Europe. But the witness has passed, and we all know it. So Vanzetta, with an unmistakable silent snicker, allows the evidence.

"But don't worry, Ted – I'll get you a full criminal history," Sonya needles him gleefully, and he does break out laughing. Stubbornly, too, he declines a delay.

THE WITNESS is a 56-year-old mope by the name of Robert William Matson the Second – double I, the Roman deuce. Which is silly, because he sure didn't come from a mold.

He had handles galore. He called himself Robbo, usually. He'd use Rob on slightly more formal occasions, like unsolicited phone calls. Most tweakers seemed to call him "Matty," and to a couple of old-timers he was "Little Bob," because his late dad, of course, was also Bob. The "II" would bollix the courthouse computers, because sometimes it would make it in there, sometimes it wouldn't, and he had as many cases in the archives as any nine normal tweakers. And then, like any long-standing patron of the legal system, he'd cluttered the computer with an AKA or two, and two or three plain old misspellings from over the years – Madsen, Mattson, Masson.

But to the sheriff and to us he was Matchstick, or just Stick, from the beginning, and it took no imagination to surmise why. He was at least six three, if a little hunched, and I doubt he ever weighed a hundred and fifty pounds. He was a lifelong doper, lifelong county resident, lifelong jailbird and probationer. And he was also, easily, the most useful, longest-running snitch our small world had ever known.

I wasn't there for most of his career, of course, but things pass into legend. For years simple possession of meth was a felony in California, and for a deal he was sometimes willing to give up at least one of his sources, particularly if he didn't like the product.

But he always had other stuff, because he was always talking to people. He could tell you who was hanging out where with who, and stealing what, and where stuff was stashed, and who beat up who next to the Circle K, and who put bullet holes in whose back door. He knew who had gone to work for the high-dollar marijuana grows, and who was doing skinhead recruiting, and who was vandalizing the Hammonds library, and who was digging up piping for the copper.

When he'd suddenly land in a probation pat-down, he'd just shrug, pull it out of his pocket and invariably say, "I barely got *shit*." They'd grin and bring him in, gently cuffed; everybody knew the drill.

Back at the station he'd give them a dealer, or at least a parolee at large, a burglar's stash, even just a couple of good felony warrant-holders. They'd say great, tell him to hang, and he would, eating snack-machine treats for an hour or two, chumming with the detectives as they would pass through.

They'd make an arrest based on his info and call it in, and then somebody would cite-release him out the back door so the guy he snitched on would never see him, and he'd have another possession of paraphernalia misdemeanor, another couple of years on probation with full search terms. Rinse and repeat.

Sometimes things reached a natural limit. He'd come through with two open probation cases, now charged with a third, and so it was time for him to go do a stretch in jail. It never fazed him. He'd nod earnestly to the judge, give a quick goodbye pantomime to his long-suffering girlfriend, and head out the back door.

IT WOULD NEVER have surprised anybody if Matchstick suddenly ran into a shank in one of those stretches, and for that matter we had to worry about him on the streets, too. We'd see him by the side of the highway, or briefly employed changing tires someplace, or he'd be standing outside the courthouse having a bummed smoke some morning, and we'd entertain ourselves working up a list of the people who should have done him in by now. We could usually come up with a dozen, at least.

He had snitched in the jail, too, before Rodarte. There wasn't as much to gain, normally, and less margin for error, but he still came through here and there. It helped that he had that goofy laugh, and an apologetic sort of air, and, of course, we fought hard to keep him off the witness stand, using every kind of protection the law offers for a "cooperating witness."

When the guy he gave up wouldn't take our generous probation offer, in most cases the drug cops would tell us just to dismiss rather than blow his cover. But more often the motley accused would sign up for plea deals, because they usually risked prison time and were hemmed in by other evidence that came to light after ol' Stick helped out the sheriff.

A couple of times, on more serious cases, he'd gotten bunked up with a target and heard pretty strong stuff, and once he did have to testify at a preliminary hearing. He first tried to take the Fifth Amendment a couple of times, which didn't apply because he was not incriminating himself, then pretended he didn't even understand the meaning of what the targeted guy had told him. But he held up well enough on cross – acknowledging he'd been put in there on purpose, but adding (in a phrase that broke us up) that nothing about that agreement "altered reality." And that dude, slinging illegally-modified assault rifles all over our backwoods, went down too.

Eventually we thought Matchstick would want to wrap it up, stop adding to his enemies list, but that day never seemed to come. He wanted to smoke meth and booze it up with the minimum of consequences, and since he'd basically never gone a month without being on some form of probation, he pretty well knew that the next bargaining session was right around the corner. That kept him motivated to stay informed.

And here he was, now, to close the circle on Andrew Rodarte.

YOU CAN'T, AS A RULE, use a snitch in jail after the target gets arraigned, which means he gets a lawyer. A jailhouse informant then becomes a government agent, even in his jumpsuit, and if the state sends him in to ask questions, it violates the right to counsel.

But there is a narrow loophole, long finessed: you can put an informant in the defendant's vicinity, any time at all, just to *listen*. And if the target starts running his mouth without prompting, and the snitch does nothing to direct him beyond responding politely, whatever the suspect is dumb enough to say can normally be used.

Since he's charged with rape as well as murder, Rodarte has been in protective custody from the beginning, away from the masses. The Stick, on arrest, would normally have gone in general population – he typically preferred the risks of mingling to getting "fitted for a snitch jacket" by being seen in PC. But Wade, inspired, pitched him a detour to the protective unit, with a bonus: if he'd go hang for a few days, he'd get a great deal, whether he heard anything or not.

This time, too, Matchstick had come into a lot of meth and bagged some up to sell around, so there was a *chance* we could have bundled him off to prison. With the stars aligned, the Stick went along.

There was still reason to be nervous.  Matson had never snitched on anything violent, best anyone could recall, let alone a murder with special circumstances, and it was also plain that he was winding down. He had developed a visible tremor, his remaining teeth were a heinous yellow, his hair was thinning, his smile was still ready but wan.

PUTTING ANY SNITCH on the stand at trial is a gamble, of course.  In the worst cases there may be risk to his life, and a lousy informant can torpedo a case faster than almost anything, making the jury believe you don't think you can win the case in an aboveboard way.   Naturally, any private agreements with a witness must be disclosed, meaning cross-examination will be savage.  And, of course, the jury usually has little trouble identifying the witness as a dirtbag and a liar by trade – if they don't already know him by sight or reputation, in a pond our size.

But on another day, in another case, what a snitch has to say may be simple and clear, just a recounting of words out of somebody else's mouth that he could never have made up, and that's where we are. We'll knock his felony down to a misdemeanor, no matter how it goes. And in the end, he's only building on to what the jury already knows.

He ambles in the side door, a little tidier than usual.  I think he combed his hair.

♦

MATCHSTICK IDENTIFIES Andrew Rodarte, and explains he was in jail with him the last six days.  They crossed paths in the day room, a few times for meals.

"Did you speak to him at all, get to know him?"

"Just hello, nothing too deep."

"Did he tell you what he was charged with?"

"Well, we all knew.  So it was more just small talk, to me direct."

"Now why are you in there, Mr. Matson?"

Here Ted could put on a small show. The question invites Matchstick to incriminate himself in his own case, and Ted could politely suggest to the court that, based upon this line of questioning, perhaps his public defender should be brought into the room to advise him. Vanzetta would likely just deem it irrelevant and tell Sonya to leave the issue alone, but if she argued hard for bringing it in he'd probably end up in the position of agreeing with Ted Stauber.

With an open charge, the PD would then sit near Matson and tell him to invoke the Fifth Amendment and decline to answer such a question. But of course Ted knows that none of that matters with Matchstick, because his deal is simple and unconditional, and so he's bound to answer anyway. And Ted is also just about as happy to cross him, knowing that since he answered freely on direct exam, the Stick can no longer invoke the Fifth.

Ted doesn't object, and Matson gives a sheepish grin. "Holdin some meth," he says. "No mystery."

"All right. Now, Mr. Matson, how many felonies would you say you've been charged with, over the years?"

He snickers, winningly. "Aw . . . lost count."

"A dozen or so, maybe?"

"We're in the ballpark." Another half-grin. "And don't even try on misdemeanors."

"Drugs the issue, normally?"

"You could say so. Goin back forever."

"Now have you ever gotten clean?"

"Well, yeah. The jail can't keep all the dope out, but what there is ain't normally good, and you're odds-on to get caught. So I basically get a break in there whether I want it or not, and then I've had treatment in a deal a couple of times. Finished the program once, six months, good folks. Stayed clean a few months after. Then the wrong people showed up one day." He grins again. "Same old same old."

"Mr. Matson, over the course of these years, you have cooperated with the police on many occasions, haven't you?"

His eyes twitch by reflex. "Time to time."

In a minute they've gone briskly through his deal.

"Now I think you'll agree that when you're using, you'll tell lies. Right?"

"Well, sure."

"To who, though?

The eyes go soft, but Stick is smiling again. "Whole world. Ol' lady, kids, probation officers, cops."

"All right. You ever come to court and lie?"

He grins again. "To the judge, or up here?"

I nearly break out laughing myself.

"As a witness, under oath."

"No ma'am."

"And you aren't planning to start today?"

Now he's serious, stone-faced. "No ma'am."

"GREAT," SONYA SAYS, turning a page. "So over the days you've recently spent around Mr. Rodarte, did he say anything you heard about the killing of Haylee Branch?"

Ted could now stand and repeat his objections under Miranda and the Sixth Amendment. But that's all been dealt with, and he's already made his record.

"A few things." Matchstick swallows, repeats it. "Not direct to me. But loud enough I heard 'em."

"Can you tell us about that?"

The Stick clears his throat, almost importantly. "Well, we're in the day room couple mornings ago, another dude comes around. Big dude, can't remember his name, don't know what he's lookin at but I think it's serious, and he brings it up. The murder case."

"While you're near enough to overhear?"

"Yeah. And so this Andrew just answers him, just starts talkin right back."

"Do you remember what he said?"

"Well, high points, anyway." There's a first time for everything, and we see it – Matchstick Matson is frightened. He passes his tongue over his lips, and twitches, and harrumphs in his throat, and he leans forward. But I'm happy to see that he looks away from Sonya, away from what anybody could think is a cue.

"Well, what he starts saying is, how he was just in a rich guy's house, and they got drunk, him and two girls, and then there was some kinda dope and one passed out, and so he says he ends up with the other one, and they end up in a bed.

"And what he tells the guy is they're having sex, and then she wants it rough, he says she wants his hands around her neck, he decides to go for it. He says he gets into it, seriously worked up, and then he hears a crack, and basically that's it. He realizes her neck's broke, and then – well, look, wasn't the plan, guess I don't know my own strength, and gets this sad kinda face. But, you know, once it happened – *I couldn't leave it there*, he says. *I couldn't leave her gurgling, her neck broke, and I'm goin down for it either way.* So he says, you know."

"What?"

"That he finished her off. Killed her."

The room is still.

"OK. Did he talk about what he did next?"

"Well, he just says he freaked out and he bailed, then somehow got caught way downstate and flown all the way back in the chopper."

"Now did you ever hear him mention a plastic bag?"

"Can't swear, but I don't remember that. I didn't hear every last word, but he's more, *geez, I don't know my own strength, and I guess she didn't either,* and like *how does that happen by accident, when they're just wantin to get it on* – well, you know."

201

Sonya pauses, a study in concentration, though I'm sure she's planned it to the end.

"How did Mr. Rodarte look, telling that story in the day room? What was his demeanor like, to you?"

Ted objects as vague and irrelevant, Vanzetta shakes it off. Sometimes, of course, the judge himself wants to hear the answer.

"Not real happy," old Stick allows. "Voice was low. Didn't look excited about it."

"But said it like he meant it?"

"Speculation," says Ted.

"Overruled. You may answer."

Matchstick shrugs, but then nods. "Sounded to me like he meant every word."

TED MAKES A FACE of controlled outrage.

"Who directed you, again?"

"Directed?"

"Asked you to get close to Mr. Rodarte?"

"Well, it was Mr. Wade brought it all to my attention."

"I see. What did Detective Wade say to you?"

Our cue. Sonya stands. "Objection, hearsay and relevance. 402 hearing."

Vanzetta nods. "Sustained."

"Now you knew the case, did you not? Before you went in there?"

"Mostly just who he was. Back when it happened they were saying the victim was a rich girl, and it kinda made him a celeb. Nobody on the street seemed to have the details, though. Probably 'cause they weren't people anybody knew, her and him. Some people knew the house, the girl who lived there, but then it came out it wasn't her who got killed. And nobody knew the actual people."

"But by now you know lots of details, don't you?"

"Much as most people, I guess. Maybe a few more."

"And the detectives gave you some tips, too, didn't they?"

Vanzetta glances at Sonya, expecting another objection, but she stays seated. Matchstick blinks and pauses, but then he clears his throat and his voice surges through. "Tips, I guess, but more like what not to do. I'm supposed to just hang out and listen."

"So that's all you did?"

"Yeah, that's it."

Ted nods, his own gears turning. Again there are ways he could push, but I see him resist tempting fate. "Now, you have custody experience. Agreed?"

"Pretty much my second home," agrees Matchstick.

"Lotta time in county?"

"Lost count. The food really ain't as bad as its rep, though."

Ted forgets to be furious, can't help laughing. "Guess we'll take your word."

"Beats my 79-cent TV dinners, anyway."

Half the room, and the box, is giggling now.

"Ever known anybody to make stuff up, in jail?"

His grin widens. He's relaxing now. "Only when their lips are movin'."

Even louder. Now Ted purses his own lips.

"No borrowing lawyer jokes," he says, mock-scolding, and gets a titter spike of his own. Suddenly it's a rollicking comedy routine. "So fair to say, you've heard people brag about doing big criminal stuff?"

"Plenty of times."

"And you knew some of those stories were, basically, a crock?"

"Sure. Knew for a fact, a lot of times. People claiming they did stuff and I knew they didn't, 'cause I knew who did."

"And that covered all kinds of crimes, didn't it?"

He thinks. "Well, sure, pretty much. People'll talk big about almost anything."

"Why do you think that happens?"

I want to blurt an objection myself – any answer is speculation in the legal sense. But Sonya doesn't move, and after a moment I reflect that she's right. Matchstick can't read minds, but he reads people.

STICK TURNS IT OVER for a bit. "Well, guess it's about image, not getting pushed around. Specially if you're new. If you're gonna talk, better sound like you're somebody not to mess with. Assuming you're ready to back it up, but that's another story."

"All right." Ted is plainly nowhere. "So, Mr. Matson, it wouldn't shock you if Mr. Rodarte was making this story up, would it?"

But this won't get past. "Objection, speculation."

Vanzetta gives it a long moment, reading his screen. "Yes. Sustained."

Ted grimaces – he counted on that last little hook. *The People's own witness said it sounded like plain old jailhouse bragging – that's all it was.*

"So, just so I have it – the only one who reported this is you?"

"Think so."

"And you reported it because the police asked you to tell them anything you heard?"

"Yup."

"While you're also in jail, with your own felony case in progress?"

"Yes sir."

"And you're a storyteller, aren't you?"

"Been known to," says Matchstick, and then he smiles again, realizing he's home free. I think he's proud of himself, and he has an exit line. "Not this time though."

THERE IS CERTAINLY no need for redirect, so it ends, and Matson gives a little stiff nod to Vanzetta as he steps down. He's soaking in sweat, seems to have aged decades in a week.

For a second time, the People rest.

# 25

*September 1 – Afternoon*
**(JPH)**

VANZETTA HAS GIVEN TED the lunch hour to decide if he has anything else. The exultation in Sonya's eyes can't be missed.

Again I flop carelessly in her guest chair, irreverent as I've ever been in this room. "An expert, maybe?  Somebody to talk about why they lie?"

"They just heard from an expert," she says, beaming.

"Yeah.  Nice going."

The smile stays.  "You've helped."

I return it, catch a full laugh in my throat.  "You haven't needed any."

"Not true.  And you've kept me organized."

Despite myself, I glow at the thought.  "Well, the job's almost done."

Sonya flashes back a classic prosecutor's look, a mingling of determination, pride and better-not-tempt-fate.  "We can dream."

◆

WHEN I ROLL BACK IN, an hour later, Graves waves me into Vanzetta's chambers.  The jury isn't due for another 45 minutes, and we don't have the court reporter.  Some judges would stress about that in a murder trial, but not ours – he trusts all of us, and not seeking death turns the heat down.

In fact Vanzetta is wrapping up a phone call about a horse.  Sonya sits with her chin in her hand, looking at the far wall, and Ted Stauber hovers over his file, mordant amusement on his lips.

Vanzetta signs off, raises his eyebrows at us.  Ted takes the cue.

"Ahem. I have alerted the court that well enough may not be let alone."

"English for dummies, Ted." Sonya's still chipper.

"There may be another chapter yet. The accused has some desire to expand on his original testimony."

As Sonya breaks into cackles, I'm puzzled enough to speak. "Well, doesn't he get to, if he wants?"

"One might assume, but it does not appear to be a settled point of law. It is possible His Honor might be in a position to refuse."

"Oh, we'd better protect the record, Ted." She's beaming a mile wide. "I say he should get another crack at it. Don't you agree, Judge?"

Vanzetta nods. "The stakes are far too high to deny him." He turns to me, perfectly poker-faced. "Counsel, your thoughts?"

I'm composing through gurgles of laughter, but Ted shakes his head. "*Ruthless*, I call you all."


SO VANZETTA DOES a handful of arraignments, and Ted goes back in the hallway with his client. But less than half an hour later, it's Ted who is smiling as he glides back into the courtroom.

Vanzetta's brows lurch cheerfully.

"Ready?" he asks. "Or . . . ?"

"Door Number Two," says Ted. "The defense will pass on surrebuttal, Your Honor."

"All *right*," the judge says, and seems content.

The jury comes back in to learn that evidence is over. The quiet anticlimax is common enough, but in the sudden calm the batch of them seem disjointed and dubious – a large family readying to leave the storm cellar at three AM, not quite trusting that the tornado has truly passed.

♦

FINALLY, LAST OF ALL, we huddle with Vanzetta to settle the jury instructions.

Since the state of the law isn't normally in dispute, most are non-controversial. The battle is always over the facts, and whether the jury heard enough to support a given verdict or defense.

Here, as always, I simply scratch notes and listen.

Ted gets instruction on his fantasy outcome: involuntary manslaughter. This is essentially what the jury would be left with if they bought every bit of Rodarte's story: that he had no knowledge or awareness that he was putting Haylee's life at risk, and killed her entirely by foolish accident.

"And voluntary, while we're at it," Ted adds, matter-of-factly.

"Oh, *Ted*."

VOLUNTARY MANSLAUGHTER – in its simplest sense, murder mitigated by emotion – is the classic "escape hatch" for the jury if it can't quite get to murder, and in a case where the killer's state of mind is truly hard to know, it has been known to make both sides happy. But it is really meant to apply only in two broad situations – when the defendant has overreacted to a perceived threat, or been provoked into a sudden "heat of passion" by events.

"This fits how?" asks the Court.

"Well, *passion*. Are we disputing the 'passion' involved in sexual congress? And the heat, for that matter?"

Sonya scoffs, but Vanzetta grins. "Off the record, doesn't that depend on the night?" He straightens up, or tries to. "Passion as lust?"

"The instructions must align with our impenetrable codes," Ted continues, ignoring them both. "And unless my spectacles fail me, the instruction says that 'heat of passion' does not simply mean anger. Rather, and I'm paraphrasing – we are told that it can be *any* strong emotion, at least in theory, that is potent enough to cause a person to act without due consideration of the consequences of their actions."

"But what emotion is that?" Vanzetta's eyebrows rise. "Unbridled sexual longing?"

"Passion. Purely and simply. Wild feeling of a kind one might associate with an intense sexual communion, progressing on to exceptionally reckless and dangerous behavior, and then – just perhaps – a sudden *thrill,* brought on by, shall we say, the victim's vulnerability. I am speculating, thank heaven."

He and Vanzetta are grinning like pranksters, but Sonya has been on a slow burn.

"Ted, why don't you read it again," she says now, with drawn-out tolerance. A sixth-grade English teacher at the end of her rope. "See, the entire concept starts with *provocation.* You want to explain how she provoked him, in any version? If you are seriously suggesting that the very idea of sex on its own can derange a man so badly that killing her in the middle of it isn't murder – not that this girl ever went along with sex at all, *ever,* before he drugged, raped and killed her – then, Jesus, put me on a raft and sail me out to sea right now. Is that actually what you're saying? Please tell me no. *Please.*"

"Well –"

"Plus it's an objective standard. Twelve people would have to believe that a man of *average disposition* could get so damn worked up over plain old sex that it mitigates killing the girl he's doing it with – and, by the way, the defendant never hinted at any such thing in all the hours he was on the stand. Am I Alice now? Has the world gone blithering mad?"

"Well, he did not precisely –"

"No, he *was* precise! Accident accident accident!" She's furious, swerving her head from side to side. "I mean, in my own foul mind he killed her in cold blood because maybe it was just a fun idea, or because he sure didn't like thinking about the possibilities if he just left her there for the fog to lift. Per him, though, it's just a terrible misadventure, for which he'll *maybe* take one little bite of the blame.

"What it isn't, I will tell you now, is a spot for a sympathy pitch, some decent-folks-take-pity line of argument, some look-at-this-poor-boy, he may have killed her and lied, but the *temptation* –"

"Yes, but –"

"And if we need provocation, you're providing it! So help me, if you're even sitting there *thinking* of arguing that the provocation was her waving her ass at him or something, Ted, and somehow that excuses *any part* of this – be it known that I will lacerate your liver with a shoe. Or plural. And I have the *sharp* heels today."

Vanzetta has turned his head, desperately trying not to laugh.

"Bailiff!" Ted shouts, near collapse himself.

"Better back off, Mr. Stauber," the judge says. "I've been on the wrong end of it myself."

"Now that you mention it," Sonya agrees. Flushed now, aglow. Still furious.

In the end, on the record, Vanzetta *does* give the instruction. But he gives us a close one, too, on flight from justice, and all in all we can live with the tradeoff.

The next day is Friday, but this week Vanzetta has cleared the decks, wanting no delay before closing argument.

◆

AND SO WE COME DOWN to the wire.

My work, to be clear, largely ended with pretrial motions. Other than researching the small, one-day issues, all I've really been asked to do is keep the file organized, get the exhibits marked each morning and make notes, which Sonya patently does not need but occasionally humors me by requesting.

So on this night of nights, as Sonya finishes bullet-pointing her closing argument on PowerPoint – it's been in progress for days – I volunteer to stay, review in real time, research any late law, even contribute a phrase or two. But she's a lone wolf, my value is debatable, and it's a solitary task by nature. She asks only that I get there an hour early for a read-through of the final product.

It dawns on me that she may not go home.

"I can do that." I'm smiling. "But call if you need anything else."

Sonya looks over her reading glasses, nods, actually beams at me. "You bet."

♦

ROSE'S GRILL AND TAVERN is the newest local restaurant of any consequence. Five minutes east of Millsford, it's just a couple of years old, and city-ish – sports plaques, framed pictures, dark back tables under low-hanging lamps, old-school steaks and chops to supplement the pub grub. They have Stillwater Amber on tap, a fine, oddly hard-to-find local brew, and they've gone full-on with flat-screen TVs in the corners. The dining room is crowded, the bar near full. There's the cheery clatter of pool. I've been here six or seven times, and from all appearances they're making it.

I don't have a fancy TV yet myself, in September 2005. The Oakland A's are on there, pounding the Yankees, and I watch the crawl long enough to see that the Angels, the American League erratics who finally won a title and are now on their fourth name, at least have a modest mid-inning lead. For no sane reason I'm still a fan.

Then, as I approach the bar, a sudden lurch. The bartender is tallish, blonde, long-limbed – beautiful, and there's just a *hint* –

She half-turns, I catch her name badge – "Terin." The smile I get when I order a draft is, I'm sure, not Haylee at all, who hadn't even fully acclimated to her beauty. Like any pro bartender, Terin is watchful beneath and radiates outward, familiar by default.

Yet there's an ease and grace to her movements and a calm to her body language that seems akin. She crouches below the bar, holds a mug to the light and wrinkles her nose, then slides it back and walks down the bar to another stash, grabs one and pulls it from that tap, leaning over.

*In a minute I'll be in love,* I think – as if drunk already. Haylee seven, eight years later. A disappointment behind her, maybe two. Gearing up to go to grad school, realizing the horse-boarding life won't quite get her there. Tough enough, now, for the likes of this.

Now she's turned, coming back to me – smiles again as she sets the beer down . . . she *knows,* somehow. She knows something I don't know myself.

Under minimal stress, I may be cracking.


BY THE TIME she takes away my plate of chicken bones, we've exchanged a few dozen words. I've even mentioned the trial, to little effect. "I'm a hermit," she says, shrugging. "Sorry." But she smiles right after it, as if to suggest I try another path.

My eyes are darting to her long slim hands as she rinses a glass, then a snack plate and a platter and a pina colada glass from down the bar, the whipped cream having started to cake around the rim, and I have the senseless urge to tell her she carries something of that other, vanished girl – of whom she's never heard.

I have sense enough not to, I have my best tie on, the mood is soft and this seems to be a moment for courage. So after a few small inroads and another great smile back – I had made some lame crack about our meager tourists – I do manage to introduce myself, and even to ask whether I would see her again if I came back soon.

To which she tells me I'd better hurry. She'll be resuming her online master's program the following week, working just part-time, mostly days.

"Motivation!" I say, grinning, easing away. It's enough to feel a win. "I'll see what I can do."

She wrinkles her nose – a what-the-hell gesture, but her eyes sparkle, and again there is *something* –

"Take my cell number."

Startled bliss. *Sure.* I fumble as I punch it in. *Take mine, too, while we're at it.*

I WALK OUT into another idyllic night. None of the credit is mine, but Rodarte is toast. The near future has a radiant glow.

My cell phone warbles. It isn't Terin, yards away. And not Sonya.

## *26*

**(JPH)**

IT'S MAYBE 35 MINUTES to midtown Hammonds, where our one full-on hospital rises in an incongruous four-story gleam; it seems an hour, all in smothering silence, lest the phone ring again.

I've been to Contenta Regional Medical Center only once, so I manage to turn down the wrong street, waste extra minutes getting parked. There's a flashing sign when I reach the ICU, visitor badge affixed, telling us it's a monitoring and medication period, no visitors until 10:30. Forty minutes away.

TOM'S IS THE FIRST FACE I see in the waiting room down the hall. Our DA is seated unobtrusively in a corner, still in his light gray shirt and burgundy tie, feet flat in front of him. Four seats over is one of my favorite colleagues, Celia Kim, in jeans, hunched forward with her long, austere face in her hands.

"Tom." We squeeze hands. "Good heavens."

"Thanks for coming."

"Jesus," I mumble, sliding into the next seat. "How? When?"

"In her office. They think a ruptured aneurysm," says Tom, very low. "Vitals OK, apparently, but that doesn't prove much. Kids are in there" – her three grown progeny – "they didn't make 'em leave. They're waiting on their best guy."

"And then?"

"They operate, apparently."

"Operate." I seem limited to single words. "Who? Why?"

"We know him – German guy. Schults with an 's,' I think?"

"Ah, right." I can picture him – wide-faced, tall, accented. He testified brilliantly for Celia once, proving up a child's head injuries, and I happened to see some of it. Drives a Corvette – I remember it pulling in in the lot. I gather my nerve. "What are her chances? They have any idea?"

Tom shakes his head. "Unknown at last report. But they've probably told Ed something by now."

"Ah." I've always had the strange feeling I know Ed Brandstetter better than I do Sonya. He retired as assistant county fire chief and works now, when he wants to, as a fishing guide. Always a highlight of the holiday party, seems never to have a bad day alive. We've wondered whether Sonya's general dourness is a reflex, an *I'd better be the realist.* Now he's with her in the ICU.

DOUG LAHTINEN appears in an old gray windbreaker. His orderly, fact-driven mind won't stop for preamble. "How's it look?"

"No clear word," says Tom. "Not yet."

"Stroke, was it?"

"They're saying aneurysm, not that I really know the difference. And they're going in. That's all we know."

"At home?"

"At the office, where else? By a fluke I was still there, heard her fall into her desk."

Doug just accepts it there, looks around. "No sign of media?"

"No," Tom says, suddenly cheered. "Now that you mention it."

NINETY MINUTES drain away, somehow. We don't dare talk; we don't dare distract ourselves. We just sit. I look over at one point and realize Doug is praying.

My own thoughts are useless. *She worked too hard,* I think, knowing she's chugged until midnight many nights, forgotten about weekends, stayed cemented in her office every lunchtime for a month or more. Drafted a novella of notes for her cross of Rodarte, spent her patience with Wade and her empathy with Marta Branch, while I have largely just sat and watched.

I recall a Japanese word – *karoshi*. Essentially, death from overwork. But it's a dumb parallel. Sonya is no expectation-driven drone, no helpless company loyalist – more a panther returned to the hunt, tracking a worthy target. On a quest, not a death march. Utterly absorbed.

Then I'm pondering the idea of the unknown weakness, the bane of my occasional late-night imagination – *a ticking time bomb*, it will later be reported. A readily treatable condition if caught in time, but *she was unaware* . . . our physical self as secret-carrier.

In my twenties I read about ventricular fibrillation of the heart, the phenomenon where, after tens of millions of regular beats a single warped impulse comes through, often with no warning, and kills the average person dead on the spot. The ultimate equalizer – no matter *who* you are, you can't know for sure that you'll survive the next beat of your own fucking heart. Any one of us – Bill Gates, the Pope, J-Lo, the worst of despots – could die in the next half-minute.

So how could she have any clue at all that something was coming apart in her head? Maybe ten seconds – a "terrific headache," FDR had said before he keeled over. That's all you get.

CELIA, EVER-ATTUNED, leans over at my elbow. "Has anyone contacted the victim's family? Would you like me to call?"

"Tom may have. Better ask him."

"If he hasn't, I can."

"Thanks. But we may want to wait for more news."

"I'm thinking to ease the shock, and tell them no session. She was supposed to close tomorrow, right?"

"Right. And Tom may not have had time." As I say it I know I'm ducking my own task, yet the thought of Celia's calm voice on the phone with Marta is far more appealing than my own.

But Tom has had time.

DOUG HOVERS CLOSE, expressionless even by his own standards. "My wife's uncle had one burst and lived through it. A friend's mother didn't, when I was a kid. I don't know what to think."

"It's all new to me."

"Time is critical, of course. My friend's mom had it on a camping trip, nothing they could do."

"Brutal."

"She's in great shape. Sonya. We used to run sometimes, you know, until my own knees gave out. Not hers, and she's got ten years on me."

"Yeah."

Doug keeps nodding. "It's awful that she didn't get to finish this case. Whether she lives or dies. She'd been needing an inspiration, these last years, and this was it."

"Yes. It's a mission."

"We've talked plenty. Like you have."

I'm nearly jealous. In truth we haven't – not much. Only now do I realize my feeling of disappointment. Nuts and bolts, my low-intensity suggestions, the Danny Tarrant story, what it means to Marta. All at slight remove. *And that's all there will be.*

"Sure," I agree.

Doug pauses, shakes his head. "Awful to have to think about it, but – you gonna need some extra help? Got her notes and things?"

I smile, faintly. "I'll have to figure it out. I've made plenty of notes, but I've barely seen hers. And there are times I've just watched."

"I get it." He sighs. "It's been a good production."

AN HOUR LATER the doors do open, Ed Brandstetter steps out, nods to Tom and Tom follows him back in. We all hold our breath, I'm sure, but after only a couple of minutes Tom comes back out, poker-faced – not peppy, not funereal. Then just a little smile, as we huddle together.

"She's still with us, and they've stopped the leak," he says in an undertone. "But that's about all the good news. If she makes it, there aren't any guarantees about her state."

"Permanent neurological damage, you think?" Doug again.

"Very possible. Across the board. Speech, walking, you name it. And might be days before we know."

"Likely to live, though?"

Tom opens his hands, half-smiling. "They didn't go that far."

We nod, fumble, and he continues.

"There's no rope needs pulling, nothing any of you can do. Nobody has anything to prove tonight. I'd urge you to go."

"I'm here," says Doug. "I owe it."

Tom bows. "The rest of you. We're at midnight already."

NO ONE LEAVES, and it's another silent hour before the door opens again and Ed Brandstetter steps out, barely moving, eyes reddened, pale, clearing his throat, as we all clench and brace. But in a very soft voice he tells us she has stabilized for right now – they reckon she'll at least get through the night, and hope to learn more in the next twelve hours.

Tom nods and tries a smile. "I guess we'll take that."

Ed nods, numb and feeble. "That's as good as it gets."

As he shuffles away, Tom turns back to us. "Go home, people. You'll hear anything that matters."

This time we do.

# 27

*September 2 - Morning*
**(JPH)**

IT'S VAGUE TO ME if I actually sleep, but morning seems soon. There's no email update, which must be good. We all do the normal thing and come to work.

"Nothing new," Tom calls out as I reach his doorway, heart in mouth. No good or bad in it. Unknown is unknown. "But word's gotten out."

That's suddenly obvious. As I peek out our front windows, there are three reporters in the waiting area, others milling around in the hall and at least a couple of TV crews fanned out in the hallway behind them – a relative mob.

"How'd they find out?"

"Well, the med helicopter landed in the middle of the parking lot, and I'm sure most of the new arrivals were staying down the street. Woulda got noticed. I'm just glad nobody descended on the hospital."

"Maybe they didn't know where to find it," I try, lamely.

It doesn't register. "Most of 'em were here for closing argument, I'm sure. This just got 'em all out of bed earlier. But they were on me in the parking lot when I got here, and of course I had to confirm it. Now they're waiting for a status update after we talk to Vanzetta. And obviously it's more than a rumor now, so we may get a few more big-city rubberneckers."

I hear the masked agony in his studied calm, but we both know the path is forward. The case may pause, but it will not stop. Once a jury is sworn, the defendant normally must agree to any significant delay, or the conviction may be reversed. And he will not, for the plain reason that no living DA, let alone me, could scare Rodarte as much as the one who's nearly dead.

*Guess I'm up*, I start to say – but then don't. I'll embarrass Tom if he's made other plans. After all, he could move in now, do it himself. Many an elected might jump with both feet.

But Tom isn't average, and has no campaign to worry about, and anyway is not wired that way. No way on earth he will come swooping in now, demanding justice in a loud voice when the accused has already confessed on the witness stand.

No, of course it's me, and there's already a fear to fight down. Failing now would be like dropping a crystal bowl. And if I fail for Sonya it would mean I fail Marta and Ashlyn Branch. Which Sonya would have a terrible time forgiving.

"So, guess you're up," Tom says, smiling as if I just taught him the phrase. "Let's go see His Honor."

♦

FRIDAYS ARE THEIR OWN sort of mess in our sleepy tiled hallways. I see from the posted calendar that there are three cases being called for trial readiness in Department Two. I see the family law crowd at the end of the hall – scrawny tweaker dads with sandy goatees, too young, wearing fresh-bought button-up shirts with their mothers alongside, staring daggers at the exes, who are 22-year-old moms of three-year-olds and dressed up fine, in heavy makeup, heels and tight blouses, to tell their side to the judge. The attorneys, mostly middle-aged women, talk it over with them as they sit on the benches and wait.

I see deadbeats here to fight their evictions on the unlawful detainer calendar. A couple of familiar faces, out of custody for a change, for misdemeanor arraignments. One repeat loser is present to surrender for his jail time. Even here, far from anywhere, it all just *keeps going*. The wheels groan, and turn, and churn – one life, one agony at a time.

As he greets us, Vanzetta's face is pale, his eyes hooded. He bows his head, a rare picture of deference.

"Tom."

"Tony," says Tom softly, using the name he knew Vanzetta by for the first dozen years of his career, when he occupied my current office.

"I figured her indestructible. Any history, warning-type signs?"

"None known. She's 62 and runs six mornings a week. Anything you saw?"

"No, but I guess I wasn't looking." He turns to me. "You?"

"No," I answer, by now confident. "Needed sleep, I'm sure. Maybe a lot of it. Wasn't eating much. But no more than that."

"In a murder trial, in other words."

I have no actual basis for comparison. "More or less."

WE ARE WAITING for Ted, but it's only a minute or two. He steps in softly, turns to Tom, lets out a long sigh, bows his own head.

If Vanzetta will give the half day, we'll have the three days after that, but he might not. "It's a service, not a sentence," he says more than once, talking about the jury. And the close calls will, of course, sway toward Andrew Rodarte – now in particular.

But Vanzetta sees the raw trauma in Tom's eyes, something near it in Ted's, and at least a shade of it in mine. That and the dimness that came with the night. And he's numb himself.

"Closing on Tuesday," he says. "Nobody's ready for this today."

Ted, bless him, nods along. "Amen," he intones.

◆

TOM FOLLOWS ME into my office. His smile is spreading and kindly, which is to say typical.

"Ready, sport?"

"Guess I better get that way."

"You will. It's your time. And when it happens they'll be all the more impressed, realizing we had two aces on it all along."

I feel myself blush – *glowing, you ass, with Sonya near death.*

"I'd better go look," I say, thumbing to the hallway.

Tom finishes the thought. "I know. Let's do it together."

SONYA'S OFFICE has always been the brightest, best room in the building – one small way Tom may have made things up to her – and it is largely as tranquil as ever. Mid-morning splashes indirectly through the south-facing window. Later, when the west window might invite afternoon glare, the sun ducks neatly behind Gray Hill most of the year, leaving a clear shot toward the edge of Marsh Lake, the smaller but more idyllic of the two, and the moneyed ridge beyond.

Her laptop shows a screen saver, her coffee mug is next to it, and a great maroon binder lies open, cluttered with pens and markers – her master compendium of witness notes and outlines. But the only hints she collapsed here are a spilled container of paper clips and the misplaced guest chair, shoved hard aside to make room for a gurney.

Two other binders are off to the side – the two volumes of the "murder book." Those and the master binder were there every day. But when I circle around the desk I discover a box I never knew about on the floor behind it, and in that box are five more binders.

The thinnest reads *Theories of Murder.* Next comes *Cross & Impeachment.* Then *Wade and Foundation.* Then *Science and Medical.* And finally *Closing and Rebuttal,* which contains a color printout of her presentation – 89 slides, hand-numbered. The last few – only a *few* – are still works in progress. That was the task for the final few hours.

Abruptly something comes back to me. My early days. Tom in somebody else's office, leaning back, talking about a case of his own, years before. A lead, a late witness, and how he decided what the hell, he didn't really need it, letting it slide.

221

*Guilty in 20 minutes, but I got that look that melts lead*, he says, remembering. *SHE never leaves anything in the gun.*

I ATTEMPT a lame little whistle.

"Whew.  First I knew."

"Light reading for the weekend," Tom says, beaming.

"To say the least."

He checks her email now, forwards me a couple, cures the blinking light on her phone.  Then swivels back around in her chair and smiles again.  "We got no better hands to be in."

"Well, that's debatable."  But I'm smiling along, and then I see there's a second box, *behind* her chair –

*YOU GOTTA BE KIDDING.*

It's transcripts, day by day, of *this* trial, in real time, bound and read and marked, purchased from and cranked forth by the court reporter, Ellen Tomkins, long into the night after I'd rolled off home. While I *slept*, probably.  God knows when Ellen did.

By now Tom has a distinct smirk.  "Did you sell her short?"

I pause to think about it.  "I probably did."

"I did once.  Early Eighties, I think."  He shakes his head, half-smiling.  "Never made that mistake again."

# 28

**(JPH)**

OVER THE THREE-DAY WEEKEND the updates are regular and monotonous. Sonya's condition remains stable but critical – no dire complications, no obvious progress, no margin for error. Ed's never gone home, Tom is there chunks of each day.

I've proposed stopping back by, hoping to be talked out of it, and Tom is right there to tell me no, she's not to the point where she'll know you're there, and you're a little busy, JP. So while they linger with her, I am wading, at my kitchen table, through the force-field she left behind – closer to her, in a way, than I've ever been.

With the program open in front of me, I grind my way through her printed-out PowerPoint slides, gradually solving her handwriting in the margins. They're large-font, not too cluttered. One point at a time, occasional pictures. She goes 60 slides just on the case in chief.

Rodarte's evisceration on the stand isn't even mentioned directly until slide 68. By then, furious, she is ready to hold him taut and naked in plain sight, explaining in terse single-line splashes how there is nothing more to explain.

Five pages of bullet points, more scrawls in the margins, to catalog the lies. He lies because he is conscious of his guilt, because he fears the consequences, because he is pathological. Because his story is a lie, the obvious beneath it is the truth. And the truth, Sonya is saying, is cold and simple.

You could easily decide there was nothing to add.

BASIC MURDER, curiously enough, is not a legally complicated crime. You just need proof that the defendant committed an act that caused a human death with "malice aforethought" – in essence, the unlawful intent to kill.

Murder defaults to second degree, carrying fifteen years to life i
California, but can be promoted to first degree (which buys you 25 t
life) if any of nine conditions apply.  Two fit the case.  The killing d
Lee Branch is murder in the first because, we allege, it was *willfu*
*deliberate and premeditated*.  And it is also first-degree murder, we asser
because it was murder in the course of rape – which also creates th
"special circumstance" that could have triggered a death sentence,
the jury were to find it true.  But since we will not seek to put Rodart
to death, his worst-case scenario is life without parole.

Then time ticks past, and I pause – jump forward, then bacl
looking at her page 85.  Two stern sentences, large font.

"REASONABLE DOUBT," of course, is what we have to overcom
– the alpha and omega of every defense argument.

**The only reasonable interpretation of the evidence is that th
defendant thought before he killed her, and raped before he kille
her.  And this means there is no reasonable doubt that this crime wa
murder in the first degree**.

I stare awhile, and a while longer.  Ambivalence – my intrepid an
enduring companion.

*What proves willful, deliberate, premeditated?*

The roofies, to start.  Rodarte came with roofies in his pocket.

*But the roofies just prove intent to rape, not kill.  And we can't prov
they were his.*

Who else's?

*Who's the druggie?  Jacinta, of course.*

Get outta here – why?

*Because she's a druggie, anything and everything.  Don't claim yo
doubt it.  So she could've had 'em herself, saved up for a time just like this –*

But he'd have seen them, and told everyone.  He denied eve
seeing any roofies.

*Doesn't prove anything. She was drinking, Jacinta got the drinks. Jacinta was probably where he couldn't see her – she could have dropped it in Haylee's own drink, thinking it was a favor –*

But she knocked herself out – that makes no sense.

*She wouldn't really know doses, if it was new to her.*

It's not even a legal drug – where would she have gotten it?

*Where did Rodarte get it? Can't be that rare. And Jacinta knows people.*

OK, so then –

*We have no direct proof that Rodarte brought flunitrazepam.*

*If he did not bring the roofies, he did not drug them.*

*If he didn't drug them, they drugged themselves.*

*If they were willing to drug themselves, everything we believe is in question.*

*If we can't rely on our beliefs, we haven't proven deliberation and premeditation.*

"FOR FUCK'S SAKE," I mumble, out loud. Haylee, at least, did not drug herself. Jacinta not impossible, Lee no chance.

*Wouldn't matter anyway. And how do you know?*

Completely inconsistent with everything we know. Too mature, responsible, *not* a druggie –

*Barely 20. Coming back from college. Could have changed.*

Still would've had to be Jacie who got 'em.

*Right, and so what? All that would matter is it wasn't him.*

OK, let's imagine – they took roofies themselves, God knows why. Then he took advantage, waited until Lee was *out*, then did the rape. It's still willful, deliberate, premeditated.

*This assumes a lot. What if it happened the way he said, Haylee was psyched to fuck him* because *she'd taken it?*

Take it and pass out?

*We don't know she did – just think so. She had less in her system than Jacinta did – if he did it, why?*

Because he poured it in beer bottles, and Jacie drank more.

*Maybe, but it probably just went in one bottle each. So as long as sh* *finished the one, they'd have been even with it –*

You're guessing – and physiology, for fuck's sake –

*Jacie's not that much smaller, and this isn't booze. Who knows how it gets metabolized?*

Haylee was tested postmortem. She *died* while it was in her system. Everything stopped.

*You know that, or you're speculating?*

THERE'S A SORT OF POUNDING above my ears. I shake knot in my neck. My refrigerator rattles in a tedious thrum.

*And WHY did he kill her?*

Because he raped her, couldn't risk ID –

*But wasn't she out?*

Sure, but let's say she stirred, opened her eyes –

*So then he panicked, figured he had to kill her?*

Well, makes sense –

*That's deliberate and premeditated?*

I swear, literally, and threaten my shadow with harm – fuck you Captain Counterpoint. A name Ted gave me in my very early days I'm grinding, squinting –

THEN, ON A WAFT of breeze, I hear a late-night avatar. Brian Flaherty, of course.

"Two things, dipshit. We *know* there was rape – either all along or at least after she zoned out. In every version there is rape. The guy who *admitted fucking her to death* is the guy who drugged her. Making it willful, deliberate, premeditated murder. Full stop. He killed her washed up, left, acted cool when they found him. Cold-blood calculated murder one."

*But Rodarte left the door open, the condom behind, beer bottles behind, body in plain sight. And a witness who could've nailed him far worse than she did. Drugged unconscious, but still —*

"Stop looking for logic. Crimes like this don't make sense. People panic when they kill. It isn't A must lead to B must lead to C."

*So he's blurry one moment, stone-cold sober the next, killing Haylee in frigid calculation, then forgetting about Jacinta, who can ID him?*

"Cut it out, JP. Under no theory did these two girls set out to render themselves unconscious. If they wanted to fuck Rodarte, they'd have damn sure stayed awake. If they didn't want to, they sure wouldn't have dosed themselves while he was there."

*Ah.*

"Then they found Jacinta in outer dreamland. There's no possible way Lee was fucking him like an animal with the same dose of roofies, so he lied. And he lied for the obvious reason."

*Right . . .*

"Then the thing he's *never* explained, JP – get back to that."

NODDING AS IF somebody's there to see, I settle down, grab another Diet Coke and return to Sonya. And eventually I find the path.

# 29

*September 6*
**(JPH)**

SONYA ENDURES through the weekend, but isn't much improved when Tuesday morning comes. I get down to the courtroom a few minutes early, stare at my laptop with such dour preoccupation nobody even says hello. I sit *alone* now, where Sonya sat, on the left end of the table. This is for decorum's sake, if nothing better – it would be odd to hunch next to Ted Stauber and leave the gap.

Brian is along a few minutes later, double-checking the connection to the overhead projector, and I don't dare wonder if he'd like to swap places. Or if *I* would. I can't do anything but smile and wince, somehow a single gesture. He grins, balls his fists and does a tiny boxing flurry. *Knock him on his ass, stud.*

Then Tom is there too. I check his face, see his own small thrill of eagerness even under these circumstances, and it's a comfort. He's not going to watch, doesn't like how it would look to the jury. But he slides by the desk, looks down and smiles.

"Your time. You got this."

When I've mumbled thanks and leaned back it's still ten minutes to showtime, and then Vanzetta himself keeps us waiting a few more. Graves, the bailiff, leans over Lucille, the clerk, makes her chuckle. I have the pleasant thought of talking it out with him later, however it may go. He tends to hear things clear.

VANZETTA EMERGES and heads straight into the jury instructions, which are a solid 20 minutes. The court explains the rules of law, drip by drip. The orderly-minded prosecutor would be pondering a last subtlety here, a final angle, a phrase. I'm farting around PowerPoint adjusting margins and font size.

*Your time*, said Tom. A theme for random sleepless nights – *what is time? How is it now? How did we turn just this many times from the original blast, the first spin? Who counted them all? How* did *we come to hallucinate together here, where a golden orb pierces endless darkness, greens and blues surround us, and there are children's voices in the breeze?*

Then as it all ticks down, a cold blast of sanity returns – a friend from a long way back. It asks me how many trials I've had where a guy can't possibly walk.

And I'm seeing Haylee, now, in three dimensions, when my eyelids close. I open them, stand up and do alright.

◆

MOSTLY SIMPLE THINGS.

First the rape – common sense. We know they had sex, because he admitted it, he drugged her for the purpose, and his story is absurd. *I'll come back to that.* Then the murder.

The marks around her throat are NOT consistent with a bag, but with a ligature – a jacket, a belt.

The tiny fibers beneath Haylee's nails – a solid match for Rodarte's jacket. They got there as she clawed, barely awake, in her very last moments of awareness.

He told lies, and then ran, in consciousness of his own guilt. He immediately searched for DNA information, in consciousness of guilt. And he was calm when the police turned up, because while conscious of his guilt, he had an even deeper belief in his ability to lie his way out of anything.

The time frame, the two calls to Tamara Roberge. The first shows his original lie. The second shows another one – by 11:28 there was no more mirth and commotion in the gleaming, endless living room, and Rodarte was still on the premises. The neighbor, Dumaret, established on the first day that the white SUV hauled off at 11:45. Rodarte had already taken Haylee to the killing ground when Jacinta rolled in her daze and auto-dialed Tamara, her cell phone found beneath her.

His fondness for sexual aggression, the unwelcome choking. The holes in his testimony. And then what Matchstick heard in the lockup, laminating the lie – Rodarte killed her on purpose, not by accident.

I build toward the best stuff, and in the moment I like the way it ends. But then I've heard an assuring and resonant sound in my voice several times before, including twice, at least, before defendants were acquitted. And I remember how the jurors who lingered made no sense, talking of theories never even pitched by workaday counsel who expected to lose, of twitches and trivialities by the least of our witnesses, even of the grudges they inferred through their own notions of dark and light, cause and effect, what merits blame and shunning. It all blurred, in the end, and I learned nothing.

My last trial was check fraud. Now murder. I'm arguing for Haylee, in case she's listening.

"IT'S OUR JOB to prove to you, beyond a reasonable doubt, that the defendant *committed an act that caused the death of another person*, and we must prove that he committed the act with *malice aforethought,* another of those antique phrases that still frame the law.

"If this is all that we prove, then you have a second-degree murder. For a second-degree murder to get elevated to first-degree, by the law, I have to show that, beyond a reasonable doubt, at least one additional factor has been proven to you by the evidence. And here there are two.

"First, when you take the law you've been given and consider the evidence you've heard, it will fully support the idea that this crime was willful, deliberate and premeditated.

"In fact, Haylee's death was not caused by a sudden impulse, nor an accident. It was a crime of opportunity – Andrew Rodarte meeting Haylee Branch entirely by accident. And after he drugged and assaulted her, her death took long and terrible minutes. Minutes in which Mr. Rodarte could have changed his mind . . . and let her live.

"But there is a second way, as alleged here, to arrive at first-degree murder, and from there to special circumstances. And that's for you to find that Mr. Rodarte committed rape against Haylee Branch.

"The evidence that Mr. Rodarte did sexually assault her is more than sufficient, particularly considering the condition of her body when it was found, half-nude, underwear up her leg – and the drug that incapacitated her.

"Just recognize that she was indeed helpless, not an engaged and demanding sexual partner as he claims, and this was, indeed, the rape of an intoxicated woman – sexual intercourse when her resistance was overcome by drugs, and the defendant knew that. It's enough if he *should have* known. Here, clearly, he actually did know.

"This is all powerful evidence that tells you your natural instincts are right. Haylee Branch did not voluntarily take roofies, and she did not have consensual sex with Mr. Rodarte, let alone violent and aggressive sex, and she surely, profoundly, did *not* invite him to cut off her breathing. That all began – and ended – with Mr. Rodarte."

THIS HAS BRIEFLY SOARED, I think, and I feel the jury's eyes locked tight.

"He admitted to you that Haylee died there in the *casita*, underneath him as he had forceful sex with her, suffering first from her broken hyoid bone, and soon after being asphyxiated – the very oxygen being withheld from her lungs.

"To accept it as anything less than murder would require you to accept the story Mr. Rodarte told you from the stand. And that story, his *third* account, was an act of desperation – full of things left not only unexplained, but unexplainable.

"Mr. Rodarte lied about when he got to the house – Tamara Roberge's evidence showed that. He twice estimated 10:45, with the drinking after that, but at 10:31 Jacinta was at home, a male in the background, and she was already well on the way to drunk.

"He denied knowledge of DNA, didn't explain his frantic computer search for information in the moments after Detective Wade left him, denied it all until he came here, under oath, and admitted his blame for Haylee's death – and at best, his account was reluctant and implausible.

"Mr. Rodarte described fleeing in a blind panic from the *casita*, from the house on Sundown Road – then had to admit that in his 'panic' he paused to rinse out his condom. He described in detail many of the events of that night – but he couldn't even estimate how long they had sex with his hands around her throat.

"But more critically, Mr. Rodarte took the stand and claimed that Haylee's death was an accident during a consensual sexual encounter between strangers.  And in this telling, it was an accident that she brought about herself, by supposedly asking him – *while in fact she was probably semiconscious, if not passed out entirely* – to perform an act that he already happened to know about and like.  Which he needed, of course, to support his amazing new story on the witness stand.

"His problem is that this conflicts with virtually everything else you heard from the stand – all the witnesses, police and scientific and medical and personal, who did not have his obvious motive to invent. And that evidence tells you that this was sex *without* consent – rape - not just rough sex between two willing partners.

"We know that Haylee Branch and Jacinta Cantrell both ingested flunitrazepam – roofies. They did it *after* Mr. Rodarte entered their lives that night.  And they did it, almost certainly, without knowing they had done so.

"There's nothing in the evidence you heard, even from Mr Rodarte, to suggest that either she or Miss Cantrell took them willingly and also no motive.  Why should either of them render themselves unconscious, or at best semiconscious, with handsome Mr. Rodarte there?  And there is no evidence of any other person being there on the premises. So the only logical conclusion you can reach is that Mr. Rodarte administered them to the two young women himself.

"Now the simple fact that Haylee Branch had substantial levels of roofies and alcohol in her system, both highly sedating and each accentuating the effects of the other, runs directly counter to Mr. Rodarte's account, the wild consensual sex with a fully awake and engaged partner that got out of hand. Beyond what you learned from Dr. Stanley about her probable state, her levels of flunitrazepam were not much lower than those of Jacinta Cantrell, who was found essentially unconscious, and did not even awaken fully enough to speak for almost twelve hours after she was found.

"But past that, the fact that he drugged Haylee Branch – which is the only reasonable conclusion to be drawn – also tells you that *consensual sex was never his motivation at all* that night. He wanted sex entirely on his own terms. And it was only one small step from rape to murder."

I PAUSE, GLANCE AT a nonexistent window in the wall above the jury. Then at the floor, then the slide on the projector, then back at their blur of faces. I inevitably look *toward* the jurors, not directly at them. Eye contact, if any, is a momentary thing.

"Now you heard from two People's witnesses – and a defense witness, too – about incidents where Mr. Rodarte did engage in air restriction. But the larger point of that testimony was how it showed you his sexual aggression even toward women he was in relationships with, not his preferred technique.

"After all, he couldn't go around drugging his partners – he had to save that for strangers, like Haylee Branch and Jacinta Cantrell. And his fondness for erotic asphyxiation, rendering women *momentarily* unconscious, is what gave him the inspiration for the crazy story he told on the stand, after the evidence against him became too clear.

"But his story was a lie, and the truth is simple. It's horrible, it's unthinkable, but it's simple. Andrew Rodarte drugged Haylee, then raped her when she was incapacitated. At some point in the middle of that rape, she began returning to consciousness, and managed to partially open her eyes. So, fearing that she'd identify him, he brutally strangled her to death with his hands and a ligature, probably his blue jacket. Then he rinsed out his condom, grabbed his jacket and fled.

"When the topic came up in the jail, he had to spin it into a marginally less appalling story, where somehow her death became a mercy killing. But any way you slice it, the forcible nature of how he killed her is clear from the one thing he couldn't even try to explain: the breaking of Haylee's hyoid bone.

"That alone would tell you that even in *his* story this was not an involuntary manslaughter, nor a mere assault. Rather, it was a purposeful killing in the act of Mr. Rodarte assaulting Haylee when she not only had not consented, but was likely unable to do so.

"Accept that the sex between them was nonconsensual, and this is rape. Which means that Haylee's death was a murder in the act of rape, which makes her death a murder in the first degree, and a first-degree murder with special circumstances attached."

PERIOD – STOP *HERE.* But then, like I'm listening to someone else, there's a last deep breath, and then a caveat.

"Folks, that's what happened, what the evidence truly tells you.

"But even if you find anything to struggle about in that, any small hesitation, any *flicker* of doubt . . . even if there were anything at all in Mr. Rodarte's testimony you wanted to credit, even if there *were* actually something accidental about Haylee's death, well, he is still guilty of murder. And that is because at a bare minimum his actions showed a wanton, willful, reckless disregard for her life, and those physical actions killed her. That is murder in the second degree, not first – but it is still the crime of murder.

"Mr. Rodarte murdered Miss Branch, from any angle you look at it. Giving him every imaginable benefit of the doubt, it was murder in the second degree. Giving the evidence you heard the weight it deserves, bringing everyday reason to this terrible act, it was murder in the first degree.

"I am here to ask that you draw the only rational conclusion the facts support, which is that Mr. Rodarte's ever-changing tales have all been lies, the actual *evidence* you heard was clear, and this was murder. He didn't kill Haylee Branch by accident, he killed her on purpose – after he raped her. And he left her there, exposed, assaulted, and extinguished, on the bed in the *casita* on Sundown Road.

"I ask you to convict him of murder, and of rape. And there is more than enough evidence to show you that he is guilty of murder in the first degree."

I sit as the jury stretches and resettles, the theater seats creaking.

♦

TED STARTS WITH SONYA – genuine and personal, more than just good politics. I admire it.

Then basic things. Rodarte's lack of violent history, his acknowledgement of the Alina Nieves incident, him going home to his mother, not fleeing. The "desperation" in putting up Matchstick Matson, the lack of any direct witness.

Then, over and over, reasonable doubt. Doubt that he drugged them, that he raped Haylee, that there was enough to prove Haylee's state, that he actually assaulted Alina, that he fled south due to guilt rather than fear.

And, finally, his grittiest and best, Ted's weathered voice resounding through the courtroom, his tiny beads of sweat because it's *still* too goddamned hot in here.

"NOW WHAT YOU HAVE HEARD is a tale of tragedy, for which my client, Mr. Rodarte, knows full well he is responsible. Let me save the People the effort of repeating what is long since past dispute. If it was not for Andrew Rodarte, and the events that began in the back of the SpeedyGrab mini-mart in Walkersburg, a beautiful young lady named Haylee Branch wouldn't have died that night. It's as simple as that, and you know it because you heard it directly from Mr. Rodarte's own mouth, here on the witness stand, where he assumed the responsibility that he was unable to face when first confronted.

"We aren't here to excuse him for his actions, or for his half-truths, or his outright lies. I don't ask you to do so, and you may apply whatever weight you find appropriate to the original accounts he gave of that night.

"But I *will* ask you to recognize that these stories, false as they were in many respects, were not the lie they might have been. And if you will bear with me, I'll explain what I mean.

"Mr. Rodarte, that first day, was contacted by the police hundreds of miles from the murder scene, and indeed, all they really had to link him to the death of Miss Branch was a set of tire prints that might, might not, have put him there in the driveway of the house where she died. But even though he fudged the time, minimized his role there and denied things that he later admitted to you here, he promptly acknowledged that he was there, that first time, and the reason why.

"And then the second time, at the point of his arrest, he moved nearer yet to the truth. He admitted to the hunger he felt, his desire for both young women, the natural impulse that, finally, he expanded on when he told that full story to you at trial.

"This is not, I submit to you, the psychological pattern of a sociopath, a killer in cold blood. Rather, it is the mental workings of a still-young man with a minor, largely non-violent criminal history who found himself, unprepared, in an extraordinary situation with a beautiful young woman, and did not respond rationally to it.

"The prosecutor assures you that there is no way this crime could have happened as Mr. Rodarte claims. But indeed it could have happened just that way, and there is a real chance that it did.

"I don't know that it did, because none of us knows, but please remember that it is not my task to prove that to you. The prosecution must prove every element of murder beyond a reasonable doubt, and Mr. Rodarte's account, maybe rough around the edges, maybe vague on a detail here and there, handily meets the reasonable test.

"And because of that, as a matter of reasonable doubt, the act that caused Miss Branch's tragic death really should be found less than murder. Instead, you should find it a form of manslaughter, a killing that had no malice aforethought, and, indeed, lacked any intent at all."

Ted's smile is beatific, his hands are outstretched – his patented gesture – and it's all I can do not to nod along myself.

"BUT THIS DOESN'T take us everywhere we need to go. It can't. Because in its wisdom, the law says that even when a crime is murder, the worst crime we can imagine, not all murders are the same.

"You've been given the elements of murder, and when we boil it down it's simple. Even if you decide that Mr. Rodarte's testimony here was just another tapestry of lies, folks, that does not leave him guilty of murder in the first degree.

"And this is because any of you, all of you, can readily understand this distinction: when a murder is not committed in a willful, deliberate and premeditated manner, it is not first-degree murder unless it's part of a specific type of felony, or falls under one of a number of theories that are not in play here at all.

"Such a felony – rape – is alleged. If you find beyond a reasonable doubt that this was a rape and a murder in the course of that rape, you may rightly find the murder to be of the first degree, and also uphold the special circumstance created by that finding. So says the law.

"But what proof do you actually have that this is rape, rather than consensual sex?

"You are asked to infer it from the drugs in her system, but there is no actual proof that Mr. Rodarte administered them to her, nor direct observation by any witness of how the flunitrazepam actually affected Haylee Branch.  You're also asked to infer it from postmortem observations, but these did nothing more than hint at the *possibility* that the sex between them was not consensual.  But speculation, possibility, is not proof beyond a reasonable doubt – it can't be.

"And counter to that, you do have what the defendant told you, while making the remarkable admission that he caused Haylee's death: That this was consensual contact, at the urging of Miss Branch – who, after all, was certainly of a suitable age to be sexually active, and might, not unreasonably, have been attracted to Mr. Rodarte.

"There is plenty to show that sex took place between the defendant and Miss Branch, much as he described it, but there is not enough to show this was rape.

"You're free to conclude that even if Miss Branch did have experience with erotic asphyxiation, it was Mr. Rodarte, not the victim, who initiated it.  But that still doesn't bring us to the level of rape.

"And even if you conclude that Mr. Rodarte initiated the asphyxiation in the course of their sexual encounter, that he grabbed her as he admitted doing and then kept his grip past the point of safety and even consent, this is the concept of 'implied malice,' not the actual malice you need for first-degree murder.  It lacks premeditation, deliberateness, willfulness – there isn't any of that, because there was never an actual intent to kill.

"Holding the People to their burden of proof beyond reasonable doubt, you are justified in concluding that no murder has been proven here at all, and that justice lies in the crime of manslaughter.  And if you were to conclude that it is murder because he accidentally choked Haylee to death, it was murder in the second degree, and not the first."

TED COULD STOP, too. I'm expecting it. Instead he pauses his pacing feet square at the midpoint of the box, moves toward it and sighs. His voice softens and drops.

"But there is also one last possibility for you to consider. What if, accepting everything the prosecutor had to say to you, you were to decide that it was no accident, that Andrew Rodarte intentionally strangled Haylee Branch, all the way to the point of her terrible and heartbreaking death? What if he really is such a cold, awful monster that he could do such a thing?

"And the answer to the 'what if' is this: Under the reasonable-doubt standard, you must conclude that even if they had sex, and even if Mr. Rodarte *actually killed Haylee Branch on purpose*, on the evidence before you he did not kill her in that manner, that state of willfulness, deliberation and premeditation, that the law requires.

"And it also does not tell you that he killed her in the act of rape, because you must look at the evidence of rape without being swayed by the fact that Haylee was also killed, and that evidence is weak.

"You shouldn't conclude there was an intentional killing, because the People haven't proven it. But even if you do believe it happened that way, it can only be understood as simple panic, a sudden stress reaction by a young man who had gradually been losing his battle with the legal system, was just free of jail, could not admit to this, could not turn himself in, could not walk away from what had happened.

"We have all experienced tragedy, in one way or another, and what is before you here is a tragedy beyond measure. The loss of a life, the loss of a beloved daughter and sister, the loss of spirit and generosity, of beauty and promise, of intelligence and achievement.

"Mr. Rodarte is the cause of this tragedy, and he is not here to be excused for Haylee's death. How could I ask you to do that, after him telling you himself that he's to blame?

"But I ask you to mitigate it, and I do this confident that you each look at the world with fairness and perspective, and follow the law.

"Mitigation is manslaughter, whether involuntary or voluntary, and mitigation is warranted here. But even if some of you cannot come to the point of mitigation, this was not a first-degree murder.

"The People have not proven beyond a reasonable doubt that Haylee Branch, may God rest her soul, was raped by Andrew Rodarte, and that means it is not a first-degree killing on that basis.

"And the People have also not proven, beyond a reasonable doubt, that this was a willful, deliberate and premeditated killing.

"That means that your choice is between the two forms of manslaughter and second-degree murder. I ask you to see this horror as the case of unintended consequences that the evidence so clearly indicates, which leads you to manslaughter.

"Mr. Rodarte is guilty of involuntary manslaughter – or voluntary, if you can find some level of intent. And if any murder could be found on the facts before you, it is murder in the second degree, not the first."

◆

THE JURY BREAKS for lunch, I absorb Ted's good effort, and then I stand up to rebut. I'm rational, I'm sincere, I'm repetitive. I'm tired.

It gets a little better at the end.

"Mr. Stauber spoke of reasonable doubt, and rightly so, because that's the place where it starts and ends. It's what you have to grapple with, and it's the lens through which you look.

"If you find it, for any charge in any case, the defendant must be acquitted of that charge. But if it's not there, your obligation is to convict. And the difficult part for Mr. Rodarte is that there *was* no reason or rationality to the story he told you.

"We've been through the many things Mr. Rodarte did say including on the stand. But let's think now about what he *didn't* say.

"First, he was completely unable to account for how both Jacinta and Haylee were drugged with flunitrazepam, also known as roofies. It's a drug never even legalized in the United States, yet well known for the purpose of aiding sexual assault by causing unconsciousness and amnesia – just as happened here. The events that ended in her death at Mr. Rodarte's hands, literally, all flowed from that assault.

"Next, he never tried to explain how a young woman with a powerful dose of flunitrazepam on board, mingling with alcohol in a combination that figures to have left her nearly or fully unconscious, was not only wide awake but sexually ferocious, right before her death.

"But the critical thing Mr. Rodarte did not say was how he broke that bone in Haylee's throat. He had nothing for that, not even a made-up story – and neither did Mr. Stauber.

"Mr. Rodarte very reluctantly admitted that he *must* have broken it. Yet he couldn't, or wouldn't, tell you *how* – even though he admitted choking her with his hands, and then, in his version, a plastic bag.

"This fact hangs out there all alone. Her broken hyoid bone, that classic sign of strangulation, sits there bleak and mute and empty, yet loud and clear in what it tells you.

"Now he *could* have admitted it, claimed that it happened in the middle of wild sex. Kind of like he could have claimed that Haylee and Jacinta dosed themselves with flunitrazepam. Or that there was some mysterious stranger in the house, some phantom who decided to drug both girls, left Mr. Rodarte to have his way with Haylee, then returned later to kill her when they were finished.

"But he knew that admitting breaking the bone was too risky, so it just sits there. And that broken bone tells you, of course, that his story at trial was a lie, just like his two earlier statements to the police.

"The thread of lies shows you not only the calculating mind behind it, but Mr. Rodarte's acute consciousness of his own guilt – because he knows, all too well, that what happened that night was not an accident, it was not manslaughter. It was murder."

A LAST DEEP BREATH.

"There's another path to this same place, though – to the point of first-degree murder. And that is the strong evidence that yes, indeed, this was rape as defined in the Penal Code, it was rape by Andrew Rodarte of Haylee Branch, facilitated by a drug known for this purpose, a drug that can render a victim completely incapable of consenting to – or resisting – a sexual advance.

"And if you recognize it as rape, you need not even decide whether the killing was actually premeditated, because it is first-degree murder for that reason alone – and in fact a first-degree murder with that rape as the special circumstance. Because the rape was *not* incidental to the murder, but a separate goal – indeed, his *first* goal – then the special circumstance applies, and you should find it true.

"This was a murder, not an accident. That's all it's ever been, or will be. Murder. Mr. Rodarte extinguished Haylee's life on that bed, not by accident but on purpose.

"It's not your job to avenge her, or to protect the community, or even to remember her and act in her honor. You need only look to truth. The true and just verdict is the verdict of murder, and there is far more than enough before you to call it murder in the first degree."

With a nod I sit down, washed by a brief, familiar bliss. It never fails. Not from adrenaline, but from the knowing I am done.

♦

AT SIX O'CLOCK I'm still at my desk, immobile with fatigue. The jury's packed up, having only had an hour to start their deliberations.

There is a tap on the half-open door, which is certainly Celia Kim – ever-fleeting, typically still here at dinnertime for abstract reasons of her own, possibly my favorite person in the building.

We exhort each other through the days, and her sharp, sympathetic eye does wonders for me. I don't fully credit it, her default encouragement and praise, but it's nice to think you have a secret ally. We are the observers and assessors, the devil's advocates.

In her usual delicate way she pushes the door to but not closed, and balances her delicate frame against it.

"Sorry," Celia begins, needlessly. "I just wanted to drop in and say that – it was great."

"If you say so." I wrinkle my nose at her. "The case does have a few helpful facts."

"And you covered them all. But it was great."

There's significance to the word choice, too. *It* was great, she says – implying the substance, not just the selling. But she would never, in these circumstances, fail to cheer me.

Cold-eyed, though, I have to set it aside. "The good part is that it's over. Unless it's the bad part."

Celia just smiles, rightly amused. In this situation the supportive colleague usually can't resist asking the exhausted trial jock what he/she expects to happen, and the other will answer in deathly fear of jinx. Unless, of course, trial went so poorly the only surprise can be pleasant, and then you talk blithely about how fast you'll lose.

Or, more subtly, you'll be asked about the jury. Were they alert, focused, nodding, with you? Do you think you were soft, weak, didn't phrase something right, went off course, started putting them to sleep? Did you get some doubtful looks, signs of annoyance? Or just, in that rare case, pure affirmation?

But for Celia it's always the subtext.

"You'll do great, but I don't care about the result. Strange as that sounds. I just wanted you to know I *get* it." She's nodding. "For whatever it counts. I get telling them there isn't just one way. That it isn't an absolute."

I smile full. "All right."

"And this wasn't even like being an understudy, right? You jus suddenly got tossed in there – here's the play, go read it, see yo tomorrow night."

"Ah, well." I've noticed that Celia abbreviates me. "Manageable.

"And if it's first with the special, you'll be happy." A sly smil "Won't you?"

*Well, for Sonya*, I nearly say – banal and gutless.

Life *without parole*.

I give it a few seconds, a buildup nod. "Odds are."

WE WALK OUT TOGETHER, turning off lights.

# *30*

*September 7 – Morning/Afternoon*
**(JPH)**

THE USUAL RESPONSE to the agony of waiting for a jury is to try to occupy yourself – catch up on email, pull other files, think tepidly about the next one, tell yourself there's nothing you can change.

Once in a while, of course, you even go back-to-back, dragging the next batch of binders to the next room of citizens, sitting down and steeling yourself to the thought of another new beginning even as the prior twelve work out how the last one ends. But that's no fun either, and most of the time you just wait.

There's nothing to pull my mind away. I've been stripped of other duties even as "second chair," nearly scolded by the clerks whenever I bring anything else up. Trial makes it necessary to thumb through your email a solid ten times a day, so I'm well caught up, and I also learn that, out of deference, I've been removed from the circle as minor issues arise.

"Read the sports page, eat a sandwich, wait for questions," Tom tells me kindly. There are always questions from the jury. I only remember one half-serious trial without questions, and that was because they acquitted, a criminal threats case, in no time at all. And I had expected to win.

On cue the phone rings, two minutes later. It's a question.

THE NOTE IS one clunky, scrawled sentence: "Does female passing out during consent sex make crime of unconc. rape, intoxicated rape if drugged, or no crime?"

We have it charged in the alternative, the two versions – rape of an intoxicated *or* unconscious person. Either or. Haylee was both.

Vanzetta's answer is the judicial default. "I'm referring them back to the instructions. Both crimes got defined, so it's all in the facts. Any problem with me doing that?"

Ted has a little smile on his face. Maybe a daydream. "I don't believe so."

"People?"

"No. No sir."

But as he formally prepares his answer I am cheery. This has to mean they are looking for a way to make rape. If they are willing to make rape, they are ready for first-degree murder. They are ready to take him down. There is no ambiguity in the fast electric flash.

◆

LUNCHTIME NOW, and the twelve have dispersed. This means it's a sure bet to bleed toward mid-afternoon, at best.

"Dimwits!" sputters Brian, loyally, as he wears out my office carpet. "How is this anything but a first? He admits he killed her, he broke her fucking neck, and the rest of his story is seven dozen lies patched together with bubble gum. He drugged her, which means he killed her in the course of sex she sure as fuck never consented to. We call that rape. He can spin it 153 ways and it's still that. Willful and deliberate, special circ for rape. Period paragraph end of story."

I nod, stiff. Nearly convinced. What did he think of the jury?

"Well, with brutal candor, I saw two I didn't like," he continues. "Didn't figure you'd appreciate hearing it, particularly since I'm wrong about 94.8 percent of the time." (Brian likes numbers.) "But there were the two. The older dude with the gray mustache in the back row, and that small Hispanic girl up front. She did a lot of scowling."

"I think she's just had enough," I say, a forced lightness, remembering that the young woman has a two-year-old. And the guy in the back row doesn't worry me – rents farm equipment, married 38 years, his granite face shyness, not hostility. *To see if the pieces fit together, I guess*, he had said of the juror's task.

My own biggest worry is a tall, hefty platinum blonde I recognize from the Hammonds branch of my bank. Fiftyish, brightly dressed, hair in a pile atop her head. I've caught her looking at Rodarte with a kind of frank appreciation, and her face has seemed to redden with the passing days. Either she drinks or the whole thing's getting to her, I think morbidly. Maybe both.

It's her and one of my original favorites, a well-known local merchant with a great bald head and soft blue eyes, law enforcement friends, eleven grandkids, self-evident common sense. He's carved bears and bobcats and squirrels out of redwood for what must be 40 years – nobody remembers a time before his shop in North Lake Village. But he has begun blinking a lot, leaned back for long stretches of my close, and wrote more notes during Ted's. Expressions, too – perplexed, dubious, tired. All likelier to mean nothing than something.

"*Ass*holes," Brian continues, and then snickers at himself. "*Ooh*, feels good. When it's my own case I won't call them names out loud."

"They're trying," I offer.

"Trying my patience."

I give it the smile it deserves. "Tomorrow afternoon, that's my hunch." Untrue – I don't have one. "Whatever it may be."

"It better be right," he says, shaking his head, but he's easing toward the door.

I WAIT ALONE, brooding, stretching, gulping ramen noodles. Nothing else seems sure to stay down.

At about three Tom does slide by again, and with true news. He tells me that Sonya Brandstetter stirred late this morning, opened her eyes halfway and made a few hesitant attempts at speech. "Vocalizations," a doctor called them.

There's a momentary thrill from it, then careful hope settles over us both. But – *vocalizations?* What might Rodarte think, after what she did to him with words?

If she has to learn language again, I decide, I'll take a turn at her bedside and read straight from the transcript. No matter how this all turns out.

THE CLOCK SLIDES to a quarter past four. I'll show my face to the press and leave when the jury does. I'll leave and I'll drink and maybe, not sure, I'll sleep early, and then we'll start again, fresh morning hope for deliverance.

The phone trills, a blocked number. I'm puzzled enough to answer.

It's Tom on his cell phone, from inside the courtroom.

"Better come down here," he says.

I'm nodding. "What now?"

"For a verdict."

# *31*

*September 7 – Afternoon*
(JPH)

MY LEGS DON'T WOBBLE, I guess, but my nerve endings all seem to hum and quiver as I plod glassy-eyed through the courthouse hallway. Trailing ten steps behind, in a collective clack of footsteps, is a posse from our office. Reporters follow in their wake, and I count six TV cameras along the way, surely a record.

Tom – bless the man – stands framed in the courtroom door, holding it open, smiling, trying for lightness, though for once he shows the strain himself. I pass through and shuffle to my chair.

IT'S A SETTING from an ancient stage. Bailiff Graves, out of character, is stone-faced. Deputy Aziz stands grimly against the box rail, perched for a conviction and the off-chance Rodarte thinks of bolting when he gets the news. Lucille, the clerk, sits back straight in her chair with her hands folded in her lap, idle for once. Ellen the court reporter scans her screen.

I sit down in Sonya's place, conscious of the space around me, squeeze my eyes closed, lean back. It's nearly funny how terrible these moments are, the suffocating nightmare before a verdict is read, but I've never met an attorney who felt it differently.

Irrational as it is, there is always the sense that a verdict carries not only the defendant's fate, but the prosecutor's too. We dread being exposed as inadequate, handing the celebration to the other side. And in the most important of our cases we risk letting down brave and human victims, who have no one else to rely on. Wins dissolve under the pressure of the *next* case, but the losses tend to stay, even as we remind ourselves that the goal is truth and justice, not marks on a ledger. And while we're at it, I think we fear our own mental process, the probability that any loss will linger and clutter our vision next time.

Better yet, you often get bonus time to think about it. The jury will be taking a well-deserved break before the revelation, or the defense attorney is off-site and en route, or the judge is in the bathroom. And that is extra-special torture, full of ghastly forced small talk through a clenched throat, pointless glances at notes, blank-eyed staring at the wall art, all for who knows quite how long.

But not this time. Ted hasn't left the building, so he has beaten me here. The jury, late in the day, just wants it over with. And the judge is waiting with the rest of us, standing behind Lucille, then sliding over and sitting.

From there it's only a minute or so before the back door opens, the bailiff catches Vanzetta's eye, and in they come. Just the twelve now, of course, with the alternates long since sent home.

They are properly solemn and blank. Yet as they turn and start down their rows I look at my lap, avoiding both the chance of an eye link and the prospect, far worse, of seeing one smile at Rodarte.

When they're seated I exhale and look back up. Here I tend to glance at the defendant, and almost always he seems to look much more relaxed than I am.

Today I don't. I strain for emptiness, trying to clear all noise.

VANZETTA MAKES his blankest face.

"We are back on the record in the matter of the People versus Andrew Rodarte. The prosecution is present, the defendant and his counsel are present, and all jurors have now returned to the courtroom. My understanding is that the jury has arrived at a verdict. If I may, who is the foreperson?"

To my mild surprise the woodworker bows his huge head and raises a hand. Despite my earlier concern, I feel a comfort at the sight of him. There's nothing smug about his humble face, no *we knew better*. And no way they could have acquitted this fast – no way. Not possible – *he admitted it* –

"Juror number eight. Thank you. You have reached a verdict as to all charges and allegations against the defendant?"

"Yes sir."

"Very well. Can you please hand the verdict forms to the bailiff?"

He does, and Graves hands them to Vanzetta.

The silence is absolute as he thumbs the pages. It seems to take a full minute, though surely not. Finally he hands the sheaf gently to Lucille, who stands and reads.

"THE SUPERIOR COURT of the State of California, County of Contenta. The People of the State of California versus Andrew Marcelo Rodarte, case number CCF031213.

"Count One, the charge of murder in the first degree, in violation of Penal Code Section 187.

"We the jury in the above-entitled action find the defendant, Andrew Marcelo Rodarte, **guilty** of the crime of murder in the *first degree,* as alleged in Count One of the Information . . ."

The air, clenched, trickles out, and sweetness stirs.

Me and my circling around, my wanting it both ways –

"Sonya," I breathe. I didn't ruin it.

Or, maybe: *the jury knew better than I did.*

I glance at Rodarte, who seems to have frozen in place.

Then the second.

"We the jury find the defendant, Andrew Marcelo Rodarte, **guilty** of the crime of administering a controlled substance to Haylee Maureen Branch, to aid a felony . . ."

*A first because he drugged her – fuck all the rest of it –*

By now you feel yourself on stage – eyes on you, curious how you handle victory.

Now the third charge – never our focus.

"We the jury find the defendant, Andrew Marcelo Rodarte, **guilty** of the crime of administering a controlled substance to Jacinta Rae Cantrell, to aid a felony . . ."

*It's everything.* They must have disbelieved every word he said. They'll find the special circumstance true, if they've come this far.

I lean back, blank, feel a twinge in my neck. Lucille shuffles the last pages as I fold my hands in my lap, affecting a humble face –

"Count 4, the charge of rape of an intoxicated and/or unconscious woman, in violation of Penal Code section 261(a), a felony."

I would swear there is incredulity in Lucille's voice.

"We the jury find the defendant, Andrew Marcelo Rodarte, *not* **guilty** of the crime of rape of an unconscious or intoxicated person, as charged in Count Four of the Information.

"These verdicts are dated September the seventh, 2005, signed by Juror Number Eight."

IT JUST FLASHES across Ted's face – startled joy, in the rubble of the worst. No rape, no special circumstance. No life without parole. Andrew Rodarte will have a shot at freedom one day.

Brian says I never changed expression, and neither did Tom.

◆

WE LIMP THROUGH the last formalities with my brain in low gear, straining and grinding.

The jury is polled, Vanzetta gives the twelve their parting instructions, and they rise briskly and pass out the way they came in. Then he sets a status hearing late in the month, where we will expect to set a sentencing date.

TOM WALKS OUT into the hall ahead of me, running interference as I slip past him, and the cameras train on him with no hesitation. He's offered me this moment, I've declined.

He could wait to absorb before he speaks, but that's not his way. As ever he's ready to ease into the light and wing it. I pause when I'm past the crowd and turn to watch.

He holds up questions with his hands, revs up.

"Good afternoon. Let me first address you all together. Thank you one and all for being here to see justice done in Contenta County.

"We are pleased with a conviction for first-degree murder, and other felonies. The jury saw this for what it was – a first-degree murder, in cold blood, whether for self-protection from criminal fear of prosecution or some unimaginable pleasure.

"As her family knows all too well, nothing we can do will bring back Haylee Branch, or undo what has been done, but we are grateful to the system we have and the people that make it work. A cold-blooded killer has been held accountable, and will be spending the majority of his remaining life, if not all of it, in state prison.

"And I would like to take this moment to thank two people."

Incredibly, he takes us out of order.

"Our prosecutor John Patrick Howland" – he gestures, they turn, I raise a palm and bow my head – "who was called upon in the face of great adversity to fully take over this case, on the eve of closing argument, and through his compelling presentation helped the jury understand the crime for what it was, though in fact this was the first murder trial of his fine career.

"And then, of course, our treasured colleague, Assistant District Attorney Sonya Brandstetter, who led this prosecution all through the evidentiary phases, then suffered a medical emergency that keeps her in the intensive care unit at this hour, improving but with her long-term prognosis still unknown.

"Both contributed greatly to the cause of justice in this case, and have earned the gratitude of the community. I'm filled with enormous pride and appreciation at this hour. Questions?"

WE MAKE DO with a twice-weekly local paper. Our crime-beat reporter is our politics reporter, our school district reporter and our music critic. He's a solid three bills and not renowned for his printed grammar, but sensible and hard to dislike. Tom will make sure he gets the first one.

"Sir, how long do you anticipate until Mr. Rodarte would become eligible for release on parole?"

"Mr. Rodarte will be sentenced to an indeterminate term of 25 years to life in state prison, and will not be parole-eligible for decades. There will also be added time for his two other felony convictions. But that's a good starting point, 25 years. Over a generation, perhaps, he'll come to terms with this crime. We are surely grateful that the menace Mr. Rodarte represents to society will now be removed from its midst."

A TV reporter – NBC Sacramento. "What do you say to the jury?"

"We say what always should be said – thank you. We're grateful beyond measure to the citizenry of this county for responding with such purpose to the jury summons, and to the seated jurors for taking their duty so seriously."

A gray, bearded reporter from the *San Francisco Chronicle*. "Are you troubled by the jury's acquittal on the rape charge?"

Tom thinks it over.

"Troubled is too strong a word. We respect the efforts of this jury, and any difference of opinion is equally respectful."

Another TV reporter, a sleek Black woman in a dark green ensemble. I catch Oakland, not her name.

"Is it a disappointment to you that the defendant will have a chance of release someday, since your office was seeking a sentence of life without parole?"

Tom waits a long, painful beat, but then he smiles, with great exhausted eyes.

"That's another word I would not use.  We live in a land of laws and freedom and civic responsibility and personal conscience.  The verdict as a whole is a just one, and we continue to be grateful to the jurors for their determination and understanding."

She follows up.

"Would you think Ms. Brandstetter is pleased and satisfied by this result, in light of the evidence?"

He nods, waits another moment, and his eyes glisten.

"If Ms. Brandstetter could be here to comment, I have no doubt at all that she would echo those feelings in far more articulate language than my own.  I also look forward to sharing the news with her.  There's no feeling to have in this moment other than gratitude, on so many levels."

♦

WHEN HE REACHES MY DOORWAY I find I'm shivering, if not trembling.  I even hold my breath, I think.  He may have hated it.

"*Big* stuff," is what Tom Winston actually says, easing into a chair with crackling knees – already back in charge of himself, the half-smile that's always near to blossoming in full.  "One for the scrapbook, JP, after all of this."

Thawing, I shake my head, but there's an act in there somewhere.

"I guess.  But I better let somebody else make sense of it."

"I'd say you already did that part.  Nice fast first-degree murder."

I exhale, smile.  "It helps when people cop on the witness stand."

"Sure.  But we also know they could've called it something else.  They didn't."

"Well, if they really didn't think he raped her.  Then we did OK.  But I guess we aren't ever gonna know that for sure."

"We may not. But coming back with first means they didn't bu
into any of it. They said it's cold-blooded murder, whatever they wer
thinking on the rape. Unless he seriously mends his ways in the join
he's looking at pine-box parole."

Embarrassed now, I turn back to what it really was – a no-braine
"He wasn't getting around the broken bone. About as simple a
that, really."

"Well, he sure *didn't*." Again Tom smiles. "Nice work."

"Thanks, Tom."

"I'll tell her in the morning."

It's a hell of a thought.

♦

THE NEXT MORNING I have an e-mail from Celia, and Dou
Lahtinen hails me from his desk. He smiles as wide as the situatio
really allows.

"The man," he says. "In better times we'd raid O'Flannagan's."

"Thanks. Still trying to make sense of it."

"Well, it all makes sense but the rape."

"Fuuuck!" Brian barks from the doorway, passing by – or had h
lingered just to bitch? He has never in his life sympathized with
dithering jury. These clumps of twelve, in his view, have one true dut
– they should listen urgently to the lawyer who is sworn to advocat
for truth and justice, not a client, and who is there to defend th
community they live in.

But this was plainly a deal among the jurors, however phrased.

"Anyway, you were right it was a first," I venture now, smiling.

"Ya think? Oh right, you told 'em that yourself, didn't you?"

"Well, I tried."

A moment, even an invitation. One of them, right now, could sa
they get what I did, not leaving well enough alone. But in fact Bria

would have done it Sonya's way, only louder and longer. And Doug, who hated trial life, never projects himself in the arena.

"*Ass*holes!" Brian barks once more, sweaty-browed. "On the rape. I wish it was *their* fucking daughter."

BY NOW, THOUGH, I've seen the poetic justice. I'm the original compromiser, always reasonable, the king of the gentle win-win. Twenty-five-to-life has me walking on air.

# 32

## (JPH)

THE FIRST POST-TRIAL STEP is common enough – the defendant moves for a new trial, an extreme longshot but a freeroll, where almost any issue can be raised.

The most common basis is a claim that counsel was ineffective, in which case a different attorney gets appointed to bring the motion. But Rodarte, to his credit, isn't blaming his lawyer. So it is still Ted, and making the most plausible argument he has.

Although inconsistent verdicts will normally stand, here the jury acquitted of the rape, which not only takes away the special circumstance but eliminates one of the two theories of first-degree murder, the "felony-murder" doctrine. And since the evidence for the other theory, he suggests, is weak, the first-degree murder conviction can't truly be reconciled with the not-guilty of rape. So Vanzetta should either grant the new trial or modify the verdict to second-degree murder on his own initiative.

But Ted is just going through the motions, because the second theory still works. Under the law, a "willful, deliberate and premeditated" first-degree murder is less than it sounds like. You don't need to have schemed, or even planned in the conventional sense – the "premeditation" requires no minimum period of time. What counts is simply the depth of the reflection, the sense that the killer considered his options. Since Rodarte *admitted* minutes of sex with Haylee Branch, he had plenty of time to think. Or if she was out from the roofies but suddenly awoke, then obviously he didn't kill her by accident or anything else, but for the ice-cold purpose of eliminating the witness.

Vanzetta knows all of this before I remind him. He denies the motion in less than a hundred words, and we agree to sentencing six weeks later.

◆

I STOP AT THE HOSPITAL on a Tuesday afternoon.  I'd better, since I'm passing through Hammonds on the way west.

The ICU itself is restricted to family, but I follow a different herd through the automatic door, lugging an orchid-heavy bouquet, and manage to find Sonya in the second room.  For a rare moment Ed Brandstetter has stepped out, and she is drugged and shriveled and asleep – worse, really, than I pictured her.  Then, after just a moment, somebody wants my *bona fides*.

I could probably pass myself off as a relative – I'm certainly not well enough known for anyone to contradict it, particularly in this end of the county.  But one of honesty's many virtues is its occasional power to extract you from places you never wanted to go anyway.

So I write a note on the card with the flowers, and then I pause and gather something and I clench her left hand, cold and smooth, just for a minute – possibly the first time I've ever touched her flesh.  She doesn't stir.

◆

IT'S A GOOD LONG WAY still – first to the highway branching off northwest, then up over the ridge, past the hilltop resort, past the county line, and on the gentle downslope you come to Farr Ridge Road.  I discovered it a year or so after I came here, and would take it on an occasional weekend wander.

The road meanders along a thin creek with a three-word Spanish name, Arroyo something, and descends into a rich postcard valley.  The gentle terrain is speckled here and there with herds, periodic blocks of wine grapes, and at length a scrap of a place called Walton Glen, where you will find a gas station and garage with a sagging sign and tires piled skyward, a non-denominational country church, two or three streets of single-wides, a school bus stop, a general store and feedlot, and just past it a tiny café with a three-seat bar.

I stopped twice there and had a single beer. The visits were a year separated, at least, but I remembered the barman – which is to say, the proprietor – and he gave every sign of remembering me.

Ignoring the mountain road that branches off equivocally to the north, the tour of the valley is effectively a loop, maybe a 35-minute swing. On the back, western side I have passed a meadow full of deer, dozens and dozens, calm and incurious.

This is a bit simpler – well before the midpoint there's a right, then another onto a firm dirt road. And a mile down that, at the base of the looming, oak-covered hill, there is a handsome sign, white script on dark brown, to the left of a proud tan head.

## (Marta Branch)

BY THE FIRST AFTERNOON we were numb. She had warned us, Sonya, that it was all going to hurt – the question was whether we felt it as a duty to witness these days when they finally came. We answered yes, in principle – or did I answer for us both? And rather than driving the hour each way, we booked a room for those first days, then the next Sunday and Monday. But on Tuesday he stood up, and so did we, and left – some things are just too much.

Ash never came back until the day of sentencing, and that took all she had, but I went back for the arguments. In a way I thought it owed it to John, as well as to Sonya. It was too much for Ash. She could endure only by creating a distance, a buffer zone, where I could absorb and digest and describe for her. And even I wanted desperately to go unseen, especially after the unthinkable, our saving grace collapsed and clinging to life, and John and his whole team pulling this off in worse shape than I am.

One reporter notices, but I wave him off. And John does see me, but when I wave *him* off I'm smiling. I'm glad he knew I came.

He leaves a message for me, waiting that night when I get back, and he also explains the other things we'll have to get through after the verdict. And then he calls the next day with the word.

At the end of 20 minutes, well before we've fully made sense of it all, I hear myself invite him, recklessly, to make the drive. *Come out here one of these days, see where she lived.* Ash flinches, covers her mouth. But as he pauses, startled, I realize how likely he is to do it.

THE NEXT CALL, maybe a month later, is to tell us the new trial motion was denied. Routine, I guess, but a liberation anyway. Sentencing comes next, and it will be a few more weeks. Well and good. We're angling toward fall, the mission's accomplished. And he certainly hasn't forgotten.

So we set it up for the next afternoon, and he's about the first visitor ever to get every turn right and arrive on time, coming along through the dust and pulling up with a sort of smiling anxious face, and then I'm greeting him with an awkward hug and leading him in.

I'VE GENERALLY RESTRAINED MYSELF. The picture they used of Lee had been on a cluttered bookshelf; I promoted it to a table at the entryway, to greet him, and he did pause and look. It lasted several seconds, and I saw him nearly say something, then hold back. It was a good picture, full of light, though I remembered she didn't particularly want to pose. That had been a picnic on Mother's Day, hot day for May, Lee was complaining about bug bites, and Ash was up ahead with her feet already in a creek. But I guess some things don't need backstory.

They both still peered over the room in school photos, and there were a couple of collages, which I liked best. But I didn't have to dismantle a shrine.

IT'S JUST THE TWO of us. He gets an almost-disappointed look, but I decide it's a fake.

He's met Ash, of course, early on and then again a couple of times after trial started, but she has never been in a condition to bond. In the months after the murder she was the zombie you'd imagine, eyes like glass, seeming to shrink away, invisible as possible. She could barely lift her head off the pillow in the mornings, even to finish high school, and of course I hardly had the strength to prod her myself.

That did change at trial – by then, all we had was pins and needles, and now you could see that swirling through her every moment, and her trying to cling to the fixed objects, however few. But talking to Sonya took almost everything she had, and so I tell him she's at work, a neighboring ranch. That's close enough.

ONCE WE'RE SETTLED on the couch, he comes straight to it. Sonya will live, for now, but will never again be the person we knew.

I'm crushed and blank, trying to make sense of it. But I ask a couple of follow-up questions about her diagnosis, which makes John wonder, so I explain I was once an LVN down in Sunnyvale. Which leads to the rest – that after seven years of it I had two girls and was making $35,000 a year to sleep days, spend nights watching monitors and tending to the failing and miserable, and . . . well, a marriage near collapse, and not much to dream of, and how I sometimes doubted I could even get through it. And then, eventually, us three packing up one Saturday and leaving Jon to it. Jonathan, my husband, their dad.

He was an insurance adjuster, a poet and a drunk – a sad and gentle one, but relentless, and breaking up just rushed it all along. He died of a stroke, like an old man, when Lee was fifteen, Ash only twelve. They'd just been down there for spring break, in this depressing little mountain bungalow he'd wound up renting in Sonoma County. That's why Lee had no dad there to fly her flag.

But the split changed everything another way, because I came here. I tell him this was my parents' house, their later years, and they were the bold hearts of the family, packed up when they were pushing 70 to move up to the quiet. Land was cheap then, and they both did ride, so they started the boarding operation, very small, and eventually I picked it up. Then my mom died, my dad was alone and couldn't have sustained it, but the timing was perfect to escape. We came up, spent two good years with him before he died, and built a life.

It was a major trek each way to high school, when they got there, but they both sailed through those years unscathed, not a car wreck or a D or a pregnancy test. People gave me credit – doubt I deserved it, it always seemed hardwired into them both. Nobody got arrested, nobody got pregnant, nobody came home smelling like weed or puke or Southern Comfort (do people still drink that?). Nobody had screaming jags, nobody broke things in a rage, nobody talked about doom and oblivion, nobody flirted with the wrong crowd, nobody blew off their obligations. They had their lazy spells but got good grades, and then the SAT came and both of them did fine.

That was two years apart, not that it matters, because Lee started kindergarten later, she was almost six. Ash started right at five, even though her birthday was only two weeks earlier, early September, but I was in a different mood then, I guess, and she'd graduated at seventeen, earlier that year, talked me into letting her hang out a little while, help out here before the next thing.

John is there to listen, if nothing else. And so I talk.

I TELL HIM about trying to hold back, from the very start. The toughest part is sitting there and letting your kids learn the hard way, at whatever it is. Breaking their favorite toys. Shivering when they forget jackets. Moaning about hunger after they pick at dinner. Called to the principal because of undone homework in middle school. Cutting themselves because they grab the scissors wrong.

Then comes all the stuff you *can't* just let them learn the hard way. Stepping off the curb without looking. Walking through a parking lot with headphones on. Cheating on a test. And worse – driving a car. Picking a college. Dealing with boys, and men.

So it's the distance thing – what's close enough? We all have to figure it out on the fly, I guess. But I was proud of myself. Half-educated single mother out in the back of beyond, living on physical work and a few years of erratic child support checks from the ex. But I got through that, came through, thought I saw the finish line.

They were both going to go out there and attain something, and then find somebody and eventually start the cycle all over again, and they were going to be close enough for weekends and holidays and birthdays and all of it. Meanwhile I'd still be here under the open sky, I'd hear from them every week, and I would know I made it. I finished the task.

Lee first, of course. Lee first, to show the way.

And the worst of it – the second worst – is how it put everything on Ash. That whole vision didn't just get torn in half, it got doubled, or quadrupled. Doubled for her and doubled with me. She could only think she's supposed to go out there for both of them, carry that torch for her own sake and Lee's. But she knew she'd also have to fill the second part, staying close and having kids and being there for all of them and me too.

It's a hell of a lot to bear, and it made me look at Ash with heart to break – even as I was still fixed utterly on Lee, thinking how many times and ways I could have done more for her than I did, or at least said louder how proud I was of her every step, and how much she meant to me.

So Ash would look at me scared, just a little, of how overflowing I was. Which left me in terror of a distance, sitting there and picturing that because I lost one, I could lose them both.

AND THAT DAY John explains that there will be a little more to argue about, but it isn't going to matter, he'll get sentenced to something like 26 and a half years before he even gets a hearing for parole. All those years to think about it, those – what – five minutes, *three* minutes, when he took her away?

Even with the hovering thought of Sonya, I remember smiling somehow, at the end of his visit, and how strange it was, a feeling of something just *beginning* to lift. And I say something about there can't be perfection, I would never expect it, but I guess there could always be *right*, whether you believe in something up there or you don't. I tell how I kinda believe but I'm fuzzy on the details, I guess, and how that's brought me up short – living a life, close to beauty, drowned in love then half of all the light on earth is extinguished, and I'm left here to think about the darkness, every single day. But that's where I was, and it's *still* where I am. If a sign comes from somewhere, I'll make an effort to understand, and there will be hope down in it somewhere.

Which is odd, I guess, because I've *never* thought I understood life even for five minutes. I've wished for a belief system, in fact – even a mildly delusional one – but it's never come to me, just a chronic sense

264

of awe and mystery. And what that means, maybe, is when John and I sat in that room, after nearly two years to think about it, I didn't know what I wanted from Rodarte any more.

*You* did *know once, though, didn't you?* A pointed question. I grab hold of myself and say *yes, yes* – those very first days I wanted exactly what I ought to want –

I DESCRIBE IT – I can't help it. *I imagined a blade in my hand,* long and thick and sharp. Then I imagined finding out with certainty who it was, even though nobody *else* knows. And then . . . whew! . . . I imagined walking up to him, and casually, him not knowing who I was, and I would, some way or the other, grab his hair and pull his head back, and then . . . my God, I can hear my teeth grind. I imagined *taking my big thick knife and stabbing him straight through the soft part of the neck, right above the collarbone,* and the knife being so fat and long it would just go all the way *through* him. Right through the throat, the larynx, the trachea . . . right through, pushed through to the *hilt* –

As a bonus, he wouldn't believe my strength, not just that I chuck hay around, but that stuff that comes from down in a deeper place. I'm not just a mother, I'm a *mad* woman. And then, while he would collapse back in horror and desperation, I would *spit* in his evil eyes, and then, as he faded out (somehow I have him still conscious, even with a knife through his windpipe), I would tell him who I was, and I would tell him I wasn't going to wait, that he wasn't going to get to tell a single fucking lie about my daughter, not going to get to waste the resources of the world on food and beds and time and government lawyers or any of that.

And I was not going to apologize either for ambushing him, refusing to wait. He was going to learn about actual consequences. Cause and effect. Right from me and my big fat knife.

In that dream there's nobody to catch me, either. Nobody happens to be a witness, I leave him there and then I'm gone in the sunset, and nobody even thinks to suspect me, no matter how plain my motive, because it's such a savage and awful thing, something a drug lord might do, not a blonde up near 50.

In fact, in my version they don't even know he killed my daughter – only a select few of us do – and so this is just random, and the unknown sicko will have a terrible record and people who wanted to kill him for a million other reasons. So in that dream the cops just don't look too hard. I'm pure avenger, in and out and gone. No muss no fuss. Leaves Lee's murder "unsolved," but fine – let them make TV shows about it. *I* will know, and I'll tip them off, too. That'd be fun.

I remember telling him, even as we talk, I can feel it *right now*. I would even go pick one up, see which felt the rightest. Stand there in the kitchen, clenching and unclenching. Wanting to memorize the feeling of it in my hand, I think.

But this was really just a few days, because the miracle happened – they found Rodarte in no time.

WHAT HAPPENED was that I had driven there for his arraignment. Nobody knew. The detectives had been out to interview me, but I hadn't met Sonya or John yet, I didn't introduce myself, nobody noticed me. I just watched from the back row, because I had to see him. And so my first look is him shuffling in, decked in a horrible puke-green, his hands cuffed in front of him. Looking at the floor, just a cloud of guilt around him.

But strange as it sounds, then and there he gained some kind of *existence* – just by standing there and breathing. You could see it faintly, the rise and fall. How crazy is that? I saw him human because I saw his breath – the very thing he took away.

He looked like a coward, I think, with a public defender there telling him what to say, some skinny little bitch I wanted to walk up and kick, even knowing it's just her job. But when I saw his human breath, Rodarte, I realized I couldn't have done what I meant to do.

I'm *not* an avenger, after all. Just someone who has to get through.

FOR SOME REASON I think of a prairie town after a tornado. *I'm* a flattened house, a pile of sticks, empty and cold and twisted into an unrecognizable shape. Yet it always amazes me to think that that no matter how brutal it gets, in this remarkable world, order does come back to win, eventually, and the flattened things rise up again.

From somewhere come the people who live to reconstruct, knowing the lost people and places aren't returning, but putting up a plaque and building a new school, new clinic, new house. Whatever it is. Remembering, digging down for truth, and moving on. That was Sonya for me, and then it was John, and for that I can only give thanks. Then, a last left turn – I am going to think about this wretch himself. The part I couldn't watch, but I got it word by word – that was our last conversation, actually, me and Sonya – chapter and verse, how he squirmed and floundered and told his lies and tried to sell himself to the jury, but him *admitting* it to the jury – *that he killed my daughter*. He says yes, *yes, I – made – her – die*. So that, after all, I could *know*. Always and forever, I could know who the other half was, in that little room – I could always *know*, not have to wonder.

Yet, small epiphany: he is human.

And then, too, I could look across and see her, *his* mother, and imagine how she was going to suffer, the ways in which the agony would be similar to mine, and the ways it would be different, and how she would blame herself and wonder what she could have done to make him safe – for others, and for himself. It also hit me that she'd still have luxury of trying to talk herself into hope, which caused me a violent moment of jealousy, but it passed.

AND SO, IN THERE SOMEWHERE, I knew it was right not to try for a death sentence. Since I'd realized I couldn't kill him myself, couldn't hate him that much even if I tried with all my might, I didn't want a surrogate doing it either.

There was another thing, too. Obviously I want to believe she went to sleep before the worst of it happened, over that bright horizon without any fear or effort at all, but the problem is I *can't ever know* – and the reason for that is that there is only one living person who could tell me. If she was quivering, if she was awake, if she looked at him with conscious eyes, if she struggled, if she spoke, if she flailed – because he is the very last soul to lay eyes on my living daughter – my first-born, my eternal joy – it means that I am connected to him, and he to me.

If we had gone the next level, hauled him in and decided that h
must actually die himself for it someday, my mind would jump there
jump, even though I'd probably never live to see it happen – and think
*and if he goes, her last witness vanishes with him, forever and ever.*

AND I TELL JOHN how you think about all the nevers.

I'd never hear her yawn at the breakfast table on a Saturda
morning again, or see her across the valley in some late afternoo
light, or lend her another book, or shop for a wedding gown – wel
she'd have taken about half an hour, bought something ridiculousl
simple and nobody ever would have forgotten how she looked.

She'd never surprise me again with a gift, a smile, a new interest
She would never be a mother, never wrinkle, never worry.

I borrowed her for 20 years, maybe left a little of me in her, an
she took that with her when she flew.  If we are lucky beyond a
deserving, I said, maybe I would see her again one day, and then he gc
tears in his own eyes, and around there I finally let him leave.

THERE WAS A HUG, a talk about the sentencing process, and the
he left.  And as he kicked up dust . . . well, there was suddenly a *gleam*
out of a movie.  A *flash* of her in a ray of light as the sun came out fror
a cloud.  Evanescent and completed.  I think he saw it too.


## (JPH)

MARTA WAVES as I pull away, in a landscape that seems arise
whole from the world of dreams.

Half an hour later, back over the county line, I wend down the las
of the second ridge, Crown Lake filling the top of the horizon.  A mil
or so ahead lies Red Branch Road, the cutoff just this side c
Hammonds.

I glance down and have a signal again, which need not mean m
phone will ring.  There's no reason it should.

It's a quarter to five. I'll take Red Branch, veer northeast through the dry brown hills, buy some late-season peaches at Cavendish Farm. Then around the northern shore in the late summer light.

The phone does ring.

♦

SHE SUGGESTS, CAREFULLY, that we meet somewhere. And so that Saturday night we convene beneath an old stone archway outside the Coldbrook Cavern Ranch, up the winding creek road in the far northeast of the county – my proposal, her instant trill of happiness, since I've struck a nerve of memory. *I went there as a kid.*

Fall colors blare along the roadway as the day fades out. About two days a year I remember my sunroof, and this is one – until I imagine her seeing it as a virility play, and grind it closed again.

The roadhouse, almost 75 years old, is amid a clearing. They've long since tacked on vineyards to keep it afloat. The sky behind her is an orange-pink revolt as Terin approaches me across the dirt parking lot, through the waft of steak over open flame. And almost *yes* – not Haylee returned, no dark obsession, but that distant hint – confident in bearing, self-possessed, heart-skip lovely, and with a self-effacing first smile and a fast apology for being four minutes late.

There's a hum in my chest, no point pretending. I've done what can be done, or close enough. Marta and Ashlyn will remain even if Sonya departs, and Rodarte has been convicted, and here in the settling dust, out of nowhere, I have Terin's beautiful eyes to meet.

Is she a lure, a light – a change of life? An artifact of my front-row imagination – or a bridge across the rest of that brutal night, when we all condensed and changed? Just another looping canyon, where I'll have to find a dream-route home, or the end of my circling path? As we saw through our steaks and sip tempranillo the question turns raw, and its curious cloud should by rights scare her off, but it doesn't.

Terin declines a brownie sundae but volunteers for coffee as we stay, and sit, her back to crystal darkness, my heart awake. Seeing her with just the *flicker*, maybe in the bones, of someone I never saw alive. And as herself, far better, across that broad divide.

THE TIME DISSOLVES. And I'd go back to look and linger in that wondering place again.

# <u>REVIEW</u>

Eric Ferguson

## 33

**(JPH)**

MEMORY TENDS TO SPARE US the clutter, but the record certainly doesn't. Here the final four-volume Reporter's Transcript of Andrew Rodarte's trial, prepared for appeal, runs almost twelve hundred pages, every word transcribed by Ellen J. Tomkins, C.S.R. And it takes up half a banker's box, grimy and tactile, the blurry-edged *now* that was then.

The summer of 2005 was when strangers came to take note of our doings, 70,000 acres and a hundred homes burned at the far north end of the county, Sonya Brandstetter had a ruptured brain aneurysm and Andrew Rodarte got sent away for first-degree murder. But I'm only able to return to it now because it was preserved intact.

Twelve-point Courier on cheap printer paper, bound with plastic fasteners, verbatim. In places crude and cryptic, in others crisp and masterful. Near the end, one small batch of me. The cold record, its purpose served after appeal, still radiant with the flame of Sonya Brandstetter.

◆

THERE WASN'T ANY MIRACLE.

Sonya did survive the ICU, got some mobility back and finally left the hospital late that fall. Though her speech was badly slurred and her motor skills ravaged, she had regained a basic knowledge of who we all were, was oriented to place and time, and here and there would seem to recapture something intact. It was reported after a while that she could get through half an hour of TV news, had managed to have a conversation on the phone, and would make an attempt with magazines and music.

I would bring up the trial the few times I saw her, of course, and when I went back through the verdict she nodded, haltingly, and there was something like a smile, probably with irony in it.

But that's as good as it got. A nurse came in full time, Ed took her for walks and fed her by hand, played bluegrass for her and kept up the yard.

We saw her one afternoon before Christmas, and eventually she made one trip down to the office, a Friday morning in mid-winter, leaning on a walker, and fended off hugs from every direction. But she made only a very brief effort to talk, eking out *thanks* and *glad to be here* and *I've really missed you*, raising her left hand to wave, and the most lucid part of her was her eyes: hating every moment, angry at the spectacle of herself, powerless as a ghost.

As she was helped into the back of her own Mercedes, now formally retired, we all realized it – Sonya the fierce, the manager, the intellect, the cosmopolitan, all gone in a flash.

THERE WERE LITTLE UPDATES throughout the year, but it was a bleak business, and that next October she had a stroke – a risk factor, apparently, from the surgery that had saved her life. Tom saw her, urged the rest of us not to. Now her whole right side was immobile, he said, and her face near-frozen, though she could still try to talk in a terrible, saliva-flooded way. *How did this happen?* she asked him once.

There wasn't any answer – it shouldn't have. And on a sparkling morning the following March, Sonya died in a wheelchair on her back patio, and the first thought everybody had was that it was a blessing for them both.

Tom, of course, gave the best oration. I wrote scrawls of it on the back of the funeral bulletin, couldn't read my own writing and asked him if he kept it on his computer. *Nah*, he said, and what notes he had he pretty much ignored when the moment came.

♦

RODARTE APPEALED, of course. I half-expected his mother to go into debt hiring somebody out-of-pocket, and was happy for her sake when they just accepted the appointed option, a venerable name from the standard appellate list.

He griped about Matchstick, of course. That's a loser. He argued the change-of-venue motion. Futile, because Vanzetta knew the record he needed to make. He argued the admission of Tanya Melendez's evidence over the discovery objection, argued an instructional error, argued Miranda one more time, complained about the prior act evidence. And then, almost as an afterthought, he got to the question of inconsistent verdicts, which had always seemed just fuzzy enough to complicate things.

No fear. The "unpublished" opinion from the Third District landed like a ripe tomato from low height, nothing but a soft *splat*. In typical workmanlike fashion the Court of Appeal had lined up his arguments, the scattershot verdict among them, then knocked them down like toy soldiers, one by one.

So Rodarte then petitioned for review in the California Supreme Court – a last, predictable desperation move. It was denied, as usual, with no comment at all, and the conviction officially became "final" about a year after the verdict.

The night the denial order arrived there was a trial win, somebody else's, so we paraded down to O'Flannagan's, as ever, and there was a general shout-out my direction, too. Which I deflected by saying he'll be back on habeas corpus, because everybody is.

SONYA DIES, Rodarte's conviction stands, time slides effortlessly past. The name of Haylee Branch is seldom mentioned, yet she hovers in her unobtrusive way, and I'm reminded, over and over again.

♦

TERIN'S LAST NAME was "Ree" – Scottish, it turned out. She was from Santa Cruz, had a degree in environmental science and a monthly stipend from her father's trust fund, and was living alone in a hilltop bungalow, family-owned, seven country miles from the seat of an afterthought county, starting grad school on a computer screen.

So I had asked, that first careful night – why here, why now?

"Memories and money," she said, just half-smiling. "Or maybe that's the wrong order. I came here a lot of summers as a kid. No rent, and figured there wouldn't be many distractions."

I laughed. "There shouldn't be."

She gave a shrug, a watchful look, finally a smile. "That's sort of an upside, for me. It was always kind of a secret joy. And I have no real idea where life is taking me anyway."

A second date, for a movie, got us to a third, checking out a new Mexican place near the north shore. Her eyes, darker blue in the dim light, rose up from a margarita and a mediocre chicken burrito. There had been ease to things, a strange lack of urgency.

"So you're still wondering why I'm here. My life path."

I may not have deserved that much credit, but I smiled. "Maybe a little."

She gave a wry smile in return. "Disclaimer first. It's my only drama. But I had someone to get away from."

"Ah. Boyfriend from back home?"

"Naturally."

Nodding, I felt acutely aware of the seven years between us. Which hat to wear? Public safety operative, supportive friend, local tour guide, lover-to-be?

"Serious stuff?"

She nodded. "Bad family. Irredeemable, him included. Which, of course, has that crazy-ass allure."

I didn't actually understand, because I never have, but I nodded along. I'll always think of Bricks Bocannon coming through the courthouse, over and over – a biker way up in his fifties with a matted beard, broken teeth, a huge gut, great craters and pockmarks on his face, scars on both arms and several past trips to prison, and never once was there not a yearning, younger female face in the audience, there with a loving and loyal heart in support. Two rivals even got into it in the hallway one afternoon. A deputy waded in and got his nose broken for his trouble, and didn't much like it when we weren't inclined to file any felonies.

It was a solid ten minutes, I guess, but she kept on point, and after all the highs and lows she tried to break up with him as they sat in a car, to which he responded by dragging her out and flinging her down on a grassy median. At which point she wound up wiping *his* tears away and moving in with him, that very night.

WE'D ORDERED ANOTHER ROUND, I'm sure, and Terin was hunching her shoulders down as she told it, mortified. Soon enough he got sore on a Saturday night, shoved her hard against the wall, came up with fists clenched. And when she ran out the front door into the courtyard of the apartment building, he caught her, threatening mayhem, flung her down and tore a lock of hair from her head.

For all the commotion, it only added up to a couple of misdemeanors and a criminal protective order, a nine-month sentence in county jail that would get knocked down by a third, and she didn't wait. She finished out the school year, then lit out for here, where her mother kept a rifle and where Noah, by a mercy, had never been.

By this time he was out, and she knew he'd been looking. He'd even gone to her mother and begged. Meanwhile she had made a friend of the widow next door, deflected drunken attention from the Rose's clientele, and he hadn't found her.

Most of what I had sounded like platitudes and encouragement, but when we eventually stood up to leave she smiled fully, eye-rolling, self-aware.

"More than you thought you'd learn tonight, I bet?"

I smiled back. "I guess so."

Somehow I must have cleared a hurdle, though, and when I pulled up to her bungalow an hour later I decided the new information merited a walk to her front door.

I've spent my life not forcing answers to questions, less Zen than laziness. The rewards have varied. But at the threshold she invited me in, and a couple of months and several blissful nights later we dined on the back patio of Greco's, the Italian place on the southwest shore of Marsh Lake, and at the bottom of a second bottle of house red she decided to come live with me.

IN A WAY it was a test of self, because of the asterisk that came with it. If Noah ever found her now, he'd find us both. Maybe once in our lives we all want to see ourselves as a guardian.

I gave it only passing thought. If he didn't know of the cabin, no way he'd think to target Contenta County, and Rodarte was one of the few people who ever found it by accident. For good measure, I now *did* have a shotgun, because that's what you do on the fringe of the woods, with tweaking burglars abundant, bears near enough, and the sheriff eager to teach you "firearm use and safety" as a public service.

And there were better questions to ask. I'd flamed out of a relationship in law school, worked up a futile longing for a law-firm colleague after that, and dated just casually since – watchful, I think, of my easy life. I could still imagine marriage in due course, and a life path beyond it. But could I see my someday children, with baby teeth and third-grade photos – then middle age, cars and college funds? And beyond, my senior sunset, Terin in her sixties, grandkids wanting to rent a paddleboat some summer afternoon, me little help due to creaks and arthritis but wanting, of course, to ease out into the beautiful blue?

They were too dense to answer, so they just hovered over these early days, and I marveled. Terin was smart, alluring, kind and serious. Tolerant of me, I think, even when I *did* see a pointless chimera of Haylee Branch in her, in tiny glimpses. *Did you ever see her picture?* I once asked, near the bottom of another glass. *You could nearly be related* ... She just smiled and shook her head, but I saw a tiny flinch first.

Terin pulled the taps three or four days a week, plowed through her program, prettied up the house. I waded through the daily routine, tried a few mundane cases, cooked a lot of mundane dinners, paid the mundane bills. Congratulated myself.

She met the office gang at a couple of work events and one curious group trek to the movies. I took her to a friend's wedding in Santa Rosa. At length I met her mother and her sister Bryn, over a weekend in San Francisco. And then, on the last day of 2007, by pure accident, she got pregnant.

MEN NEVER FAIL to panic at such news, I don't think. Mine lasted an hour or so.

Then, with conscious effort, I rallied to the thought – but more importantly, so did she. Terin smiled and grasped my hand at random, started to muse about the logistics, talked about fate and fortune, how it would be easier now than after she started a career, even dared murmur a few possible names.

She seemed cheerful, almost nonchalant, about the binding it would do, the permanent link. The "m" word didn't come up at once, but it hovered. And I nodded along through the weeks that followed, warming along with the season, even as the question ping-ponged around my head – is this *it*, then? Is this my life?

We trekked to a baby superstore on a Saturday in early March, two counties distant. As we navigated the green valleys I thought just briefly of Haylee Branch, who never had this chance, and died as the world went bare.

We spent a long couple of hours shopping, had mild arguments over the car seat, the diaper strategy, the infant toys. Me still not quite believing, imagining, envisioning.

I remember a loud exhale as we looked at cribs, her weary eyes flashing. *I realize we're not very domestic, but could I just take the lead, you trust me on this?* And so I did.

After we got back we went for a long walk, our four-mile loop. The late afternoon was a fuzzy golden-gray and cold, the sodden ground at last draining toward spring, the streams awash, seeing wild yellow blossoms springing out here and there. I watched her with a certain awe, and when we got back she was humming, did that all evening.

She rose in the night, and eventually I stirred just enough to see the faint light through the bathroom door. It did not jolt me, just stuck at the border of my awareness, and she came back to bed soon enough. She didn't sleep, and she didn't wake me up.

WHAT I FELT was a jumble. Sympathy for her above all, I guess since she had already committed her own heart. Mournful emptiness, certainly, at a life being canceled. A low-grade anxiety based in arithmetic – even as I did very little to pursue it, I'd always thought fatherhood would have to happen by 40, and time was waning. But down there somewhere, too, there was at least a granule of relief, no less real for being near-impossible to explain.

I had platitudes at the ready, which she gratefully consumed. *I guess this wasn't quite the time . . . Well, now we know it's possible . . . It's there if we want it . . . We'll try again when you're ready.*

We packed the unisex things we'd gathered that day, to go with the many Bryn had already sent. They sobbed together on the phone and Bryn, glowingly kind, came up to cheer her a few weeks later.

At night it was warm enough now to sip outside, and we plowed through local vintage – "the upside," Terin mordantly observed. And I watched as she did push through the hurt, moment by moment

280

understanding it, head bowed, face clenched in sympathy, in awe of her – yet still at my watching post, eyes to the horizon, not in the harrowing trench.

The last day of the visit, I remember walking out to Terin on the patio after Bryn came inside, and her telling me she was "mostly cured." I squeezed her hand, repeated it – *We'll try again.* But we never really did.

♦

TWO MONTHS LATER Noah went off the side of a mountain on his motorcycle. She laughed out loud at the idea he'd done it on purpose – *he couldn't go on without her!* – but it was easy to see what it changed. Terin's rationale for staying in Contenta County was now me alone – not me as father-of-child, nor shield-and-protector.

She had just finished her master's in environmental science when it happened, which had long been the hovering question mark – the chances were slight she'd land a forest or river protection gig in our backyard, and she'd originally meant to stay near home, working for coastal non-profits on stuff like erosion and spawning grounds and tide pools. So that summer she was still tending bar when she saw a chance, a good fit – on the north coast, three hours away.

She built up to the topic as we sat by the fireplace. Methodical, rational. She was even lovelier than when we met, I was no thrill but a familiar harbor, and she thought just *maybe* we could both live with the foggy coast, chilly summers and redwood trees – did I think . . . ?

It shouldn't have knocked the wind from me, but it did, and I think she read me right away. All I could do was ask for a few days to think it over. And then a week later, eyes to the ground, I said no.

I'd found a home, a path, a belonging. I was tethered by my first-day, wild-grass epiphany, my deed of trust, my memories – and then by Haylee, through Marta, to Sonya, and now a tranquil after-place.

Eric Ferguson

I do want you, want us, I told her. But I didn't have the nerve to secure it, so I gave the choice to her.

In plain fact, I wanted her to stay. And for excellent reasons, she decided to go.

◆

WE WERE IN the driveway, her Kia full. She hugged me.

"I may hate it. I might come back." It's been a mantra. "We'll meet up."

I was numb, empty, still admiring. Maybe you do only know love when you lose it. "I'll see you anytime."

"I'll make time. Come up when I'm settled. Or I'll come down."

"Those are good thoughts."

"I'll see you soon."

"I hope you will."

She pulled back and looked at me, damp-eyed, but smiled. "What might have been, huh?" She meant the baby. "But life's full of that."

All I really had left was a nod.

◆

IT HAPPENED ONCE EACH DIRECTION, three months apart. Dinner, smiles, the rest. *Maybe* we could stay long-distance committed – she had no competitors for my attention to fend off. And she may have stopped to ponder it. But a month after the second time she told me they were offering her a can't-resist job in Alaska.

I drove up, and there was one last dinner. This was a wrap, but we were calm and warm together.

I circled back to that night at the bar, as if we hadn't a hundred times before. The double lightning bolt – Terin and Sonya. And that night I came up with a line: "I'm only sorry about half of it."

282

That earned a smile. "Our half's all I know, and I'm not sorry either."

"That's nice to hear."

"You thought you were home free that night, didn't you?"

She meant the trial, I think, but I gave it a big, woozy grin. "Oh, I wasn't looking to be free."

AS IT TURNED OUT she married the chief engineer. And a year later came a photo card, "Jed, Terin & Tessa" under the Christmas tree. It took a moment to realize how happy I was for her.

# *34*

**(JPH)**

TOM ANNOUNCED HIS RETIREMENT well before the 2008 election. He had tipped us off much earlier, naturally, and by then there was no real suspense about his successor. Doug had ascended to Sonya's role, first interim, then permanently, but had no interest in the final leap, and it was equally obvious that Brian not only wanted the job badly, but would win it with ease.

Brian's wide, guileless everyman face was made for billboards and TV ads, and Tom endorsed him at the starting line. Even with months of lead-in no serious opponent ever emerged, and so on the first Tuesday of the next June he got 73 per cent of the vote in the primary election, and spent most of his victory speech talking about Tom Winston and Sonya Brandstetter.

The retiring hero worked to the very last day, though we thought he had vacation he stood to lose if he didn't use it. Somebody finally brought it up, and he burst out laughing. "Where do you think I'm going to be from here on out?"

*Close enough to bail me out when I start fucking up*, came Brian's cheery bark from the back of the room.

HE RETIRED TO his boat, more or less, on the west shore of Tahoe. But Tom has never seemed that far away. Age has slimmed but not shriveled him, and he still turns up at our Christmas fete, most years, in time for at least two large belts of champagne. We still lure him down to formally consult every once in a while, and he's lax at best about submitting invoices.

I had always wondered what he really thought of the verdict, and finally – years later – I dared to ask. Tom smiled, and said that you do what you can do with what you have, and you trust in the rest of it because there's nothing else you can do without going mad. They give you the rules, you take your oath, you see what comes downstream, and you make the best of it. But the good news is, there's no other thing you ever have to do.

I nodded, warmed to the core, and only later reflected that he had not entirely answered the question.

♦

IT'S EARLY JULY 2011 when I see Alina Nieves through the one-way glass, easing up to join the back of the security line, just outside the courthouse door, edging forward in jeans and a red-and-white blouse, her long raven hair parted in the middle. I know her at once.

It comes back in a slow rush, the early evening the night before she testified, Sonya interviewing her with me adjacent and investigator Steve silent at the end of the table. She was wearing the skirt and blouse for the next day, I remember, having only removed the jacket, and she was calm and steady even in the face of three of us.

Our office is the first right turn in the building, and when she reaches the window she asks for me.

THE YEARS HAVE ONLY ACCENTUATED her luminous face. She's as ethereally beautiful as blown glass, an ice sculpture, a dragonfly. Her serious mouth is bowed into a delicate hope-you-remember-me, and I manage to smile, make that apparent, and gesture to a chair.

"I was in the area, delivering my son to camp," she says. "Thought I should stop."

Somehow I have his name. "Nathan, was it?"

Alina sparkles. "Amazing that you would remember. I had to leave him for two weeks. I didn't do too well saying goodbye."

"I can imagine."

"Kids?" she asks, almost playfully.

"No. And I'd better get a move on."

"Well, never too late." She laughs. "Or too early, in my case."

"This was a trek for you, wasn't it?"

"Yeah, still in Red Bluff. I bought a little house, though."

"Very nice."

"Yeah. Things break, and I'm not exactly handy. But it's good."

"And what do you do?" (A *house?*)

"Bank," she says, with an embarrassed half-smile. "I'm a branch manager. Sounds better than it is."

Then I start to tell her about Sonya, but she already knows. She followed it looking at our local paper online – a task only for the determined – then googled her later and found the obit. *Did she ever really understand?* she asks. *I mean, how it ended?* I mumble equivocally, talk about her guts, talk about the verdict, and then we get to Tom, now Brian. Then back to her life, her boy. Finally a gap, and she brings up Andrew Rodarte.

IT MUST TAKE ME eight minutes, settling back in the chair, to provide a half-minute's worth of bullet points, but she at least feigns interest all the way along. Basically he's down to habeas corpus because he's had his appeal, and other things too. He hasn't sought i yet, but he's bound to. After that fails, eventually he will be entitled to parole hearings, but not to release until they believe he's no longer an unreasonable danger to society, which might be never. He's probably been screwing up in prison. And in any case his first hearing is still decades from now.

Alina exhales, nods. "Thanks. Thought maybe I was being silly and it was an extra drive. Plus I didn't even know if you were still around. But somehow I wanted to come back."

I'm startled, a little touched. "That's a rarity. People we drag here don't usually get attached to us."

"Well, right. I'd never call it fun. But I think I've always wanted to process it a little more." She sighs, looks away, battling something

"See, I realized when I came down that I hated what he did, but the truth was I didn't hate *him*, at the time. He crossed a line, but he may actually have thought I'd like it, that we'd get closer. But then to hear what he had gone on to do – maybe he hadn't meant to kill her, but whatever, he did. He hadn't lost control with me, really, but I could piece it together, that there was a point of no return with him."

"You could sense danger, at some level."

"Looking back, at least. It's not easy to see it through my eyes at the time. I just remember sensing that I was in over my head, didn't have control of the process, and that was enough to scare me off."

"Understandable."

She nods, looks out the window. "So he spooked me, but I don't think I felt my life was in danger. Yet it fit his big excuse, right?"

"Pretty much." A bulb flickers. "Wait, you followed that, too?"

"A little bit. Since I was done as a witness I thought it was OK."

"No, you're right. It is. Well, the bottom line is that he's tucked away, no danger to anyone for a long time now."

She nods. "Good. I just . . . wondered."

I smile. "Nobody's forgotten how you helped the case, nobody's forgotten Haylee, and nobody's forgotten him."

I GET HER CELL NUMBER. To update her, is the idea.

"He's staying where he is."

"Great." Alina stands up with a sunburst smile, her hand outstretched. "Thanks."

Reeling, I grin and repeat history, following her out into our lot. When she backs out in a white Ford Escape, a half-decade old but sparkling clean, I see rosary beads over the rearview mirror. She turns out of the lot and pauses at the stoplight, and she runs her hands through her hair before she pulls out, heading north.

# *35*

**(JPH)**

SOONER OR LATER there is always a petition for writ of habeas corpus – the ancient failsafe and freeroll. This is the evergreen way that the defendant can allege a wrong, even after appeal has come and gone, and there is no real consequence for trying and failing.

To have any prayer of undoing your conviction on habeas corpus, you normally have to show one of two things – that your attorney was harmfully incompetent under the United States Constitution, or that you have some convincing newfound evidence that you didn't commit the crime after all.

At least nine out of ten inmate habeas petitions in state court can't even meet the initial burden of pleading and are denied on the spot. Most of the rest will be rejected after a preliminary response. But a handful put forth enough of a case to be litigated out, or – less often – resolved for some kind of relief.

The higher courts can hear a habeas petition, in theory, but it's best to start in the trial court, where you're at least due a few sentences explaining a denial. Our county, like many, picks a single judge to deal with the petitions. Here it has long been the grandmotherly Marjorie Pearce, who goes all the way back to Ted Stauber's DA days. She's sensible and has always seemed to like me, with a maddening trait – on everyday things like motions to suppress evidence, she'll sometimes smile and twinkle my direction right before she rules the other way. But in the years since I took over the habeas task from Doug, I've never lost an important battle.

RODARTE'S PETITION ARRIVES on the eleventh of May, 2012, though I somehow don't see it until two Mondays later. It's just five single-spaced, handwritten pages, stapled to the envelope it was removed from, date-stamped, with an attachment beneath. It's in rudimentary form, properly sworn, most of the right legal terms, but no real brief – just a couple of basic paragraphs, and beyond it a declaration, two pages long.

I race through it standing up – then, eyes already ablur, the attached letter to me.

I read the letter, then read it again, then the petition and declaration again. The petition alleges neither of the standard statutory grounds for habeas relief, or even close. The declaration –

Dizzy, I set it aside, then thumb down in the neglected stack of mail, past an ABA circular, two DUI reports and a thin legal journal, and I find an order from the Hon. Judge Pearce asking us to respond.

BARELY PAUSING TO THINK, I google a number and dial it. I'm asking the wrong question, though, and leave a message that isn't answered for days. Then I stagger out the front door, jaywalk across the street and collapse on the shadiest bench in Municipal Park.

Ten minutes drift by, fifteen. Shoreline squeals, pigeon flutters, the squeaky wheels of the ice cream cart, a bright red kite bouncing above the trees on a near-invisible string. And the sense of time collapsing.

Eventually I do figure out a starting place.

♦

BRIAN LAUGHS, which I counted on. As a trial dog he would charge a hill, and his instincts usually got him to the summit. I think he tried 70-something cases, believed every one was just and true, and lost maybe four.

But what he really had was a brilliant sense of evidence. While good cops were his soulmates, he read police reports with a jaundiced eye, always wanting more clarity and follow-up, and could see a case from the defense point of view almost as readily as from his own. Then he'd frankly acknowledge the unknowable things to the jury, even as he bundled them into a small parcel, tied it at the end and set it aside, where it would be dwarfed by the steamer trunk full of evidence that *did* make the case.

So after the laugh he sobers right up. "But how does this even fit habeas?"

"It doesn't."

Brian makes a face. "So we oppose on that first?"

I form a rueful smile. "Well . . ."

He cocks his head to the side. "You think there's an actual chance?"

"Well, I can't even form an opinion yet. But I don't think anything in the record would absolutely refute it." I pause. "And – well, crap. He's asking *me* to look."

"Because he doesn't get counsel yet, right?"

"Well, right. Only if there's an order to show cause."

"And he's not demanding it?"

"The reverse. He's telling me he *doesn't* want it."

"Doesn't – ?"

"Flat doesn't want representation, at this point."

Brian is rarely dumbstruck, but it's close. "Be-cause . . . ?"

"I don't know." Smiling. "If it's a fairy tale, maybe he thinks he can sell it better than a lawyer could."

"What about an investigator?"

"I assume he'd take it, but he probably doesn't get that either without an OSC."

"But that's chicken and egg, right?"

"Sort of, though that'd be his argument to make. We're back to whether he's made a prima facie case."

"And this is? Or – it isn't?"

I don't have to do more than wrinkle my nose.

"Who the fuck knows, right?" Now he's nodding, patiently, like we have all day. Tom's worthy heir. "So what's our duty, JP? What's the professional rule?"

"I don't know, down in the weeds. It can't be that we have to follow his lead. We aren't ever his agent." I hitch, take the step. "But you could see it as the right thing."

He's nodding, but hedging too. "Wouldn't it be safer just to go to bat for him about counsel, and then figure out what our duties are?"

"Bound to be, if there's actually a basis. But if he's not asking, and we aren't at OSC stage yet, why would the court jump the gun? And he says he'd say no, clear as day."

"Have you talked to Wade yet?"

I shake my head meekly. "No. Been trying to clear my own cobwebs first."

"OK."

"But there's a starting place, of course. There's a certain somebody we can ask."

Seven years on, it takes him only a couple of seconds. "Aha. Right, of course."

"If she says no, we'll press her hard, try to make sure of it. If she says yes . . ."

"Do we accept it, under the circumstances, and see where it goes from there?"

I just raise an eyebrow – *yes*. And that's good enough.

♦

FIRST, THOUGH, I make a stop, down the hall and around the corner from Brian. Our one windowless office. Celia Kim chose it, likes the door half-closed and the lights half-lit. With Brian out of the regular mix, she's now our best – even if she seems to actively obscure the fact. On the verge of a double-homicide trial herself. A few words pass, not much more, and I hand her the pages and leave the room.

She's through it in three minutes, going back to the early paragraphs when I meander back in, foolish, almost pins and needles.

CELIA SMILES, AS USUAL, with the barest hint of pity in it, nothing personal. She is invariably a pace ahead, and wants to give me a chance to catch up.

"I don't know habeas, of course. But is there really a question?"

"Of our duty?" I squint at her, half-shrug, truly unsure. "Probably not."

It's relief I see in her eyes.

"That's what I'd think."

"And that's your specialty."

# 36

**(JPH)**

JACINTA CANTRELL had finished her diversion soon after trial, then turned up as a bystander witness in a DUI-causing-injury case a couple of years after Rodarte was convicted, but that was it. That case pled out long before trial, and beyond it we got no courtesy updates about her, pro or con – she dropped from our sight, and even Wade's. To the extent she crossed our mind I assumed she'd left the area, either for a degree or something more permanent, though we were dimly aware that her father still owned the Sundown Road property and maintained some local connections. I started to wonder why I hadn't wondered, so to speak.

I'll wait to tell Wade. There's bureaucracy to solve, I'm sure – the case is closed, the die is cast. We'll start in-house.

♦

THERE'S A NEW LEAD DOG in our four-officer Bureau of Investigation, Steve Waterford having retired. He's a former detective sergeant from Kern County named Craig Hustedt, and he's already shown a genius for finding people.

There are two phone numbers for her in Probation's records, neither of help, and an address. So that first afternoon Craig gears up.

"Well, I'll go out to the last known."

I think for a minute. "I'll come with you."

FULLY BRIEFED and comfortably silent, sunglasses on, Craig drums his fingers along the steering wheel of the aging white Taurus, a rhythm in his head.

I've lost track. Will I know her right away, seven years on? Will she know *me*?

At length we come to a faltering road past a couple of the higher-end wineries, and I've been down it. I know where the branch-off is too, onto an eroded, well-worn dirtway called Summit Camp Road. It veers gently down toward a creek bed, then along it.

After a half-mile in a shroud of foothill pine and buckeye, there's a low place and the road cuts across the trickling water, which looks ripe to become the Johnstown Flood in wet winters but apparently doesn't. Soon we're down into a small valley.

The road bends and swirls, gradually regaining altitude, and at length we pass another dirt road, branching left, better tracked – the artery, it turns out, from the Hammonds end of the county.

We keep going another mile, mile and a half. The road is overrun with squirrels, a rabbit here and there. Something flashes that might be a raccoon.

Abruptly we come to it. There's an iron fence and gate, a driveway, a paddock to the right and a wide white house on a rise, maybe a football field from the road. Money is evident. The property is elegant, well-fortified and well-cleared – the forest of dry oak and high brush at the perimeter is all too easy to imagine ignited.

"Looks like someplace an asshole would own," Craig mutters, for no good reason at all.

CRAIG PUSHES THE BUTTON at the gate.

"Yes?" A woman's voice, middle-aged, many miles on it.

"Good afternoon. We're here from the District Attorney's office. Wondered if we could trouble you a minute."

"Umm, can I ask – what about?"

"We're hoping to locate Miss Jacinta Cantrell."

You can almost hear the flinch, and the pause excites me – "she no longer lives here" would have rolled right off the tongue. A moment later she buzzes us in.

THE BUZZER'S NAME is Cari Lett, and I place her within ten seconds – she's a counselor, formerly one of the program managers at the Drug Court, which I manned for a few months in my earlier years. Like all of them she'd lived it. In the doorway of Cantrell's successor house she is craggy and bottle-blonde, with a wandering left-arm tattoo and a California poppy in her hair. It's the season. She's well into middle age by now, but looks little different than I remember her, as if the years are catching up to the face she already had.

She greets me like she remembers me well, but then even reformed tweakers shoot angles by reflex. Invites us in.

"Nice place," Craig says.

"Well, I just caretake," she says, closing the door. The foyer is huge, the living room and kitchen beyond it vast, bright, tiled. She leads us to a set of stools around a white center island. "Land, animals and people."

I TAKE THE LEAD. "For Mr. Cantrell, is that right?"

The smile is just slightly forced. "Well, he's not up here much. So I mostly deal with his business manager Brad."

"I see. And what about Jacinta? Is she living here too?"

"Well, kinda sorta." She's nervous, and suddenly it's obvious why – she's still on the payroll to make sure Jacinta stays clean, and the two of us are every clue to the contrary. "It's her official address, and she's got a bedroom and a closet full of clothes. But she does a lot of coming and going."

"Why is that?"

"Her job takes her away about ten days a month, event organizing. Then she takes trips of her own – San Fran, the Rockies. And lately she's been spending a lot of time at Todd's place. Her boyfriend."

"Todd?"

"Todd Karchner. You know his dad." We do – Bob Karchner owns the sporting-goods store, two fast-food franchises and several dockside operations, spent a term as a county supervisor, puzzled everyone by not running for reelection. Wags said he was too rich to take an interest in bribes. "He has a place in Hammonds. West Hills. Dad has him running the big store."

"Has she stayed here lately?"

"Well, two nights last week. Monday and Tuesday, I think it was." She gathers her courage. "Can I ask why you're looking for her? No trouble, is there?"

"No trouble." I go further than I need to. "We just had something to ask her about an old case."

"Her own case?" Her face is stricken.

"No, no. Her friend's. Who was – killed."

"Oh Lord. Rodarte. I should have known." But she's relieved.

"It'll be quick," Craig promises.


I LOOK OUT the wide front windows. "Does she ride the horses?"

"Often as not," she says, and now new fear leaps into her eyes. "Should have told you first that she's stopped by today, just gone for a ride around the hill. You see Daisy, brown-and-white mare?"

"No, haven't crossed paths."

"How long ago did she leave?" Craig asks.

"Fifteen, 20 minutes. Probably take her another half-hour."

"Ah, OK."

"You're welcome to wait. Get you something to drink?"

"Nah, thanks. We'll just hang in the car."

She nods, maybe half-relieved, and then I hear my own voice. "Where's the path she took?"

"I think she took the trail across the road. Loops up past the lake, over the crest, back along the creek, winds up right out back."

"Lake?"

"Shadow Lake. Just up the hill."

SURE ENOUGH – a fleck of blue on the county map.

"I'm just gonna stroll up there a minute," I mutter, closing the glove box.

"You got time," he agrees mildly. "I'll camp here."

The path is a gentle incline, littered with tread marks from county trucks, crumpled Bud Light cans, horseshit aplenty. It climbs a fair way, around a bend, and then suddenly I'm looking down at a perfect shallow bowl below the looming hill, with the slow late spring light fading gold upon the water, maybe a hundred and fifty yards across – a tiny auxiliary reservoir. Human-contrived or not, it sparkles and it moves, ever so slightly, and there comes a memory and an echo from long, long ago – in fact a place on a hilltop in Los Angeles, a soundless city far below, that *simulated* just this, and even that was enduring.

I stand for a minute, hands in my pockets, forgetting Craig and Jacinta Cantrell – even Haylee Branch – in a cloud of utter silence. And then, as a county-stocked fish breaks it by surfacing, the question washes over me: *How can everyone on earth be somewhere else?*

Another minute along the trail angles down into a valley, and I see the horse a quarter-mile away, and a tousle of hair beneath a cowgirl's hat. But even if it's her, and even if I closed the distance, I can't interview her alone, so I head back down the way I came, psyched up.

Craig is leaning against the car.

"They texted. Jacinta says 20 more minutes, come in and wait."

IT'S BEEN ABOUT THAT, I guess, when Cari Lett peers out the back door, puzzled.

"Well, that don't fit."

"What's that?"

"I see Daisy . . . but no Jacie."

We follow her out across a huge patio, through a small rose garden, down the shady incline. A couple of home runs from the house she reaches the riderless mare on a dirt path, talks to it, pivots her head one direction and another. In a minute she nods our way.

It's easy enough to see where Jacinta dismounted, and the bootprints head down into a gentle hollow.

Craig, in the lead, passes down through the wash. I trail along pointlessly as a minute or two passes, and then we hear the engine. Scrambling to a vantage point and looking back toward the house, we see a white two-door pulling around the side and up the long driveway, then turning onto the battered roadway and making noisy tracks south.

A SIDE DOOR IS AJAR – Jacinta had run in to grab her purse.

Cari Lett is quivering and apologetic – did not mean to tip her off, can't understand what "triggered" her, no red flags about her "recovery." We just shrug, not too kindly. I doubt all of it.

Craig calls the sheriff, they run DMV and he confirms the car, a tricked-out white Infiniti. Then he catches Todd Karchner in the store.

"Claims they fought last night, hasn't seen her today, and doesn't know where she'd go. Promises to tell her she isn't in any trouble."

It's enough for now.

Cari twitches us out the door. "I'll tell you if she calls, for sure."

"Thanks."

CRAIG FROWNS as we buckle our belts. "She thought we had a warrant when we showed up – I'm sure of it. And she thought we were gonna find something."

"That fits," I agree. "No way she could guess the real reason, and she knows we weren't just passing through the neighborhood."

He nods. "I'll call her back, squeeze a little. Keep her spooked."

# 37

**(JPH)**

THE INFINITI TURNS UP the next afternoon in the parking lot for Wilder Falls, down near the southern county border, well off the beaten track.

I'm told of jumbled footprints, apparently all hers, around the car. At least one set leads to the pavement, others less clear. There's no car damage, no blood, no signs of scuffle in the dirt – there *shouldn't* be. The deputy who noticed the car did poke around a little, but it's a stretch of dense pine forest that has managed to avoid burning these last many decades, not much underbrush, difficult to track.

*She walked to the road, got picked up,* I assure myself – even as I ask, carefully, how far they looked. *She was tweaking, thinks we know. She dumped the car, she called a ride.*

Todd Karchner is cooperative again, but he has nothing but a missed call, sends a screenshot of his call log. The time is right – maybe an hour after she bolted – but that's all. *Did they go to the falls – could she – Christ, could she have – ?*

BRIAN AND I go huddle with Wade, give him a thumbnail sketch. I can boil it down to a couple of paragraphs.

And he listens. He has the *next* one to worry about, like all cops, but he's now the detective sergeant, and Rodarte and Haylee Branch come up every time we talk.

Our pitch is simple – Jacinta is soul-scared of something, we can't reach Frank Cantrell and Cari Lett has nothing useful to add. So Wade buys it as a missing-person case, and his higher-ups will too. If nothing else, I guess, everyone can imagine the lawsuit from Cantrell if Jacinta turns up bleached bones a few months on.

Then he softens. "And when we get her, tell me what she says."

I nod, grateful. "For certain."

♦

THE NEXT MORNING I ride along, to the falls, as a rook deputy drives and a newly minted corporal asks me questions about criminal procedure. Four members of the county's volunteer search-and-rescue team, strong, tan and worthy, follow in their own SUV. And we spend four solid hours to find nothing.

Quickly forgotten, I trail many yards behind, baffled by their search techniques, strangely confident it's pointless. But when we circle out to the falls I do feel relief. There's no corpse at the base of the cliffs, and it's plain that for all the noise it makes, the falling water loses much of its force in the deep trough at its base. This means that the power of the gently-sloping stream that flows out wouldn't be enough to take a body any major distance, and in any case the bed is clogged with branch and rock.

Nor is there a scrap of fabric, a hairband, a sock. Jacinta, however scared, did not jump. She panicked and called someone. She ran away.

♦

IT'S FRIDAY, TWO MORNINGS LATER, when Jacinta's father calls back. Wade and I had both left messages, but he and Cantrell had always loathed each other. By plain good luck I've never spoken to him myself.

I have a roar of fear as I reach for the phone, threefold: He may have bad news to give me, or he's been out of the loop and expects to hear it from me. Or – likeliest of all – he's just enraged at the unanswered questions.

"John Howland."

"John, Frank Cantrell." To my surprise his voice is light, almost facetious. "I gather you're part of a hunt for my daughter."

"Yes, yes sir." I'm groping for a notepad. "As we've advised you by message, she is regarded as a missing person. There has been a search –"

"Don't speculate," he says, and pauses. "Jacinta is safe."

I literally shudder in relief, the gathered dread starting to ebb out of me. "Is she in your hands, sir?"

"After a fashion."

"Out of our area?"

He lets it settle. "Someplace safe. Let's leave it there for now."

"Right now," I repeat, almost blankly. "But, if you would –"

"What?"

I clear my throat and try to do my job.

"Well, the fact is the sheriff has an open missing-person case. So we very much need to close it out, and we also need to ask her about a separate issue dating back to what happened in 2003, which was the reason we went to your property in the first place."

"I appreciate that. I understand the job you do, and of course we want to end your search. But for right now, it's her safety and state of mind that matter most."

"I guess I don't understand." The loaded question. "Safety how?"

"That I can't expand on," he says. "Her – well-being. Both her physical and mental state."

"Well," I mumble. "Great to know she's all right. I'll be happy to stop thinking about the alternatives."

"Right. And you're doing what needs doing. So am I."

Frustrated, impotent, I make it worse. "The point to alert you to, though, is that we may have to speak to her. Conveniently if we can. But we are confronted with something that's big and it's unexpected, and getting answers to just a few questions would be extremely important to us."

"Understood. But I don't anticipate her returning to your jurisdiction right away. And I don't believe she is of a mind to speak to you by telephone right now. Your appearance, I would say, rekindled something very deep and dark for her. She still has a lot of trouble with this case – as you would expect, I'm sure. Now she's calm and safe and getting her bearings back. It won't take a long time, but it won't be overnight."

"We'd be happy to come to you, if that's what it takes."

"And what, slap a subpoena on her? No, I don't see that."

"Sir, I don't know whether a subpoena would even be necessary. This is threshold information, and we're far from any sort of hearing. But please understand that she can be subpoenaed anywhere in this state, if it becomes necessary."

"Well, you'll have a challenge with that," he says, his voice still light. "Is my daughter facing criminal charges?"

"No, no."

"Is she under investigation?"

"Not at all. It's simply –"

"Under subpoena at this moment?"

"Not at this time. No sir."

"Well, then. I think we're in the working-together phase."

BRIAN GOES INSTA-RED. "That fuck beetle! Who does the jackoff think he is?"

"Maybe just a dad after all," I say doubtfully. "Maybe it's her more than him."

"Well, I know she was a shaky reed, back then. Tweaker, fragile psyche, spoiled brat. You reckon she still is?"

"No clue, except that we haven't filed charges on her for the last seven years."

I SCRAWL THOUGHTS at all hours, but it all flows from question one. Confirm or deny. I expect to believe a denial. I'm sure I'll believe her if she tells me it's true.

WADE IS MADDER than Brian, but much less surprised.

"Not asking your help," I add, after mutual rants. "Just keeping you in the loop."

He raises his eyebrows. "You can ask."

◆

EARLY THE NEXT WEEK Cantrell calls back with an offer.

"Provide the questions, John, and Jacinta will answer them by way of declaration."

*Fuck no*, I think instantly. *This is not a negotiation.*

"I appreciate that, sir, but that's awkward and it may not meet our needs, as law. At least not in the longer term."

"Why wouldn't it?"

"Well, the question is the foundation. We'd need information like the date and place of making, strong identifying detail, sworn under penalty of perjury. We would have to aver that the doc we provide is authentic and true, and they could still object." I'm babbling, really – this is a rabbit hole. "I'm not sure how to make that assurance."

"She will swear it, of course, and date it. Notarize it, if you like."

"Well, I appreciate that, but then it becomes evidence the judge may or may *not* accept without live testimony behind it."

"Hmm."

"Under these circumstances –"

"What circumstances? No jackass judge can tell me I can't protect my daughter when she is not under the jurisdiction of the court and doesn't have an order to appear, magic robe or not. This is America."

I clench, unclench, make a last effort. "It's just process, Mr. Cantrell. That necessary bureaucratic stuff to do our job, get it lined up, get to the truth – the things we have to do. Again, we may not even need her to act as a formal witness."

He grunts, barely pauses. "So what's your bottom line?"

"Well, it's getting the questions asked, and answered, I hope. They're simple ones. Then *maybe* it goes to court, or maybe not. But every passing day ups the chance that her answer will be seen as tainted, just because of her choosing to run away and stay away."

"Hmm."

"And then, third, there's the fear that's worse yet." I hear myself sigh. "Which is that we *might* be dealing with a true story – and if there's any chance of that, your daughter is in the best position to know. We're not out to punish her if she left out something important, I promise you that. But we need to know."

"I get that." Cantrell pauses, drags it out. I swear we are almost there. Then his flat, affectless business voice. "But look, John, you had your crack at that, back in the day. What I can do now is get you a plain answer in writing. You're going to have to make it work."

I have a capacity for fierce, sputtering rage, and it's never done me a lick of good. Maybe I wait three seconds – nah, less.

"Sir, *please* don't attempt to dictate to me. You do not hold the power here, and neither does your daughter. *I* hold the power. *This office* holds the power. You are not above the law. I can bring you here I can bring Jacinta here. We know where to find you, wherever you've put her. We can sit on your *house*. We can go to the *press* . . ."

Somewhere in here I realize I'm talking to myself, so I smash the handset of the telephone against a filing cabinet. Rather to my surprise the cabinet takes the worst of it.

THE NEXT DAY, as it turns out, he does call back, asks for "somebody senior." They pass Cantrell to Assistant District Attorney Doug Lahtinen, terse and windowless, and maybe it rattles him.

She's in some kind of rehab, Cantrell explains, strangely halting Soon done. And when she's through it he will bring her in.

Brian tells me the guy's a *double* fuck beetle, but I'll settle for it And two weeks later she does come in.

♦

I EXPECT SHE'LL TURN UP with her father, and probably a lawyer too, but in the end she's delivered in a silver SUV, and climbs out alone. I'm watching from my window as it pulls up, lets her out and rolls down to the end of the parking lot to wait.

The differences are clear enough, and interesting. Jacinta has gained a healthy few pounds, now light blonde and rounder of face. And rather to my surprise she seems to recognize me.

She's dressed in a routine, professional way, and has a sort of holdover glow, the residue of expensive rehab. It's equally clear that she is scared.

We've settled around my desk, our victim advocate at her elbow. Craig starts recording. And the answer is yes.

♦

WHICH LEAVES TWO MAIN QUESTIONS. One's out of my hands, the other just occurred to me.

It's been a little while, I guess. The lid is askew, and there's dust on the plastic cover of Volume 1. That's the starting place. I crack it open, spend two minutes. Then dig farther down the box.

CRAIG IS A SPORT, fires up the Taurus again.

"Fun's just getting started," I say, not meaning it at all.

"Oh, I'm here all week."

It's a shorter drive. This time we're lucky.

# 38

**(JPH)**

IT WON'T BE Judge Pearce, in the end. With so much still unanswered I need more time, and by now Rodarte has decided to ask for an investigator. So she issues an order approving both requests, and in it she explains that she will retire the following month.

Such news normally leaks in advance, but this didn't – nor the next part: since no successor has yet been assigned, the case will return to its point of origination. The Honorable Anthony J. Vanzetta.

By then, though, I'm already reeling, because the appointed investigator is none other than ex-Sheriff's Department detective Mitch Marks, of the long-lost Danny Tarrant robbery case. Marks finally *did* fuck up for good, got fired for cause and didn't even challenge it, and was too lazy to go start over somewhere else. So he's been living on scraps as a defense investigator, and now he's next on the running list for appointment. That's how they all stay afloat, of course, and in any case the alternatives are precious few – we've never had more than a handful to choose from, and far fewer who were worth a shit.

"Careful what you wish for," Brian cracks.

◆

AS THE NEXT DEADLINE NEARS, in mid-July, Rodarte has done nothing to supplement his cryptic petition for habeas relief, almost certainly because Marks has done nothing.

I've learned enough to know that I can't oppose it outright – and not nearly enough to believe. So I suggest that Vanzetta issue an order to show cause, the defense's first objective, and set an initial status hearing a few weeks out.

Rodarte could demand that a different judge hear it, but he simply joins the request and asks to be transported from prison for the hearing. And he gripes for a solid page about his appointed investigator.

A WEEK LATER Vanzetta summons Marks to court. I'm in there just to watch.

"You've been able to pursue the identity question for Mr. Rodarte?"

"Well, the cellie first." No cellmate is actually involved. "Figure that leads to the rest of it."

"All right. What result?"

"It's a moving target, I guess, yeronner. Lotta records to dig through, tryin to work through the AKAs, goin off the description, lookin for the name."

"So no luck yet?"

"Not just yet, Judge."

"You've obtained jail records from Palomar County?"

"Well, gettin started."

"Subpoena still pending?"

"Little less official. I know a few folks up that way. They did some lookin for me, got me some possible names, but I don't have the whole picture."

"You have names to pursue, on Mr. Rodarte's behalf?"

"Got me a couple, but haven't tracked 'em down yet."

"And why not?"

The question seems to baffle him. "Well, still got sorting to do."

"You, or them?"

"Us both, I guess."

Vanzetta, at his limit, glares down.

"You do realize this court has already issued an order to show cause, do you not, Mr. Marks?"

Marks goes from pink to red to maroon, and frantically clears his throat. "I don't, sir, you don't have any cause. I'm not tryin to put one over on you, sir. I'll swear under oath."

MARKS SHUFFLES OUT in a blaze of sweat, still technically on the case. Rodarte hadn't actually demanded someone else, and there may be no better option to provide. Vanzetta turns to me, desperate.

"Have you made *any* sense of this?"

We're *ex parte* and off the record, but there's a simple answer. "A little, Your Honor."

As he nods I have no trouble reading his eyes. *It shouldn't work this way, but you're the best hope we have.*

"Any progress you may make will be a great service to the Court."

♦

THERE'S PROGRESS the next week, and then we get to August.

# 39

## (JPH)

ALINA NIEVES has never tried fried mozzarella, so on the first Saturday in September I order it in the cheery tavern at the Indian resort an hour north of home, where we have developed a curious habit of meeting.

Whatever this is, it happened in increments. There were a few more emails first, then a long phone call. She asked to see the opinion affirming his conviction, which interested me – I ran her off a copy. I didn't particularly want to hang up the call.

A few days later she called again to say that she had something she wanted to tell me, and to show me. Sort of about the case.

So we met in the middle, a Starbucks in this hotel late on a weekday afternoon. I was greeted by a fleeting glow of a smile, and she gave me a card that Andrew Rodarte had sent her a week after she broke up with him.

SHE WAS EMBARRASSED. She had misplaced it at the time, then found it in a box in her closet thirteen years later. No bombshell, just him saying sorry, saying he cared for her, saying he'd always messed up good things, that he'd never known how to do things right. Hinting at another chance but not asking for it.

I was still reading when Alina abruptly crumbled, turned away and buried her head in her sleeve.

"Hey . . ."

"Sorry. Didn't see that coming." She daubed her eyes. "It's just, I wonder sometimes how things happen the way they do."

"You're still thinking it could have been you?"

"Sure, of course. I didn't answer the card, but what if I had? Would I never have gone to college? Would my son have never lived? Then I'm thinking about *her*. I do that a lot."

"Just reflecting?"

She nods. "Yeah, the stuff with no answers. Like what if I had more nerve, told people this charming handsome guy had a dark side to look out for? I'm not sure I even thought it was a crime, what he did, but it scared me. And maybe I could have shaken him up, scared *him* somehow. Like hey, watch yourself. And then . . . maybe –"

I reassured her, watching, wondering, and we lingered an hour or so. At the end there was a cheery parting – *hope I see you again sometime* – my friendly emphasis on *again*, no suggestive stress on the *see you*. We're twelve years apart – rounding down – and, long ago, she was our witness to protect. The Contenta County District Attorney's Office won't need her again, but we did once.

BUT THE NEXT MONTH there came a follow-up text, and she pitched a return visit, for a strange new reason: she was thinking about law school, wanted my thoughts.

In the mirror I noticed every sag and creak and gray hair, but this ended up *two* hours, two drinks across a round pub table, long detours from our starting place – and something that carried over.

So there was a third, at my intrepid suggestion. This was a Friday. I had books and materials, Torts and Civil Procedure and LSAT prep. She had scanned the appellate opinion, wanted to give it back, didn't want her son coming across it.

Soon we were past all that, deep into likes and hopes and histories. Her son, trending tall and athletic ("at least he got one thing from his dad"). Home economics. Comedies. National parks of the West.

I waited a long time to order a third drink, and when I did she said she hoped I wasn't driving back.

"Yeah, I decided to camp here tonight." I laughed aloud, at nothing funny. "In case I lose my better judgment."

Somehow she laughed at the laugh. "My own sometimes comes into question."

# Cold Record

TONIGHT, ABOUT OUR SEVENTH – we've seen each other nowhere else – she takes a tiny, delicate nibble when the crusty cheese arrives, flinches a bit. Dunk it in the sauce, I say, to balance it out. Then it's pretty much crunchy pizza, but lower in carbs.

I smile as I say the last part – she struggles to stay above a hundred pounds. I've urged nachos and beer and cheesecake on her, these months, to stink-eye and laughs. She's been eyeing the grilled tilapia as she sips her mojito.

I've told her nothing beyond the bare minimum, these several months – that Rodarte made a claim, and we're taking a deep look. In some way, perhaps, I'm protecting her; in another, remote way, I'm protecting the record.

It's been fun, too, the little game of it. And now I can tell it all. But first she needs to read what he wrote, so I hand it to her and take the long stroll to the john.

I'VE LEARNED SHE READS everything twice, and slowly, so when I reemerge I know there's a further moment to kill. I look across the soaring open-air lobby as the incongruous cigarette fumes waft upward, suddenly almost too tired to move, and listen to three-quarters of a Journey song cranked out by the cover band at the far end of the floor.

As I amble back, her eyes are still on it, now restless – she is biting her lower lip. I'm wondering how much she already figured out. Then a quick head-turn to me . . . She lifts up the page, now, then casually sets it aside.

Her eyes are bright. "Oh my God. But –"

"Right." We have all evening.

I grab it back and read it through again myself, as if I haven't already committed nearly every word to memory.

## SWORN DECLARATION OF ANDREW MARCELO RODARTE IN SUPPORT OF PETITION FOR WRIT OF HABEAS CORPUS

1.    I was convicted of first-degree murder for killing Miss Haylee Branch, age 20, in Contenta County, CA, in 2003. I testified at trial that I killed Miss Branch, by inadvertent strangulation during consensual sexual contact.

2.    This testimony was false, I did not in fact kill Miss Branch, not accidentally, not intentionally and not personally. Yet I am also not innocent of her death.

3.    Miss Branch was strangled in front of me by a white male I knew only as Rust, aged 40s, who I met through a jail friend in Palomar County.

4.    The friend from jail, a mellow Mexican guy I knew as Cheeto, did favors for me when he got out, while I was still in on a probation violation. He had a long last name I never really learned, I think it also began with C but can't remember it now, even though I recall many things about him.

5.    He had mentioned having links to some biker-type outfit up there possibly involved with meth, though he didn't look or act biker at all, but he brought up a friend named Rust.

6.    I learned on release that "Rust" wanted me to drop him off with a package in the Bay Area on my way back south. The idea was paying back Cheeto's favor. Feeling pressured, I agreed, and brought Rust, whose true name I never learned. I assumed the package was drugs but do not know.

7.    On November 21 2003 we reached the Contenta County area by taking back roads across the mountains. We did this to avoid police contact. I met Miss Cantrell at the mart, and assisted her as described, following her home at her request. The unmentioned fact is that Rust was with me.

8.    At the home I met Haylee Branch. She called herself Lee. I found her intelligent, beautiful and kind, but she also seemed unhappy.

9.    Rust and Jacinta quickly became drunk, and she began to pass out. I went outside with Haylee, and we talked. We connected with each other.

10.  Meanwhile Rust had drugged Jacinta, and when we came back in he then drugged Haylee, without my wish or knowledge. I believe it was by way of beer, as to both of them. Haylee also then passed out, unconscious.

11.  Rust showed me the drugs he had used. When Haylee was out he took her to the guest house, and demanded I follow. I did, out of fear, though I fantasized that I would rescue her.

12.  In the guest house he raped her. She was unconscious and did not consent. It occurred directly in front of me. I could have easily have stopped it. I did not, I did nothing.

13.  Then, after quite a few minutes, she began to wake.

14.  To protect himself, Rust strangled her to death with his hands and then my jacket, which I had removed. I stood still as this happened, never going to her aid. I did nothing. She died because I did not intervene.

15.  We fled the property and the area in a panic, barely pausing to think. But once south we ended up delivering the package. A senior biker, having learned something happened from Rust himself, held me at gunpoint and threatened me and my family if I incriminated Rust, or them in any way.

16.  Rust had given them my name on the way down, and they knew where my mother and sister lived. I said I understood, I left, I never mentioned Rust, and never saw either of them again.

17.  I am now prepared to tell the truth at last, in part because I have learned that "Rust," name still unknown, has recently died, and I no longer fear the threats. But I have also waited to tell the truth because my imprisonment is just.

18.  He got away with murder, but I also accept deep moral blame, and am asking only that my conviction be modified in light of the truth.

19.  I will explain all of this under oath if the court were to convene a hearing on this petition, and would then make my request of the court. I am neither innocent nor the man portrayed at trial. I'm haunted and I believe in truth as the final goal.

AND A COVER LETTER, personal to me. Asking *me* to get him to the starting gate – to put a name on Rust, and to go ask Jacinta Cantrell to remember.

♦

AFTER THE BLOWUP with Cantrell, and before Jacinta came in to answer, Brian had reared his contrarian head. It's late some afternoon, he's fully reclined, his feet on the desk. He's been thinking.

"Let's say Rodarte somehow proved it – that Rust is real. Wouldn't that just leave us one handsome lad and one sloppy ball-sack of a biker tromping around this palatial abode, and *one of the two* doing rape and killing? And if they're both in the room, wasn't Rodarte aiding and abetting?"

"Possible, but we'd still have to show knowledge and intent. If he went there with no idea, then really did nothing but stand and watch the other guy kill her, he's not good for it."

"What if he helped out the rape? Where's that leave us?"

"Maybe we could have argued murder was reasonably foreseeable." Time to grin. "But, uh, they acquitted him of rape."

"Aw fuck." He laughs at himself, as always. "There is that. But he'd still be copping to being right there and then driving the getaway car, wouldn't he? Getting the second shithead outta Dodge?"

"Yeah, but same thing – not enough if he had no plan to kill. Gotta have knowledge to aid and abet. Accept all that and he's probably just an accessory."

"*Pffft*. Maybe. But why should we buy his version anyway?"

"We don't have to. Sort of interesting if it's a lie, though, because he's clearly saying he's still liable for a big crime. He's hoping for a lesser, no doubt, but it's pretty unusual to run a habeas and admit guilt in the same breath."

"Maybe so. But the jury never woulda let him off as an accessory, even if he could prove this other guy was there. Not up here. They'd buy the rape and say BS, you both did it, probably took turns on her."

"Possible, sure. But if they heard about both guys, a lot of jurors might want to think that the skuzzy biker was the heavy and the handsome kid was just along for the ride, wouldn't they? And if somebody buys that now, we can see where we are. He's way past his max sentence for just being an accessory, and all the extra years would eat up parole, unless there's some last-ditch bone we get. Murder gets tossed and he probably strolls out free and clear."

Brian twitches his head, disgusted. "That's a bracing fucking notion, ain't it?"

"I'd say it is."

"So you want to keep digging. Or think we should."

I reflect. "Both."

Doubt, but no hesitation. "Then dig, man."

♦

SO FIRST JACINTA, who hated remembering.

Craig's there, in the background, and our victim advocate silent next to Jacinta, a calming hand at her left wrist when things get rough.

But *yes*. Right before it all went dark, there was a second man in Rodarte's white Suburban, and he must have come along to the house.

I DON'T PLAN to explain.

"OK. That's where we needed to start." I smile lightly, catch her eyes. All friends here. "What else can you remember?"

"Well, I remember *him* a lot better, and everything I said about him was true. Andrew – Fuckface, I just call him, or Psycho – I hate saying his name. Who he was, where we met, what I said. Please know, whatever I tell you, I never lied about any of that, to you or at trial. Everything about him was true.

"The earlier part is pretty clear. Haylee's there with me, I drag her down to the store, she stays in the car, I find this good-looking guy at random. And he's pretty mellow when I come up on him, and he says OK to buying it.

"I remember wanting him to come back to the house. I can't even remember if I was actually short on cash, or just lied about it. But at some point, probably at his truck, I tell him he needs to follow me home. And – I guess he goes along with it."

"So there was an ulterior motive?"

"That's how I operated. I know I'd had partying in mind that night before she called, and that's why we had to go get beer. Lee didn't care – she'd have drunk diet iced tea all night and talked about books. But she was an afterthought. Of course I would've wanted to add a hot guy into the mix." She shakes her head. "If he wanted my space-cadet ass, I'd've fucked him."

"And Haylee wouldn't have liked the idea?"

"Well, I remember telling myself maybe she would. But that was a bullshit excuse, because I knew what she was like – she was shy really, and wouldn't drink enough to let go, sure wasn't gonna do some strange guy at random, no matter what he looked like. She always stayed in control, aware. It was just who she was.

"And I had to know it wasn't what she wanted, she just wanted to hang out that night. None of it stopped me. I get him to follow me home." Jacinta exhales. "But, right. There was another guy in his truck, and I never told anybody about him."

CRAIG AND I are nodding in tandem.

"Now I only saw him for a minute, at the truck. I know it was quick. We didn't interact, and then almost everything does fade out at the house. All I had after that were these little random snapshots, like *pieces* of memory. That's all true. I don't think I ever lied about it, an the whole world was fuzzy, I didn't remember everything at once. But, over time he kinda started to come back."

"Do you remember what he looked like?"

"Well, kinda. He's on the passenger side, it's at night, I think the dome light's on, but I see him. I remember he looked a lot older than the fuckin first guy. White dude with a scruffy beard and a red face, sort of a mullet. Kinda fat and grungy. Not too much more than that."

I strain to sound casual. "You didn't happen to get his name?"

Jacinta shakes her head. "If I did I don't remember."

More casually still. "You never heard the name Rust, did you?"

"For him, you mean? No – or at least not when it could stick."

Jacinta picks at her manicured nails, faces up to it. "But I do know he came along to the house. I realized that pretty early on. I mean, it makes sense because he was in the truck, but it's also because his laugh came back to me. Almost everything's blank, I really *didn't* lie, but I remember him laughing at something, there at the house. Being loud. Obviously we were drinking. I *think* he was there in the living room, with us. But that's all."

NOW JACINTA LOOKS squarely at me, and her voice shakes. "Are you saying – could he be the one who dosed me? And could he have been – part of it? Both of them?"

"We aren't sure yet." I wait a minute, trying to judge her resilience. "And we don't know who he was. But if we pin him down, do you think there's a chance you'd recognize a picture?"

"I could try." Now she makes a wry, hesitant face. "How bad have I fucked up? Am I in trouble? I'll take what I deserve."

I muster a smile. "No, that's not the point. And if you answered every question honestly, you didn't do much wrong. But can you explain why you never mentioned him?"

Jacinta turns her head, wraps her arms taut around her chest. Thinks it over. Shakes her head reluctantly.

"Not that well, I guess. It was . . . like a bomb went off in the middle of that night. I remembered him at the store, sort of remembered going to his truck. But after that it's just random flickers.

"Then I'm out for a million years, and even when I come back it's all super-dim. And when I wake up in the hospital, practically the first thing that happens is they shove these photos at me, and I recognize the first guy. I didn't even have a name for him in my head, I don't think, and I don't have the whole picture, but he's there.

"So they're happy, they ask if I met him at a liquor store, I say yeah, and they ask if I remember being with Haylee and I say I do from earlier in the evening, we went to get beer but it all goes dark. Which definitely *isn't* what they want to hear. And . . . then they tell me – about her." Jacinta bows her head, bites her lip. "I wanted to disappear – I wanted to kill myself, then and there – I *knew*. I knew I'd caused it. I felt like I cried for a week. I couldn't even move."

"And you weren't asked about anybody else?"

"They never mentioned anything about a second guy that day, and I don't even know if I would have remembered him then. And next thing I can tell, it's like the case is solved.

"The main detective guy comes back a couple days later, but again it's all specific stuff about the first guy, I guess trying to check whatever his story was. And I'm still no help, because it all went dark so fast.

"At some point I do start to remember seeing the second guy, and after a while I can kinda recall him at the house. But I tell myself they'd have asked me if he was important, and the more time goes by, the more scared I get about saying something. I start thinking that if I bring the other guy up this late, I'll be in deep shit for holding back and it might mess up the case against the first guy, which sounded totally clear. So I decided to stay quiet unless somebody directly asked me, and no one ever did. And I sure wasn't gonna bring it up at the trial."

I NOD ALONG. "So you've held that memory for nine years?"

She makes a half-smile, a rueful click. "Yup. It never went away. You nailing him was endless relief – it's like I knew then that Lee could sleep. But I'd always kinda thought it might come back to haunt me, because I realized nobody seemed to know about the other guy, and how was that possible, what if they were *both* involved in it?

"Then all these years later you guys show up, Cari texts me and says you've got questions about the case, the nightmare. And it's like my worst fear coming true, so I panicked. Somehow I knew you'd found out, I was to blame, and it meant I'd fucked up all over again."

"Well, we'd have understood. But I get being scared."

Jacinta sighs. "You should understand what a fucking catastrophe I was, back when she was killed. I didn't tell you, but I'd actually gotten caught selling prescription drugs in my high school in San Francisco, if you ever wondered why I was up here. Nobody told the cops, but the school kicked me out.

"My dad had just finished getting the house built, thinking he was gonna make wine on the side, and he thought I'd be safer here than among some new batch of jillionaire kids. Pretty ironic. He got me settled, came up almost every weekend at first, then gave me more slack. Did his best. But I was a fuckup, and it didn't improve with extra freedom and a party estate."

Now she raises her head, but her voice wavers.

"Then . . . I made this friend out of nowhere, who's smart, normal, sensible, even kind of wants to teach me about life – like how to get your act together, not be an idiot forever. She's also gorgeous, more beautiful that I'd ever be, but I couldn't even be jealous of that, because she barely seemed to care herself. And she wasn't like anybody else I knew. She looked at me in this way of her own. She didn't care I had money – she liked me for me, and I *loved* her, those days.

"But when she left for college I practically forgot about her. And when she comes back to see me, to see *me*, because she cared about me

319

– I get her killed.  First because I had to go get beer, second 'cause I invited him home.  A guy who rapes and kills, and drugged me too. She gets murdered at my own house while I'm not even awake to know."  She finally unwraps her arms.  "I brought her *death*."

I JUST WATCH HER for several beats.  "Well, it's not quite that simple.  Things never are."

"Maybe not, but – it starts with me, and now somehow it was gonna end with me too.  I panicked.  Messed you up, freaked out my dad.  He figured I'd relapsed.  But I've never told him the truth either." She pauses, back in charge of herself.  "Will I be a witness again?"

"Too soon to say.  First we have to find him, ask some questions." I don't mind her assuming he's still alive.  "Could be there's some kind of new hearing, could be not.  I'll keep you up to date."

"I hope you do.  I hope . . . *fuck*."

Time for diplomacy.  "You're back, you're laying it out.  We appreciate it.  Thanks for coming in."

Jacinta brushes back her hair now.  Her smile turns bitter.  "Fail the test, get a pass.  Story of my life."

◆

AS I CONDENSE IT for Alina I watch her eyes – turned inward, somehow, absorbing, asking *herself* the questions first.

"So this is true."  I watch her gears keep turning.  "She admitted there was a second guy.  And now you know who?"

"We do."

"OK.  But – couldn't it still have been Andrew who did it?  Or even both of them together?"

"In theory," I say, smiling.

Now all she does is cock her head and give me a look.

"It's Saturday," Alina says.  "Be kind."

# *40*

**(JPH)**

RODARTE WAS DELIVERED to Contenta County on Monday, August 27, 2012. He'd written first, two paragraphs, asking to meet me face to face. It happened, with Wade's help, that Wednesday afternoon.

It was strange to look at him square-on – save for his misery on the stand, it had been all profiles. But I could see he was not much changed. Somewhat bulkier now, a crease or two, and the eyes darted around a little – prison vigilance, no doubt. And anxious. Truth or lies, he was scared I wouldn't believe.

We exchange a professional shake and settle across a metal table in the sheriff's interview room. Craig starts the recorder, confirms our voices, then slips out the door and lingers beyond the security window, where he'll wait and watch.

HE STARTS WITH a tight smile. "Thanks for coming over."

"Sure. Glad you made it."

"I'll get her name wrong, but I did hear about her. Ms. Branstander? That she didn't make it back."

"Yeah." I'll be lean with words. "Tough business."

"No doubt. I mean, she was pretty strong up there."

"She was."

"Her eyes – man." Tries a smile. "Like laser beams. I couldn't imagine anything taking her down."

"Yes. It's hard to believe."

"Already a long time ago, me on trial and all that."

"What, seven years?" We both, of course, know exactly how long.

"More or less. And nine since, well . . ." He shakes his head, looks away. "Strange being back here now, really. This long after the fact."

I see him gearing up. "I mean, it's a trip. But it seemed like the time had come."

I nod, wait a beat. "So are you ready to tell this new story under oath, if we get there?"

He nods back. "Whatever it takes to make things right."

I'll mark territory. "Well, that's kinda beyond our power at this point, isn't it? We can't bring her back."

He flinches. "Uh, right. Bad word choice. But – well, next to that I'd think maybe it'd help her family to know. And you too, if you've ever wondered."

Much better. "Sure. There's always more to know, right? Truth is the main objective."

"And justice, right?" He looks scared he's misquoting.

"You bet. But I think you need truth to get there."

His eyes flicker, and he nods. "It's all I have. The truth."

FIRST THE STRING-BEAN in the Palomar jail. Rodarte figured "Cheeto" came from how skinny he was, like maybe he could eat all the crap food he wanted. He heard his real name called by the guards a few times, but it was long and unusual, and did not stick. But they made friends.

"What *do* you remember about him?"

"Well, we were from the same area, south end of the Valley, so we clicked over that. His folks worked in the fields, so when he heard mine had a farm he'd give me shit about it in Spanish."

"You fluent?"

"Not really, that's the funny part. My granddad came up from Sonora right after World War Two, worked his ass off to get a farm, went all-out American. So even my dad spoke English at home growing up, and most of what I learned was from workers or at school. But I could follow enough to laugh it up with him.

"We're in there together maybe ten days, I guess, before he's released. I still have a few weeks to go. But I've been complaining about getting the VOP, no time to plan, my life already a mess, now it's nothing but loose ends. So one day he offers to sort things out for me when he gets out, best he can – talk to my landlord, clean out my fridge, get my truck running, all that stuff.

"I'm like hell yeah, thanks. I've already decided I'm done with it up there, coming straight back down, can't wait to clear out. I know I'll owe him one, but whatever. I'll do something for him."

"OK."

"Now along the way he's talked about knowing some bikers up there, which is funny because he's anything but a ride-or-die-lookin dude himself. But he goes hey, they're pretty decent guys and they get good weed.

"And he's a champ, does what he promised, picks me up in my own truck when I get sprung. That's the Wednesday. We go straight to a bar, what else, and then it takes a left turn.

"Cheeto's a little embarrassed, goes hey, wonder if you can do something back for me, this biker friend of mine needs a ride down the way you're going. Because I've told him I'm heading down to San Ricardo. And he goes hey, if you can do it, call it even for my help.

"I get the feeling right off it's kinda dicey, because Cheeto's a little nervous and he's normally a sunny sort of dude. But before I even give an answer, in walks this scruffy short guy from redneck central, grungy beard. He's the friend, and Cheeto introduces him as Rust.

"We order another round, and then right away this Rust starts squeezing me about it. He goes hey, I got something needs to get from here to there, you know? And we're kinda connected up here. I ain't asking lightly, and you help me you help Cheeto, too. Says I'm just a one-way trip, I'm picking up a bike down there. I'll buy the gas. He's basically in my face. So I say OK."

I stir and shift. "And Rust is all you got, to ID him?"

"Well, later he used Chuck, but he said that was fake."

"OK. So how does it all go down?"

323

"He meets me in town and we head out around midday Friday. I've left most of my shit in a storage unit, not knowing where I'll end up next, so all I have's a couple suitcases. He's got this big bulky overcoat and a gym bag, not just a change of clothes, I'm sure of that.

"He gives me fifty bucks, which I appreciate, and goes hey, his license is suspended and he has probation search terms, so that's why he's not driving down in his pickup. And we go sailing off.

"Then, maybe half an hour down the road, I suddenly remember my expired tags. I tell him and he gets pissed, starts to freak out. Obviously he's scared shitless of getting pulled over, and I realize it ain't gonna go well for me if we get stopped, either. So he goes OK, then we need to avoid 101, take back roads.

"So next I know we're cutting across country, and it's a disaster. He's reading the map, but it's steering us crazy. We keep coming to closed roads and gates and rutted dirt trails. Pretty sights but it's a nightmare, we're zig-zagging all afternoon, the mountains never end.

"But we finally come down and hit the top end of a lake, and we're starving, so we stop for food and gas. Then afterward we make our way around the shore and then realize there's a second lake, so loop around that, keep going. By then I gotta piss, and so we stop at the mini-mart."

"Right."

"And it's the way I told it. I parked around the side, he stayed put. I take a leak and then go to the cold section, thinking maybe grab a couple of cans. She's hovering there, Jacinta, and then she kinda shuffles on up." He heaves a sigh. "Fate, basically. And really I don't want any part of it – I'm tired. But she had a way with her, kind of a devious smile, party attitude and this sloppy-chic look. There was something appealing about it, and she mutters hey, could I hook her up with some beer. She goes she knows the clerk and he's cool if she's not buying herself. He was pretty busy and she wasn't too hard to look at, so I did it. Wish I said no, but – I said yes."

RODARTE WOULD PAUSE on that, I think, but I push.

"So you bought it and then she came over to the truck, like we've always heard?"

"Right. And I just want the cash, plus I've got Rust in the car, who oughta be enough to put her off. But now she's digging in a purse and giving me this story, I don't have the cash but follow me home and I'll give you full payment, we can hang a little, have some fun, all that crap.

"Now we have the package to deliver, whatever it is, and on this crazy trip down he's been droppin hints that it's part of some serious arrangement, that he's making a connection with some big-league outfit, basically this is some high-priority shit. And I'm thinking we're already running late. But he's like yeah, what the fuck, why not?

"It all leaves me confused. I don't know jack about biker gangs, but I'm thinking it can't be standard to slide off in the middle of a drug run, or whatever it was. And it also didn't make any sense her inviting us, really, since now she'd seen Rust and after I saw what she was driving I figured she was rich. It was all overkill for a few bucks – I could've just kept a few beers, whatever.

"She was acting into *me*, though. Total flirt vibe. The funny part is I wasn't that interested in her, or in partying. I wanted to get back to my mom's place and take a sanity break, and something told me all along it was a mistake.

"But with Rust up for it I'm a weak spot, so I tell her OK, she pulls out in her loaded Acura, tears off and I manage to follow along, barely. And when I pull up the driveway behind her I'm already nodding – uh-*huh*. I can see there are vineyards, the house is huge. It's an estate.

"So Jacinta pulls in her garage, I park in front and she comes around and opens the front door, lets us in that way. And . . . there she was, standing back behind. *Her*."

"Haylee."

"Yeah."

HE HESITATES NOW, exhales through his teeth.

"Could even be she'd been in the car – I wasn't close enough to see. But Jacinta introduces her, calls her Lee." He shakes his head. "And, I mean, everything I ever said about first seeing her was true. Instant dream girl. Long legs, sparkling eyes, the hair, and I got this smile with her mouth closed, right *at* me, but kinda like she wanted to keep it a secret. I nearly melted on the spot.

"But you could also tell she was a little wary, 'cause we didn't fit the vibe of the place. We're in a palace and we pretty well look like the convicts we are."

"And Jacinta?"

"Not bothered at all. She just busts out the beers and offers 'em up, and Rust says hell yes. And so I sit down in this fancy room thinking one, maybe two. It was a helluva place, no question.

"Pretty quick things get weird, though. Jacinta seems to get hammered at warp speed. After ten minutes she sounds like she's drunk a twelve-pack, slurring her words, laughing at nothing, falling back on the couch, acting totally blitzed. I don't understand it at the time. I'm just trying to look cool and work up the nerve to say a few words to this other girl, Lee. I get through a couple of beers fast, go for another one and I get a chance, because Lee somehow spills the last part of hers on the couch, and starts laughing about being a klutz. So I bring her a couple of napkins and a new beer, and she smiles and takes a sip or two but basically just leaves it there.

"Meanwhile, this Rust motherfucker is acting like he's hangin out in some buddy's garage. Jacinta's barely there at all, and he's telling her about having a pet rattlesnake, talking about the Sturgis rally, ridiculous bullshit. And she's only like a quarter listening, sort of laughing at random – completely bombed.

"Then I look over at this Lee, our eyes lock, and then she suddenly goes hey, you wanna see the outside, it's pretty nice. And next thing I know she's over in front of me, smiling, dragging me up off the couch

"Now I can guess even then that she mostly just wants out of the room. But what do I care, I'm in a dream world – I'd follow her anywhere she wants. So I grab my beer, we go out the sliding door to a terrace, stop to take it in. And it's like . . . nothing was settled."

I GIVE THAT a long moment.

"How so?"

"Like there was a different path." Rodarte swallows, stares at the far wall. "I mean, I never believed in fate anyway, I've always been sure we make our own decisions. That's the core of life. And I still am. I *could* have done different. He could have. Jacinta could have. Except nobody did. We all did – what we did."

"OK, I got that. But what happens next?"

"Well, the rain's gone and there's all this nice lighting out back, in the yard and along the walkways. The main walk down from the terrace comes to a stone path, and we go across toward the sound of water, there's a creek there, you can hear it rushing along. And there's a fence to lean against, so we do.

"Then we just hang out and talk. Looking at each other in the glowing pathway lights, like we're alone under the stars. I'm worrying a little about Rust and a little about time, but the beer buzz helps, and I'm with her, and it's like a half-hour of heaven."

"Sounds pretty nice."

"It was. And thing was, I'd been assuming she was rich, too. But then she tells me she's not local, her mom has a horse place somewhere, and she's at Sacramento State. I remember I saw a normal-looking Hyundai up there. And I realize we're both just tourists, so to speak. We don't belong there – but there we are anyway.

"I do worry a little she's gonna ask about Rust, what the hell we're doing on the road together, who he is, what he wants. For which I have no answer worth shit. But instead she asks about me, which really oughta be worse, because somehow I don't want to lie to this girl.

"So I'm vague – came from a farm, been around the state, blue-collar jobs, didn't make it to college, unattached, no kids . . . heading back to see my mom. Back in '98 my dad got killed in a wreck, and my mom decided to sell the farm. I was already gone, and she loved the Bay, so that's where she went. Left the ag life flat. Got a state job, house prices hadn't gone totally nuts, and my sister finished high school. I'd come back through there a couple times already after leaving, going around in circles.

"It's lame, and for all I know she figured me out right away, but she's just smiling and cool. We get talking about likes and dislikes, animals, weather, places, whatever. Everything she says is kinda thoughtful and sincere – no pose. She didn't have life all figured out, but she had hopes and plans and courage. And – that smile."

HE KNEW IT WAS a dream all along, Rodarte tells me now.

"She's no casual hookup, that's pretty obvious, whether she likes me or not. I wouldn't even try, and I know there's no chance I ever see her again. Plus what shot would I ever have anyway, my past over me like a thundercloud. All we got in common are back roads. So it's like a beautiful dream to be living for a minute, but I know I'm gonna wake up, so I'm trying to memorize her, freeze the moment in time.

"Finally we do hit a little pause, and then she kinda sighs and goes well, hey, guess they're gonna be wondering about us by now. I remember thinking they might not be even giving a fuck, either one of them. Can't really say that, though, and I can't leave that freak there, meaning we do have to leave, sometime. So I'm reluctant as hell, but go sure, guess so. Hoping she knows I'd rather stay with her all night. But we go back inside, and – that's the end of the dream."

I give him a noncommittal eyebrow and a layup. "So what did you find when you got there?"

Rodarte stares past me now, his eyelids limp and heavy. *What else?* "The start of the nightmare."

# 41

## (JPH)

"ALL RIGHT." I'm still acting, carefully flat, but it's *his* story – I have nothing to win. "So now you're back inside. Then what?"

"Nothing good." Rodarte twitches his neck, squeezes his eyes shut, collects himself. "Rust is drunker, the TV's on, and now Jacinta's sagged back on the couch, her eyes barely open. It still doesn't register that it's more than beer, though.

"When Rust sees us he looks at Lee and goes hey, where'd you two go without permission? Like it's his own castle – creepy as fuck. I'd been ready to tell him dude, we gotta go, kinda been rehearsing it, but now there's something dangerous in his eyes. He's like sit down, chill out, and – I do. I'm hoping Lee comes to my side of the couch, but she slides over where she was.

"I grab another beer and slam it. Didn't make sense, since I'd been planning to go, but I just wanted to escape. Then I go get another one, start belting it and I look back over at her, Lee, and I see she's miserable. Whatever it was like out by the creek, she really just wanted a night with her friend. Now that's all gone, Jacinta's lying there next to a drunken dirtbag who's barking orders at us, and I sure can't save the night. I can picture us all just slamming beers until we pass out, fuck the consequences, and that almost seems like the best plan of all.

"It's gotten clear enough to me by now that Jacinta has a problem, and Haylee says yeah, and it hasn't gotten better since they've been apart, which bums her out, you can tell. So she leans back, picks up her own beer and downs most of it in one shot, like it's what she needs to deal with the whole thing. And then right away she hiccups and laughs, the last happy face I saw, and she goes shit, I can't drink. I laugh along, you know, thinking it did seem out of character. And wishing I could help somehow.

"Obviously we should've left. I shoulda told him fuck, I'm driving, we're leaving, brutal as it would have felt. But now Jacinta is completely out, and as I'm looking over I see Lee's own eyes start to get cloudy, and a couple of minutes later she suddenly just falls back and passes out, too.

"And then I see that fuckin Rust just sitting back grinning, and he waves this little vial and I know what it has to be. *Don't leave home without it*, he goes. *Sweet dreams*."

"You're saying it's roofies, and he's just carrying it around in his pocket?"

"It had to be. Maybe in his jacket."

"And dumped it in their beers, you think?" This had been a sore spot – thanks to a screwup, the dregs of the bottles were never tested.

"Well, that's all anybody drank. I think he dumped it in Jacie's right away, but Lee's first bottle was too far away. But she left the second one there when we went outside – perfect invitation."

"So I go oh dude, naw, *naw* – and now I'm *sure* we've got to go. She'll realize I'm pure trash when she wakes up, this Lee – I want to write a note and put it in her purse, say here's my number, I'll never forget you. But leaving was our only chance."

THEY DIDN'T, THOUGH.

"I just don't say anything." Rodarte leans back here, staring at the space in front of me. "That's what I live with. And next thing Rust leans over to Jacinta and slaps her on both sides of the face. She just kinda twitches, and so now he does it to Lee. She moves a little more, but doesn't wake up either, and now I start getting scared as fuck.

"He finds Jacie's purse, roots through it, grabs her keys. And he goes she told him it's like the fuck pad for parties. But if he has a choice it ain't her he wants – I should have known that all along.

"He turns, grins and picks up Lee, right off the couch, strong little fucker, and he goes come on, wingman, we're goin places. He goes this is something for the spank bank, kid, and when they stir we're gonna be five counties away."

"And you followed?"

Rodarte nods, very slowly. "I went along. I'm buzzed, and in shock, and scared too. I know this is getting sick, but after the shit he's said I still thought he had to make good on the delivery. When we found a signal he'd called somebody down there as we rode, telling 'em he'll be late and blaming it straight on me, giving 'em my name as the dumbass with expired tags. So I know I better not leave him to get arrested when they all wake up sober. And if I do I'm thinking he'll probably give me up to the cops, blame whatever happened on me.

"But basically I'm just a gutless piece of shit, so I follow them on down to this building, she's over his shoulder. I'm lookin at her closed eyes, picturing that I'll save her from it when we get there, somehow – mister white horse. And – I don't."

"OK."

Rodarte clenches his eyes, takes a good ten seconds.

"It's the place, the guesthouse, and he finds the key from the ring and we go in. I had the rest of a beer in my hand, set it down someplace. And Rust had to leave his bottle back up there, because he needed both hands to carry her. So mine's the only one."

I STAY BLANK. "OK. Now who does what?"

"He just dumps her down flat on the bed, no sign she stirs. She's out, helpless. I'm still thinking fuck man, I *know* her now, what's behind those eyes – and, fuck." He shakes now, gathering breath. "Whatever I thought, I did nothing. He reaches over, grabs a pillow, puts it under her head, I remember, and then he changes his mind, moves it back. Then he looks at me and goes hey, you'll get a turn.

"Now look, I know damn well I'm never doing that to her, and it's not just morality, or already being in love with her. But once he nuts he'll turn sane, realize Jacinta is lying there unconscious, and that he

331

better flee for his fucking life. But right now he's like *chill, dude, they can't ID us* – guess he figured using a fake name was that powerful.

"I *had* to stop him. But I didn't. I stood there and watched him do what he did earlier, slap her on the face. And it's like she flinches a little, but she didn't open her eyes. So he just goes to work, while I stand there like a statue."

"OK. What did he do?"

He scowls at me now – the most authentic face yet. "Fuck, man."

RODARTE TRIES. Rust pulled her pants off, he says, opened her blouse, undid her bra, shoved her breasts out. Then the rest.

Haylee was *not* a virgin, of course. That juvenile fantasy crossed our minds, but Marta doused it right away. There had never been anyone serious, but they talked. And then she'd gone off to college.

"Where are you, when this starts?"

He shakes his head, looks down. "Maybe five feet, to the side."

"And he's in her, going full bore?"

"Well, workin at it. And I'm standing there fixed in place." Rodarte shudders and exhales. "Thinking about my own skin. Even if nobody walks in, I was sure there were security cameras everywhere. They'll have my truck. There's probably meth in it, and I'm part of a rape. They'll nail us just from the plate on the truck – it's pathetic how easy it'll be. Basically, I'm realizing I'm toast, I'm gonna go to prison, never mind what's happening to her."

"Now did he have the rubber on from the beginning?"

"Nah. It wasn't. He started in without one." Rodarte frowns. "I don't actually know when he put it on, but it wasn't right away."

"You don't keep watching, though?"

"No, man. Before God, I'm turning away, trying *not* to watch. It's brutal – and then what if I actually got excited, as beautiful as she was. Where would that leave me? Fuckin dark thought."

"So how long did this go on?"

"Hard to know – time was like mud, somehow. But after a few minutes he suddenly he goes hey, you need to go back up to the house and look for the vial." Another bitter shake. "He goes Jacinta won't wake up, it's on the couch or the table, just grab it and come back."

"To drug Haylee more, you thought?"

"I'm figuring he's suddenly scared of it sitting there, like that would be the worst of our problems. But now I think mostly he just wanted me out of the room."

"What did you do?"

"I faked it. I walk up and see Jacinta still passed out through the window, but can't risk her waking up, and I can see it's not on the coffee table anyway. Plus I'm not putting my prints on anything, forget that. I just stall a few minutes, trying to think, and then go back down, ready to say I can't find it, we gotta put her clothes back on, take her back up there, pray she won't remember, get out *this minute*."

RODARTE'S EYES squeeze shut, his head shakes, his body trembles. I *want* to believe.

"When I get back he's still going at her. And I freeze, I just stand there again paralyzed. But then I realize he's struggling with his dick, of all things. He's trying to talk *himself* into getting through it. He knows I see it too. So he pulls it out, trying to work it himself.

"Maybe he's slipped the rubber on by then – not sure at this point, I'm turned away." As if in contrast, he lifts his eyes to face me. "But then I see her eyes flicker, right as she lay there on the bed with him half-limp inside her. Then she opened them enough to see."

*It had to be.*

"What was that like?"

"Well, it was slow, and not even halfway, just barely lifting the lids. But then you see panic, and she flicks open wider, like – trying to come back. And she tried to talk, but that's when he wraps his hands around her throat."

"Did she see *you* there, you think? Off to the side?"

Rodarte rubs his temples. "I don't think so, because I moved back away. That was thought number one . . . I was worried about what she was going to think of me – *while she was being killed in front of my face.* When all I had to do was pull him off, be her hero, surrender to the cops, testify against him. And – Jesus. I – fucking didn't."

I SAY NOTHING, and it takes a while. Rodarte runs his hands through his hair, turns away and back. His face is drained.

"Now he's throttling her, still his hands – there never was a plastic bag, don't even know why I made it up. But it's his hands around her, her eyes still flicking open, and she's grabbing now, but like quarter-speed, totally useless – she's *trying* –"

"To save herself?"

He nods, dumbly.

"And what did Rust do?"

"Fuck, I don't even know – I'm trying to understand *myself*. It's like I can't move any better than she can, somehow, can't lift an arm – even as I'm watching her be killed." He's a man on a pitching ferryboat. "*Her*."

"You knew that, by now?"

Another mute nod. "All I even tried to do was yell stop. Not really a yell even, more like a croak, nothing behind it. He's bare-assed, with a half-limp dick, out of his fucking mind – I'm not small – I could've knocked him away from her . . ." He shakes his head, clears his throat, then leaks angry tears. "The best I do is I say *stop*. One pathetic word. And then I hear the crack of her bone."

IT WAS PROBABLY ENOUGH to kill her. But not right away.

"I hear her gasp. And see, I had my jacket, but it was warm in there, so I'd tossed it. So Rust grabs it . . . he wraps it around, and she clenches at him, at it, but her muscles barely work. And I *still* don't do anything. I clench my eyes shut, praying maybe – I don't even know."

He's shaking now. "But it's still like two or three minutes, the longest in my life, before finally I open my own eyes and I see her, her eyes just cracked open, and staring now, slack and limp."

"And what's your reaction to that?"

"That's the sick thing – *now* I can scream what the fuck, now I have volume. He's a shaking mess, and says fuck, it wore off, or I got the dose wrong, or some shit. I'm crying now.

"I should have checked her pulse. There might have been a chance. But I was so fucking scared I didn't even wanna touch her. There were hand marks, and the other marks from the jacket, which he'd tied up tight. I couldn't bring myself to do anything to help.

"And that makes me a collaborator. I'm not guilty the way you said it, or even the way I lied about it. But I'm still guilty as fuck, and I don't know how to live with it. That I let *this* girl die in front of me."

I DON'T THINK I've ever changed expression.

"What about the condom afterward?"

He shivers. "Well, I tell him rinse it, and he does but he goes hey, look, I didn't even fuckin – finish." Shaking his head. "How sick is that? She died because he couldn't get off. I mean – he nuts when she's still out, fuck, it's rape and we both go to prison, but he's not gonna kill her. He goes they don't remember afterward, that's the whole idea.

"Not this worthless piece of shit, though. He grabs his clothes, sloshes the rubber under the bathroom faucet, then manages to drop the fucking thing on the way out the bedroom door. We're both in a panic, pretty drunk, insane. I'm too freaked to even grab my bottle.

"So we left her there and went out the door, wiping down the handles with our shirts, but right there it's confrontation. I'm like let's go, get the fuck out, and he says we need to go grab the things we better not leave, put back Jacinta's keys, shit like that. I say fuck, I won't do it, so he says fine, bolts off to the main house to do it himself, grabs whatever. Maybe the roofies. Not sure what.

"We're so fucking out of it we leave the door half open. I think I tried to pull it shut and it grazed him in the doorway, got deflected. Makes about as much sense as everything else that happened.

"I go up through the trees, get to the truck, and right then he gets there too, must've raced. Goes he wiped the door handles and the beer bottles. So we just jump in and haul off blind to the south. He looks for cops and lights, I focus on the road. Buzzed, nearly drunk. Insane. All the way down."

"But you stopped to make your drop?"

Rodarte snorts. "Yeah, sure enough. Still Job One. Eventually we get to this place in the hills near Concord or somewhere, must be 2:30 AM. I'm fuckin cross-eyed by now, but the beer's worn off and I'm thinking just, Christ, get rid of this fucker and then see if I can even start to process it.

"But we find it, big open ranch-type property, up a dirt road, pull up to a building. I tell him OK, thinking fuck you, never gonna see you again – though I'm a little scared he'll *try* to stick with me, thinking I have some kinda plan. But he says hey, hang a minute and we'll talk."

IT'S MORE LIKE FIFTEEN, but Rodarte stays.

"Then he comes back with this major scary-ass older dude with him, fat but full of muscles, shaved head, lotta ink, gray beard. Whether he was actually Hells Angels, I don't know, but he was the real deal, total badass-enforcer type. And somehow I can tell Rust's admitted something to this guy – I'm sure not the truth, but that we did something bad and stupid, that's why we're late, cops might be hunting us. It's all over his fuckin guilty face.

"I can see they're both tweaking now, and the big fucker climbs right up in the passenger seat, sticks the snub of a gun in my side and I can feel death an inch from me. I practically don't care. But he goes hey, first, you better forget my fuckin face, and that asshole's too. Forget this place, this trip, everything about this night.

"And then he says hey, you say one word, we've checked you out, we know where to find your family – down San Ricardo way. My fuckin blood runs cold and I go right, yeah, I'm forgetting everything, and anyway I don't even know his name, or yours, or anything else.

"He goes good, but remember that if the shit hits the fan and you drag him in, you fuck us, because he's an associate. Then we find you, hurt you bad, and then we hurt the people you care about. We clear?

"I just nod and he stares at me a minute, the gun still in my ribs, then he slides it right up to my ear, and I manage to mumble yeah, absolutely. And he gets out, I drive off and I never hear a word from either one of the motherfuckers again, though I'm always half scared I will, somebody'll come after me in jail or once I get to prison."

"So how'd you act so calm at your mom's place, after all that?"

"Well, she's calm herself, that helps. Always is. She wakes up, but doesn't press me. She figures we'll talk after I've slept. So I just say goodnight and head in the shower, like I can somehow scrape this horror off myself. And then I lie there, mind racing everywhere, but I take some PM stuff eventually and somehow I do go to sleep. At most I'm out an hour when the knock comes."

"You pulled it together, though."

"Don't know how, except I wasn't that shocked. Either cameras got me or somebody saw me, got the plate. And that would show my mom's address, so they were pretty much a lock to hunt me down. I was gonna come up with a story and head right back out again, if I could. But when they're at the door that fast, and I haven't slept, I don't know what to do but admit I was there, give the real explanation.

"Now it hits me Jacinta will remember stuff, including Rust. But then I think well, she wasn't in the room, she was drunk and drugged, and she didn't know his name, so really she can't even incriminate him.

"Otherwise I'm just wanting to not get hauled away in front of my mom. The detective is cool enough to take me off to the side, but no way he's buyin it. Then, by a miracle, he doesn't arrest me."

"So what did you tell your mom?" I'm nothing but curious.

"Well, if I tell her the truth she's gonna try and get me to admit it all to the cops, and I couldn't face that. So I say it was a bar fight, we took off, got followed by the cops."

"And then you get back to the plan of running."

"It's all I could think about, really. I skated on getting arrested but he's circling me, that's obvious, plus he took the DNA sample and I know that's somehow gonna nail me.

"But for like two days I'm paralyzed, can't figure out what the hell to do. I'm basically scared to breathe. Finally I come up with a story I'm going to San Diego, gonna do a training in truck electronics. She knows that's a lie, too, but as always she just goes along. She'd tell you now she was always too soft, saw my potential, ignored the fucking loser I was actually turning out to be.

"So I pack up, take off real early, can't really see anybody following, and for a while I think I'm clear. But I get nailed halfway to LA. I saw the fuckin deputy tearing down the ramp in my rearview mirror, but then he slowed down and tried to make it seem natural. The reg would just be a ticket, but I have the fake license, too. He doesn't say a word, but I know I'm in the net. Then here comes the helicopter. I nearly laughed when I saw it."

I FOLD MY HANDS, look past him. "So what did you hope to gain from that second lie, after Miranda?"

"It was just the jacket – that's what really had me freaked. It was mine, they'd seized it and it's the last thing he killed her with. Then go look up DNA after he swabs my cheek, and see there's stuff how can transfer just from touch. I mean, I know it's fine that I'm on it, since it's mine, but I got more and more sure they were gonna find her on too, after it had been wrapped all around her and she'd grabbed at it. And from my first story she'd never have touched it, so if I get caught I'm thinkin I gotta come up with something. Then I do get caught.

"I realize I'm fucked once I get a look that old owl, he'll never believe me turning her down, or even that other wiseass. But I'm in too deep, got nothin else, so I put it out there, thinking even if it's pretty obvious BS, I've got the doubt on my side, and if even one person buys it maybe it's a hung jury and you get tired of the case, make me a deal with some kind of hope, something to look forward to. But after I get it told and realize I'm still screwed, he starts fucking with me – I knew I *wasn't* under her fingers. So that's when I got pissed."

"And then we get your big story at trial."

He shakes his head. "Yeah, I'm a true fuckin mastermind. It was just the life without parole. That's what I couldn't face, and she terrified me. I'd messed around with the choking stuff, obviously, and thought well, it kinda fits. I can't really explain breaking her bone, or the frickin drugs either, but I get the reasonable doubt, and I've heard there's a chance you get a manslaughter on this, involuntary even.

"Earlier I'd asked Ted, what if they found it that way, and basically he goes hey, you oughta dream at night, plus they'd stack a bunch of years on it if they find rape too. But I was sure I was going down, and thought it still had to be better."

HERE, I THINK, I finally smile – I've saved the money question for seven years. "And you got Ted Stauber to go along with it?"

To which Rodarte laughs, and for once in my life I've been right all along. "No, man. Decided to shock him right along with everyone else. Which I did, and he was royally pissed off about it."

"I'll bet he was." For a moment I marvel at how Ted passed it off. "Whew. And I don't really think the jury thought much of it either."

"Hard to know. For sure they hated me, and I hated myself just as much. Making her into a freaky sex monster who couldn't resist me, then having to keep building on it, when she was nothing like that. But again, I couldn't think of any other plan. Even as I did it I'd apologize to her in my mind, as if somehow she'd understand."

339

NOW I NOD ALONG. Almost there. "So you really never thought about bringing up Rust?"

"*Thought* of it, sure. A million times. But the guy with the gun was a killer, I knew that much, and if I told the whole truth I figured I go down right along with him anyway. Then before I know it I've told two layers of lies. So by the time we go to trial I'm thinking fuck, it won't get believed, and then word will get out anyway and it's the worst case of all. I'll have to watch my back forever, and now I've put my family at risk for no gain. I never did tell my mother."

"Why not?"

"It was just too much. I swore to her I never touched Haylee which was true, but if I told her all of it she'd never quit till I put it out there, and fuck, I've still had to worry about 'em, these years. And since I held myself responsible I couldn't really rant and rave about doing the time."

"OK. Now what about your story in the jail?"

He wrinkles his face. "Just more covering. Trying to act hard and not finger Rust. Back in those earlier days I'm still thinking anything say is getting back to his people somehow, jail grapevine. Didn't know what to do but steer it as far away from him as I could."

"So you still assign a lot of blame to yourself."

He stares away for many seconds, eyes ablur. "What else? I'm almost as responsible as he is. I mean, I should have had the nerve to save anybody in that spot – but *this* girl, I could stand and watch her be killed, arms at my sides? There's a moment in everybody's life where you learn your own character. I did. It's simple as that."

FULL STOP. What's left is a question I've already learned the answer to, so I ask it.

And his answer is the truth, so I make a face of mock regret, retrieve a police report from a folder, and hand it across the table.

"Well, Mr. Rodarte, you're entitled to this."

# *42*

**(JPH)**

OLD DUMARET HAD ANSWERED on the first ring that afternoon in June, after Jacinta came back. So Craig and I went back to Sundown Road, turned left this time, climbed the rise.

It all made sense. There had been *two* big hints, and nobody ever noticed – because there was no reason to think it mattered.

DUMARET IS THERE for the duration, and his house is nearer a shrine than Marta's. His wife, silver-haired and serene, occupies as much display space as his kids and grandkids combined. They dined and ballroom-danced, trekked the globe, sweated together over their tiny vineyard. Bottles abound, and apparently he's still at it, labels as recent as 2010. But then Dumaret still looks like he could still scale any hill in the county in full gear and fend off mountain lions on the way.

We settle across his kitchen table, cracking open frosty bottles of spring water. His eastward view is as good as the west.

"Sir, we'll keep it quick. The transcript of your testimony at trial shows that you stated you 'heard car doors slam,' plural, right before the SUV roared away. But in the courtroom I think we heard it as 'a car door slam,' and that's how it reads in the police report. Do you happen to remember what you said, and what you meant?"

"I do remember. And that's what I said at trial. Best I could tell there was a double thump. Thought I'd told it that way to the detective, too, but he didn't have much left in the tank that day."

"*Two* doors." I have a sudden impulse to laugh.

"Can't be positive, obviously – long way away, and happened quick. But sounded like two. I didn't even know it mattered."

"Well, we didn't either." I exhale, bracing myself. "And then you were asked, sir, about whether, specifically, you saw or heard anything before the SUV took off – 'for example, a female voice?' And you replied 'not that I could make out.' Remember that too?"

"I do."

"Did you hear something that *sounded like* voices?"

"I did. But it wasn't quite the question, and nobody followed up."

"How would you describe it?"

"Well, just the hum, very low register, before the truck hauled off. Maybe five seconds long. Nothing you could make out."

But we didn't know, because we never asked. All that mattered was Rodarte bolting away.

IT WILL ONLY GET WORSE if we linger.

He shakes hands on the porch, squints in the afternoon glare.

"Been a while, hasn't it? You worried you sent the wrong guy up the river?"

I blink, give the world's feeblest laugh. Craig just stands there trying not to smirk at me. "No sir," I say. "Not quite that."

◆

SO RUST WAS REAL, and Rust fled the murder with Rodarte. That left the obvious.

Then one late July morning Craig had loomed at my threshold fighting to keep a straight face.

"Bad news good news, JP."

"Have a seat," I say, un-fooled. "Whichever order."

"First, I find nobody alias Rust that fits the situation in the statewide databases, or the fed for that matter. Nobody I could find with any real Palomar links, it's so remote, or even a good fit for age. And I got equally little help on Cheeto." But a grin starts to creep. "The good news is we found the mystery snack food anyway."

I lean back, thrilled. "Tell me all about it."

"Tried the other end of the stick. Palomar wasn't ever going to do it, and of course their shit's not digitized, but they offered to let me come up and dig through the jail records for '03.

"So I went up last week and managed to pull everybody who overlapped with him there, which was only a few dozen over the four months – and mystery solved. Not Cheeto, Chi-*lo*, with an I-L. Easy to hear wrong in a day room. Another nickname – chill, mellow. And that's him. He's legit."

"For certain?"

"Direct confirmation. Has a mouthful of a name, Arturo – Mancia – better spell it, C-o-l-l-a-g-u-a-z-o. Two-bit misdemeanor record. They were twelve days in the same wing in the fall of the year 2003, and he was out the door before Rodarte.

"By hook and crook I got a cell number to try, and I got lucky. Guy has a little food truck nowadays, goes up and down the coast frying fish and selling knick-knacks. He's real. And he remembered all about Mr. Rodarte."

I'm squinting. "So –"

"In fact" – he's restraining me with a finger – "they were bona fide pals in there, way he tells it, and Chilo's even kept in touch."

"You mean –"

"Said in fact he even once went to see Rodarte, way back when he was at Hartsville. I haven't had the logs pulled, but no reason he'd lie. I asked why and he goes, out of guilt – because he says, quote, 'I steered him wrong.' And reason for that, JP, is that Chilo says that when Rodarte got out, he paired him up with 'a crazy dude named Rust,' and it all went so bad he 'went down for killing a girl.'"

"Wow." I take a long pause to absorb, believe it. "Damn."

"IT GETS BETTER. He says Rust has a salvage yard, near Bay City. Chilo did some work for him there under the table, they got along, and so he started hanging out.

"Sure as shit, Rust does have his own little biker outfit. He says
they mostly just showed up in their vests and hung around there
getting loaded, but they were a group, they'd raise some hell and talk
big. Chilo actually liked Rust, he said. Kind of a maniac but generous,
treated him pretty decent.

"And *then* he says that around that time, when Chilo had gone
back in, he knew Rust had made a connection with somebody down in
the East Bay, might even have been a Hell's Angels branch but he
wasn't sure, and started making some deliveries, trying to get linked
up as an affiliate. Kinda how that shit usually works, I think."

"Did he know what they were shipping?"

"He figured it was meth but they also slung weed, like everybody
probably trafficked in guns. But anyway, something was stirring."

"So they did connect after he got out, him and Rodarte?"

"Just like he told it. Rust decided Chilo's hard work was billabl
for the club, and he tells Chilo he needs to arrange the connection."

"And so he found out about the murder case, after the fact?"

"Well, everybody heard about it, and I guess he did some piecin
together. Then Rodarte would've filled in a few blanks."

I turn it over, make a wry face. "Now let me understand. Thi
mellow, non-riding Hispanic dude was hanging with a white outlaw
biker gang, hearing their secrets?"

Craig wrinkles his nose. "Well, we're giving all of it too muc
credit. Ol' Chilo is no tough guy, and I can't see any serious outlaw
gang tolerating him even as a hang-around type – just no menace t
the dude, plus he's Mexican and the groups normally keep it pure. Bu
let's face it, this was a small-time bunch in the middle of nowhere.

"Chilo couldn't remember the club name right off, so I talked t
an old connection up that way, who asked around for me, and he end
up telling me they must have been some low-grade dickwads wh
called themselves the PC Haters. Highway 1 joke, I guess.

"He said they'd gotten into a few things over the years but neve
amounted to much, and the task forces up there didn't really eve

bother with 'em. He didn't know a Rust offhand, but said he'd try to find out. And when I ran the club name by Chilo, it rang the bell."

I'M STILL MARVELING. "Now are you saying this Chilo got squeezed in the whole thing himself?"

"Hard to say, really. He lives up to his nickname, carefree sort of dude, and it sounded like pretty distant history. But the last thing is he tells me, *before I ask*, is that he heard ol' Rust just cashed in his chips."

"No shit. When?"

"He thought six months maybe. Vague who told him, but said it was solid info. Then he tells me he figured he ought to let his old pal Andrew know, so he found out where he was and sent him an old-fashioned letter, U.S. mail."

*Click.*

Finally, abruptly, it's time – there's a pulse in my throat.

"Did he happen to know *Rust*'s name?"

Craig smiles. "How did I know you'd ask?"

♦

IT TURNED OUT Chilo had the first name, most of the last. So it's only the next afternoon when Craig is back at my door.

"Got him, JP." He's five feet off the ground. "Once and for all. Name of Wrathley, W-R-A-T-H-L-E-Y, Raymond Eugene. Date of birth 6-23-60. Three felony convictions, one for possession of meth while armed that very year, probation. Never went to the joint. And DMV had him near Bay City for decades."

"Just not Rust as an AKA?"

"Well, not on his RAP." By now he could burst. "But if you were to, for example, get the police reports on his transporting case from four years before the murder from Palomar, you'd learn that it's used by everyone who knows him – and his biker outfit, *the PC Haters*. They faxed it to me this morning."

I'm full-on cackling. "Brilliant. And let me guess?"

Craig's already nodding. "Five months back."

But it isn't quite glee. For me it feels more like something settling, reverberations dying away, the still after a three AM earthquake.

◆

JACINTA CAME BACK without a fuss, and Craig assembled a photo lineup. I watched. Ray Wrathley in the third position, top right.

Maybe five-Mississippi, then a firm index finger, a soft, almost resigned voice. "That's him."

"You sound sure."

She nods, bites her lip. "Didn't think I would be." Then she looks up with a smile. "But I am."

CRAIG IS GRINNING after she's been ushered out.

"And now we got his widow, back up there in Palomar."

"Uncooperative, we can assume. You fixing to go up?"

"Hell yeah. Just tell me how to play it."

"Well, let me make a call."

WADE HAS BEEN WAITING, of course. I don't *think*, by now that he's surprised.

# 43

## (WADE)

I MIGHT HAVE RESISTED, in another life. Putting a big case together first means dealing with your own doubts, and wanting to *know* is the greatest motivator of all. So you don't ever want to imagine getting it wrong, and after I got over those first hesitations, the DNA came and I'd satisfied *myself.* I was sure, and stayed that way – Rodarte going down for murder was justice.

But the case always stayed near to me, as you'd think, and when JP told me the rest of it, I knew I had to go. Not much more to it than that. I had to go, and we needed a warrant if one could be had.

As it turned out we got lucky with the rotation that week, since Judge Bright had his turn as the warrant judge. This wasn't your average affidavit. Jacinta's positive ID was gonna be enough, most likely, but this was for service in another county – hadn't tried pulling that off before – and, basically, to prove a case against a dead man.

But whatever we found could change things for Rodarte, who *did* have an open case, and old Jim Bright was a gut-instinct type. Plus like everybody of any local tenure, he remembered the case, and I think he knew we'd try to keep it civil, tossing a dead guy's house.

He'd actually kept his head down, the Dirtbag Formerly Known as Rust. Nothing but one dumb misdemeanor after the murder. Then he died, property records showed no transfer since, his wife's name was on it too.

Whatever the odds against us, this long beyond, I had to go look.

WE'D HAVE GONE no matter what, but the warrant gives you the high ground. Smile, seek consent, then bring it out politely once they've told you to shove it. You'd be amazed at the attitude shifts you see.

It ends up three of us at her door – me in a tie with my badge on a cord around my neck, Craig from the DA Bureau in his usual island shirt, a smartass young deputy named Bicknell, in uniform, who's good with tech. Told JP I might Skype him, just to keep him on his toes.

This is a hike, let me add, an hour to 101, two more to the coast, then another 75, 80 miles up the 1 along the rocks and the redwoods. We left in the pitch-dark, and in the end it's a raggedy old two-story farmhouse painted robin's-egg blue in the shade of a forest south of Bay City, a couple of miles up an old, broken-asphalt road between the hills.

It's maybe a three-acre property, chain-link fenced. There are chickens loose in a side yard, a couple of goats, and naturally dogs, though they're just wannabe tough guys, mostly curious about visitors. But a woman lives there, so there's some effort. The front porch is swept, the flower beds weeded. There's a welcome mat, yard décor, a little old turning windmill out front.

Her name is Trish, and she's about as happy as you'd figure to see three mismatched cops out of nowhere. She lets us in against her better judgment, steps back and looks at us like shit-caked boots on a shiny-clean floor. Suffice to say we don't get offered coffee, even though I know I'm smelling a nice fresh pot.

AND SHE REALLY OUGHT to be telling us to go fuck ourselves from the jump, but when we ask about looking around she just scowls and goes yeah, whatever, knock yourselves out. Maybe that matters.

It seems to me she's not surprised, and no beginner, maybe does figure we didn't drive all that way without a warrant anyway. So I kind of expect she'll tell us she's cleared everything of his out, or send us to a storage unit.

But she doesn't, just points us to a bed-less bedroom with a grungy desk, a closet and a chest of drawers, a few bankers' boxes in a corner. Mentions the attic, says don't leave piles on my fucking floor, and then just sort of hovers around and mutters as we look.

Maybe anyone would, in that spot. For all the attitude she had to be an upgrade over him, big tall gal with flashing green eyes, wide hips, scarf on her head, grandkid in the back bedroom. She's buried the fuck, and she's broke – even if he did junk cars, he's not doing it now, and we can assume he didn't leave a 401k.

And even though she's accusing us of trying to bust a dead man, I'm sure from the beginning that she has no idea what we actually hope to find. Which more or less makes us even.

AN HOUR YIELDS LIMITED RETURNS. We find a quarter-ounce of weed, a few porn DVDs, a fistful of IOUs. A prescription bottle that says amoxicillin but is plainly heavy pain pills. A handwritten bill of sale for a bike.

Group photos from a trip to the Colorado River, the women draped over the Harleys behind the men. With helmets and shades I can't even pick him out. A new receipt for a pair of generators.

Then finally a folder of receipts, mostly innocuous, but down in it we get a little warmer, sort of. They aren't recent but they tell a tale – there's red phosphorus and acetone, and then some handwritten scrawls about "PE," which was bound to mean pseudoephedrine. Names on a sheet – monikers. Phone numbers.

Eventually I realize she's gone quiet. And finally, when we're through the garage and the master bedroom and the junk room, and then the little girl's bedroom, I limp back into the kitchen on stiff knees.

"He hadn't been well, your husband, or was it sudden?"

She flinches, but that's all. "He'd been short of breath. They did the stress tests, he bombed, they diagnosed heart disease. And a week later he goes to have a nap and it gives out, just like that."

"Mmm. Well, sorry for your loss."

"The fuck you are. Nobody is, really."

"I'm human, ma'am. I can see you hurting."

She shakes her head. "Two months behind on the mortgage, still sorting out his shit. I'll have to sell. Get to begin again at 48."

WE LOOK IN THE CARPORT, the attic, a falling-down storage shed. Clutter, cobwebs, oil stains. Little else.

I'm ready enough to leave with nothing, really. He's had years to purge stuff, God only knows what he'd even have kept around in the short term, and none of it's necessary. Just didn't want to leave it undone.

There's a quiet gray in the sky outside, and now she's receded a long way, shrinking back somehow. Bad's gone to worse.

I circle back through the kitchen, gathering the scraps I'm taking. I'd decided to search first, then talk to her. Nobody will be charged with making meth or anything else, obviously, but maybe it's something to build off.

WHILE I'M THINKING all that, Trish Wrathley reaches in a drawer, rattles, comes out with a key. Shudders, angry a new way, holds it out.

"Look, since you'll find it and ask me anyway, this is to a shack on the road up to Lookout Peak."

"OK, sure. What can you tell me about that?"

She shakes her head, eyes hooded and miserable. "It's all federal land this side of the state park, and there's a bunch of 'em. Mostly prefabs, I think. They've got power from someplace, couple of portajohns, but that's about all I know. I was there a grand total of once, and only because I found out about it and threatened to snap his neck if he didn't show me.

"Road up is maybe a mile ahead, dirt, left-hand side, little ways past a bank of mailboxes. Rough. But you may as well go knock yourself out up there, too."

I haven't done anything but gaze back politely, I don't think. Then she looks at me full on.

"I mean, I've been trying to forget it existed, but the fact is I can't afford to keep caring about everything, and whatever you find up around there ain't gonna matter now. Karma already bit him in the ass." She starts to tear up, but fights it back. "I didn't ask questions – no gain in it. I figure they had a little pot grow, out of sight of the big operators, and maybe a lab in one of 'em, too. Ray claimed they didn't even deal meth anymore, because he knew how I felt, but I never really bought it. And that probably means they were cooking too, someplace up there. I'm not gonna act dumb and innocent for you."

Straight-face time. "Well, thanks. It's bigger than Ray, but as far as I know nobody's ever implicated you. If that counts as good news."

"Yeah, well I'm not guilty of anything. If you're trying to bust his piddly-ass crew, go ahead. They're basically scattered anyway, most of 'em couldn't even be bothered to get here for the funeral. But I don't know anything about his connections, and I personally hate everything to do with meth. It's the devil.

"My nephew got his arm blown off, *then* went to prison over it. My daughter's in inpatient right this minute, if you're wondering why grandma's in charge. I mean, I know she didn't get the shit from Ray, and he didn't do it around me the last few years, but it's all one giant cluster-fuck up here.

"It was a fight that was gonna go on forever, so he mostly had the good sense to keep it outta my sight, and I didn't ask a lot of questions about how we were getting by."

I nod along. "What's it look like, this shack?"

"Well, before we went I stole a couple pictures off his phone. He took his women there, too, all right? I figured *that* out. Way to wine and dine 'em. Fuck on a mattress, clean up in the porta-potty, cook a can of chili over a wood stove. God knows how many there were, but I'll bet on that cunt with the curls in that shot you found from Havasu. Niece of one of his crew, ain't that sweet? You should've seen him talk me out of goin down there with him. But this was his grand ol' getaway place."

"Can I see?"

There's enough to identify it – a creeper bush, an off-colored door, a screenless window. I take a picture of the picture.

"Burn it if you're in the mood," she adds. "Don't wanna know what's in it, and I don't know who the fuck I'd sell it to – assuming I can even prove he owned it."

"We'll have to get up there and find it."

"You will. It's just this side of where the forest gets thick."

THE ROAD IS PRETTY AWFUL, but we'd brought the right unit, and the shack is easy to find. The key snaps the padlock right open.

It's a dive, all right – a couple of lamps, a filthy old couch, a card table with three folding chairs, a mini-fridge, a small wood stove. In the one bedroom there's a double bed flat on the floor, a battered end table next to it, and a ratty closet. In the closet is a bin that latches but doesn't lock, and inside the bin is an old plastic shopping bag.

The bag contains a manila envelope, and in it I find two newspaper clippings and two other stories printed from the web. And then everything really does go numb, in a second and a half, since they are all about the same news story, and one has a picture.

"Fuck me," is what I manage.

"It's the memories that matter," observes young Deputy Bicknell with a straight face, like this happens every day. He's also found a laptop tucked beneath the end table.

THE BATTERY'S DEAD, the power pack takes a while to find. We find it, though, and I'm not waiting four hours. So we stop back by the house, go into the repurposed bedroom, close the door and plug it in.

He was considerate enough to forgo a password. There's a folder called "Media," then a subfolder "Fun." We click, up come thumbnails.

There are five, in all, and when you click you get short clips, none more than half a minute, dude filming himself from above, a little of his hairy gut creeping out, drilling away.

There's only one half-visible face, a redhead; three of the others are olive-skinned, smaller. No curls – we're way off the radar, even hers.

They're limp, make no noise. They're drugged. They're raped.

And sure as fuck he can't resist – he pans up a couple different times in a mirror. There he is.

I get to a sub-folder within the folder, titled "Admin," and then two more levels down one called "Survey," and you open that and there's no thumbnail but a link. This one he hid.

I click, and then – no warmup, no preamble, no anything –

IT DIDN'T ENTIRELY make sense. The others might have been later, but in '03 they hadn't invented smartphones, so he'd have needed a camcorder for this stuff. But those had shrunk way down by then, I think – hard to remember, with all that's changed – and easy enough to digitize it later. If he's carrying roofies around, it's a regular thing, and there had been this perv in the news that year who videotaped all his knockout rapes, so I guess he was inspired. Maybe he dragged the damn thing everywhere.

Nothing can brace you for it. But the worse, in a way, the better.

*Got a prize*, I text JP. In the moment it's the best I can do.


## (JPH)

WADE JUST HANDS ME a disk, tells me to close my office door, and I don't even try to prepare myself. I click and at once she's there, the *living* Haylee, beautiful and breathing, helpless and violated. Her head lolling, eyes closed, arms askew, her breasts tumbled out, her underwear pulled off the right leg, caught on the left.

He's in her, grunting for a half-minute – then lifting the camera to the mirror on the dresser. He pulls out his dick, sheathed in the rubber. Whacks it above her. Mumbles to himself.

My guts clench from nausea, and a kind of numb apprehension, too. I've been coming to belief – and what if now, in the darkest place, Rodarte appears? What if he never imagined this could be found?

It's a different hell, though. It's two and a half minutes of self-love and grunts, and yes, a pathetic struggle, the javelin sagging at points, just half-inspired. The auteur eventually pulls back, then a pan, Haylee with unmarred neck, still living in this twilight place, rising and falling and raped and *almost* aware – stirring, rising to the surface despite herself – coming *back*.

Awakening to die.

Rust alone with his rape. No Andrew Rodarte. And at 3:19, it stops in mid-grunt.

# 44

**(JPH)**

I'M WATCHING CLOSELY, since Rodarte can't possibly guess what he's about to read.

In fact he's shaking and wet-eyed by the time he's to the bottom of the first page, and when he gets to the description of the video he abruptly turns his head away. Then slowly back, pale.

"Jesus. I never saw him with a camera at all."

"He got you out of the room – that must be when he filmed. You said he had a big jacket, camcorder was probably a mini. Maybe it was in the truck, and he went to get it when you were out back with Haylee. And he clicks it off when he hears you coming back."

"I guess he could have . . . Jesus."

"So we know you didn't invent this story," I add. "And I guess that means we have things to talk about."

He looks at his lap, gives a tiny shrug. "That's all I've hoped for."

"But the thing is, Mr. Rodarte, I'm still not sure what you want."

SLOWLY HE SETTLES, sighs, nods – getting psyched, really. "Well, right. I'm just, God, down nine years, had a story nobody could've believed, and now . . ."

"Is there more?"

He shakes his head, not too firmly. "No, man. It is what it is, and I've just tried to endure, knowing if I had any balls . . . *fuck*. But I didn't, so she died, Lee, right there in front of me. I would've hitched my life to that girl after knowing her an hour, gone anywhere on earth she wanted to go, would have dumped everything I ever knew. But I wouldn't grab a fucking naked slab of dung off her. Not even with minutes to think about it. Basically stood there pissing my pants, couldn't even make my muscles move. And now it's like I want people to see me cold and clear, hate me in a different way just because it's the true way. What I've always been, really, is a fraud. Big guy with no balls. I'm not a sociopath, I'm a fucking coward. But somehow I gotta get someplace right, and I'm still dreamin I can."

"And what is that place? What is right?"

He's shaking his head. "Just, going back to it, maybe you tallying it all up again, knowing about Rust." Looking up now. "And if you believed it . . . maybe giving it another name."

"I see, sure." I pause, let him rehearse his thoughts, map out my own. "But if it happened that way, what do you think is justice?"

He'll want an involuntary, settle for a voluntary, at least in his dreams. He'd still be close to release.

RODARTE EXHALES, turns his eyes away, but his voice is flat and firm.

"I'm *not* who killed her. Rust did it. But she's still dead 'cause of me, too. So just change it to second-degree murder, drop the roofie charges, send me back. Parole at fifteen if I deserve it, on me if I can't figure it out. That's all."

I sag in the chair, amazed. It's fifteen seconds to get my bearings back. "So you're thinking second is justice, and you're showing me how serious you are? Or are you figuring that's as far as I would go?"

"It's justice. I know you aren't gonna set me free because of this – I don't deserve it. I'm accountable, and hell yeah I want you to know I'm serious. But if I'm ever gonna live again I have to pay what I owe."

"To the people, the county?"

Too easy. "To *her*."

BY NOW I'M NODDING like a bobble-head doll.

Rodarte plows on. "Look, I watched her get murdered right in front of me, real-time. Can you even imagine? How bad you have to fuck up to land in a spot where watching a fat rapist kill a beautiful girl you just fell in love with is the best choice you think you have? And it takes a long-ass time, too, not like the movies. Goes on and on. All as I'm standing right there, right *there* –"

A question springs from nowhere. "And you didn't help, right?"

Rodarte's eyes go wide, and he quavers. "Strangle her? Lord, no – no sir. I didn't, I didn't, I *couldn't* – I never touched her myself –"

I've always been ready to believe it. Rust existed, and he raped her, and filmed the rape, and there had *always* been a little hitch for me, even next to Sonya. I'd been shocked when he confessed. *But –*

I GATHER MYSELF – middle-aged now, no sweating kid.

"Well, let's add it up. We have Rust on the video, and if he was still living he'd be arrested for rape, at the very least, and no doubt charged with murder too. And I'll have to give you full discovery on him, if we go to a hearing – the video and everything else we know.

"I can pretty well buy the threats and you being afraid for family. And if we're going off RAP sheets and pictures, he looks more like a guy who'd choke the life out of a girl than you do."

The rest of this could still explode on me. Yet I can't turn back, not if I'm ever going to understand.

"But at the end of it, Mr. Rodarte, I have to side with justice. If new information tells us somebody shouldn't have been convicted, our job is to fix that."

"Right." He's barely breathing.

"And there's a very strange problem here. Which is the fact that if I believed every word you told me, then I don't know if, in good conscience, I could sign that deal.

"If what you're saying is gospel truth, then you didn't mean to kill, you didn't help in killing, you didn't conspire, you didn't encourage him to kill. You didn't even directly set the events in motion, other than being a good sport about buying beer.

"You didn't stop the murder when it was happening in front of you, and that'd haunt anybody. But as weird as it sounds, Mr. Rodarte, you probably had no legal obligation to do that. Since you'd done

356

nothing to put her directly at risk, you had no duty to save her life, no matter how you felt toward her. The law and living with yourself are two different things. So how would this deal ultimately be fair to *you*?"

HE'S BEEN NODDING for half a minute now. He expected it.

"I think – just pure justice. Maybe in a higher way. I've had a lot of time to think, process my own life, my own acts. Whatever the law says, I allowed it, I could have stopped it, I *let* it happen –"

"And so you think you *deserved* to go down for a life tag?"

He can't wait to agree. "Yes. Yes sir. I know I did."

"All right." I wait to see if he'll add on, but he doesn't. "Well, I can't get inside your conscience, Mr. Rodarte, but I have to look at it on paper first, just to get to the starting point.

"At best you're an accessory to murder after the fact, which is nothing to be proud of. But you've done nine years, and the max for accessory is three. Your sentence would be deemed served if your murder conviction got undone, and at worst you do a little parole. You'd be on the street with nothing more than a pretty low-end felony conviction. Are you telling me you'd take twelve extra years in state prison – *at least* – even if you aren't legally guilty of anything worse?"

He goes stiff, nodding, fighting through the question like a dust storm. Ten seconds, fifteen, 20. Finally he shakes his head.

"I don't know. If it was that simple, with a choice maybe I wouldn't. But I'm not gonna argue law with you, sir, 'cause I'll lose. I just think the right way is a second."

It's a long, dense moment in the silence, and then a switch flips. A rare moment in my life – seeing through fury to a goal, and knowing I can get there. The truth, once more, is angling toward the light.

"Well, I can't do it." The words startle my own ears. "Sorry, Mr. Rodarte. I can't, in the name of justice. Unless you trust me at the end."

Which gets us, finally, *to* the end.

357

# 45

**(JPH)**

VANZETTA IS ALREADY on the bench when I roll in that Friday, the last day of August. I catch Rodarte's eye and he nods in agreement.

He waives counsel again, for the record, and Vanzetta turns to me. "Where are we on this?"

Now I smile – enjoying it, really. Maybe my first-ever moment of advantage over him. "We have reached a resolution of the petition, Your Honor, subject to the Court's agreement."

AFTER THE SHOCK, the first thing I see is the disappointment. He wanted this last opportunity to consider the case, easily the best-known of his judicial life. But he's also curious, and in theory doesn't have to accept it.

"Resolution."

"Yes sir."

"Can you elaborate?"

"Yes, Your Honor."

And I can. For once I'm on my game. The bottom line, of course, but the rest in small bites, simple language, having managed to anticipate it all. I give him the minimum, pleasantly, and shut up – quietly daring him, I guess, to insist on more.

He pulls a solemn face, certainly, and I think he makes us wait for the fun of it. But I'm never actually in doubt, and it's not more than a minute. Vanzetta raises his eyes from his now-irrelevant notes and he smiles, a grudging concession.

"For the record, this petition makes a very provocative claim, but Mr. Rodarte is taking an unusual stance about it." He sighs. "And the Court is not yet in a position to make any determination at all, because the People" – raising his eyes – "declined to address the merits in their initial response." Another five seconds. "Mr. Howland, you're an officer of the court. And I know you know the case. Are you representing to me that this disposition serves the cause of justice?"

"I do. The People don't even see it as a compromise, Your Honor, but a modification that ensures justice for everyone involved."

"And Mr. Rodarte, what about you?"

Not a hitch. "Yes sir. It does."

Vanzetta's eyebrows rise. He wants just a *little* more – maybe another day. But in the end he'll stand for justice, too, and so he nods.

In a five-minute record he grants the petition for writ of habeas corpus. And then, with the full authority that this confers, he modifies Rodarte's first-degree murder conviction to second-degree, vacates his convictions for drugging Jacinta Cantrell and Haylee Branch, and sends Andrew Rodarte back to state prison, resentenced to fifteen years to life.

IN THE STALE ANTICLIMAX Vanzetta comes up with a friendly smirk. "Never expected to see you back here, Mr. Rodarte."

There's low-hanging fruit here – *And you won't see me again, I can promise that.* But he resists, just thanks him, waves and shuffles out, and as he does, once again, I think of Sonya.

◆

I'VE STUCK TO THE HIGH POINTS, but Alina is dead pale herself. Yet thinking.

"If Rust raped her, I can't see how he didn't kill her. But can we know Andrew didn't help?"

"Good question."

"And he only wanted it dropped to the second degree."

"Yes."

"Even knowing you had the video of the rape."

"Yes."

She squints. "A coverup?  He hid evidence?"

"No, not really."

"Something after, or before?  He did a favor for him?"

"No."

Her machinery whirrs, the clatter recedes.  I look at her, keep looking, and then suddenly Alina lights up.

"The *jacket*."  She turns to me, eyes afire.  "Is that it?  Rust didn't grab it himself.  Andrew gave it to him."

And so it was.

When Haylee's eyes blinked open Rust had panicked, squeezed her throat, kept at it and her hyoid cracked.  Then, as she lay there gurgling, half-conscious, Rust gestured for the jacket and Rodarte handed it to him.

He told himself it was already too late, repeated it for months, for years, until he nearly believed it.  But not quite.

NOW ALINA IS STILL, ready to cry at last.

"Oh, God.  What a thing."

"Right.  He hesitated, I'm sure of that.  And if he wasn't gonna pull him off, it didn't matter anyway.  Might already have been too late.  But in the moment of truth . . . well, that's what he did."

"And that's murder, by the law."

"Absolutely.  Direct aiding and abetting."

She lets this settle for another long spell, head bowed.  Finally she looks up.

"And this was the most he could ask for?"

"No.  *Could* have asked for lots of things.  Like manslaughter."

Her eyes widen, then narrow, and she appraises me.

"But you wouldn't have agreed, once he admitted the jacket?"

"No."  There's relief in a simple answer, but an echo behind it.  Then louder.  "No, I would not."

# 46

(JPH)

THE SECOND TRIP to the ranch – the Thursday of the Rodarte week – is another full afternoon. Again it's just the two of us. I bring the reports, knowing I don't need to. Marta won't doubt my accounting, or my corroborated faith that what Rodarte finally admitted, at the very last, is the truth.

(Marta)

I DON'T THINK the years had softened me. What ground I had given was at the start, when I decided I didn't want him to die. John would report to me on the appeal, and that's as much as I could do – listen once, seal it away. Then all that was over, but he did warn me he could still, someday, have a way to come back.

It's protocol, I guess – talk to your survivors before you go making deals – and I had stages. All distinct. In the moment I doubt he understands any of it. He tells me, though, and I go numb.

That's what the body does, I guess, when with waking eyes you see the scalpel, and understand that your most vulnerable parts are about to be sliced open, brought out in the harsh glare all over again, and that whatever crippled narrative you've managed to accept is about to change.

But then, as that ebbs and we try to get through, I feel this savage rush of hate for *both* of them in that room that night. Lee didn't *have* to save herself – she didn't have to die – *he simply stood there and watched.* And I become as angry at him for lacking the guts to save her life as I am at the sociopath who actually raped and killed her.

John has expected that, I think. And he has the sense to wait me out, let it all spill out through my clenched fists and closed eyes, saying nothing, and after a time my fury seems to shrink into fear. It's like I'm down to my own core, where you run out of answers, in my living room in the middle of a sunny afternoon – who *are* we, at the very end, the final nakedness?  How have *I* lived nine years in this labyrinth of loss, this forest, and how can this man live with how he failed himself, in that room?  Let alone Lee?

That's two hours, at least, fits and starts, inner convulsions, but finally it also gives way, and to my shock there is a slow, subtle wave of joy and relief behind it – the pure blessedness, I guess, of getting to the truth.  Beyond all of it, in some way I have always wanted to *know* – not the who, but the how, and the why.  No more or less.

EVENTUALLY, once I can fully re-engage, we come down to the fundamentals.  I have no veto power, but a blessing to give.  Rodarte will return to prison, where he'll have a choice of paths.  And John says five solid years until he gets a chance at parole.

No vision, this time, as he pulls away.  Exhale, shove it beneath. I'll try not to count the time.


**(JPH)**

MY MATH ISN'T BAD.  We've stayed at fingertip-length, noted our changes.  They calendar his parole hearing in Tehachapi for a July Tuesday in 2017.

# *47*

**(Marta)**

ASH IS IN HER THIRTIES now, long finished with vet school. She's gotten married, and at the reception held my hands and told me there won't be kids for a while. *Too much to process. Give us time.* It's been three years when I go to Tehachapi. And I've gotten married, too.

A couple of weeks before the hearing, John calls to tell me what I was already sure of. He talks in a slow, soothing voice, praying once more I'll find the good.

I'll be there. Ash won't. It's how she's survived.

**(JPH)**

MARTA'S NEW HUSBAND is lanky and lean, several years younger than she is, a graying goatee. They met in an online support group. His name is Dave, he's a contractor, and his son got shot, seventeen, outside a burger joint in the middle of a Sunday afternoon.

He's only seeing her to the gate, so it's just the two of us who sign in and are ferried in a golf cart to the main building at the prison.

The inner gates whir and clang. We pass through and descend to a day room, the hearing room beyond.

Rodarte has accepted an attorney for his parole hearing, faintly and absurdly disappointing me. She's Indian-American, from the name, still young, with oversized glasses and bright black eyes. Precise and eloquent – a future judge in her formative years.

ATTENDING FAMILY MEMBERS sit behind the DA, in plastic chairs along the wall. There are five chairs, but they are a forlorn sight.

The last cold truth of murder is that by the time a killer's chance comes around, the next of kin have often fallen by the wayside, felled by age or illness, by fear, by futility. Even for that first hearing, there's often no one on hand, including us – we attend in person, rather than by phone or video link, only when there are survivors to accompany. And for those who do persist, it worsens, in a way, when the inmate gets a predictable denial and comes back for his second try, much better schooled in the game, while the survivors have done nothing but struggle and shrink, slowly fading away.

A WOULD-BE PAROLEE is grilled by a commissioner and a deputy commissioner, and there are three basic trends in response.

Usually, by reflex, he minimizes his actions, his state of mind, or both. But as a rule this fails, because being anything other than frank about the horror shows a lack of "insight" – the magic legal word.

Less often the inmate denies guilt entirely, which in theory should never fly. The opening disclaimer makes clear that the verdict and legal findings are conclusive, and the case isn't being relitigated, but in a very rare case a pitch for actual innocence by an otherwise strong candidate may sway a panel just enough.

But the wisest of them take full responsibility for the killing, because the law has changed: where once the circumstances of the original offense alone could be enough to deny parole, the Board must now link the murder directly to the inmate's *current* risk of danger to the public. Which means, at least in theory, that even an inmate who disemboweled a dozen nuns can hope for freedom, assuming that he had a banyan-tree moment early in his sentence and has walked the righteous path ever since.

ANDREW RODARTE takes full responsibility for the death of Haylee Branch, including his jacket around her neck. I don't catch a single change from what he said to me, or for that matter to the psych evaluator, who quoted him at length and, critically, rated him a low risk to reoffend. He has also authored a letter of remorse to Marta, another to Ashlyn, a third to Jacinta Cantrell.

Where the iffy candidates often try to barrage the board with low-grade plaudits, Rodarte has used his time productively and efficiently, kept his head down, stayed out of trouble.  He's earned two online junior college degrees and a paralegal certificate, done well at every measured task, followed the rules.  He has a reasonable plan for parole – transitional housing first, then a warehouse job in Stockton, a place to live.  His mother, never wavering, will help him along.

He cries a little, but it's a shuddering brief wave and the words that leak out through it stay in key.

WHEN THE TIME COMES for our brief argument, I'm sure Marta's eyes bore directly into my neck, for all I warned her.  There's no doubt how this will end.

The crime was brutal, I say, and he acknowledges his blame.  But the story he has told was corroborated, and the relief he asked for was relatively modest.  The years have passed without incident, he has achieved, he has learned, he has humbled himself.  And so I can't in good conscience argue against his suitability for parole, not even with the victim's mother four feet away, strong-wristed enough to snap both our necks before the fat guard in the corner could get his taser drawn.

It's still a good half-minute before the two commissioners fully take it in, but this once I will keep it short.  The office of the Contenta County District Attorney will not advocate for Rodarte's parole, because that is not our place.  But we will not oppose it.

HIS LAWYER ARGUES, calmly and carefully, and Rodarte then – to my surprise – waives his own right to make a statement.  So finally it is Marta's turn, and as I pivot to watch there is a dull hum in my ears and a needle in my chest.

I'm afraid, and I think she *wants* me to be.  She realizes, late, that I default to the safe.  I'm a bracer for bad news, a low-bar-setter, a friendly face amid turmoil.  And that *wasn't* Sonya – which Marta presumes I long knew, but in fact I learned only from her.

In their darkest moments, Marta tells me, she would rise up. *They'll try THIS, but we'll oppose like hell.  They're arguing THAT, and I have a case that says they're wrong.  They'll want to bring in X, and we'll hammer them with Y.  There is nothing gonna knock us off the path.*  Sonya was that, at least for Haylee Branch.  And now she's gone.  Here at the end of advocacy, Marta has every right to compare.

She has donned reading glasses, but needs only a few downward glances at her notes.  Her voices wavers slightly at the open, an engine revving on a sub-freezing morning.  Then a steady thrum.

"COMMISSIONERS, COUNSEL, THANK YOU.

"I'm here because I had to be.  I still live suspended someplace between dark and light, dreaming one day I'll come to terms with something so unthinkable as the murder of my first-born child.

"I still can't really make sense of what happened, or grasp how everything could have been ripped away from my daughter, and this great hole torn in everyone who loved her, on that terrible night.

"It's a cliche, I guess, the mother-daughter bond, but we were fragments of the same soul, Haylee and I, and despite a whole lot of trying I know I've never fully processed what it did to me, both the loss that was her death and the horror of thinking about how she suffered.  That suffering – and mine too – transcends easy understanding.  There is no real way to accept or come to terms with it.

"But I know that hearing accounts of the pain of murder isn't really the purpose of this hearing, and by now I've learned that the law offers its own path to redemption, independent of me, the prosecutor, the judge, even of you.  You will decide whether he's truly followed that path, I guess, and I'll try to see it in the best possible light.

"Jesus says to forgive.  Buddhism says there's a place, eventually, where suffering ends.  They may both be right.  I'm still trying to fight through my own jungle, still searching, almost fourteen years after the fact. In the end, though, I've learned that flight is foolish, and that all I can do is accept my changed world and count the good that remains.

"Learning that the circumstances of Haylee's death were far different than the jury believed them to be has not consoled me, nor even learning that the man who actually snuffed out her life has now departed this life himself. But I do recognize that Mr. Rodarte as he sits in front of me today, who came to admit his direct involvement in my daughter's death, has himself been working toward truth and atonement in his own way. It's clear, especially after hearing him, that he is vulnerable and haunted and profoundly aware of his own guilt.

"And I've realized, eventually, that the core of our humanity is the capacity to forgive – especially the things that are, for want of a better word, unforgivable."

Now she turns her gaze to him, a slight protocol break but there's a trance to the moment.

"So, Mr. Rodarte. At first I wished you dead – violently dead. There was a time I longed to kill you myself. But time and my reflection changed that, and left me content with your exile. That banishment was just. Yet over time, your effort to change and live in truth has moved me, maybe even against my will, and I know that this is the culmination, the moment to take account.

"And so, here on a permanent record, I . . . forgive you now, Mr. Rodarte, for your role in the death of my daughter Haylee, just as you must forgive yourself." She closes her eyes, shuddering. "I hope that whether you are freed now, or later, or even if that day never comes, that you will reflect not only on what happened to my beautiful girl, and your part in it, but on the principle of atonement, making right.

"I hope, Mr. Rodarte, that whatever the path you take may be, you'll never for a moment *forget* her face, or even mine. I hope that if you do return to the wider world, it's with a purpose, some objective that will elevate you and that you can share with others.

"And should our paths ever cross again, I would hope for strength of my own, because I will want to look you in the eye and ask what use you've put your life to, once it was given back to you. What *did* you do? What *will* you do? How will you live your life in tribute to Haylee Maureen Branch, whose path you crossed by happenstance, whom you claim you fell in love with the very night she died? Can you *see* her, *remember* her, even now?

"I don't know these answers, but I've decided my own road is toward hope. And I'm willing to share the idea of hope – that there is a place at the end where the darkness turns to light." Only here does she falter, battle down tears. "I hope, Mr. Rodarte, that on the strength of your own effort you will travel as a free man to that same place. And there, in a light of reconciliation, we might yet one day meet again."

THEY'RE OUT 20 MINUTES – long, really, for a formality. We sit across the waiting room from each other, nearly silent. Then they come back in the room and find Rodarte suitable for parole.

He cries again, head down, near-inaudible, then raises his eyes and looks over. To my great relief, he thanks us only with the look.

AS WE PASS BACK through the gates, I nod, eyes to the hills, and can't think of a single sufficient thing to say to Marta Branch.

But she abruptly squeezes my shoulder, and in the parking lot there's a concluding hug. Perceptive husband Dave approaches, waving his iPhone, folding us together for a picture.

◆

THE GOVERNOR LEAVES IT ALONE, and the grant goes final. After the last bureaucratic belches Andrew Rodarte is paroled from prison the following May, and my eventual reward is a postcard from the beach in San Clemente.

# *48*

(JPH)

AS HIS EIGHTIES CLOSED IN Ted Stauber had a couple of bouts of vagueness in the courtroom, to nobody's pleasure, not even the newbie DA sent in to try a misdemeanor against him. But he adjusted meds or something and came back strong for another year or more, then announced his retirement so suddenly – just a couple of months before Rodarte's parole hearing – that we feared he was deadly sick. Turned out it was his third wife Liz, though, who pulled through, and by then he'd realized it was time to make full-time use of his fairway location – walking his round most days, according to reports.

Since Rodarte had never accused Ted of ineffective assistance, the attorney-client privilege remained intact throughout the habeas litigation, meaning that Ted could not have helped me make sense of the claim unless Rodarte waived it. So I had never done much more than tell him the outcome, and Ted had not pressed. The logical thing, were he curious, was for Ted to ask him directly.

Our conversation did waive it, of course, and about a week after Rodarte's release I call to make sure Ted knows. He doesn't, it turns out, though he figured it was soon. But there's no cloud cover in his voice at all, and he promptly invites me to stop by at the cocktail hour.

WE SETTLE ON HIS DECK, sun umbrella open amid the green rustle and the *thwack* of seven-irons, mutually armed with vodka and cranberry juice, and once I've been through the parole chronology I start in with the truth.

Ted's mouth falls half-open, then curves into a smile, his eyes light and grateful.

"My *God*. So it was that! That all along."

"He said he never told you. Was there a hint?"

"Not as to that. I suspected there was more to the story, because there is always more to the story than the client will tell you, but it never took form, and of course he got shoved to the stand by Miss Nieves and others, at which point all our expectations went up in flames. But, no – that remarkable scenario never crossed my mind. It seemed so obviously a one-man crime."

"I though maybe you'd planned it all along." I offer, very delicately. Still playing a bit dumb. "Going for second-degree."

Ted looks at me sidelong. "Not at trial, no, when all outcomes are still possible. In those days life all too often *did* mean life, and the girls were drugged – that wasn't going to help. I couldn't see an upside to steering the jury toward any sort of murder. I had assumed our path was reasonable doubt, come what may."

I'm nodding. And as I'd realized that long weekend before closing argument, Sonya's plan made sense. Though Alina could have helped his pitch for second-degree in one way, she was there to show his general sexual aggression, the *impulse* that made him rape. But if Ted tried to put it in the context of erotic game-playing, to sell it as implied malice at worst, the roofies and brutality would refute it.

So instead Ted had started where anyone would, looking for reasonable doubt, assuming for argument's sake his client was innocent without, as usual, directly asking him. Should an accused privately admit guilt, it can limit the questions his attorney can ethically ask him on the stand. Easier for all if he comes up with a story and sticks to it.

Rodarte didn't do either one – just said he wasn't a murderer, and that he was willing to testify. But otherwise he gave him nothing, not even trying to explain his story change from his first statement to the next. And innocence seemed off the table, Ted said, with the stories, the time frame, the single set of tires, the beer bottle, the broken hyoid bone, the attempt to run.

Cold Record


THEN ONE DAY long after prelim, out of the proverbial blue sky, Rodarte told him that he *would* plead guilty to second-degree murder.

"Which frustrated me, as you will appreciate.  I didn't want a confession, of course, but I also didn't want to hear him denying guilt and pleading to a life tag in the next breath.  And so I stalled, got him to let me think, and then I went back and said look, don't tell me more than you have to, but let's wait on that."

"And you offered manslaughter."

"We-ell," he says, now sheepish himself.  "It was my place, but I fear my heart wasn't in it.  There was no chance Sonya was coming back with an offer of second, whether he'd ultimately have taken it or not, and of course she was by nature never somebody to bluff.  So she laughed at our suggestion of voluntary, and when the young man brought up a murder plea again, I talked him out of it – I *knew* she'd never take it, and you didn't need a confidence boost."

"So we just went to trial."

"Yes, off we marched, Sonya made the case, and I saw no path other than him testifying, as he'd always told me he wanted to do."

"Even though he'd already told two versions?"

"Because of it, almost.  But I had seen his sympathetic side, too, and there was an earnestness to him, which I thought might come through.  So I was going to let him say what he had to say, hope it went over well and they'd give serious thought to a second, or at least consider scrapping the special circumstance."


HERE I SMILE.  "And then he drops that yes sir on you."

For a moment his eyes flash – he's there and angry all over again.  But it passes quickly, and now Ted smiles, too.

"The grand piano of cartoon legend.  From about five stories up."

# *49*

**(JPH)**

BY THE SUMMER OF '18 I'm up to third on the List. A couple of years back, now a bona-fide veteran, I've been nudged into Doug Lahtinen's old job, cranking out charges, sifting the daily skirmishes and light-handedly supervising the everyday folks. And then, that summer, Doug retires as Assistant District Attorney.

As his last weeks tick down, Celia Kim sidles up to me in the parking lot. Her usual secret-keeper's smile. "So, have you?"

"Have I what?"

"Doug's spot."

Stone-faced. "Me? Absolutely not."

"I think you'd be fabulous."

"I think you're officially full of it," I say, and then laugh out loud as she does, because for once I've caught her out.

The Friday before she'd convicted another child molester, and we'd gone to O'Flannagan's. She allowed herself one whiskey sour, then eventually excused herself for the powder room. Whereupon Brian, ever impolitic, told us that the new Assistant District Attorney – vaulting me, since I hadn't applied – was going to be Celia Kim.

A MONTH LATER she's nearly settled. Sonya's old office is *still* the best room in the building.

"Comfortable?" I ask my new superior.

Celia hunches slightly, intimidated by the desk. But not the work. She laughs. "Is that the goal?"

I pause a minute, come up with a line. "That and all the rest of it."

"The pesky doing-justice stuff."

"Yes," I say. "That."

She glances out the excellent window. "It's easy in the abstract."

HER THING NOW IS TO REMIND ME, straight-faced, that I always wanted to do another murder trial. Except I didn't, and I haven't, and now I won't, and she is kidding. We still don't get many.

Then every now and then, bouncing off some distant reference, Celia will smile and tell me again in that flat, discreet voice that it was great – and that it's equally right that Rodarte is free.

I've never been sure if that's an achievement, or just a fact. He is free, Haylee is gone, and Marta and her living daughter have husbands to stare down midnights with, when flooded again by what they lost.

♦

ALINA REMAINED at a beautiful medium distance. It never really got a name. But at 34 she finally decided it was time, and so I encouraged her through the next three years of law school, online in her evenings, and then the bar exam.

Her Nathan got into Berkeley the year she finished, so in a minor way history repeated itself – not long after the exam ordeal, months before the result, she made a drop-off run, then veered to Millsford.

This is different, though. For one, I know she's coming. For another, I have a skein of wandering roads to show her, expectation-free. For another, he's *off to college* –

"We're hiring," I add at dinner.

A squint and a scowl, if a scowl can be happy. "Can I remind you I haven't passed the test yet?"

"For future reference."

She looks at me hard but fondly, purses her lips. She'll pass, I'm sure. And then I'd say it's four to one against – but there's the one.

I'M NOT SURE how I got here. Her receding lights leave a hollow, and most of my ships have sailed. But there's a moon above the slough and a rustle in the trees, and I'm not going anywhere at all.

Eric Ferguson

# ABOUT THE AUTHOR

Eric Ferguson, born in Texas and raised in Los Angeles, graduated with honors from Chapman University School of Law in 2004, where he served on the editorial board of the *Chapman Law Review*. He has been a prosecutor in southern California since 2005, primarily focused on habeas corpus and post-conviction litigation. He and his wife Susanne are the parents of two grown children. *Cold Record* is his first novel.

Contact Eric via email at coldrecord23@gmail.com, or visit him online at ericmferguson.com.

Made in United States
North Haven, CT
10 November 2023

43842176R00231